Camille sat, stubbornly unmoving. The gentleman bandit slid from his horse to stand next to her wagon, his face only inches from hers. His gaze played over her, lingering on her heaving bosom before meeting the challenge in her eyes.

"You're much too spirited, my dear." His rough voice was a caress. With another mocking smile, he vaulted into the wagon and stood over her. He was entirely too close. She drew herself as far as she could against the opposite side.

"Stay away from me." Her voice wavered a little.

"Oh, no," he said softly. "Ask anything but that, dear lady." His voice was velvet, but laced with steel. Unhurriedly, he studied her.

★

Spring Will Come

SHERRY DeBORDE

WORLDWIDE

TORONTO • NEW YORK • LONDON • PARIS
AMSTERDAM • STOCKHOLM • HAMBURG
ATHENS • MILAN • TOKYO • SYDNEY

SPRING WILL COME

A Worldwide Library book/October 1987

ISBN 0-373-97046-3

To my grandmother and my mother who taught me to love books and simply to love. Also to my husband Ray and our children, David, Kristy and Lindsey, for sharing their wife and mother with her obsession. To my aunts, Barbara and Peggy, and to Maggie Burkley for their help in rediscovering Natchez. To sharing, caring friends who happen to be writers: Micki, Elzie and Mary. Also to my dad and the rest of my wonderful family for their support and encouragement.

Last, but certainly not least, to Rita Gallagher and to my editor, Kate Duffy, for their faith in me and Camille from the beginning.

Chapter One

NATCHEZ, MISSISSIPPI, 1852

YELLOW LIGHT and raucous laughter spilled from a disreputable shanty nearby, filling thirteen-year-old Camille Beaufort's heart with fear. She glanced back through the darkness at the city on the hill behind her. Natchez, with its white-columned elegance and genteel ways, was a striking contrast to these weather-beaten shacks.

Silver Street narrowly snaked its way down into the infamous part of town known as Under the Hill. It was a necessary eyesore, as wealthy planters and businessmen often conducted business there, but the aristocratic residents of Natchez were glad to have it hidden away below the bluffs.

A damp chill crept up from the river to wrap Camille's small body with its slender fingers. Hugging her arms closer to her sides, the dark-haired child hurried along the rutted road, going deeper into the boisterous den of gambling halls, bordellos and saloons.

Tinkling piano music and bawdy laughter mingled with the familiar night sounds of locusts and cicadas in tall trees covering the steep hillside behind the crude dwellings. Here, dilapidated buildings filled every inch of space, right up to the edge of the muddy Mississippi, where they stood like long-legged spiders on tall pilings, challenging the river to do its worst.

A large, colorful sign advertising a Gypsy fortune-teller banged crazily over Camille's head. Jumping nervously, she moved more quickly in and out of the shadows.

A drunken body was dumped out of a tavern window and lay sprawled across the walk at her feet. "And don't come back!" came the proprietor's loud, angry voice. Camille smothered a gasp with the back of her hand and skirted widely around the lifeless body, trying to stay out of sight.

She closed her eyes and fervently wished herself back home at Magnolia, but her father's words, spoken less than an hour ago, spurred her onward.

Fetch Charles Longmont, child. Go quickly, now!

It might be the last thing she could do for him, and she was determined to do his bidding. But Braxton Beaufort's daughter had the awful feeling that after this waking nightmare, nothing in her life would ever be the same.

Thoroughly frightened by his words, Camille had fled her father's bedroom, her hooped skirts brushing the doorway as she hurried down the winding staircase and out onto the front porch. Oblivious to the beauty of the manicured grounds stretching out before her, she had stood a moment, considering her father's request.

"Missy Cam, honey, what's wrong?" Camille whirled as Josef, elderly trusted servant of the Beauforts, stepped out of the shadows, his wrinkled, black face etched with worry and concern.

"It's Papa, Josef. He . . . he's worse tonight." Her voice trembled as she continued. "He's given up, I think, and he's asked me to fetch Mr. Longmont. But I don't know where to find him." Camille knew only that Charles Longmont had been a close friend of her father for the past year or two, and had recently purchased land adjoining Magnolia. She had seen him on several occasions when he'd been a guest of her father, and once he'd kindly helped her mount a recalcitrant pony. But she had not the faintest idea where to find him.

Josef, who had belonged to the Beauforts since childhood and served them loyally through the years, patted Camille awkwardly. "Now, Missy, it gonna be a'right. I knows where to find Mr. Longmont. He stays at the inn Under the Hill. Dat ain' no place for a lady, Missy." Josef knew that women of quality never ventured down there, and even the men went only in groups of two or three, usually armed with a pistol or a bowie knife. Why, the fever must have had his master plumb out of his head to send his young daughter on such an errand!

Ribbons of darkness slithered across the circular drive in front of her, and Camille shivered in apprehension. Josef's description had been enough to make her reconsider, but only for a moment.

"I must go, Josef. Bring the carriage around."

The faithful servant who had never in his life disobeyed a command or spoken back to one of the Beauforts, did so now. "No, ma'am. It gonna be dark soon. I jest can't take you there, not now."

"I'm going, Josef, if I have to go alone," Camille had said in a commanding tone much like her father's, and tossing her head with more bravado than she felt, she had turned back to the house.

"But Missy Cam, yo' don' *knows* what kind of folks lives in dat godforsaken place. Why, dey's rumrunners, riverboat rowdies, gamblers and Lord knows *what* down in dem saloons!''

Josef had followed her into the house, still arguing, but he knew he'd lost. If Camille said she'd go, she would, and the one thing he could not do was let her go alone.

''Yes'm,'' he said, shaking his aged head in resignation, ''I'se gonna git da carriage right now.''

Camille hugged him impulsively and ran to get her wrap.

Soon the elegant Beaufort carriage was bouncing over rutted roadways through the slumbering town. Shivering and clutching her wrap to her shoulders, Camille urged Josef on.

''We's goin' along jest 'bout as good as we kin. Don' yo' worry none, Missy. Josef here—he gonna get yo' dere.''

By the time Josef had guided the carriage to a careful stop at the head of Silver Street, the sun had dipped well below the darkening waters of the Mississippi. Camille ordered Josef to stay with the carriage while she continued on foot. Though he'd been reluctant to do so, the servant had had little choice but to do as his mistress commanded. As he watched her small form march away, Josef picked up the buggy whip and clutched it tightly in his hands, determined to go after anyone who dared to interfere with the child.

It was only minutes before Camille saw the two-story inn up ahead. Though much like the other buildings on the dark street, its steep wooden stairs and spider-web railing that led to a second-floor landing were just as Josef had described them.

''Well,'' she said to herself, squaring slender shoulders, ''I'll just have to see if he is here.'' Her soft voice full of youthful determination, Camille would do what her father asked. She would not return without Mr. Longmont, regardless of what she might have to do or where she might have to go to find him.

Struggling to control her trembling knees, she grasped the rickety railing and climbed the uneven planks of the stairway. At the top, she faced a doorway shrouded in darkness.

She rapped sharply and waited. Impetuously she had come here, never thinking he might not be home! What would she do if she could not find him? She knocked again, fear making her head swim. Still there was no response.

Numb with defeat, she turned and began slowly descending the stairs. Halfway down, she halted. Barely discernible in the dim light of the waterfront, she saw a group of roughly clad men huddled on the boat landing across the road.

Camille strained her eyes, almost certain the man standing in their midst, towering above the rest, was Charles Longmont. As she watched, the men completed their furtive business and slipped away one by one.

When the tall man turned and walked toward her, she held her breath, hoping fiercely that he was indeed the man she'd been sent to find. His long legs carried the dark figure rapidly across the road. In seconds he reached the bottom of the stairway and stared up at her in amazement.

"What in God's name are you doing here, child?" His voice was ragged and he took the stairs two at a time to grasp her shoulders roughly.

"Why have you come to this awful place?" he demanded, his cultured voice at odds with his surroundings.

Camille was thoroughly frightened at this unexpected response from her father's friend who, at this moment, seemed more like a river pirate than the gentleman her father thought him to be.

"You're trembling." His voice softened. "Come, Camille, tell me why you're here."

His grip on her shoulders had gentled and she breathed normally again. "Please, sir, we must hurry. My father is quite ill. He's calling for you. Will you come?"

Nodding, he flung his coat carelessly over his broad shoulders and took her small hand in his. "Let's be off!"

Moments later his rich voice filled the interior of the carriage. "The last time I saw Braxton, he was hale and hearty and intent on having the most profitable cotton crop ever. What has happened, Camille?"

"It's the fever, sir—the same sickness my brother Devon died of last year." Her small voice was filled with pain.

"I'd hoped we wouldn't see the yellow fever again," he murmured regretfully. "Too many lives have been forfeit already." The deadly and most often fatal disease had swept through Natchez before, claiming its victims at random, but there'd been no new cases for some time, until now.

Josef urged the horses as fast as he dared, and soon the carriage turned into the circular drive and rolled to a stop in front of the massive front doors of Magnolia.

Charles jumped to the ground and reached up to help Camille, who stepped lightly onto the covered portico, her hand resting against a stately Grecian column.

The large white plantation house was simple in design and sturdy. Though it possessed understated elegance, it was, above all, a comfortable home for the Beauforts. Camille loved it with a singular, devoted passion. It was her home and the symbol of all good things to her: the love of her mother and father, the Southern traditions she'd grown up with, and her whole way of life.

Fan-lighted front doors opened into a wide hallway used for dancing in happier days. Warm light fell across the porch from candles blazing through the lower floor, illuminating double parlors that extended the sixty-foot length of the house on the left, and the library and dining room on the right.

Camille led Charles Longmont up the spiral staircase to her father's bedroom. Dimly lit, the austere, high-ceilinged room reflected the character and plight of its occupant. The room's furnishings were of heavy mahogany, and muted shades of brown and green covered the bed and hung at the window.

Raspy breathing filled the room. Camille hurried to his bedside. "Father," she whispered, bending over him, "I've brought Mr. Longmont."

Stepping nearer, Charles Longmont took the fevered hand in his own. "I'm at your command, my friend," he said quietly.

"Charles." The weakened voice still possessed an unmistakable command. "It is imperative that you do as I ask. . . ."

The paper-thin eyelids with tiny tracings of blue veins blinked once, then opened with some effort. Watery blue eyes, so unlike those Charles had come to know in his friend, peered up at the two standing there, as though measuring them.

Her father reached for Camille's hand and brought it to his lips. "I . . . love . . . you . . . Daughter." Every word was punctuated by a heavy, labored breath. "Now . . . leave . . . us . . . please."

Stricken by the sound of his breathing and far more by something in the depths of her father's eyes, Camille leaned down and placed a kiss on his leathery cheek. With a sob, she ran from the room.

BRAXTON BEAUFORT KNEW he was dying. He must make provisions for his two daughters and for Magnolia, his beloved plantation that spread out over a thousand acres of lush Mississippi farmland. His diverse business interests, including part-ownership of a cotton gin and several smaller plantations in Louisiana, required constant supervision; and over two hundred slaves, both household staff and field laborers, depended on him.

Now that his son Devon was dead and he knew himself to be dying, Beaufort agonized over who would manage it all when he was gone. Certainly not Camille. Though she did have a quick mind and a strong streak of independence, his oldest daughter was only thirteen. And ten-year-old Jacqueline had always been a frail and sickly child. While Braxton had thought on his children, his mind had sharpened and the solution to his problem had suddenly become clear to him. Now he spoke to a man he considered to be his best friend; a man who, though much younger, had proved his honesty and integrity in many ways during the past two years.

"Charles, you must promise me you'll look after my girls and Magnolia. I have no one else to turn to."

Charles noted the toll the short speech had taken on his friend, and his heart grieving, he answered quickly, "Of course, I will, Braxton. I promise." He would not realize until much later just what his hasty promise had involved.

CAMILLE HALTED her headlong rush in the hallway outside her father's bedroom and clutched the railing to steady herself while she tried to catch her breath.

Since she'd been big enough to toddle about, Camille had been her father's shadow. She had ridden in front of him in the saddle to survey the crops and played by his chair during his many business meetings. Lately he had even begun to school her in the business of running the plantation. The two of them had been inseparable. Her father was her dearest friend and she idolized him.

Camille was hurt and confused. She could not understand why he called for Mr. Longmont now, wishing to confide in him instead of her.

A door opened behind Camille and she turned to see her sister Jacqueline standing in the doorway, her wide brown eyes almost black with pain and fear.

Moving closer, Camille noticed the telltale bright pink cheeks. "Jacqueline, are you all right? Come, let's go down and have Essie make you one of her famous 'potions.' Everything's going to be all right. Mr. Longmont is with Papa now."

Camille put her arm around her sister's shoulders and guided her down the stairs. Since their mother's death, Camille had taken on the responsibility of Jacqueline. She'd watched over her younger sister like a protective mother hen, defying anyone to cause her unhappiness. But she could not prevent her sister's pain now, any more than she could prolong her dear father's life.

Later, Charles Longmont joined them, his sad business with their father completed. His crinkling brown eyes and warm smile brought needed comfort to the two young girls. He talked with them as though they were adults, telling them of his adventures and how he'd first met their father on a riverboat bound for Natchez. He seemed to know exactly what to say to make them feel better.

Charles Longmont vowed to do his best to carry out the commission thrust upon him by his dying friend, by starting now to woo these two lovely children back to life.

Observing them, he thought Jacqueline the prettier of the two, with her chocolate eyes, olive complexion and mane of curly black hair. But he found Camille irresistible in a way quite unfamiliar to him. Something about the serious young girl was so beguiling, so innocently appealing.

Freckles had been strewn across her pug nose by a humorous God, who must have smiled as he formed the dimpled cheeks and left just a hint of turquoise in indigo eyes shaded by dark, curling lashes. Perhaps she would never be a beauty, but she was charming, and a startling courage shone from her eyes.

"Father is dying, isn't he, Mr. Longmont?" Camille asked abruptly, interrupting his appraisal.

"I'm afraid so, child. We can do nothing for him now, but pray."

"Praying doesn't help."

Camille's childish voice was flat, but oddly moving. For one so young, she'd experienced much tragedy. First, her mother had been snatched away in a raging barn fire, then her brother Devon had died of yellow fever, and now her father lay dying in his upstairs bedroom. No wonder she felt God was no longer there, he thought, his heart filled with compassion for her. What a dreadful burden for such a little one to carry!

"Ah, Camille, though God does not always answer our prayers in the way we think He should, He is there, and He cares for you very much, little one. Some day you will see that, I promise you."

The comforting words came from full lips, set in such a strangely handsome face. Why, he could not be much more than twenty-five himself! Camille thought in shock, watching the candlelight play through his dark hair almost like a halo. How could she ever have thought him a pirate? He was more like an angel, yes, an angel! Even if there were no God, there could still be angels, couldn't there?

Thoughts of death and grim despair were eased back to the corners of her mind by his banter and good humor. Camille relaxed and smiled for the first time in days. The burden of being in charge had slipped off her shoulders and onto the stronger, more experienced shoulders of this man her father loved and trusted.

From that moment Camille worshiped the man chosen by her father to watch over his daughters and his holdings. She was sure she would do anything for him, with no questions asked.

DEATH CLAIMED Braxton Beaufort that same night.

Charles Longmont stood beside the girls through the heartbreaking loss of their father and the grim ordeal of the funeral.

After the other mourners had finally gone, Camille begged a few moments alone at the grave in the family plot. Rain pelted down like millions of tiny darts on her exposed flesh—a damaging, bruising rain sent by an avenging God. She felt like pounding her fists and small feet against the soggy earth in her frustration and grief.

Hair plastered in slippery rivulets over her head fell across her face and into her eyes, but still she stood by the grave, staring at the mud-covered mound. Feet rooted in the miry ground, she was incapable of motion—a puppet with no strings and no master puppeteer.

Thunder commenced miles away and rumbled louder and louder like an offended bear, until it clapped a fierce crescendo immediately over Camille's head. Still she did not move.

Were all the elements directed against her, too? A shiver shook her from head to toe, compressing her slender form, and at that moment, Camille Braxton Beaufort stiffened her spine and slowly stood up straight.

Charles, who stood watching from a gentle slope a short distance away, saw the child square her shoulders and wipe her eyes. A smile spread across his dark features.

"What a spunky little thing," he murmured, his admiration for her growing.

Long strides carried him quickly to her side. Gently he turned her to face him. Her eyes held the traces of tears, but in their depths Charles saw an inner fire and determination sparking to life.

"Camille, child. Come away with me now. You've paid your respects. It's getting late, and you're soaked to the skin."

His cloak settled about her shoulders, its warmth spreading through her. She allowed him to lead her to the carriage and, trembling, snuggled up next to him in its chilly interior.

Through his jacket, Camille felt the steady, strong beat of his heart; the pleasant, familiar aroma of tobacco wafted around her; and, for the first time in days, she slept.

At the sound of her regular breathing, he smiled once more.

Days passed. Charles Longmont calmly and intelligently arranged matters so that Camille and Jacqueline would be spared as much as possible. Privately he struggled with the immediate and serious problem of what to do with the girls themselves until they reached maturity.

The Beauforts' lawyer, Marcus Smithfield, had failed to return from a trip to New Orleans before Braxton's death, so there was no legal power of attorney. Thus, Charles feared he might not be able to assume complete control of the Beaufort estate, as his dying friend had requested. Knowing the children needed his protection from fortune hunters, who were plentiful around Natchez, he spent several sleepless nights before arriving at a solution.

"BUT I DON'T WANT to leave here, Mr. Longmont. Natchez is my home, the only home I've ever known." Camille, in a demure morning dress, sat beside her guardian in a gazebo overlooking a placid, shaded pond.

Impatiently she slapped a closed fan against her full skirts. Trying to reason with this serious-faced Charles Longmont was impossible! She sighed and tried to smile, for he held her future in his smooth, well-formed hands.

She dismissed the crazy thought that the hardest thing would be leaving this man. It was only Magnolia and Jacqueline that concerned her. Why, she hardly knew Charles Longmont, and then only as her father's friend. And here he sat, calmly asking the hardest thing imaginable, that she leave her home and her friends.

"I know, child, I know. Still, it is the best course for two young ladies recently orphaned. Green Oaks School is highly respected, and Baltimore a much better place for you during the next few years than Natchez. Your father wanted the best education for you both."

"But he *never* mentioned sending us away! Never!" Camille fought back tears that signified childishness. She was almost fourteen! She vowed he would never see her cry again.

"Perhaps not, but your circumstances have been altered by his sudden and tragic death." His warm brown eyes softened at her valiant fight to control emotions so near the surface. God help him not to damage this wonderful child, he thought, feeling protectiveness and a sudden, stirring tenderness for Camille Braxton Beaufort.

He pleaded for her understanding. "Don't you see? It's the only way I can truly protect the two of you."

"How can you say that? How can you protect us by sending us away?"

His face closed before her seeking gaze. "I'm sorry, Camille. I wish there was some other way. But I must carry out your father's last request." The determined look that settled over his handsome features ended the matter once and for all.

Even if she could have gone against her father's last wish, there was nowhere else to turn. Her father had passed the responsibility for them and their affairs into Charles Longmont's hands. She had no choice but to do as he said.

"Camille, there *is* something else I feel I must do. I hesitate to mention it, as you will probably find it most disturbing, also," he went on.

"Disturbing?" she echoed.

"Yes, in order for me to have full control of your affairs as your father wished, I'm afraid it's necessary, that is . . ."

Why was he stuttering and almost incoherent under the steady, inquisitive gaze of this child? He cleared his throat, forcing himself to continue.

"Miss Camille, would you do me the . . . that is, the honor of becoming my wife?"

Charles's startling proposal hung in the air as he watched the emotions play across Camille's expressive face. Shock was followed by incredulity, to be replaced by faint stirrings of humor, and the beginnings of a smile.

"Are you serious?" she asked.

"I've never been more serious in my life. I've thought it over at length and I've decided it's the only way I can adequately protect you and your estate as I promised your father." No smile answered hers; he was very much in earnest about his request.

"Well, then, the answer is yes."

"You don't have to answer right away," he continued quickly, unaware of her immediate response.

"Yes," she repeated quietly.

"Yes?" he asked. "Just yes? No questions...no nothing?"

"Just yes!" Her eyes were luminous. "If you think it's best, Mr. Longmont, then I'm sure it is. And I will marry you, whenever you say."

Camille knew at that moment she would go to the ends of the earth for him, but he hadn't asked that. He had only asked her to marry him.

Her brilliant smile twisted his heart, and Charles groaned. Please, God, let me be right in this, he prayed silently, taking her small hands in both of his.

"Camille, I will give everything that I have for you and I will work diligently in your behalf while you are away, but when you return, the choice is entirely yours whether the marriage shall continue or not."

Charles had no intention of claiming his conjugal rights, but he felt compelled to marry Camille in order to have the legal right to protect the Beaufort interests. Sending the girls away to school was the next practical step to avoid gossip and to secure for them the best education available. When Camille returned, she would be a young woman and able to make her own decision about the marriage or annulment. But who, he wondered, could have predicted the bizarre string of events that had led him to a proposal of marriage to a child?

"WELL, I DO DECLARE, Indigo! Whatever is taking you so long? The guests are already arriving and I'm to be married in less than an hour—it's almost noon now. Do hurry!" Her face a paler shade of ivory than usual, Camille sat before the mirror in her bedroom, the familiar, beloved objects of her childhood surrounding her.

Her wedding veil looked out of place on an enormous canopy bed of elaborately carved solid cherry, and the brightness of the noonday sun was muted by the heavy drapes of mauve Italian silk that edged the lace panels in the room's three large windows.

The past few days had been a hectic blur, for Camille had decided that the wedding ceremony, though necessarily unpretentious due to the circumstances, would not be without some style. After all, it would likely be the only wedding she'd ever have.

Indigo grinned upon hearing her young mistress sounding like herself again. "Yes'm. I'se hurryin'. Jest as fast as I can!" Indigo's caramel-colored fingers worked efficiently at the task of bringing order to the young woman's riotous black curls.

"There now, that's jest fine, jest fine!" Hands on her narrow hips, the servant girl backed up a few steps, waiting for Camille's reaction.

"If only I could have another week or two," she pouted, turning and twisting to see the back of her hair. "I'd have time to have my hair properly done, and to order a fine dress...."

"Now, Missy Cam, you knows Mr. Longmont, he in a hurry so's you two young ladies can get to Mar'-land 'fore the first snow. He done already let you have a week longer dan he wanted to."

"Yes, I know, and I'm trying to understand, truly I am." She turned to face the black girl, as much friend as servant. "I just wish I had a little longer. And I *do* wish you were coming, too!" Tears welled up in both pairs of eyes as the girls fell into each other's arms.

Camille held on tightly, clutching not only the black girl but her past as well, terrified of the long years of separation and loneliness ahead. In spite of everything, she still nurtured a small hope that she could make Charles Longmont change his mind about boarding school after the wedding.

"Now, now, Missy. You'll muss yo' pretty dress and yo' face, too, if yo' keep dis up. And yo's marryin' a fine gen'l'man, dat he is."

A sharp knock interrupted the discussion. Camille's best friend Glory flounced into the room, a picture of loveliness in a dress that was a cloud of rainbow colors.

"Cam! Why aren't you ready? That handsome, charming fellow is pacing the floor downstairs and you're up here, taking your sweet time, and *crying*?" Glory was incredulous. "Are you really *crying*, Cam? On your wedding day? You're so lucky. . . I can't tell you! Why, all the girls we know would give their eyeteeth, I mean their *eyeteeth* to be in your shoes today! And that's God's own truth!"

Glory's hands gestured wildly as she paced back and forth, lecturing her best friend in her usual melodramatic style. Finally, seeing a smile tugging at the corners of Camille's mouth, she stopped in front of her and looked her over.

"That's better. Now let me see you." The tight-waisted eggshell satin dress was covered with tiny seed pearls, and fell in soft folds to the floor.

"You really are a sight! Oh, *Cam*!" Now Glory's arms were around her, eyelids lowered to conceal a suspicious moisture. She composed herself quickly, anxious not to add to Camille's sadness. "I can't wait to see the look on Charles Longmont's face when he sees *you*! Now, let's go!"

Indigo scampered to help Camille maneuver her impossibly wide skirts through the doorway. On the landing, the servant girl stood watching her mistress descend the spiral staircase to a sea of upturned, smiling faces.

The original plan had been to invite only a few good friends, but the Beauforts were well known by everyone in Natchez, and it had been hard to draw the line. The parlor and wide hallway were filled with many sympathetic and curious neighbors and friends.

After all, how often did one see a young heiress to a vast fortune wed to a man who, though known as promising and ambitious, was considered a rake and an adventurer, and whose Under the Hill activities were, at best, questionable?

Still, Charles Longmont was well liked by most everyone, and Beaufort had trusted him enough to leave his two daughters in the younger man's care. And Longmont *was* dashing and quite handsome in his cutaway jacket and trousers. Perhaps he would settle down and make Camille a good husband.

Rumors abounded, though, that he already had a sweetheart, and had been practically engaged when the Beaufort tragedy occurred. They wondered what would happen now, with the young bride away for several years, and probably unaware of his previous attachment.

Charles looked up at Camille with tenderness in his warm, brown eyes, and would-be gossips were temporarily silenced by the unspoken communication between the young man and the lovely child.

Camille pulled her eyes away from his to the well-loved, solid walls of the only home she'd ever known. Her fondest dream was to be mistress of Magnolia. She could run the plantation herself, even now; she knew she could. Her family and her home had always been everything to her, until one by one, she'd lost them all. Now only Jacqueline and Magnolia were left—and the big, empty space in her heart.

Under her hand, the smooth, burnished wood of the banister reassured her of her connection to the house, the land, and the people of Natchez. She would come back, to carve out her destiny here where her roots were, here where her father and mother had labored together and died.

In Natchez lay hopes for her future life. And here, standing so tall in front of her, was the man who would help her, the handsome man soon to be her husband.

On the bottom step, Camille paused, smiled and held out her hand.

The ceremony was completed quietly and in the best of taste. A bouquet of gardenias held tightly in her hands and the unfamiliar feel of the gold and diamond rings on her left hand assured Camille she was married, though she certainly didn't feel like it. A fatherly kiss on the cheek from her husband had done nothing to change that impression.

With her back straight and an unnatural smile on her lips, Camille walked beside Charles through the crowded parlor and out onto the shaded veranda where a wedding feast had been laid out. Imported champagne saved for just such an occasion as this bubbled in a fruity punch. Turkeys and hams from the smoke-house were flanked by fresh vegetables and bread, as well as coveted strawberries and ices delivered by riverboat. A three-tiered wedding cake stood proudly in the center of the long, heavily laden table.

Graciously the bride and groom accepted the con-gratulations and best wishes of the guests as they filed past them and out the double doors to set happily upon the food.

Charles's strong hand under her elbow supported Camille when her legs trembled from the effects of the punch, the excitement and the exhausting routine of the past few days.

"Hold on, little one," his soft voice reassured her.

The temporary weakness had been uncharacteristic and quickly passed away. "I'm fine, Mr., uh, Charles, uh, what the devil shall I call you now?" she mut-tered.

"Call me Charles, my little Camille," he said, chuckling.

"Well, *Charles*, let's eat!" She laughed and took his arm. She liked his name, liked the way it felt on her lips. And she was amazed at how hungry she was, af-ter all, and how wonderful everything tasted.

After the guests had all gone, and the buffet had been cleared away by the servants, the two of them stood quietly by the ornate railing. The sun sank be-yond the horizon, casting rays of pink and purple over the rolling grounds of Magnolia.

The heady fragrance of crepe myrtle drifted across the porch. Sadly, Camille watched the lovely white flowers fall to the earth as shadows played beneath the spreading branches of her favorite magnolia tree.

"Soon all the flowers will be gone," she murmured, her voice heavy.

"Yes, but they'll return in the spring, little one. They always do."

"I suppose. Yes, the spring. It just seems so far away now, doesn't it?"

"To one as young as you, I'm sure it does. But as one grows older, time passes too quickly most of the time."

A shadow fell across his face, and Camille heard the heaviness in his voice. It was a strange notion that someone like Charles Longmont would ever be sad. But then she knew so little about this man she'd just married, and nothing at all about his family or his friends.

Her new husband was wonderfully kind and handsome, but this was not the wedding day Camille had dreamed about. A sharp disappointment swept over her as they turned to enter the house.

Chapter Two

MOTES DANCED in fragments of morning sunlight across the polished marble of Magnolia's entryway. Sturdy leather trunks stacked against the wall would soon be loaded onto the waiting carriage.

By afternoon Camille and her sister Jacqueline would be aboard the steamship *Natchez*. Thinking a trip up the river too long and difficult, Charles had arranged for them to travel downriver, making connections in New Orleans with an ocean vessel for the remainder of the trip around Florida and up the east coast to Maryland.

Camille Braxton Beaufort Longmont sighed. She had been certain that after their marriage she would be able to convince Charles not to send her away. But she had had absolutely no say in the matter and Charles had been determined that it was best for her and Jacqueline to go away to boarding school. Though she had pleaded with him, he had been adamant in his refusal to change his mind. Frustrated, she'd realized how helpless a married woman was, how dependent on her husband's decisions. It was a bitter lesson.

She vowed it would be the last time any man would tell her what to do. When she returned, she would take him up on his offer of an annulment, and see to her own affairs. She wouldn't need to be dependent on him, or on any man, ever again.

Desperately unhappy, Camille wanted to hug her favorite doll to her chest and hide under the ancient oak in the back courtyard, but reminded herself firmly that she was no longer a child. She was being called upon to play a new role, and she would do it well, she vowed as she walked with a determined step toward the front door.

Outside, her friends talked and laughed quietly. She steeled herself for the painful goodbyes and stepped onto the gallery. At first, no one noticed her, giving her time to fill her heart with one last picture of each of them.

Glory sat in the bright sunshine with no umbrella as usual, not in the least upset by gossips who made snide remarks about her "disgraceful tan." Camille smiled. Glory never did what was expected of her, but she had a kind and loving nature and was Camille's dearest friend. How could she bear not hearing Glory's contagious laughter for six long years? And who would she talk to about the new feelings stirred to life inside her?

Dandy Ashton hovered around Glory like a moth drawn to a flame. He'd always been fascinated by Glory's blond curls and unconventional ways, but Camille knew Dandy was mostly enamored of himself. Camille's worried expression softened to an understanding, affectionate smile.

Shaded by the canopy of the massive magnolia tree, Marguerite Duval stood speaking softly to Indigo, her striking gray eyes wide with interest and concern. Camille sensed they were discussing her, and felt surrounded by a cushion of warmth and love.

No matter what happened, these were her friends; they would always be her friends. She must not let them see her unhappiness.

"Well, what is this, a Sunday social, or a going-away party for your best friend? I expect to see long faces and tears from this group and soon!" Forcing a wide, mocking smile, Camille joined them and they spent a few moments in friendly banter.

"Cam! It's about time you showed up! Waiting to make a grand appearance as usual?" Dandy's eyes lit with approval as he moved to take Camille's arm and escort her to her waiting circle of friends.

Dandy had never been quite sure why he'd chosen Glory over Camille. He found the dark-haired girl on his arm extremely good-looking, and was delighted by her irrepressible and charming ways. In her tailored traveling dress, Camille looked much older than her years. She could easily have been his age, sixteen, and her eyes held a mysterious knowing gleam that had never been there before.

Though he considered himself worthy of any belle in Natchez, Dandy had always felt that Camille was a bit above him and somehow unreachable. Now she was married and the time for making a move in that direction had passed.

A twinkle in her eyes, Glory took Dandy's other arm with a guileless gesture and reclaimed his straying heart.

"So!" Glory began, "You're actually *leaving* that handsome man here, easy prey for all the conniving young women in Natchez?"

"I haven't much choice," Camille muttered.

"No, I s'pose not. Well, that's that, then. Tell you what, I'll be your eyes and ears while you're gone."

"What are you two plotting?" Marguerite had joined them as they strolled arm in arm down the wide drive, shaded by oaks over a century old.

"They're up to their usual schemes, I'm afraid. Let all eligible bachelors beware!" Dandy said, with a rebuking glance first at one lovely girl and then the other. "No one is safe with these two around. Maybe I should warn Charles?"

"You'll do no such thing, Dandy Ashton, and you know it!" Glory poked him in the ribs, but did not remove her arm from his. Making a wide circle, they turned back toward the house.

"Now, Cam! You must write every day!" Glory urged, a catch in her voice.

Camille laughed. "But when would I have time to do my lessons?"

"Surely you can't be planning to do *lessons*! Why, just think of the dances, the parties, the *theater*!"

The forced laughter of the friends was stilled by the sight of Josef hoisting the bags onto the top of the carriage. Camille's throat constricted in pain, and she fought to hold back the tears as she hugged each of her friends fiercely.

Glory squeezed her hard and whispered in her ear, "There he is, Cam! Your *husband*." With a teasing giggle, Glory gave her friend a gentle shove in Charles's direction. "You *are* going to kiss him goodbye, aren't you?"

Unfamiliar, but not unpleasant feelings surged through Camille. Throwing a sharp look over her shoulder at her friend, she hurried toward Charles, who was helping a pale and shaken Jacqueline down the steps.

"Jacqueline, what's wrong?" Concern darkened Camille's eyes from cool indigo to a smoky slate as she hurried to support her sister's other arm. "You are not ill again?" she asked, fighting a rising panic.

"I think she's just very tired. The strain of the past few days has been difficult, and perhaps she has a bit of a chill, but nothing more serious than that, I assure you. Please don't worry, Camille."

Charles's soft voice had its usual comforting effect on her, she discovered as she looked up into his dark eyes full of concern for her and her sister.

"Thank you, Charles." In spite of her displeasure at being sent away, she was grateful for his steady strength and consistent support through their troubles. Her father had been lucky to have had such a friend. Could she dare to hope she might also be lucky to have him for a husband?

Looking up at him, she thought she could certainly do worse. Standing tall in his soft leather riding boots, fitted waistcoat hugging his trim waist, he looked very handsome. Over his shoulder, she saw Glory wink at her and grin widely.

Charles handed the two young women up into plush seats of burgundy velvet. Last minute instructions were recited and acknowledged, youthful goodbyes and kisses thrown in both directions.

When at last there was no excuse to delay any longer, Charles still had not given the command to leave. He strode up to Camille's window and placed one hand on the facing.

For several seconds he looked at her with an unreadable expression on his face, his dark eyes mysterious. Camille hardly breathed as his gaze held hers. He raised his other hand to reveal a perfectly shaped and fragrant gardenia.

"This is for you, little Camille. Go with God."

"And you, Charles," she replied with her hand in his, her voice husky with emotion. Though he would ride behind them to the waterfront, Camille realized he preferred to say goodbye here.

The carriage pulled slowly away, down the tree-lined drive. Eyes almost blinded by tears, Camille's last glimpse of home was of the gardenia bush at the foot of the drive, dropping its ivory blossoms one by one to the earth, and the giant magnolia tree sheltering her friends and her home.

She hugged Jacqueline tightly and the two of them wept bitterly, Camille for the first time. When the tears were spent, she felt a little better, and hope crept into the space occupied only by despair before. She dared to think perhaps everything would be all right again one day.

When at last she spoke, it was with some of her old spirit. "Jacqueline, look! There's the *Natchez*!"

From the top of Silver Street, two hundred feet above water level, she could see the queen of the river, its name painted proudly in bold letters on its side. The grandest of the twenty or so boats at the landing, the *Natchez* rode regally in the water while roustabouts hastily loaded and unloaded its cargo. Two immense smokestacks rose majestically into the air, their tops feathered with delicate white filigree, as was every spare inch of the riverboat's trim, in a display of the captain's vanity and showmanship.

This was the fourth *Natchez*, its predecessors having fallen victim to one of the many hazards of a steamship's brief life. They had either worn out, burned up, run aground, sunk or—all too often—exploded in one of the rowdy races their captains so loved.

Each time she was rebuilt, she became more ornate. Her wide decks were flanked by big wheelhouses that covered the three-story-high paddle wheels.

Camille was fascinated as she took in every detail of the scene before her. The street wound its way down the hill in front of them, teeming with people, buggies, wagons, horses and mules. It was dusty and smelly and noisy. A line of care-worn slaves shuffled down the steep road where no flowers or grass survived to soften the barrenness or settle the dust.

Camille brushed away the painful memory of that night a few short weeks ago when she'd come here to find Charles Longmont at her father's request.

"Won't it be fun, Jacquie?" She tugged on her sister's thin arm, longing to make her smile again. "It'll be fine—and great fun, you'll see," she continued, but Jacqueline did not respond.

Charles went aboard to check on their accommodations, while Josef supervised the loading of their baggage. The elderly servant shook his head from side to side sadly and bid them farewell.

"Bye, Missy Cam, Missy Jacq'line." Backing up several steps, he turned and fled so they wouldn't see the tears that coursed down his wrinkled cheeks.

Glancing toward the landing, Camille saw Charles once more astride his favorite stallion, watching them intently. He bent to hear something Josef said to him, then lifted his hand in a farewell salute. Camille knew he would wait there until they were out of sight, and the thought made her heart skip a beat.

The lonesome whistle lingered in the air as the boat prepared to pull away from the dock. Paddle wheels slapping against the muddy waters of the Mississippi echoed the beating of Camille's heart.

The *Natchez* had steamed its way to the middle of the river channel before a disturbance on the sandbar at the Vidalia landing drew Camille's attention.

Several well-dressed men stood there. Two of the men paced away from each other as the others hurried off to one side. The two turned and, in measured steps, walked toward each other. Though she could not see clearly, Camille realized with a start that each man held a weapon. Seconds later, after a scuffle, one of them lay on the ground, his blood seeping into the sand.

"My God!" she gasped in horror. "What was that all about?"

"You mean you never seen a duel, little lady?" asked a gruff voice behind her. "The famous bowie knife in action," he chuckled.

"Of course I haven't," she snapped. "Ladies never . . ."

Camille left the sentence unfinished, her mouth agape as her eyes traveled up two legs as thick as tree trunks, and across the expanse of a massive chest to a drooping white mustache and curling locks of the same pale shade laced with streaks of black that hung to the man's shoulders. His square face was alive with good humor, and he was obviously enjoying the whole scene.

"Ladies never . . . watch duels, is that it? They just cause 'em! Yessirree! They just cause 'em!" His laughter thundered across the deck and Camille's face reddened as she realized everyone was listening to them.

"How can you laugh—about an awful thing like one man taking another's life?" she demanded.

"Easy, child. It happens every day in my world." He watched Camille closely, eyes squinting. "Name's Jonathan Blackwood, Cap'n John, to my friends. What's yours?"

"I'm Camille Beaufort Longmont, and this is my sister, Jacqueline Beaufort."

"You two traveling alone, are you?"

"Oh, no, sir! My Aunt Emily is already settled in our cabin, I understand."

"Yessirree, Mrs. Emily Lawrence, from Vicksburg. You're in good hands, my dear child, but if there's anything I can do, feel free to call on me."

Though he was a strange man, Camille found to her surprise she didn't dislike this captain who spoke his mind so readily. "An interesting character, Cap'n John," she remarked to her sister before turning her attention back to the swirling waters of the mighty river.

Camille loved the familiar wild scenery and unending line of trees bordering the river on the Mississippi side, interrupted by an occasional isolated cabin or plantation. At irregular intervals, crude landings jutted out into the water. Spanish moss dripped off the trees and over the banks, looking very much like the "Spaniard's beard" it was often called.

On the deck of the *Natchez*, Mississippi cotton planters strode back and forth in their large, broad-brimmed hats, lace cuffs and ruffled shirts, an air of importance and wealth about them. Some had business in New Orleans, but others were on their way to Europe. From far-flung capitals of the continent, they would return with delicately carved rosewood furnishings, Belgian lace and other fine fabrics, Italian marble mantles, serving pieces of Sheffield silver, possessions designed to bring a sparkle to the eyes of their wives and daughters and an aura of luxury to their plantations.

Camille's heart warmed toward Charles as she was ushered into the elegant and luxurious suite he had reserved for them. Rose-colored draperies, original oil paintings and gilt-edged mirrors decorated the spotless white walls. Her feet sank into thick, luxurious carpet, and Aunt Emily grinned at her from one of the bedroom doors.

"Well, it's about time! I was beginning to think I might have to make this trip without you, my dears."

Camille was astounded at the way the elderly woman was able to gather her and her sister into an enthusiastic hug simultaneously.

"Aunt Emily, it's so good to see you. How was your trip down from Vicksburg? It's been so long since you've paid us a visit at Magnolia. We've missed you."

Emily Lawrence was a close family friend who'd always been called "Aunt" by the girls, though there was no actual family connection. Happily, her shopping trip to New York coincided with their voyage, and she had agreed to accompany them all the way to Baltimore.

"I've missed you, too, but dear Uncle Robert has had such a case of the gout, and I haven't been able to get away for a minute. Now he's much better, and, my dears, I feel just like a bird out of a cage. Oh, we're going to have such a grand time! Tell me, what do you think of this magnificent suite? Charles insisted on paying my passage, and he's obviously spared no expense. He must be a remarkable man, this Mr. Longmont of yours!"

"Yes, I didn't expect anything so grand. It *is* beautiful," Camille said, turning to Jacqueline who lingered inside the doorway. "Come on, Jacquie." She had never seen her sister in such a state—she didn't seem to care about anything, and her face was constantly pale. Aunt Emily put an arm around Jacqueline and took her into the other room to get her settled, murmuring soothing words all the while.

Camille paced the length of the stateroom several times, her irritation escalating with each step. Jacqueline should be home, not here in this strange place. She should have Josef and Indigo and the family doctor to care for her.

Camille's feeling of gratitude for Charles was replaced by a blossoming resentment. He had been wrong to send them away. Maybe he wanted them out of his way. He probably had a ladyfriend and now would be free to see her whenever he wanted.

How dare he do this to them—shipping them off like a pair of second-rate relatives? His apparent concern for them had been only a charade; he couldn't wait to be rid of them.

For Jacqueline's sake, Camille concealed her feelings and pretended to be having a good time, though it seemed to make no difference to her sister, who remained listless, and was occasionally feverish and violently ill. Aunt Emily bustled about, caring for Jacqueline the best she could, leaving Camille free to spend at least part of the time on the deck, where she loved to feel the wind blow freely through her hair.

To fill the endless hours, Camille watched the other passengers with an avid fascination. All types of people had chosen the river for travel, from the professional gamblers who loved to fleece the wealthy planters, to whole families making a happy outing of the trip downriver.

Camille found her interest repeatedly captured by a man dressed in black whose eyes blazed with a dark fanatical fire. She was frightened, but unaccountably intrigued by this man who kept to himself, taking no part in the shipboard conversations and making no effort to develop an acquaintance with any of the other passengers.

A brilliant sunset colored the muddy waters briefly before darkness fell with surprising swiftness, sending a chill of foreboding through Camille. She hurried below to check on Jacqueline, and was startled to find a stranger sitting with her sister and Aunt Emily in their cabin.

Camille questioned the older woman, "Is something wrong, Aunt Emily?"

"Oh, no, my dear. This is Dr. Resnick. He learned of Jacqueline's poor health and kindly stopped by to see if there was anything he could do. This is Camille Longmont, Dr. Resnick."

"Charmed, my dear. Charmed." His soft, puffy hands grasped hers and he smiled in an ingratiating manner she found most unpleasant.

Extracting her hand from his as quickly as possible, Camille murmured, "Nice to meet you, sir," and turned away to sit beside her sister, who seemed to hang on every word that fell from the doctor's thick lips.

"Isn't he just too kind, Camille, to stop in like this?" she asked.

"Yes, I'm sure, Jacquie, but shouldn't you be in bed?" The constant motion of the boat combined with the unfamiliar rich foods had kept Jacqueline's delicate constitution in an unsettled state for the whole voyage. She seemed to feel well only when lying quite still on her bed.

"Oh, I feel better just listening to Dr. Resnick, Camille. And he's been telling us about a minister who is also on board."

"Yes, indeed, Clement Masters is a marvelous man—a truly wonderful servant of the Lord." The doctor's praise held a false note that bothered Camille, but she said nothing as he continued speaking to Jacqueline. "You really must meet him, my dear. It is entirely possible he might be able to help you—"

"In what way, Dr. Resnick?" Camille broke in, distressed by his pretentious words and by Jacqueline's apparent interest in them.

"Why, my girl, he is a well-known healer and it is said he can effect miraculous cures. Your sister here seems to be in need of just such as he."

"I thought that was *your* domain, Dr. Resnick," responded Camille sharply, anxious to get this so-called doctor out of their cabin.

"Of course, of course. Only I'm sure you realize, there are things that go beyond my abilities—things no mere man can do," he said piously.

"And this is where your Mr. Masters comes in?"

"*Reverend* Masters," he corrected, beginning to recognize her skepticism and feeling uncomfortable and defensive. Turning back to Jacqueline, he continued, "Wouldn't you like to meet him, child, talk with him for a few minutes, perhaps?"

"Oh, yes!"

Camille looked at Jacqueline and was taken aback by the hope shining from her eyes. She actually believed all this! For her part, Camille found that she was starting to have doubts about this man even being a part of the medical profession. If anything, he was only a quack.

But she hadn't seen this much animation on her sister's part in a long time, and she couldn't bear to do anything to dim her enthusiasm, not yet anyway. Surely it couldn't hurt for her to meet the man. Besides, Camille doubted she could do anything to stop it, particularly if Aunt Emily agreed, which she appeared to be doing.

"We'll be on deck tomorrow morning at ten," Camille said, dismissing him and making sure he realized that she would be with her sister.

"Well . . . well . . . see you then. I'm sure Clem—uh, *Reverend* Masters will be so happy to meet you and talk with you."

I'll just bet he will! Camille thought, wondering what these two men were up to.

The next morning, a warm, heavy humidity hung over the river, but the dull iron-gray skies refused to give up their moisture. No breezes blew to relieve the unseasonable, oppressive heat.

Idly, Camille waved her fan as her eyes followed a leggy snow-white heron successfully snatching its prey from the water. She heard the flutter of its wings as it rose to the sky and passed overhead.

Jacqueline sat quietly beside her sister on an identical wooden deck chair, but her eyes moved restlessly, scanning each passenger who approached them. Camille knew she was looking for the doctor and his "miraculous" friend. Aunt Emily dozed, snoring softly, a few feet behind them. She would be of little help.

The rotund doctor soon appeared at the far end of the deck, followed closely by an emaciated figure, garbed all in black. With a start Camille recognized the man with the strange black eyes she'd noticed on deck the day before.

"Oh, no!" The words were out before she could stop them.

"Cam, what is it?" Jacqueline asked, but her eyes and attention were trained on the two incongruous figures moving steadily toward them across the length of the boat.

How could she explain to her sister the sudden, tearing fear that ripped through her, especially since she couldn't help noticing the welcoming smile on Jacqueline's face?

"It's nothing," she answered, standing to greet the men. But she told herself she'd soon find a way to be rid of them.

"Good day, gentlemen." Camille's false smile did not fool the doctor or the preacher, she could tell, but she was hopeful that at least Jacqueline hadn't noticed the sarcasm in her voice.

"Good day, ladies. This is the friend I was telling you about. Camille Longmont, Jacqueline Beaufort, may I present the Reverend Clement Masters?"

Hard, black eyes that missed nothing swept over the two young girls, lingering with pretended interest on the younger, more interested one.

"How do you do, Miss Beaufort?" As an afterthought he acknowledged Camille, then immediately turned his attention back to Jacqueline, whose eyes were trained on him with passionate interest. She believed this man could help her! Camille realized that this meeting had been a terrible mistake.

The "Reverend" Masters asked Jacqueline several pointed questions and filled her head with more nonsense, promising a miraculous cure if she would only believe his precepts and follow the regimen he suggested. What foolishness! But Camille was thoroughly frightened by Jacqueline's devoted response to him.

That night as she sat brushing her hair, Camille replayed the events of the afternoon, her mind dwelling on the unfeeling black eyes of the preacher and the unctuous devotion he seemed to arouse in both the doctor and her sister. Soon they would be in New Orleans, and Camille fervently hoped they would be rid of him there. No harm had been done, surely, in so short a time. But the worried frown remained on her face even as she climbed into bed and extinguished the lamp.

Following the circuitous route of the Mississippi made the 255 mile trip seem much farther, but at last the *Natchez* steamed its way into the dock at New Orleans. A bustling place, the city teemed with boats of all sorts and all sizes docked one against the other, so closely a man could have strode from one to the other without getting his feet wet. As the *Natchez* sidled up and was secured with long ropes by several dockhands, Camille's eyes swept over the portion of New Orleans she could see.

In the foreground along the levee were lean-to establishments where vendors hawked their wares, ranging from raw fish to the famous pralines. Behind these, the Cabildo and Presbytère flanked the stately cathedral. On either side of the square were the deluxe apartments built by Baroness Pontalba in 1849 and 1850, fronted by new walks and gardens. New Orleans seemed to have a life of its own that beckoned to the young girl standing alone in the prow of the boat.

Anxious to be back on solid ground and well away from the preacher as soon as possible, Camille hurried Jacqueline and Aunt Emily off the steamship. They would stay with friends of Aunt Emily for the two days until they were to board the sailing vessel *Martinique* for the remainder of the trip. Camille had heard a great deal about the Crescent City and was determined to see as much of it as she could in the short time they would be there.

Their hosts, wealthy long-time residents of the Garden district, thoughtfully arranged a carriage tour for the following day. New Orleans was an exciting, rowdy town, and the French Quarter was said to make Natchez Under the Hill look like a child's playground. It lay along the waterfront, isolated from the other parts of town. The residents were apparently satisfied that the seedy elements of New Orleans had been collected in one spot and could therefore be contained, at least to some degree.

They visited the Place d'Armes and Camille spent a few moments in the sacred quiet of the cathedral. As she knelt, she recalled the strange black eyes of the preacher, and the way they'd seemed to see right through her. Thankfully, they had not seen him again, and if her prayers were answered, they would *never* see him again.

The two-day break in their voyage was over all too soon, and Camille and her small party boarded an ocean-going vessel for the remainder of the trip. The *Martinique* was a sleek and speedy boat when under full sail and, with favorable winds, made good time through the Gulf and around the tip of Florida. The northward leg of their journey, however, proved to be much less pleasant as they were alternately battered by violent storms and rough seas, and becalmed by gentle breezes.

They had been at sea for some time before the Reverend Clement Masters made his unwelcome appearance. It seemed he had been on a circuit of the western territories, and was now on his way home. Camille was disturbed to learn that his destination was the same as theirs, Baltimore. They had not seen the last of the troublesome man as she'd so fervently hoped.

Camille's restlessness increased along with her sister's continued weakness. She was more than a little concerned by the presence of the preacher and his increasing influence on Jacqueline. Oh, if only they were back home at Magnolia! Then everything would be all right.

It was all Charles's fault! She cultivated her resentment for the man who was her husband, the man who controlled her fortune, the man who had sent her and her sister on this impossible journey.

Chapter Three

BALTIMORE, MARYLAND, 1859

"NO! IT'S NOT SAFE!" the headmistress of Green Oaks said vehemently. "Surely you don't plan to make that kind of a journey across country, Camille. Besides, I'm sure Mr. Longmont is expecting you to return the same way you arrived here in Baltimore!"

Miss Lucille Cavanaugh sat primly behind a massive Louis XIV desk in a walnut-paneled room filled with priceless antiques. Bright April sunlight filtered through the small window behind her, outlining her stiffly erect body and small gray head that bounced up and down when she talked.

During the past six years at Green Oaks School for Young Ladies, Camille had never lost her respectful awe for the headmistress, though she'd often failed to heed her admonitions. Now she must defy her again, for Camille's urgent need to return to Magnolia took precedence over all else.

"I appreciate your concern, Miss Cavanaugh," she said calmly, "but I cannot wait for a ship. I must return to Magnolia at once." She purposely avoided further mention of Charles, knowing full well he'd be furious and would try to stop her if he knew of her change of plans.

Camille would have been the first to admit that her years at the boarding school had not been entirely unpleasant, though she had fought a losing battle with homesickness. Learning had become a passion for her, and she'd taken to her studies, earning high marks in chemistry, languages, and philosophy, as well as in the fine arts classes she adored.

She would be taking home with her boxes of gilt-edged books of Plato and Aristotle, as well as the more popular novels of the Brontë sisters and Charles Dickens.

Worlds had opened to her she'd never dreamed possible and she was hungry for more, her head swimming with new ideas and notions. Private lessons from a Pennsylvania banker had introduced her to the world of business and she was anxious to utilize what she had learned in the management of Magnolia.

Camille's only problems at school had come from her tendency to follow her unconventional impulses first and face the consequences later. Curfew was meaningless to her, even when she had to pay the penalty for staying out beyond the acceptable time. The more anyone tried to apply the rules to her, the more she resisted, and some of the conventions required by the traditional school she found appalling.

"Will your sister be traveling with you?" the headmistress inquired.

"I'm afraid not. The winter has been especially hard on Jacqueline. She's promised to come as soon as she can, though." Pain etched a momentary frown on Camille's lovely face. She knew the real reason her sister remained in Baltimore was her attraction for the charismatic preacher. Recalling the strange, wild eyes of Clement Masters, Camille felt a surge of dislike and distrust that had intensified since she'd first met him on board the *Natchez*.

The two young women had argued about the return home, but Camille had been unable to persuade her sister to leave Baltimore. She was very worried about Jacqueline, and hoped to enlist Charles's help in getting her back to Natchez as soon as she could talk with him in person.

"You plan to travel alone, then?" The headmistress's stern voice broke into Camille's thoughts again.

"No, Lauren St. James will be returning with me. She is from Washington, which is just north of Natchez. We've talked it over and I've made all the arrangements. My mind is made up, Miss Cavanaugh. We leave within the week." Camille's voice was firm, making it clear she would brook no interference with her plans.

Miss Cavanaugh noted that Camille's soft Southern drawl had taken on none of the flat pronunciations of the Easterners during her years there. She smiled, deciding that was probably because the young men seemed so enchanted by it. And this was a young woman who knew how to capitalize on an asset.

Could this beautiful young woman be the same Camille Beaufort Longmont who had arrived on her doorstep over six years ago? The headmistress could still see her as she'd looked on that November morning, her freckles like fine sand scattered across an upturned nose, her younger sister's hand clasped tightly in hers.

Miss Cavanaugh's faded blue eyes scanned the face of the young heiress. The freckles had disappeared, leaving an unblemished complexion of the creamiest ivory. In contrast, her vivid black curls swirled in unruly fashion around her dainty head and shoulders. She had become a breathtaking beauty, but the same

stubborn pride and determination still lurked beneath
the ladylike exterior.

With a sigh, Miss Cavanaugh realized it would be
futile to argue further. "There's no more to be said,
then," she conceded, making a mental note to write
Charles Longmont immediately about the change in
plans.

The two women bid polite farewells and Camille
hurried from the room, more disturbed than she
wanted to admit by Miss Cavanaugh's warning.

The journey would be long and arduous, if not
dangerous. She was foolhardy and stubborn to even
consider it. If she were wise, she would probably take
the headmistress's advice and wait for the first available ship.

But it might be weeks before the spring storms were
over, making ocean travel safe, and she had to get
home as soon as possible.

SLENDER FINGERS DRUMMED impatiently on the
wooden seat of the carriage. Despite misgivings at her
mode of travel, Camille would soon be on her way! For
most overland trips, even short ones, several different
forms of transportation had to be employed, often-
times a combination of water and land travel. In this
instance, Camille had hired a coach for the compara-
tively short trip to Pittsburgh where she and Lauren
would board a steamer on the Ohio River bound for
the Mississippi. She tried to calm her racing heart and
maintain her outward composure as she and Lauren
waited for the other passengers to arrive. Where had
that coach driver gotten off to, anyhow?

Going home at last! Joy bubbled through her with
thoughts of Magnolia and her friends back in Nat-

chez. Glory's chatty, informative letters had come regularly to Baltimore, keeping her in touch with life at home, but they were nothing like the long talks the two friends had when they were together.

Glory's latest epistle promised an exciting announcement on Camille's return! She was sure Dandy had proposed, and that he and Glory were engaged. Marguerite had already been married for three years and had two babies, a boy and a girl. Things would not be the same at all. But it was the last letter she had received from Charles that was the cause for her haste in returning to Natchez. She was sure his plans called for drastic changes in Magnolia.

With her eyes closed, Camille could see her home as clearly as on the day she'd left. She loved the austere beauty of its ivory columns, the beckoning shade of gigantic magnolia trees, and the rolling grassy knolls leading down to the pond. She'd spent many happy days on those grounds and knew every slope and twisting stream.

Magnolia would be empty now, except for the houseservants. Unless, of course, Charles was living there. No, she knew he would not do that. But would he expect to move in now—with her? Or was he anxious for the promised annulment so he could get on with his life? Why should she care, anyway, for his wishes? What mattered was what she felt and what she wanted, as he would soon discover.

Although almost twenty years old, Camille still felt in some ways very much the thirteen-year-old child who'd left Natchez six years ago. She had loved the attention of the young men who flocked around her while she was at school, but she was married to a man—how old would he be now, thirty-one?

How would it feel to come face to face with her husband? Camille pictured his tall, slender body, his thick mahogany hair, and recalled the strength and softness of his touch, the sudden warmth of his laughter. In the past, she'd had a girlish adulation and respect for him, but now that she was a woman, how would she feel?

Camille had no way of knowing if she would be considered pretty by a mature man, someone who had probably known a lot of beautiful women. Would he want to remain married to her?

She shook her head and rebuked herself for pursuing such thoughts. As soon as she returned and was able to take over her father's affairs, she would demand the annulment he'd promised. Surely it was what Charles wanted, too, since he'd obviously never cared for her.

The small hurt she'd felt when he had sent them away in spite of her protests had festered and grown during the long, lonely years at Green Oaks. It was *his* fault Jacqueline was so ill and could not even come home with her. If he hadn't insisted they make that damned journey...!

No, Charles Longmont was not the man she had once thought. Why, he'd probably spent the family fortune by now and made himself at home at Magnolia with his ladyfriend. How could she ever have allowed him to persuade her to leave Natchez?

The driver returned with news that there would be no other passengers, and after a few more delays, the coach lurched into motion. Their travel was, if not comfortable, at least not totally unpleasant. The wooden seats were covered with thin padding and they were protected from direct sunlight by the high roof and shielded from blowing dust by thick windows of cloudy glass. Camille and Lauren bounced along in the private coach as far as Pittsburgh, with only brief stops for refreshment along the way.

The Pennsylvania town was full of political speculation about the new western territories and their slavery status, as well as the upcoming election of 1860, which would be critical in the sectional dispute over slavery and state's rights. Secession was almost a certainty should Abraham Lincoln be elected. He would not allow slavery to be extended to the territories and felt a fierce devotion to the Union. Serious trouble brewed.

Camille was appalled at the anti-slavery sentiment rampant among Northerners in the rough-and-tumble river town. She thought these people had no true understanding of slaves or of their status or treatment on Southern plantations, and told them so quite plainly.

Dining at a local restaurant with some new acquaintances, she had remained quiet as long as she could before bursting out, "It's not like that at all! Obviously, sir, you've never been south of the Mason-Dixon line!" Her remarks were directed toward one particular man who had been holding forth in a vehement diatribe against slavery in particular, and Southerners in general.

Flabbergasted at her blunt remarks, the corpulent old gentleman glared at her. "Women should keep silent..." he blustered, not about to be bested by a mere chit of a girl!

"I did, sir, as long as I reasonably could, in good conscience." Her Southern drawl thickened as she lowered her lashes to charm her way back into the good graces of those at the table who were looking at her in open shock. "But, honestly, I think you all should see for yourselves before you berate the 'perils of slavery.' I've lived with slaves all my life and all the families I know own slaves, and I've *never* seen a single one mistreated, as you suggest.''

His mouth dropped open and his face began to redden as he stuttered again, ''But . . . but . . .''

''Yes, sir, our slaves eat from our table, are under the care of our family physician, and have every Saturday night and Sunday afternoon to their own pursuits.''

Thoughtfully, she continued, ''I don't think I can honestly say I've ever seen an unhappy slave, sir,'' she paused, ''and I surely can't say the same thing for some of you.'' She looked pointedly at his glowering face. ''Now, if you'll excuse us, gentlemen, we have an early departure tomorrow.'' She nodded to Lauren, who had not said a word during the entire dinner but had listened with rapt attention. They both rose and bid the Pennsylvanians a good-night.

''I didn't know you felt so strongly about slavery, Camille,'' said Lauren as they climbed to their upstairs bedroom.

''Neither did I.'' Camille smiled widely. ''But I *did* love his stammering. He certainly is not used to anyone speaking their mind, particularly not a woman, I think!'' They giggled as they entered their room where a small fire crackled merrily against a late spring chill in a corner fireplace. The room was plain, but clean and comfortable. They snuggled into bed and talked for a long time before sleep finally came.

The next day was one of those rare creations of spring, with every ingredient perfectly prepared. Clear, bright sunlight sparkled across the deep blue water of the Ohio River like faceted diamonds. A soft breeze rustled pleasantly in the tops of tall trees, newly bedecked with glossy green leaves.

The entire town of Pittsburgh seemed to have turned out to greet the steamship, always a welcome sight on the riverfront. Children frolicked along the banks, itching to climb aboard the big steamer tied up at the dock.

Lighthearted and prime for the adventure, Camille and Lauren strolled toward the boarding ramp, with lacy parasols unfurled to protect their delicate skin from the awful nemesis of freckles and tanning. Lauren was shorter than Camille, and her tightly curled red hair and vivid green eyes made her a striking contrast to her traveling companion. Thus far on the trip, the two had discovered that they had little in common, other than reaching their destination. Camille found Lauren too selfish and self-centered, and Lauren thought Camille entirely too headstrong and impetuous. There had not been a clash of wills, but a kind of understanding had been reached wherein each allowed the other as much privacy as possible, and their conversations were confined to general things as a rule, preventing argument.

The tall captain in his immaculate dress uniform greeted the two stunning young women warmly as they stepped aboard. "My dear young ladies, your cabin is prepared in the stern just as you requested. I trust you will be most comfortable there. Steward!" he shouted. "Show these young ladies to Cabin Three." Turning back to them, he assured them, "You will only be two doors down from my own cabin. Therefore, I can look after you personally and see to your safety and comfort."

Warm and sincere, his smile made Camille feel they were in good hands. He did not seem the type to indulge in the foolhardy races she'd heard so much about, where the captains pushed their engines beyond capacity, until they exploded violently, killing and injuring many of the passengers. Charles had taught her to request the rear cabin, since it was farthest from the boilers and would be safest in the event of an explosion.

As the days passed, Camille's favorable opinion of the captain grew. He seemed proud of his ship, and sincerely concerned with the comfort and safety of his passengers, particularly Camille and Lauren. They took their meals at the captain's table and he frequently checked on them to see that they had everything they wanted or needed. A week passed quickly, and they made only one brief stop in Cincinnati.

Two days later, they steamed into Louisville. Tidy homes faced the river and Camille was glad they would be spending the night there. But one night turned into several as a worried captain waited for upland spring rains to raise the water level over the treacherous ''Falls'' that lay just below the city.

''The Falls,'' he explained to the girls, ''is what boatmen call two miles of deadly rapids just below here. When the water is too low, the limestone ledges become very dangerous, making it practically impassable. So we'll wait for the spring rains to raise the water level. Also, we're waiting for Beau Monroe—a special Falls pilot who knows these waters like the back of his hand. He'll take us safely through, you can count on that.''

"When will Mr. Monroe arrive?" Camille asked, not overly concerned with possible danger, but still anxious to be under way.

"Tomorrow morning, I expect. He'll check the water level, and when he's satisfied, we'll shove off! You ladies have a pleasant night's sleep; perhaps your next one will be spent steamin' down the mighty Mississippi!"

"All right, Captain. Good night."

"Good night," Lauren repeated. After the captain had gone, she turned to Camille. "In the meantime, we can enjoy some more of that wonderful fresh trout for dinner," she said, licking her lips. Camille had no difficulty agreeing with that suggestion.

"FULL STEAM AHEAD!"

The happy optimism of the captain and the Falls pilot spread through the ship as the engines built up a powerful head of steam. Passengers stood in the sunshine on the deck waving to new friends they'd made during their extended visit in Louisville. No one seemed to give serious thought to the Falls they would encounter that day.

If the captain and Monroe thought it could be done, well, by God, so it could! seemed to be the attitude of townspeople and passengers alike. It had certainly been done countless times before, by this as well as other ships.

The placid waters gave little hint of what lay ahead and, after an extended leavetaking, people aboard settled into their previous routines: the crew competently going about their duties; the passengers walking about, sitting with a book in the shade, or heading below for a nap.

Camille chose the latter course, leaving Lauren topside while she went back to their cabin to unpack and rest. She loosened her stays, plumped up her pillow, and lay back on the narrow bed. The steady chugging of the engines and the side to side rocking motion of the boat soon had her dozing peacefully.

A loud screaming of the engines woke her abruptly. Disturbed, she sat up and tried to decide what could be wrong. An icy chill ran up her arms. Through the small window above her bed, she saw only billowing black smoke. The floor beneath her feet vibrated with more and more fuel being added to the boilers. Camille remembered the pilot saying that the boat must travel faster than the swift current if they were to safely navigate the Falls.

The Falls! Of course, that explained the uneven lurching of the boat, the sound of swirling waters and the massive build-up of steam. Why hadn't Lauren come below with her? Camille worried about her being up on deck now. She would be terrified by this unusual commotion. Camille reached for her shoes and sat on the edge of her bed to put them on, but she was hurled from the bed to the floor, her shoes flying across the room, as the boat made a steep dive.

Two miles of this! Camille thought, panic rising in her throat. She must get to Lauren! They would be safe in their cabin, surely. But her friend could be in trouble up on the deck.

Inch by inch, she pulled her way across the floor until she had retrieved her scattered shoes and somehow managed to get them on. She struggled to her knees, still unable to stand, and crawled toward the door. Her hand on the knob, Camille twisted and pulled with all her might, finally loosening the door, which flew inward with incredible force, flinging her against the wall. The sound of water combined with the laboring engines was now deafening. She wanted to hide her head under a pillow and put a stop to the awful racket, but there was no time! She had to find Lauren!

She staggered out through the open door. An ear-splitting noise filled the air and she felt the floor shudder beneath her as an explosion tore through the boat.

Camille was thrown back against the wall and the breath knocked from her. She fought against the darkness that threatened to overwhelm her, and steadied herself against the railing before she continued down the passageway. Pulling herself slowly along, she reached the narrow, smoke-filled stairs and began to climb. When she reached the top, she was quickly drenched by flying spray.

She fastened her life preserver around her as her eyes frantically searched the deck. Debris was strewn about and, in growing horror, she saw the burned bodies; some writhing in pain, others ominously still. It had been a deadly blast. Screams and moans of pain came from the other end of the ship near the boilers. She had to get to Lauren!

Though the smoke burned her eyes, Camille worked her way toward the section of the boat where the explosion had occurred, stopping to cover one woman with a blanket, wipe soot from a young man's eyes, and help a youngster to her feet. She hugged the child, speaking words of comfort, and located her parents who, thankfully, had survived the blast, though they had suffered some cuts and bruises.

The blast had torn a large hole in the boat, which now listed dangerously to one side. Camille was forced to grab the rail and edge her way along. She looked frantically for the familiar bright hair of her friend. What had she been wearing? Oh, yes, a bright green dotted swiss the same color as her eyes. Diligently, Camille inspected every person on deck, her hopes waning that she would find Lauren alive and uninjured. She had noticed a few other faces that also seemed to be missing. Had they been killed by the blast or could they have taken refuge below?

Turning back the way she'd come, she bumped into the captain, who set his big hands on her shoulders. "If you're looking for your young friend, ma'am, I'm afraid she's been hurt."

Camille was so pale it appeared she might faint, and he held her firmly. "Oh, not badly hurt! Just a few bruises and sprains. She's one of the lucky ones," he said sadly. "The Monroe sisters, were sitting so near the boilers . . . the explosion . . . I'm afraid the force of it blew the two sisters over the side. There was nothing anyone could do for them." There was a catch in the captain's voice but he continued, "Miss Lauren has been taken below. Now, I wonder, ma'am, could you help me see to the others? Some are in dreadful pain and we need to get them below and do what we can for them. I think the boat will hold till we get to Owensboro where we can get a doctor. But for now—" he shrugged tired shoulders "—we'll just have to do what we can. Keep 'er goin', Beau!" he shouted to the pilot, taking Camille's arm after she'd given a quick affirmative nod to his request, and turning toward the wounded.

Camille worked tirelessly through the long night, doing everything she could for the wounded, trying desperately not to think of the dead, of the poor Monroe sisters. Much later, she found Lauren.

"Camille! Where have you been? I've been in such awful pain! You just cannot imagine. No one seems to have any time for me at all. My leg aches horribly, and I can barely move my right arm. I hurt all over. I probably have broken bones nobody has even noticed. I may even have broken ribs."

Camille thought her injuries very slight indeed compared to the others she had seen, but refrained from speaking frankly, in consideration of Lauren's condition.

"I'm sure you'll be fine, Lauren. We were really very lucky. The two Monroe sisters..." Her voice trailed off as she thought of the two women catapulted violently through the air and disappearing into the dark waters. "And there are one or two others who may not survive their injuries."

Camille's heart was torn when she thought of the crew member so badly burned he was almost unrecognizable, and of the passenger who had probably suffered a broken back in a fall down a flight of stairs.

"It was a horrible explosion! And all that captain's fault for taking us over the Falls before it was safe."

"You're wrong, Lauren, so why don't you just hush—and...and...go to sleep or something!" Camille had stalked away, impatient with Lauren's bad humor and complaints, which continued to fly even as she went out the door.

"Camille! You come back here! Do you hear me? I don't want to be alone. I'm your friend. Can't you see your place is with me?"

The next morning Camille helped the captain get the wounded ashore and to a doctor. Later, in a brief ceremony, the survivors said goodbye to those who had perished. Finally Camille collapsed for a few hours of much-deserved sleep.

When she awoke, her fatigue-drugged mind had to deal with the problem of how they would get home. The ship had been damaged beyond repair, and she learned that there would not be another downriver for some time.

"There is another way," Beau Monroe assured her. "A packet boat goes back and forth from here to Colbert's Ferry, down on the Tennessee. But from there on, you'd have to travel the Natchez Trace, and it's no place for a lady, no ma'am!"

Camille shivered, recalling tales of daring holdups and gruesome murders by bands of ruthless outlaws who roamed the Trace, an old roadway that ran from Nashville to Natchez.

"There's one man who could get you safely home across the Trace. Name's Zeb, and he sets out with a caravan fairly frequent down toward Natchez and back."

"Do you think he'd take us?" Camille had not hesitated in her decision. She would get home whatever way she had to—but she *would* get home! The Tennessee River—the Natchez Trace—it didn't matter. Nothing would stop her, not now!

"Yes'm, I b'lieve he would. I'll just go 'long with you to Colbert's Ferry and look 'im up."

A heated argument had developed when she told Lauren of her plans, however. "Camille you must be completely out of your mind! The Natchez Trace! No, indeed! I let you talk me into this crazy idea, but I won't have any more of your schemes! I'm staying right here until my father can come for me. And I'm not riding home in any wagon, you can be sure of that!'' With a snort of indignation, she had turned her face to the wall and would say no more.

''It's all right, dear,'' the captain had said to Camille when he learned of her dilemma, ''I'll be here to watch over your friend, and the kind folks who are tending to her have assured me she will be fine in a matter of days. Don't you postpone your trip on account of her bad temper. I know how much you're wantin' to get home. And when you get there, you can send her father right back for her.''

Finding the packet and getting down the small tributary of the Ohio had been easy. Finding Zeb once they'd gotten there had been another matter and had taken some doing. But at last Beau had good news.

''I've got 'im, ma'am. And he's pulling out with a caravan right away. Sez you're 'welcome as the rain' to join 'em!''

''Oh, good!'' she said with relief. ''And thank you, Mr. Monroe.'' But she was thinking, *Home at last!*

Chapter Four

THE PLEASANT-FACED caravan leader who would also be Camille's driver stood beside an open wagon. She gasped in dismay at the primitive conveyance that was to take her the rest of the way home. Unperturbed by her attitude, Zeb spit through the gap in his front teeth and grinned widely at her.

"Yes'm. It's the most sensible vehicle for the Trace. An' we got us a tarpaulin suppos'n the sun gits too hot or it decides to up'n rain on us." His matter-of-fact reply made her feel foolish and more than a little spoiled.

The few passengers who composed the caravan spent the night at a small inn. At first light, they set out. Zeb told Camille there would be occasional "stands" along the way offering at best lumpy beds and greasy food, but at least part of the time they would sleep in the open. Her sense of adventure dampened by this information, she was quiet for most of the morning.

Zeb, on the other hand, chatted unceasingly about his exploits in Texas, the unpredictable weather, varieties of forest animals, and numerous other subjects. He related the entire history of the Trace from early times up to the present. Camille listened with mounting alarm as he spun tales of the "gentleman bandit" and the awful Harpe brothers who had robbed and murdered for the fun of it during the 1790s.

Doubtless, the frightening tales she'd heard were often exaggerated. Too, it was said that the gentleman bandit was extremely handsome and could be quite charming. *It might even prove interesting to meet up with him!* she thought, with a flutter in her stomach.

Before long, though, Zeb's unabashed friendliness and the incredible wild beauty of the countryside began to work a subtle magic on her. There was a mysterious sense of wonder in the shaded tangle of trees and moss, and in the ancient roadbed itself. She could imagine fierce Indians and roaming herds of buffalo whose countless journeys had packed down the earth.

Clutching the wooden bench to keep herself from bouncing about each time the wagon's wheels met a hole in the trail, she sat by Zeb's side throughout the long day without further complaint.

Camille adjusted her wide-brimmed straw hat to keep the sun from burning her fair skin, glad she'd dressed appropriately that morning. A soft, brushed-leather skirt fell to the top of deerskin boots. Her shirtwaist blouse was open at the throat, and her fingers touched the locket her father had given her for her twelfth birthday. Inside it was a well-known, well-loved miniature of her whole family before death had begun to make its claims on them. It was her connection with her home, what was left of her family and her old way of life, and it was her dearest possession.

A feeling of loneliness and unfathomable sadness swept over her. Tears glistened in indigo eyes shaded by the big hat. No matter how hard she wished, things would never be as they once were. Wishing would never bring back her mother, her father, her brother.... Her apparent helplessness in the path of fate disturbed her most of all. She could have done nothing to prevent the tragedies of the past, and it seemed she had no control over the future. She could only face whatever might lie ahead.

Charles's last letter troubled her. In it he revealed his purchase of more land adjoining Magnolia and his plans to consolidate the two properties and build a "showplace."

Camille did not want a "showplace." She only wanted Magnolia as it had always been. Surely, when her father entrusted Charles with his daughters and management of their estate, he could not have known the power would go to Charles's head. The man must be addled to make such ridiculous plans without even consulting her!

But soon she would be home—with her husband— what a strange and frightening thought. She shivered, admitting to herself a degree of curiosity and excitement as well. As a child she'd dreamed of falling in love and marrying a handsome man, having lots of children, and being a devoted wife and mother. Well, she'd gotten off to an early start on at least one part of that dream, she thought, a wry smile curving her lips.

"Feelin' better, I see," the driver noted. "I know that kinda look. Gotta fella back home?"

"No—" she hesitated and added "—a husband."

"Uh-huh!" was his noncommittal reply. The matchstick sticking out of the side of his mouth hardly wiggled.

"Uh-huh!" she agreed, and they both laughed, feeling comfortable with each other. After several hours in his company, Camille was beginning to sincerely care for this overly talkative, but very kind man.

"Nope, it ain't gonna be a bad trip a t'all, not a t'all." He grinned and snapped the reins sharply. The pair of heavily muscled horses picked up their steady pace.

A soft breeze blew through Camille's hair, loosening tendrils about her face, though she'd tied it back in a sensible bun before they'd started out.

"It's such a lovely day," she murmured. The peaceful trail was overshadowed by trees and vines that occasionally allowed the warm sun to peep through.

Hours passed and the small caravan, consisting of five wagons and several single riders on horseback, stopped as necessary to fill their water containers or to relieve themselves in the thick trees along the edges of the pathway they followed. The Trace showed them its many faces; some soft and pleasing, others eerily dark and threatening.

Camille's slender fingers reached unconsciously to touch the beloved locket. *I still have Jacqueline and Magnolia,* she thought, vowing to cherish what remained. She would preserve Magnolia as it was when her father died. No one would ever take it from her!

She wriggled, her muscles tired and cramped from long hours on the hard wagon seat. Just then they rounded a sharp bend in the road, and Camille saw through the dim light a wagon and several riders on horseback.

"Ho, travelers!" Zeb called, and flung his big hand high in the air.

While he flashed a friendly gap-toothed grin, Zeb's right hand hovered over his pistol between them on the seat. Camille knew there was good reason to be wary of travelers on the Trace, as it was often hard to distinguish friend from foe. Many had died for their carelessness in meeting strangers.

The small haggard group had obviously been traveling a long way. A weary woman of indeterminate age clutched a small, dirty child to her breast in the wagon hitched to a pair of bony horses. Three men straddled beasts that looked hardly any better.

"Ho there!" replied a big man riding a dun-colored horse. "Ye be bound for Natchez, travelers?"

"Yup!" The matchstick hanging from Zeb's mouth barely moved. Though the pitiful band seemed harmless, Zeb's hand still rested by his gun.

"Best beware!" the man shouted. "One day back, we was jest makin' camp and *they* fell upon us before we could git our guns. I thought we was done fer sure! Why, they broke my brother's arm, there. I thought he was a goner."

"Who's that, friend?" Zeb questioned, eyes trained on the man's face.

"A rough and surly gang they was—shovin' us 'round 'n takin' what they wanted. 'Course it was precious little we had, 'z you kin see. Mayhap thet's why they left us—jest like thet!" He snapped dirty fingers. "Lookin' fer better pickin's, I 'spect. I'd sure 'nuff dig a hole 'n bury my val'bles tonight if I was you. Yessir, thet's what I'd do."

He shook his shaggy head. "Less'n ya could jest turn 'round 'n fergit the whole thing. The Trace ain't safe— 'specially not fer a purty woman!"

Camille didn't like the way his eyes slid over her fine clothing. She shivered, lowering her eyes while Zeb bid the man and his hollow-eyed companions a good day, thanking them for the warning. He pulled their wagon over to the side and let them pass.

Camille turned to watch them go by, realizing they would soon be back to Tennessee—and civilization.

And where would she be? In the middle of this wilderness, easy prey for the outlaws they'd described. What *would* such a band do to a "purty" woman? she wondered, knowing she never wanted to find out.

For the rest of the evening, she wrestled with her doubts. Maybe she should ask Zeb to take her back at least far enough to join the other group. Then she would be safe and she could take the first ship that came along. The thought was appealing, especially when she looked ahead at the lonesome trail winding deeper into wild and primitive lands.

"Zeb."

"Yes'm?"

She couldn't ask him to take her back! Camille had never backed away from anything, and she wasn't about to start now! She was on her way home, and one small scare wasn't going to send her running. No, there would be no more looking back.

"Won't it be time to stop soon?" she answered after a long pause.

"Yes'm."

The sun had dropped behind a thick wall of trees before the little caravan reached a small clearing and prepared to make camp. There was much bustling about, and Zeb chose a grassy spot for Camille, leaving several blankets for her comfort.

Camille wearily stretched out on the rough bed and gazed at a dusting of stars overhead. Though she was bone-weary, unfamiliar noises chased away sleep. She tossed and turned, trying not to think about creepy, crawly creatures of the night, not to mention the voracious wild animals roaming the woods. She specifically refused to let the idea of murderous bandits into her head. At last, she dozed fitfully.

Sometime later, she blinked, opening her eyes wide. Had she dreamed that whisper of sound? She stared into the darkness at the edge of the camp where firelight glimmered through a thick meshing of trees. Yes, the aromatic smell of pipe tobacco was probably just one of the caravan men enjoying a smoke before turning in.

Camille sat up and looked about. Everyone was sleeping soundly. She shivered in a sudden chill and the hair rose on the back of her neck. She had the distinct feeling she was being watched! Again she searched the darkness, but saw nothing. The camp fire some fifty feet away sent shadows leaping and receding through the trees and she told herself it was this that sent the icy hand of fear running down her spine.

There it was again! The whisper of a sound, so faint it could have been a leaf whooshing to the ground. Or it could be someone stepping on a leaf! She was too frightened to move or cry out.

Suddenly a menacing shadow loomed out of the darkness. Camille's breath caught in her throat. Her head pounded in panic, and she hoped with all her might she was only dreaming.

It was no dream. The dark form lounged against a nearby tree softly slapping a horsewhip against a muscular thigh encased in tight, black breeches. The soft, vibrating twang of the thin strip of leather against corded muscle was the only sound in the night stillness.

The man's upper body was swathed in shadows, and an aura of danger surrounded him. Camille felt herself drawn unwillingly under his hypnotic spell. Unable to move or utter a sound, she kept her eyes trained on the dark figure.

He seemed neither concerned at being seen, nor anxious to come closer, but stood puffing casually on his pipe. She could barely see the spark of flame when he inhaled, and the swirl of smoke above his head. Though slumbering campers were all around, it seemed as though they were completely alone. Nothing stirred.

How long did she lie there riveted by his magnetic presence? An hour? Or was it only seconds?

A breeze rustled the branches over his head. A golden shaft of moonlight fell briefly across his mane of thick hair, revealing a dark mask that covered most of his face.

Camille gasped. *My God!* she thought, *it's the gentleman bandit!* Her heart beat so erratically she feared it might stop.

His chuckle was low and seductive. She was mesmerized. Though every instinct warned her to flee or scream and rouse the camp, she remained still, waiting for his next move.

Then he vanished! He disappeared so completely he might never have been there! Only the woodsy aroma of his tobacco lingered in the air. Camille wondered if she'd imagined him. Her heart pounded and deep within a shivery yearning unfolded.

A long time passed and the mysterious man did not return. Finally her eyelids drooped, and exhausted, she fell once more into a troubled sleep.

When morning came Camille helped Zeb douse the fire and break camp without mentioning the incident of the night before. He would only grin and warn her against eating before bedtime!

Grime from the trail had settled into her hair and covered her clothes like a heavy mantle. How she longed for a real bath with warm water and scented soap! Though she'd done her best with cold creek water, she felt decidedly dirty and unattractive. But she was glad the darkness had hidden her disheveled appearance from her night visitor. Had he been real—or just a figment of her overactive imagination?

A morning downpour quickly changed the road to muddy ruts. The horses slugged wearily along, dragging heavy wagons and soggy passengers behind them. The promised tarpaulin brought little relief, for though it was some protection for her precious cargo of books and personal things, it did nothing to keep the rain and dampness from settling into her skirts and clinging uncomfortably to her legs and thighs.

By midday the rain had tapered to a drizzle with only a few big drops plopping noisily on the horses' backsides. A rainbow etched its way across the sky, taking Camille's breath away with its extraordinary beauty. She remembered learning at her mother's knee that the rainbow was God's promise of fulfillment. With a painful ache, she saw her mother sitting before a crackling fire, her skirts spread around her. And she saw five-year-old Camille climb up and snuggle in her mother's lap for a story. But it was so long ago, and now her mother seemed so far away, more like a dream than someone who had once loved her, someone whom she had once loved.

Warm sunshine followed the rains, making the afternoon muggy and miserably uncomfortable. Camille opened the collar of her cotton blouse and rolled up her sleeves as they bounced along.

"Sure 'nuff a hot one today," Zeb remarked.

"Sure is." She reached for the canteen. "How about a drink, Zeb?"

"Ladies first," he insisted, waiting until she finished.

Zeb drank with his head thrown back, so Camille was first to see several men approaching rapidly on horseback. Each of them held a gun. She tugged at Zeb's sleeve, but it was too late for him to react.

"What th' hell?" he muttered, spitting angrily. "It's the gentleman bandit hisself."

When the band of five men surrounded them, the masked leader stopped beside Camille's wagon. In the revealing light of day, she boldly looked him over.

From behind the anonymity of a mask, his dark eyes returned her stare. She felt his recognition. The mask and black hat pulled low over his face did not hide a mocking smile.

"Dear lady, we meet again."

Surely that was a line from one of her Victorian novels. She was not actually hearing it from this arrogant thief!

His voice, soft with her, turned harsh when he barked a general command. "Climb down, all of you."

Behind her, Camille heard gasps of fear and muttered complaints as members of the caravan grudgingly did as they were told. One of the bandits worked his way back, searching through each wagon.

Camille sat, stubbornly unmoving. The gentleman bandit slid from his horse to stand next to her wagon, his face only inches from hers. His eyes played over her, lingering on her heaving bosom before meeting the challenge in her eyes.

"You're much too spirited, my dear." His rough voice was a caress. With another mocking smile, he vaulted into the wagon and stood over her. He was entirely too close. She drew herself as far as she could over against the opposite side.

"Stay away from me." Her voice wavered a little, but at least she had managed to say something!

"Oh, no," he said softly. "Ask anything but that, dear lady." His voice was velvet, laced with steel. Unhurriedly he studied her.

Then he wedged himself onto the seat beside her, his leg brushing against hers. Alarm rippled up her spine as he reached toward her.

"Don't touch me!" she ordered. "Don't you dare touch me! My father's a very powerful man in Natchez. He'll have you hanged if you harm me."

A rich chuckle and flare of interest in his eyes evoked an answering quiver inside her. Surprisingly gentle, his hand toyed with her locket, his fingers brushing the bare skin of her neck.

"No!" Her hand reached to cover his. "No, take my wedding rings instead. See, this is a carat or more, and pure gold. The locket is of little value. A keepsake only!"

When his eyes met hers, she realized with surprise that he had not intended to steal from her, but she could see she'd made him angry. He snatched the locket from her neck.

"Damn you!" she shouted, reaching for his fist holding her precious necklace.

Zeb took a step toward the wagon, but the bandit sprang threateningly to his feet.

"No, Zeb!" she cried. "It's all right. He didn't hurt me."

The old man heeded her warning and backed away.

She turned flashing eyes on the bandit who had leaped to the ground. "All right. *Now* will you leave us?" she demanded imperiously.

"For now, my heart, but we will meet again." Then, giving an abrupt signal to leave, the masked leader swung onto his horse and the huge bay pivoted smoothly beneath him. The gentleman bandit's laughter echoed back over the thunder of hooves as the five horses galloped away.

"I hope we *never* meet again," she murmured, knowing even at that moment she was not telling the truth. She was intrigued, even fascinated by this masked but stunningly attractive man. In truth, she felt not the slightest fear of him—not anymore. She was somehow quite certain he would never hurt her.

She'd glimpsed fleeting pain in his dark eyes, perhaps even remorse. Suspecting that much lay below the menacing facade of the gentleman bandit, she wondered what had led him to a vagabond life of thievery.

"CONSARN IT, MA'AM! I *am* sorry. He just purely sneaked up on me." Angry at his own helplessness, Zeb was relieved the bandits hadn't hurt anyone.

"Why do you s'pose he took your locket and nothin' else?" he asked.

Camille couldn't answer. Her fingers traced the path on her neck that still tingled from the fire of his touch.

Why, out of everything on the caravan, had he chosen her necklace? Her most treasured possession would be worthless to him. He seemed not only uninterested in her rings, but unaccountably angry when she'd offered them instead.

The look in his dark eyes and his mocking laughter were imprinted in her memory. Camille would not soon forget the gentleman bandit of the Trace, nor could she easily erase the heated sensation of his touch on her bare skin. Even in her anger and passing fear, she acknowledged an unwelcome attraction for the too handsome bandit!

The next few days passed without incident, though Camille's watchful eyes were ever vigilant for another encounter with the bandit. He *had* promised they'd meet again, but she told herself he'd forgotten her as lightly as he forgot his crimes. She fought down her disappointment.

At last the tired caravan reached King's Tavern, the final stop on the Trace as it entered Natchez. The tavern, constructed of hand-hewn timbers and fitted together with wooden pegs, had weathered a century of Mississippi winters and, as it had hundreds of times before, welcomed Camille and the small band of weary travelers back home.

A servant sent by Charles had been awaiting her arrival and ran swiftly to fetch a carriage for the the rest of the trip home. While she waited, Camille bid a fond farewell to Zeb, who was returning to Colbert's Ferry to meet another caravan. She genuinely liked the older man, and insisted he call on her at Magnolia and meet Charles on his next trip to Natchez.

She had made it! It felt so good to see the familiar landmarks of home. A smile animated Camille's lovely face. She must be careful, but she was determined to see that she and her sister would have everything that was rightfully theirs. In the process, she would show Charles Longmont a thing or two.

Closing her eyes tightly, Camille tried to picture him, but his image stubbornly refused to appear. Instead she saw a dark, dangerous man, as tall as

Charles, and equally haughty. He stood with legs wide apart in a provocative stance, slapping a horsewhip against his thigh. Vividly she saw once more the mocking smile, and heard the echo of a familiar husky chuckle.

Chapter Five

CHARLES LOUIS LONGMONT nervously straightened his cravat and smoothed an invisible wrinkle from his pin-striped suit. He was decidedly uncomfortable in the elegant clothes of the successful Natchez planter, and wished fervently for his familiar broadcloth shirt and breeches.

It was early June, but the weather in Natchez was already extremely warm and humid. Charles much preferred the cool breezes that were more common in late spring, and would even have chosen clouds over this bright, unrelieved sunshine.

A worried frown puckered his suntanned brow as he impatiently brushed back an unruly lock of dark hair, admonishing himself again for behaving like a love-sick boy.

Why in thunder should he feel more like a bride-groom today than he had on his wedding day six years ago? His palms were sweaty and he fought to suppress a building excitement. He'd never expected this kind of reaction on the return of a nineteen-year-old girl, who had still been a child when he'd sent her away.

Camille. Coming home at last. His wife. Charles looked again at his image in the cheval mirror in his bedroom. What would she see? What would she think of him? Would he be only an old man to her? Would she immediately ask for the annulment he'd promised?

Though he didn't realize it, the man who stared back at him was virile and ruggedly handsome, with a new mustache that hugged his sensuous upper lip and hair longer than he'd ever worn it curling around his ears and the nape of his neck.

She's still a child, he told himself, and she deserves her chance to choose her beaux and finally her husband. And, too, there was faithful and patient Justine, who would be waiting for him to settle the Beaufort affairs and return to her. He should be glad to be relieved finally of his responsibility for the Beaufort sisters.

That morning, a breathless young servant had arrived at his doorstep with the news that Camille's caravan had reached King's Tavern. He'd immediately dispatched a carriage to meet her so that she could complete her trip to Magnolia in some comfort, and had begun to look toward her arrival with unexpected anticipation.

It was not gallant to keep a young lady waiting, he reminded himself, especially if that young lady was your wife. A twinkle in his eye was accompanied by a dazzling white smile as he turned and strode out the door.

Almost as an afterthought, he reached down to pluck a white gardenia blossom growing beside the steps. He tucked it into his lapel, pleased with himself. The subtle, haunting fragrance of the flower stayed with him as he rode toward Magnolia.

Charles didn't like to think how anxious he'd been to see Camille and welcome her back. It made him feel foolish and almost middle-aged, though there was not a gray hair to be found in his thickly curling dark brown hair.

Wanting to allow her time to rest and settle in at Magnolia, he had forced himself to wait before calling on her. She'd been home only a few hours now, but he could wait no longer.

The short distance to the Beaufort plantation was covered quickly. He reined in and jumped to the ground, his booted feet crunching the fine gravel. Camille stood waiting on the front portico.

His long strides covered the distance between them in purposeful strides. Then he stopped, looking up at her. Nothing in his experience could have prepared him for the intense physical shock he felt when he saw the young woman standing before him.

She stood regally tall. Her dusty-rose-colored dress was tight-waisted and the top cut low to reveal an enticing expanse of bare skin. Voluminous skirts swirled about a stunning figure as she took a step toward him.

Camille Braxton Beaufort Longmont had become a breathtakingly beautiful woman. Skin the color of heavy cream made a remarkable contrast to vivid turquoise eyes and cascading ebony curls that fell in tempting disarray halfway to her tiny waist.

Her bearing displayed an innocent, untouched sincerity and youth, even at the age of nineteen, but her ravishing smile revealed the sensuous woman underneath. He'd never seen anyone like her!

Her head cocked to one side regarding him so closely, she reminded him of the little girl he'd sent away. He saw anew her stubborn, independent spirit and remarkable courage—but nothing else remained of the child.

"Not even the freckles . . ."

"What?" She laughed, and the sound was a melody.

"Oh!" He hadn't realized he'd spoken the words aloud. "I said your freckles are gone," he repeated with a sheepish smile.

"Yes." Her wonderful laughter moved through him again, making him tingle with an unfamiliar pleasure. "I suppose they are," she continued. "Funny I hadn't thought of them in years!"

But I've thought of you. With the fingers of one hand, she touched her cheek hesitantly, as though seeking the missing freckles, and then held her hand out to him.

In instinctive response he drew her fingers to his lips, whisked the gardenia blossom from his lapel and laid it on her open palm, his warm hand still circling her dainty wrist.

Incredibly, her eyes widened, darkening to a smoky indigo, and filled with tears. "It's lovely," she whispered, "just like the one you gave me the day we left."

Thinking the tears were for her sister, and feeling guilty for having caused their separation, he said softly, "I'm sorry Jacqueline couldn't come home with you."

But Camille was thinking of that first blossom, pressed between the pages of her scrapbook, and her silly, romantic notions about this man, her husband.

She tossed her head, a shade falling over her eyes, hiding her thoughts and feelings. Hurt and resentment swept softer feelings away as she remembered what this man had done to her and her sister.

Charles sensed her withdrawal, but was ignorant of its source. Though he was now over thirty, his dealings with women had been limited and his understanding of their ways still woefully lacking.

"Come inside, Mr. Longmont."

"Charles, remember?" His voice was husky with some new emotion.

"Charles," she repeated softly, leading him into the library.

Camille perched gracefully on the needlepoint-covered piano bench, as though afraid to relax in his presence. He stood before the marble fireplace, hands clasped behind his back, watching her closely. She was perfectly at home in the tastefully elegant room filled with handsome rosewood furnishings accented by priceless silver. She should always be surrounded by such luxury. Yet he had sent her away from it all for six long years. Would she be able to forgive him for that?

He studied her, wondering how anyone could be lovelier. Inner and outer beauty mingled to the point it was impossible to separate strength of character from a flawless beauty. She was truly exceptional.

Somehow he knew he must not let her know the effect she was having on him. He'd made up his mind to allow her her freedom, and he didn't want his almost violent physical attraction to her to complicate things.

God knew she deserved some happiness and the freedom to make her own choices, have lots of suitors and flirt and dance and marry the young man who could sweep her off her feet.

"How was your trip?" he asked at last.

"Oh, the trip...it was fine." She laughed—that wonderful sound again. "Long, tedious, miserably uncomfortable, but Zeb was wonderful. It if hadn't been for that kind man..."

But the man who'd captured her imagination was another... tall, dark, dangerously sensual...

"Thanks to Zeb," she continued quickly, dismissing her errant thoughts, "I'm the new local expert on the Trace, the Choctaw and Chickasaw, wild musk-rats, how to locate the best camping spots, singing in the rain, and taking 'spit' baths out of a jug!'' She laughed merrily.

He laughed with her before his expression sobered. ''When Miss Cavanaugh's letter arrived, I was angry with you for taking unnecessary risks, but it was too late to stop you. You know I would not have allowed it, Camille. And to complete your journey across the Trace! It is intolerable to me that you should have done such a thing. What could you have been thinking of?''

She regarded him closely, unaccountably glad he'd changed little in the six years she'd been away. Tiny laugh lines around his eyes and mouth added character rather than age to his timeless good looks. In spite of herself, she found him irresistibly handsome. No wonder she'd been madly in love with him as a child.

But he could still make her feel like a little girl with a few carefully chosen words!

''You would not have allowed it, Mr. Longmont?'' she repeated, sarcasm thick in her voice.

He chose to ignore her tone and the challenge in her question. ''Of course not, Camille. I *am* your guardian. Your safety is important to me.''

''As you can see,'' she pointed out succinctly, ''I arrived unharmed, so you would have worried needlessly.''

Provoked, her inky eyes flashed a blue fire so appealing he almost forgot everything else. She really was remarkable.

''I see you are not wearing your wedding rings.'' A quiet observation, it was no less a rebuke.

''The Trace is no place for jewelry. Zeb said I should keep them rolled in my underdrawers in the trunk.''

She blushed. Deliberately she failed to mention that this occurred *after* the confrontation with the gentleman bandit who had taken her locket.

"I think you'd better put them back on now that you're home. We wouldn't want to give the good citizens of Natchez something more to gossip about, would we?"

"I'm sure *you've* given them plenty to keep their tongues wagging while I've been away!" Camille had heard the persistent rumors of Charles and his ladyfriend.

His left eyebrow arched inquisitively. She was jealous! He loved the way her deep blue eyes sparkled with anger.

"But then it never was a *real* marriage, was it?" she went on, her anger aroused by his casual attitude. "So why *should* you be faithful? And you did promise me an annulment."

"There's no need to remind me." His tone was cool. "It's yours for the asking, of course. But there's still the matter of a year and a half until you'll be old enough to take complete responsibility for your estate."

"Damn it, Charles! Why must you always treat me like a child?" His raised eyebrow made her more furious than ever. "I may have been thirteen when you married me and sent me away to school for my 'protection,' but I'm not a child any longer!"

"I can see that." Golden brown eyes moved over her slowly, and he was scarcely able to conceal his admiration.

Abruptly he scowled at her and said curtly, "We will discuss this another day—when we can be more reasonable. Good day, Camille.'' He spun on his heel and walked briskly out of the room.

More reasonable, indeed! She stomped back and forth, pacing the length of the double parlors. Her stormy temper kept her sputtering and mumbling unladylike oaths as she trod across sumptuous Aubusson carpet.

She'd show him reasonable! He thought he could order her around, control her life, walk in and out and over her heart! Oh, no, Charles Longmont, not anymore!

''And I'm as reasonable as I'll ever be!'' she shouted. Realizing ruefully just how foolish and unreasonable that sounded, she smiled, her anger cooling slightly.

Hurrying up the winding staircase to her bedroom, she crossed to her dressing table. Lifting a delicate vase, she turned it upside down and shook it. Her wedding rings dropped into her hand. She slipped them on her left hand, vowing to play the part of Mrs. Charles Longmont to the hilt—at least until she had the promised annulment. Her silly notions and jealousies must not be allowed to put Magnolia in jeopardy. With a start, she realized they had not even spoken of his plans for her home, the main reason for her haste in returning to Natchez. Neither had they discussed his living arrangements. Apparently he did not plan to live at Magnolia.

BACK IN HIS ROOMS Charles Longmont also paced and argued with himself. His sense of honor and fairness demanded he stay away from her, but his heart and his body vehemently demanded otherwise.

Why couldn't he be one of her suitors? he asked himself. But no—that was impossible! The whole situation was impossible! What in God's name was he to do?

As a lad of eighteen, he had fled Scotland and the squalor and hardships of his youth for the bright promise of a young America. For the seven years since his ship had docked at New York, he'd worked hard and struggled, making his way across the country until finally he had arrived on the banks of the muddy Mississippi.

At Natchez Under the Hill he had shrewdly invested his savings in speculative ventures that proved more profitable than he'd ever dreamed possible. The purchase of land next to Magnolia had been the beginning of the fulfillment of all his desires and plans. He was determined to make it the biggest and best cotton plantation in the South. He would not allow himself to fail.

But his carefully laid plans were being complicated by a bewitchingly beautiful and independent child-woman who was working her way into his heart against his better judgment.

A FORTNIGHT PASSED before Camille's first chance for a long talk with her best friend. "Glory! How wonderful you look! Come, I have to know *everything* that's happened while I've been away."

Putting her arm through her friend's, Camille urged her along the shaded pathway. Below them, the Mississippi followed its relentless course southward, crowded with barges and other smaller craft, and an occasional whistle shrilly punctuated the conversation of the two reunited friends.

"Cam! Oh, *Cam*! I don't know where to start! It's been so long since we've had one of our talks!"

Glory's familiar voice, full of the usual exaggerations, sounded marvelous. Listening to her chatter on about local gossip, Camille felt truly at home for the first time.

"I can't believe it's been two weeks and this is the first time we've really talked! It's all your fault, you know, Glory. You've been so busy, you don't even have time for your old friend."

"You've not exactly been a wallflower yourself, Cam. Haven't I seen you at every important Natchez event since your return? But the attractive Mr. Longmont *has* been conspicuously absent, I've noticed."

"You would notice, of course. Well...I don't understand him at all, I really don't. First, he seemed glad to see me, and then he disappeared. I haven't seen him since." She would not admit, even to Glory, how hurt she'd been by his unexplained disappearances and his aloof manner.

"He's away on one of his frequent business trips, then?"

"Yes—no—I don't know. He's such a strange man."

"He's also your husband, Cam."

"I certainly don't need to be reminded of *that*, Glory." Camille smiled in spite of herself, remembering how much in awe of the handsome Charles Longmont she'd been at thirteen—and still was, though she wouldn't admit it.

"No, I suppose not, still . . ."

"Still, what?"

"Still, you certainly don't act married."

"It was not exactly a conventional marriage, if you recall."

"Yes, I *do* seem to recall..." Glory smiled. "I recall a young girl who was quite smitten by a handsome man who came to her rescue like a knight in shining armor and..."

"All right, all right. You always were hopelessly romantic, weren't you?"

"Yes, and so were you!"

"Perhaps not anymore." Camille thought of her sister and that awful preacher and all the years she'd spent away from her home and all the people she loved so much. She thought of all the changes Charles planned for Magnolia. "Perhaps not anymore," she repeated softly.

"You *can't* mean that, Cam. Speaking of romantic, you haven't forgotten the yearly costume ball at Moss Rose next week, have you?" Not getting anywhere with the present line of conversation, Glory was off on another track to divert her friend and, hopefully, to cheer her up.

Camille loved parties and the Moss Rose Ball was renowned as one of the finest and most elaborate, even for Natchez society. "No, I haven't forgotten. I've even been asked to provide some entertainment for the evening."

A sly smile was all the information Glory could finagle out of her friend about either her costume or what kind of performance she had planned, but she had at least succeeded in changing the painful subject of their earlier discussion. As she left Camille, Glory wondered what surprise was in store for all of them, knowing her friend never did anything in a small way.

Chapter Six

CAMILLE STRETCHED and allowed herself the luxury of wakening by degrees. A brilliant summer sun played leapfrog through wide-open windows, and a playful breeze ruffled the tops of tall oak and magnolia trees.

"Mornin', Missy." Indigo bustled in with her breakfast tray. The young servant girl had an uncanny way of arriving at just the right time; never before her mistress awoke, but usually only minutes after. She knew Camille perhaps better than anyone, and was fiercely loyal. The black girl had been born on Magnolia months before Camille and the two had grown up together. Indigo had grieved by Camille's side at her mother's death, and had shared her pain in the loss of both her brother and father that had followed so quickly.

Camille yawned widely and returned the greeting. "Good morning, Indigo." The aroma of warm, buttered biscuits and steaming coffee drifted across where she lay propped up in bed.

"You'd best be gettin' yo'self up an' 'round, Missy Cam. Tonight's da big ball at Moss Rose."

"Yes, and I have a million things to do." Camille cast a worried glance at the door of her wardrobe, where her surprise outfit hung in readiness. No one but Indigo would see it before she made her entrance at the ball.

Camille didn't regret her choice of costume, though she admitted to a few misgivings. Her plan for the evening was outrageous, even scandalous, but certain to catch the attention of Charles Louis Longmont. He would be there . . . he had to be there, didn't he?

She would prove to him he'd made a big mistake in discounting her as a woman. By making other men want her, she would arouse his jealousy and show him she wasn't a child any longer. A satisfied smile curved her full lips as she pictured him falling under her spell.

He had a lot of nerve—being so cool and distant, making her the laughingstock of Natchez society. How many times had she been asked, ''Where's your husband tonight, Camille?'' She *never* knew where he was; had no idea what he did with his time—or with *her* money for that matter.

A desperate hurt and building anger had prompted her thoroughly outlandish preparations for the ball. He acted as though she didn't exist—and no one could do that! She would show him she was very much alive—and very much a woman. Yes! The ball was her chance, and she was up to the challenge!

SOFT AS A BABY'S BREATH, the pulsing rhythm of the Spanish guitar wove its way through the crowd, stilling conversation and movement, casting an enchanted spell on all who listened.

Burnished to a high sheen, the dance floor shone bright and empty, expectant. Enormous French mirrors framed in gold leaf hung on both ends of the room, reflecting the splendor of the wall coverings and magnificent chandeliers, making the double parlors seem even larger than their seventy-two-foot length.

Mysteriously, the lighting dimmed as strategic candles were snuffed out in the massive room. The soft guitar music continued, imperceptibly building in speed and intensity.

Through the wide arched door to the center hallway moved a vision; a creation, surely, of some ancient imagination. Statuesque, shoulders back and head high, Camille swayed into the room with hypnotic grace. High-heeled cordovan boots began the intricate foot-tapping of the flamenco, taking her to the center of the floor. Delicate arms and hands coiled above her head were representative of the hooded cobra, and her agile fingers picked up the rhythm with clicking castanets.

Inky eyes the color of a starless midnight sky flashed the pride and hidden fire that are a Gypsy's birthright. Her hair swirled about her like a blue-black cloud of smoke, restrained only by high combs covered with a lace mantilla.

Wine-red, her dress plunged to a deep lace-trimmed V, molded like a glove to her tiny waist and clung to curving hips before falling in flounces from her knees to the floor.

Charles stood on the fringes of the rapt audience, a soft smile playing across full lips. His eyes did not move from her and his heart pounded in rhythm with the thrumming guitars and Camille's rapid footsteps. Her fiery snapping eyes were a dark mystery that held him captive.

He was lost. He knew it without the slightest doubt. Camille had been dear to his heart since she was a freckle-faced child. He'd always cared for her, but since her return to Natchez as a sensuous, beautiful woman, a powerful new feeling had been growing within him.

He admitted to himself that this disturbing feeling had been the cause for his frequent absences.

Now it burst into full flame and he could no longer deny it. God, how he wanted her! He had never desired anything so desperately. "And this entertainment is not helping, my little Gypsy flower," he murmured, wondering where she'd ever learned to dance like that.

His lips curled upward mischievously as he reminded himself that this fascinating and beautiful creature, this obviously passionate woman, was already his wife. What a provocative thought!

His attention, like that of everyone in the ballroom, was riveted on the voluptuous young woman who stamped and twirled with such abandon, who seemed tied by invisible bands to the beating tempo of the accelerating guitar.

Camille twirled and flipped her flounced skirt, revealing a white satin underlining and a shocking glimpse of shapely leg. A collective gasp greeted the display, followed immediately by an electrified silence. Then, one by one, a few younger men began clapping and stamping along with her, and soon were joined by others. An occasional exuberant *olé* could be heard.

The soft glow of candlelight played across her dewy skin and her moist lips parted, revealing a row of straight sparkling white teeth. The exertion of the dance heightened the normal glow of her cheeks to a deep dusty rose and her magnificent indigo eyes burned with an inner fire of their own.

The pace quickened even more, and the rhythmic clicking indicated her feet were still on the floor, though Camille felt as if she were floating or flying, having lost herself in the frenzied movements of the dance. Pleasure bunched up inside her and a tingling spread to her fingertips as she finished with a flourish of lifted skirts and a deep bow to the floor.

The stunned crowd seemed to hold its breath for long seconds before a smattering of applause began and built, sweeping rapidly through the room.

In that moment Camille searched the enormous room for Charles, whom she had not yet seen. Young, handsome men stared at her with open admiration, but she looked for the familiar brown eyes, the shock of curly mahogany hair. He was nowhere to be found. A sharp disappointment swept over her, even as she hurried from the center of the floor. The dance, she admitted, had been entirely for his benefit, and he hadn't even been there to see it!

"Cam! That was extraordinary, absolutely *extraordinary*! And I'd say that, even if you weren't my best friend." Glory, waiting with two goblets of punch, offered one to her friend.

"A drink! Glory, you're wonderful!" Camille drank thirstily, continuing her surveillance of the room.

"Looking for someone?" Glory eyed her suggestively. "I think I just saw your *husband* go out that way." She pointed toward the double doors at the end of the center hallway, flung open to catch the gentle night breeze from the back courtyard. Glory had watched Charles's discomfort during the dance with growing interest, smiling when he had practically run out the back door just before it ended.

Camille gave her friend a haughty glance and handed her the empty goblet before turning toward the courtyard. So he *had* seen her dance!

"Be careful, Cam. He did look very forbidding!"

"Oh, pooh! Glory, dear. Don't worry about me—I can certainly handle the formidable Charles Longmont!" She threw the fearless words over her shoulder, but her heart beat faster as she made her way toward the door. She stepped outside to be met by the cool breeze blowing off the river and a sky peppered with millions of stars, shimmering with the soft glow of a full moon.

"A perfect night, is it not, *señorita*, or should I say *señora*?" The familiar voice sent shivers cascading up and down her body. Charles stepped from the shadow of a giant oak, breathtaking in the elaborate garb of a Mississippi gambler. Tight black pants and high-topped boots encased his long, muscled legs, and a white satin shirt was open entirely too far at the neck, revealing an intriguing glimpse of dark curling hair. A wide-brimmed hat, pulled low over his eyes cast shadows over the chiseled features of his face.

"Charles," she breathed.

"Yes, my dear wife." With a lazy smile, he bowed and reached for her hand.

He was mocking her! She snatched her hand out of his, and whirled toward the house. But before she could take a step, he grasped both her arms firmly, yanking her up against him.

His warm breath stirred the hair behind her ear, and for long seconds she stood, not moving. This treatment was beyond her limited experience, and she hardly knew how to respond. That it was intensely pleasurable to feel his body next to hers, his arms tightly around her, she was not ready to admit.

Camille's hesitation fueled the fire burning deep inside him. With a muttered curse, he twisted her around in his embrace until she was facing him, the top of her head below his chin. Her embroidered shawl fell to the ground, unnoticed, and a thin strap of her gown slipped down, leaving one creamy white shoulder bare. His lips fell to the alluring spot, trailing fire across her satiny skin, into the hollow of her neck.

Camille's head arched back, her breathing suspended. She dared not move for fear he would stop this delicious torment.

His nuzzling sent shivers of delight coursing through the lower part of her body. She was acutely aware of every contour of his body pressing so intimately against her own.

Planting a series of small, teasing kisses along her neck and across the smooth, classic line of her jaw, his lips finally claimed hers. She kissed him back with a passionate fervor that shocked them both, her arms stealing up around his neck.

It was the depth and the strength of her physical response that made her push him away at last.

Camille had not meant to feel anything, only to make him feel. She'd sought a reaction from him, and she hadn't been disappointed. But her response to him was unnerving. Always before she had been able to control her emotions, and she couldn't understand what was happening to her now.

''The fire is not only in the dance I see, little Gypsy,'' he said, chuckling.

''Don't call me 'little Gypsy,' '' she hissed. He was still treating her like a child! She had wanted to arouse his jealousy and make him angry, but it was obvious he could not be as easily manipulated as the boys at school.

Surprisingly gentle fingers under her chin tipped her face up to his. ''Camille...''

Before she could resist, he was kissing her again. The tumult of the dance was nothing compared to the effect of that one kiss. It lasted forever . . . but only seconds. It was frightening . . . but wonderful. It was terrible . . . and delicious. . . .

"Come dance with me, love." His touch was soft, but she thought the mockery lingered in his voice.

"I'm not your *love*," she argued, but her protests came too late. She found herself on the edge of the dance floor. Illuminated by thousands of candles, the ballroom was crowded now with dancing couples.

He laughed softly, crushing her against his lean body, audaciously holding her much too closely. "Smile, my dear, you wouldn't want anyone to think you weren't glad to see your husband, now would you? Especially as he's been gone for two long weeks?"

"Damn you!" She stepped down hard on his instep, gratified to hear him respond with a curse of his own.

"Do be careful, my little spitfire, or I shall have to take control like a true husband." The unveiled threat in his low voice silenced her, but only for a moment.

"A *true* husband you could never be, sir! Nor I a true wife to you. Why did you bother to come back?"

"To take care of some *personal business*, my dear," he growled fiercely. "I did leave rather in a hurry, as you may recall."

"I certainly do recall." A frown marred the smoothness of her brow. "You were in imminent danger from a group of your ragamuffin acquaintances, as I remember."

"Nothing so serious as all that." He laughed. "Merely a small misunderstanding, my dear."

"Will you please stop calling me *my dear*? I'm not your *dear*, nor will I ever be anything more to you than a child you feel responsible for."

He ignored her petulant words. "Ah, you smell of flowers, love. I see you are wearing one in the usual place." Roguish eyes swept over silken breasts her low-cut bodice did little to conceal, and lingered on the petals of a white gardenia nestled in the valley between them.

"What I wear is no concern of yours, not now or ever!" How had he known she always wore a gardenia? She would have sworn he never noticed anything about her! She tried to pull away, but was trapped even tighter by the viselike grip of his hand on her bare back. She had started this, but she had no idea how to stop it.

"Oh, but it is, my dear. It most definitely is. And what you do *not* wear is of equal or even greater concern to me." Camille felt naked, stripped as much by his suggestive words as by dark eyes that raked her longingly.

She whispered sharply, "If you will listen carefully, *sir*, you will no doubt notice that the music has stopped. If you will look around you, *sir*, you will no doubt notice that everyone else has stopped dancing. Now, will you kindly take your hands off me, *sir*!" Indignantly, she stomped a small foot and wrenched herself out of his grasp.

"Well, it seems we've given the very proper society of Natchez something further to titter about tonight," he said with a chuckle, releasing her.

In a louder voice, he continued, "Thank you, madam, for the delightful dance." His eyes mocked her, a smile tugging at the corners of his lips, but his voice held the ring of sincerity for the benefit of those around them.

Throughout the rest of the unbearably long evening she did not see him again.

IN THE EARLY HOURS of the following morning, Camille sat cross-legged in her wide bed, unable to sleep. Charles Longmont had successfully turned the tables on her, and she was agitated and completely bewildered. She hardly knew what to make of his unruly, unpredictable behavior.

Was it possible he was only punishing her for her unconventional behavior? That would not be beyond him. Whatever the case, there was more to this man than she had thought. And the feelings he'd aroused in her had been both unexpected and unwelcome. Camille flopped back on overstuffed pillows. She would need to be much more careful in her future dealings with her husband.

She would have been glad to know that Charles's anger had been very real. At that very moment his dark brows were knitted in a fierce frown, his body coiled tightly in the saddle as he rode his bay stallion pell-mell through the streets of Natchez. The big horse slid to a stop in front of King's Tavern. Flinging himself to the ground and whipping the reins into a quick knot around the hitching post, he stomped up the well-worn steps to the Tap Room. With a few drinks and some pleasant conversation, he hoped to ease the hungry fire burning in him.

Charles threw some coins on the bar and downed a stiff drink in one swallow, then roughly demanded another. It did not help. In his mind he still heard the steady, driving beat of the guitar and saw the dark

Castilian beauty moving through the intricate steps of the mysterious dance. Camille had the classical features of a Southern aristocrat, but for the few minutes of the dance, he'd been convinced she was a product of ancient Gypsy caves.

She was so enchanting and desirable he'd ached with a feverish longing to possess her completely. But he had harshly reminded himself she was only a child, just nineteen, and the daughter of his old friend. And he had promised Beaufort protection for his daughters! Protection, hah! When he thought only of ravishing her? Who would there be to protect her from him?

How could he allow such thoughts to roam unchecked through his mind? His behavior in the courtyard and later on the dance floor had been inexcusable! Unreasonable jealous anger had driven him to act in a most ungentlemanly fashion. What in the world had come over him? Had his costume rid him of inhibitions so easily that he had played the role of an unscrupulous gambler to the hilt? Or could it have been several glasses of the very potent champagne punch?

As it appeared he would not be successful in avoiding Camille completely, he had to find a way to control himself when he was around her. But how to rein in the whirlwind of desire building in him?

He glanced up then to see the beautiful hostess of the tavern enter the room. Of course, Justine! Hadn't she always been there for him? Hadn't she waited patiently for him to settle the Beaufort estate and return to her? She had even understood his need to marry Camille. Justine would be more than willing to appease the gnawing ache inside him.

With a welcoming easy smile on her attractive face, she walked toward him. She was soft and pleasant; he'd always found her appealing. But as she came closer, he was aware that the fire, the excitement of his young ward—his young wife—was missing from this woman who'd been his mistress for years. He felt no leap of sexual attraction, no burning desire to capture her body and soul, no protective surge of affection. That little raven-haired vixen had thoroughly bewitched him!

"Charles?" Justine questioned, seeing something amiss in his troubled eyes.

"Justine." He rose and placed a perfunctory kiss on her cheek. "I needed a drink. Will you have one?"

"No, thank you, Charles. Is something wrong?"

"Nothing I can't handle!" He spoke more sharply than he meant to and winced at the puzzled hurt in her eyes. He knew that tonight at least being with Justine wouldn't help. "I'm sorry," he said quietly, putting his hand gently over hers, "but I think I'd better go."

Wisely, she did not argue, but watched him slap another coin on the bar and stride quickly across the room, slamming out the door. For a long time she stared after him. Then with a small shake of her head, she set about seeing to the needs of her customers.

Charles rode hard for hours before fatigue finally claimed his body, assuring him he'd be able to sleep. Even in his dreams, though, he was tormented by visions of the voluptuous dancer and the memory of the sweet honeyed taste of her lips.

Chapter Seven

FOR THE NEXT several months, Charles put all his energy into his many business interests, through wise speculation becoming an important capitalist. He spent much of his time traveling between Vicksburg, Jackson and New Orleans, seeing Camille as little as possible. When they chanced to meet, his studied behavior was impersonal and more distant than ever. With vigilant care, he kept a tight rein on his emotions and passions, at least outwardly.

Camille was troubled and confused by his apparent indifference and the fact that she saw him so rarely. She assumed he still directed her father's affairs, while scrupulously avoiding her. Without the catalyst of his presence, she soon found herself bored by the endless flurry of social events in Natchez; the parties, dances and theater she had so looked forward to seemed insignificant.

But his absences did give her the opportunity to take over, little by little, the supervision of the field hands and the household staff at Magnolia. She managed it all superbly and began to spend more time at her father's Natchez office, studying contracts of his various ventures and making small decisions with surprising business acumen. Even Matt, the office manager, who at first had been appalled to even see her there, grudgingly admitted she was capable, even gifted, at making good deals and wise investments. He allowed her more and more input, and soon she was working with bankers and other important business-men from as far away as Memphis and New Orleans. She insisted Matt take the credit for an astute maneuver that had added a saw mill to their holdings. Her father had loaned money to a local merchant to open a saw mill some time before his death. The mill had done well and had begun to show a handsome profit when the owner was drowned in a freak river accident. Camille had been able to call up the outstanding mortgage owed the Beauforts and assume complete control and ownership, despite vehement counter-claims by other creditors.

Camille loved what she was doing, but when Charles was in town, she carefully avoided revealing her in-volvement in the business, fearful of his reaction. He might order the men to have nothing to do with her; as her guardian and her husband, he had that right. She was amazed that no one had yet given her away, though she had become a familiar sight on the streets of Natchez, her abundant hair subdued into a neat chignon on her neck, tucked skirts rustling over full petticoats, kid slippers peeping out below.

In the man's domain of business, what she did was not the accepted thing, and certainly not ladylike. But for some reason, there seemed to be a conspiracy of si-lence on the part of the townspeople as far as Charles was concerned. At least for the moment, no one breathed a word.

In truth, they all seemed amused, even impressed with her unique combination of business sense and striking beauty. The men were completely under her spell and, though they wouldn't admit it, a trifle intimidated, as well.

They were accustomed to women in the role of pampered ornaments. But as long as she wasn't *their* wife or daughter, they'd do nothing to gainsay her.

On an unseasonably warm day late in the fall, Camille met with Marcus Smithfield, the family lawyer, on the gallery at Magnolia, seeking his advice on some legal matters. After their business was completed, they sipped mint juleps and lapsed into a discussion of the past.

"Yes, sir. I always admired your father, Camille. I surely did. He was a good businessman and a fair and honest man, right up to the day he died."

"Yes, Mr. Smithfield, he surely was."

"And he showed his good sense, even then, in selecting Charles Longmont to manage his affairs."

"What do you mean?" Her voice cooled. Personally, she hadn't been that impressed with Charles's handling of matters regarding her and her estate, and she was still concerned about his plans for the future.

"Well, ma'am, Mr. Longmont is solely responsible for the additional accumulation of your wealth since your father's death and it *has* been quite considerable."

"Indeed?"

"Oh, yes. Every investment has turned to profit in his capable hands. And the property that he bought adjoining this for a song, why, that was a stroke of brilliance!"

"I can't say that I agree."

"But Miss Camille, the combination of that property with this should make yours just about the largest and most profitable plantation in the entire state of Mississippi!''

"Yes, and Charles would control it all, wouldn't he?"

"Well . . . as your legal guardian and your husband, he would, of course."

"Of course." *Just as he controlled everything else!* She was so tired of his continual domination of her she could scream. And he had probably used *her* money to purchase the land, anyway!

"And I was *truly* amazed when he insisted on using his own money to finance you two girls in school."

Her mind, having strayed from the conversation, was jerked by this remarkable revelation.

"He *what*?"

"Just like I said, ma'am. Every penny to Green Oaks School came straight out of his accounts—transferred on to Baltimore by myself, of course." With a self-satisfied smile, the lawyer waited for a response from her that did not come. When he realized their conversation was at an end, he soon bid her a good day, leaving her to her own thoughts.

Charles had paid for their schooling—not a small sum! Camille thought, watching the lawyer's pudgy body amble toward his coach. *Why* had he done it? What did he stand to gain from such an expenditure? Not her gratitude, surely. Besides, he had shown little interest in her feelings, gratitude or otherwise. He was only carrying out his responsibility to her father, though paying from his own pocket exceeded that responsibility. It suggested something else. But what?

Had he felt guilty for sending them away and chosen that as a way to make up for it? It hardly seemed in character for the Charles Longmont she'd come to know. Still. . . .

"Missy Cam . . . yo' takin' yo' tea out here? It sure is a beautiful day, yes'm, warm ez summer t'day, it is."

Without allowing her mistress the chance to answer and without interrupting her own steady stream of small talk, Indigo vanished back through the French doors into the parlor, presumably heading for the kitchen, although one could never be sure the girl would get wherever she was headed.

Camille smiled indulgently. Indigo would reappear soon enough with the tea—unless something side-tracked her on her way to the brick kitchen out in back.

The early afternoon sun warmed Camille and slowly eased away the tension caused by her discussion with the lawyer. Still puzzled by this side of Charles that had been revealed in her discussion with Smithfield, she swept heavy curls away from her face in the same way she'd tried to sweep that troublesome Charles Longmont from her thoughts.

Enormous, almond-shaped eyes closed in response to the indolence of the warm sun, but flew open at an unusual sound that disturbed the peaceful quiet.

Full lips curved upward and her classical nose flared when she recognized the sound that had startled her. Booted footsteps on the gravel walk! That authoritative stride could belong only to one man and she straightened, fully alert, but maintaining her lazy, regal appearance as Charles Longmont rounded the corner.

"I thought I might find you here." He chuckled, taking the stairs up to the side porch two at a time. "May I join you?" Sweeping his tall hat off and bowing in the chivalrous, though exaggerated manner of the Southern gentleman, he proceeded to occupy the chaise next to hers.

No one seems to be waiting for my reply today, she thought, with a moment's petulance as Charles sat in the seat vacated by Mr. Smithfield. But his presence filled the patio in a way the elderly lawyer's had not.

"Do join me," she said with a mocking, but not unkind smile. "Indigo's bringing tea, or at least I think she is." She looked toward the doors impatiently. "I swear you never know where that girl's likely to end up."

"She is a bit, uh, unpredictable, isn't she?" Charles smiled broadly at her laughter that rang with the unaffected merriment of a child. It never ceased to enchant him.

Tiny flowers tucked into her ebony curls bounced delightfully and the white flower in the bodice of her lace-trimmed dress beckoned him irresistibly. His unruly thoughts were straying entirely too much in the direction of his young wife, and he breathed a sigh of relief as Indigo chose that moment to appear with the tea.

"I haven't seen you in some time, Charles," Camille said as Indigo set the tea things on the table between the two of them and vanished again. With an impatient shake of her curls, Camille reached to serve the tea.

"Please, allow me."

His warm hand covered hers and guided it back to the arm of the settee. Her hand tingling from his touch, Camille watched him with a lifted brow. She'd never seen a man serve tea before. His tanned, capable hands were surprisingly gentle as he poured from the china pitcher, added two lumps of sugar and handed the dainty porcelain cup to her.

Settling back in his chair with a steaming cup, he turned toward her and answered the question she'd only implied regarding his whereabouts.

"I've been in Jackson on business. Only arrived back in Natchez this morning." A worried frown puckered his brow, but he said no more. She already knew him well enough to recognize his quiet, stubborn refusal to discuss business with her.

"Mr. Smithfield was here," she told him.

"Yes?" he responded politely, but his expression was devoid of curiosity. Obviously he assumed the lawyer had been paying a social call and found that far from interesting.

Should she mention what she had discovered in her discussion with the lawyer? If she did, she would have to show some gratitude, she supposed, and Charles's aloof manner irritated her so badly, she wasn't at all sure she could. No, she would let the matter drop for now.

"Yes, but he left some time ago. Did you hear about the murder Under the Hill last Friday?"

"I'm afraid I did. A terrible thing . . . but how did you know about it?"

The frown was back on his handsome face. Why did he have to be so damned protective? Didn't he realize she was almost twenty—and well able to take care of herself?

"I saw it."

The words were out before she thought about them, and his reaction was predictable and immediate.

"What!" Charles was on his feet, glowering down at her. "What were you doing down there?"

"Why, Mr. Longmont, tell me if I'm wrong, but don't you still live there?" It was a direct challenge, but if he could live there, why shouldn't she be allowed just to visit there? She wondered again why he chose to retain his Under the Hill quarters.

"Camille...." The threat in his deep voice sent chills up her spine in spite of her outward bravado.

"Oh, sit down, Charles," she snapped. "I wasn't really there. I don't know quite why I said that. I suppose I just wanted to see your eyes snap." She smiled then.

He dropped back down onto the overstuffed chaise and drew the back of his hand slowly across his forehead, almost visibly erasing the worried lines.

"Camille, what am I to do with you?" The words were serious, but an indulgent smile played at the corners of his mouth. She was irascible and unpredictable, but so thoroughly charming that when she really tried, she could persuade him to do almost anything. Which made for a dangerous combination in this child-woman he was pledged to protect, and who also happened to be his wife.

"How about taking me on a picnic?" Now she was teasing him unapologetically. "It's such a beautiful, warm day. Let's not waste it." Her deep blue eyes danced with childish excitement. There was no way he could deny her, though there were endless demands on his time, countless matters that required his attention, and he knew better than to allow himself to be alone with her.

"Well, just for an hour or so."

Camille was on her feet and summoning Indigo before the words were completely out of his mouth. "Oh, thank you, Charles! What fun we shall have! Let's have our lunch under that big old oak on the bluff over the river."

The sweeping curve of the Mississippi on the southern edge of Natchez fronted a portion of Magnolia's grounds. The place she mentioned was one of her favorites, far enough from the house to be out of sight, and well above the water. It was pleasant and quiet, a wonderful spot for picnics and lazy afternoons watching the boats below.

Essie agreeably put aside her churning and gathered up what she could lay her hands on for the impromptu picnic. She thought it was good to see the young miss smiling and happy again, and bustled about, singing to herself as she worked.

Camille changed into a soft dimity dress, more comfortable for walking with its softly swinging skirt and lack of the detested hoop and stays.

They soon set off, carrying the hamper between them. Companionably they strolled beneath the massive oak and magnolia trees, down the sloping green hill toward the pond. There they rested for a few minutes and Charles skipped stones across the glassy surface, smiling with masculine pride at the increasing length of his throws. Half reclining on the bank, Camille seemed to be enjoying the sun, but was indeed watching him closely through slitted eyes.

With a start, she realized that the lines of care she'd noticed lately on his face were not permanently etched there. When he smiled happily as he was doing now, he had the carefree look of a small boy. She wished with an ache unfamiliar to her that he might always look thus. Had she been the cause of some of those troubled lines? she wondered, vowing to do her best to eradicate them, so he might always look as he did now. Hatless, the sleeves of his shirt rolled up and his collar open, he was the picture of relaxed, refined elegance.

"Now you try it!" Grinning, he challenged her to a contest. "Bet I can skip stones farther than you can!"

Camille had never skipped a stone in her life, but wasn't about to admit it. Certain she could throw one every bit as far as he could, she jumped to her feet and searched about for smooth stones, finding five that were perfect.

"You first, my lady," he said mockingly, motioning her toward the water's edge, shaking his five stones confidently in his hand. "Are you sure you don't need me to show you how?"

"Of course not! Why, there's nothing to it! Watch this!" Trying to throw side-armed as she'd seen him do, Camille wound up and hurled the stone as hard as she could. With a decided plop, it landed almost at her feet, having not skipped a single time! "Oops! It must have slipped out of my hand!"

Charles smiled indulgently; would she never admit there was anything she couldn't do, and do better than any man?

His smile faded slightly as her second stone took several lively skips across the water. "Not bad," he admitted as she turned to him with a smirk, and beckoned for him to try a couple of his stones.

Charles's first stone landed in almost the same spot as her best try, but his second fell short of that by a foot. He tried two more that only exceeded his best by several inches. Saving one stone for last, he said with a mocking bow, "Your turn, my lady."

Camille had three stones left, and was determined to prove to him that she could do something as well as he. As hard as she could, she let the first one fly, and it did a credible job of sailing, then skipped rapidly, landing farther than any of the others. One more fell far short, leaving her only one. "Your turn, gallant sir." She would save her last one until she saw how far his would go.

"All right. You have this coming." Charles walked with a firm step to the water's edge, and a look of concentration on his face, flung the stone as hard as he could. This would have to be the longest yet, he was sure of it. And it was!

"Top that if you can."

"Okay, watch this." She was sure she could do it, and somehow it had become too important to her; after all, it was only a child's game they played. With her eyes glued to the spot where Charles's best throw had landed, she prepared to throw, releasing the stone with just the right flick of the wrist. She watched it soar, then skip—one, two, three, four, five times—before it landed beyond his last throw!

"There!" she said triumphantly, turning to him for her congratulations. "I've beaten you!"

She thought a strange expression flickered in the depths of his amber eyes before he assumed the role of the wounded male ego and grinned at her. "But you see, I twisted this arm just yesterday, and besides, I knew you wouldn't be fit company all afternoon if I didn't let you win!"

"Let me win! Charles Longmont, you cad. You liar!" Grabbing a handful of clover, Camille flung it at him, and chased him with another handful around the pond, until they both collapsed, laughing, on a soft bank covered with sweet clover and wildflowers. Plucking several of the fragrant flowers, Charles tucked them into her dark curls, and tickled her nose with them. Laughingly, she tucked one behind his ear and another in a buttonhole of his shirt, her hand brush-

ing the curling dark hairs on his chest. The tickling she
felt then was a long way from her nose, and hastily, she
scrambled to her feet, retrieving the basket and motioning for him to follow as she headed for the bluffs.
Still grinning impudently, hands in his pockets, he
trudged after her.

While Charles spread the blanket for the picnic,
Camille wandered to the edge of the bluff and looked
down at the water. She remembered with pain the
carefree times she and Jacqueline and her father had
had here, such a long, long time ago. So much had
changed. Funny, though, how she didn't really feel any
different. She was still the same little girl who had
happily thrown stones into the water and hounded her
father until he'd reluctantly let her climb down the
steep hill to dip her feet in the muddy water.

"I'm going wading," she suddenly called over her
shoulder. Before Charles could protest, she had stepped
out of her slippers and peeled off her stockings. Holding up her skirts, she started down, stepping over the
edge of the cliff. Her left foot found a rock, but as she
put her weight on it, the loose, wet clay underneath
gave way and the rock began to slide.

Horrified, she could see herself plummeting straight
down into the swirling water and grabbed for the edge.
Her hands clutched only air, and she cried out in fear.
Time stood still for long seconds. In panic, she closed
her eyes, expecting at any moment to feel the cold waters close around her.

Instead strong hands grabbed her arms. Swinging
her in a wide arc out and away from the drop-off,
Charles set her easily back on solid ground. Stum-
bling, and awed by his unexpected strength, she fell
against him. The deep rumble of his heartbeat against

her ear where it rested against his chest was comforting. Camille recalled the day of her father's funeral, when she'd been wrapped in his cloak and had snuggled against his chest. She felt again the same happiness and security that had allowed her to sleep in his arms on that long-ago day.

Abruptly, Charles held her away from him. "God! Camille, you'd try the patience of a saint! Why can't you act like a normal person just for a little while? It would certainly make my job easier."

She was completely taken aback by his unkind reaction. First he had saved her, and then he had held her tenderly; now he had the nerve to refer to her as his *job*! His job indeed! She stomped her foot in anger, but when her bare toes sank in the sand, the gesture lost a great deal of its intended impact. She thought she heard him smother a chuckle, but when she glanced up angrily, his face was still serious, set in those implacable lines she knew so well.

His hand still firmly grasped her arms and she had to tilt her head back to look up at him. How could he say such outrageous things to her, and look so boyishly handsome with his thick chestnut hair curling around his ears, all at the same time? It was maddening!

When he glared at her as he was now, she felt like nothing so much as a disobedient child.

Far from finding her childish, Charles was having great difficulty keeping his hands off her fetching shoulders, his fingers out of her hair. Her wide, innocent eyes were the same deep blue as the sky reflected in the waters of the Mississippi behind her. But in their depths lurked the very real threat of whirlpools and quicksand ready to suck him in and swallow him until he would be completely helpless.

The thought of her plunging into those swirling waters and being swept away in the swift currents and undertow still sent his mind reeling with the aftershock of fear. He couldn't have said what had compelled him to follow her over to the edge, but if he hadn't...? She would have slid all the way down the steep bank and into the rushing waters. In his mind, he could see her struggle, her head going under as she was carried farther and farther away from him.

His mind could not deal with that awful possibility.

And now she'd stiffened her spine against him again and actually tried to stomp—he chuckled—her dainty bare foot in the sand. He looked down at the toes covered with clinging sand and suddenly swept her up in his arms. He held her tightly until he deposited her, none too gently, on the picnic cloth.

"Charles..." she protested when he knelt and lifted one foot, carefully brushing away the particles of sand.

"Charles...?" Was it intentional the way his fingers seemed to caress her ankles, her instep and finally her toes as one by one he attended to them? No, it was only her overactive imagination playing tricks on her again.

She was sure she'd been wrong when he brusquely gathered up her stockings and shoes and dropped them in her lap, turning his back to her.

"Let's go back," he ordered.

The day was ruined. Though she could not have explained it, Camille realized something had happened, something was happening between them. She did not understand it, was powerless to stop it, and was not even sure she would if she could.

Wouldn't it be wonderful if Charles really loved her and wanted her for his wife? They could work together and make Magnolia what it could be and have a lot of children and . . . How you do run on, Camille, she chided herself. She knew Charles was fond of her, when he wasn't reproaching her for something, but she doubted he would ever see her as a woman, much less desire her as his wife.

When she'd danced the flamenco and he had kissed her, she'd been angry, but secretly she had dared to hope he might have some feeling for her, and today, just for a minute, when he'd held her . . . but no—

Dejected and trying hard not to show it, she'd helped him gather the picnic things and had walked silently beside him back to Magnolia. He bid her a perfunctory goodbye at the door.

Essie's raised eyebrow revealed her dismay at the untimely end of the picnic, even before her tongue started its insistent clicking that always drove Camille to distraction.

"Oh, hush, Essie! We changed our minds, that's all."

Dumping the basket on the dining room table, she flounced out of the room before the nosy kitchen maid could begin her prying questions.

Deciding she'd try to find a good book to while away the rest of the long afternoon, Camille strode across the wide hallway and into the comfortable dimness of the library. She stopped abruptly inside the doorway, her skirts belling out around her. Her hand flew to her heart. This was Father's room! How could she have forgotten? She had not entered the book-lined room since his death.

She could almost see him behind the massive desk where she'd found him so often, his head bent over the account books, puffing the pipe that was so much a part of him. She could smell the woodsy aroma, even now.

Though he'd been very busy, he'd always had time to hold her in his lap and even to tease her unmercifully. Her heart ached with the memories, the pain worse than it had been six years ago, and she remembered all too vividly how she'd grieved for him as a child.

"I wish you were here now, Daddy," she said to the empty room before she turned on her heel, shutting the door firmly behind her. She had not gotten a book, but she no longer felt like reading anyway.

In the hallway, Essie waited for her with a letter, rather than the lecture she'd expected. "Here y'are, Miss Camille—dis came fo' yo' t'day. I knowed yo'd want ta see't."

Camille's eyes fell to the Baltimore address—a letter from Jacqueline! It was the first one she'd had since she'd been home. She had been so afraid her sister was too angry with her to write.

Hurriedly, Camille ripped open the heavy vellum envelope and unfolded the surprisingly short letter.

Dear Sister:
Glad to hear you arrived safely. I still think it foolish of you to travel across that wretched Trace! Was Mr. Longmont very angry with you?

Clement is about ready to begin our morning devotions, so I must hurry off. I'm in good health and good spirits; hope this finds you the same. We may be seeing you before long.

Your loving sister,
Jacqueline

Camille crumpled the fine stationery into a small, hard ball. The little minx! She had her nerve, rebuking her sister, and calling that awful little preacher by his first name, practically in the same breath! What in the world was happening? And hadn't she said *we* when she talked of coming home? Camille would have to have a talk with Charles right away: surely he'd begin the necessary steps to bring Jacqueline home alone—without that damnable peacher—right away!

Camille's anger quickly turned to distress as she thought of her sister in the clutches of that seedy little man. She had to admit he could be quite persuasive. She remembered her last confrontation with Clement Masters before she'd left the east coast.

The night had been dismal and cold, and the wind howled, beating itself against the windowpanes, hurling itself at the doorway of the parsonage, demanding admittance. Insidiously it snaked its way inside the smallest cracks, and crept across the plain wooden floor to crawl up her bare legs, her heavy woolen skirts and stockings providing little protection.

Camille thought with a start that the preacher had stood the whole time in front of the fire, deflecting the heat from her, and absorbing it all for himself. Funny, she hadn't noticed at the time, though she had been aware of the eerie outline of his thin, darkly clad body silhouetted in the fireglow that had haloed around him.

"My dear Mrs. Longmont," he'd said, his voice as smooth as heavy silk, "I'm so glad we could talk before your precipitate departure for Natchez."

"Precipitate, sir?"

"Yes, Jacqueline tells me you are traveling against the expressed wishes of Miss Cavanaugh."

"Miss Cavanaugh is much too conservative. No, my departure is necessary and timely; not in the least 'precipitate,' I assure you. But I am quite distressed that Jacqueline refuses to accompany me, and I lay the blame for that entirely on you, sir. What do you have to say for yourself?" Camille knew the little man would pounce at the slightest sign of weakness, so she was determined not to reveal the extent of her concern and distress.

"Oh, my, my, my. We mustn't be upset." The more he tried to be conciliatory, the more Camille could see right through him. He continued, "No, no, no. That was her idea, hers alone. Of course, I do think it better, due to her unstable condition that she remain here where Dr. Resnick can continue to care for her, at least until she's better."

"And you've both been promising that 'miraculous cure' for the past six years, haven't you, *Reverend* Masters? Funny, I haven't seen much improvement. I feel strongly that Jacqueline should be home where those who love her can look after her."

"Oh, but my dear, there's where you are so wrong. She is loved here. Dr. Resnick and his dear wife have treated her like their own lost child. Now surely you would have to admit that?"

Camille frowned thoughtfully. The doctor and his very young wife certainly seemed fond of Jacqueline since she'd dropped out of school because of her health, and they had insisted she live with them. Jacquie seemed happy enough there, and though her health had not improved as promised, her younger sister still had faith in the combined efforts of the doctor and the preacher.

Jacqueline had flatly refused all Camille's pleas that she return to Natchez with her, forcing Camille to request this meeting with Masters and seek his help in persuading her.

Looking into his hard, beady black eyes, Camille realized with a rush of unhappiness that she would never get anywhere by appealing to his conscience; he had none.

"Sir, I believe I'm in a position to offer you a tidy sum of money to help me persuade my sister to return home." She pulled out her reticule, and drew out several large bills.

"Wait!" Apparently highly offended, he held out his hand as if to ward off an evil spirit, and took a menacing step toward her. "You must not attempt to bribe a servant of the Lord! Blasphemy!"

Camille was amazed. She'd never dreamed he would actually turn down money. His threadbare clothing was mute evidence of his need, and he could certainly stand to eat better, she thought, looking at his emaciated form. The greed in his soul had been plainly revealed in his black eyes. What was his game, then? She knew without question that he was up to something, and that it involved her sister.

But what else could she do? She could not physically force her sister to go. Jacqueline was sixteen now, and quite impressionable, except when she really set her mind to something. Then she was as stubborn and stiff-necked as the rest of the Beauforts, Camille thought with a sigh.

Except for her urgent, driving need to get home, Camille would have given up and remained in Baltimore with her sister. But her sense of impending doom, though she couldn't understand it, drove her relentlessly.

"All right then, if that's the way it's to be. But rest assured, she'll soon be hearing from our guardian, who will demand she come home forthwith! Why, he'll probably set right out to fetch her himself!"

Camille had turned toward the door, but his thin, white hand had ensnared her arm. Long, bony fingers circled her arm like talons and held firmly, though she pulled away. For the first time Camille was truly frightened of this wild-eyed man, though she knew she mustn't let it show.

For long seconds his gaze hypnotized her and they stood without moving. Finally, with a small shake of his shaggy head, he released her arm, and said with a slight smile, "Do allow me to escort you to the door, Mrs. Longmont."

"MRS. LONGMONT!" A shout brought her from her reverie and Camille saw before her in the circular drive of Magnolia a neighbor, Melody Copeland, who seemed so distraught that Camille hurried out onto the porch, Jacqueline's letter still clutched in her small hand.

"Melody, do get down off that fidgety horse and come into the house this minute and tell me what's wrong." The stallion's eyes were rolling as he pranced and pawed the gravel, as though anxious to be under way again.

"No, Camille! There's no time!" she shouted. "Is Charles home? Roland sent me to find him. Our barn's afire—and it's threatening to spread to the house. Willows is in danger, Cam! We need every hand we can find!''

"Charles is not here, Mel." Camille thought, *as usual*! Even as she spoke, though, Camille was running for the barn, shouting orders for Josef to round up the field hands and get them over to Willows in the wagon. The two wide-eyed stable boys helped her saddle her mare and a small horse for each of them.

She heard Melody's horse streaking down the drive, gravel spraying from under flying hooves, as she flung herself into the saddle and yelled, "Hurry up, you two!" They scrambled up into the saddle and hung on for dear life as their horses briskly moved out behind their mistress's.

Josef was rattling toward the field in the wagon, buckets that he'd quickly gathered madly bouncing about in the back, field hands running along behind him and clambering aboard.

As her horse flew across the first low fence that separated their property from the Copelands', Camille could already smell the bitter, acrid smoke.

No! I won't think about that now, she thought—shoving painful memories forcefully out of her mind. They would need all their wits and all the help that could be mustered to fight this fire.

Fire was a feared and respected word in Natchez. Whole plantations had burned to the ground as the result of one tiny spark. Water had to be hauled long distances, from a well—or from the river—and it took many hands working together to keep one from getting out of control.

A bucket brigade had been formed and was working steadily by the time Camille and her troupe of servants arrived. They all pitched in and worked frantically, dipping and passing and throwing bucket-loads of water on the blazing barn.

Camille was astonished to see Charles, sleeves rolled up and covered with dirt and soot, working the last bucket nearest the fire, throwing water onto the burning barn. Her heart quickened to see him so near the deadly flames, but she had no time to wonder how he had gotten word and arrived there ahead of her.

Thankfully all the stock had been turned out to pasture, so their main task was to contain the fire, save the barn if possible but, at all costs, keep it from reaching the Copelands' house.

Camille worked without thinking, passing the heavy buckets up the line, hand over hand, her back muscles screaming from the unaccustomed strain. The intense heat burned her face, and she occasionally closed her eyes to shut out the flames.

Her fractious mind flew back to another fire—a fire much, much worse than this one. It had been a horrible, consuming, killing fire. She would never, as long as she lived, forget it, nor would she ever recover fully from the effects of it.

For in that fire, she had lost her mother.

Chapter Eight

A RUSH OF MEMORIES swept over Camille, memories so painful she felt as though the breath had been knocked from her slender body. With a soft cry of anguish, she felt the horror sweep over her again: the snickering of the terrified animals, the horrible smell of singed horsehair, the fierce and deadly heat, the awful crackling and roaring of that other fire as it had consumed everything.

"No! *Ma mère!*" the child Camille had cried out, "Do not go in there! It is too late, too late!"

But her beautiful mother Charléna had heedlessly plunged into the flaming barn in a vain attempt to rescue her precious saddle horse LaBelle, so dear because she'd been a wedding present from Braxton.

Camille had been too small at the time to understand anything except that her mother was in terrible danger, and she would have run in after her had Josef not grabbed her and held on tightly to her thrashing young body.

Camille shivered. She was still mindlessly passing the heavy, sloshing buckets of water toward the fire in the Copeland barn, though the scene from her past was more real and immediate than the present. Then suddenly she was filled with a desperate need to beat *this* fire. She shouted orders down the line for increased speed and, grabbing someone to take her place in the line, she ran nearer to the fire, hoping there might be something more she could do.

"Get back, Camille!" Charles shouted angrily when he saw her approaching.

"But Charles, I just wanted..."

"Do as I say, right now!" The black scowl on his face sent her backward a couple of steps. He could be such a tyrant, she thought, watching him turn his complete attention back to the fire, his muscles bunching from the effort of swinging the heavy buckets of water onto the blaze. He stood so close to the burning barn, he was almost inside the doorway, but seemed unaware of the danger. Camille looked up and was terrified to see the heavy timbers supporting the roof begin to sway outward. A groaning and creaking was followed by a fearful snap. It would fall on top of him!

"Charles!" she shouted, pointing upward, "Run!" Her voice had penetrated the roaring and cracking of the timbers, and he turned to her with a puzzled look on his face, before he looked up to see what was coming. He lunged toward her, propelling them both out of range of the collapsing structure.

Her heart pounded and she thought she might never draw another breath as she lay beneath him, his body shielding her from flying sparks and small pieces of debris that rained around them. Her skirts were wrapped tightly around her legs, and she had twisted one leg in her fall, but she didn't think she'd been hurt. She looked up into his face, surprised to find the familiar grin and quirk of an eyebrow. "I did tell you to move back, now, didn't I?" he chided. "But when did the headstrong Mrs. Longmont do as she was told?"

"Ooo! Let me up—I demand that you let me up right this minute!" How could he turn everything around so successfully and make her look so foolish and childish?

He smiled. "It doesn't seem to me that you are in a position to be demanding anything at the moment, my dear wife. But it would seem the propitious thing to do. We still have a fire to fight." The look in his eyes, though, said there was more than one flame they needed to be concerned with as he pulled her to her feet.

They joined anew in the struggle against the diminishing fire. Since the timbers had fallen, it seemed to be burning itself out: there would be no further danger to the house.

Exhausted almost to the point of collapse, Camille gathered her servants, wagons, and horses to begin the trek back across the rolling pastures toward Magnolia. They were all bone-weary and their disheveled clothing reeked of smoke.

In the semidarkness, Camille rode slowly, silently letting her eyes roam, taking in the beauty and the lush stillness of the land. What a contrast to the threatening sparks and the thick, black smoke of the fire!

How could she still love this land so unreservedly? With all its hardships, it was stealing from her one by one all those she cherished. Yet as her mother and father before her, she knew she always would love it, and that she would always fight to preserve and protect it.

Charléna LaMont Beaufort, a sensitive French aristocrat, had been filled with abundant amounts of love for her family and for the wild, beautiful land on the Mississippi. Over a hundred years earlier, her ancestors had settled there, carving out a place for themselves and their descendants in the fertile ground above the river.

Camille had been born on this land and it was a part of her; it was hers. She could never understand why anyone would choose to live anywhere else. All those years in Maryland had only reinforced her strong ties to these Mississippi bluffs. Camille was glad to have been born here and to be part of the gracious, easy-living South, where charm and culture were the usual and expected thing, and where gallantry and chivalry still reigned.

As Magnolia, standing proud and magnificent, came into view, small scenes of the good times from her childhood flashed across her mind. Those happy times danced over the grim despair of her recent losses, blurring the edges of the pain. She was surprised at how good it felt to remember now, and she freely allowed her mind to play backward in time to the summer day her mother had laughingly despaired of ever teaching her small daughter skills with the needle; to the day of Jacqueline's birth and the excruciating joy of at last having a baby sister; to her first pony Muffin, who had been her best birthday surprise ever.

Finally she thought of one cold, dreary evening the family had all gathered around a crackling fire to listen to yarns spun by her father of Natchez in the early days—of the first French settlement and the uprising and massacre of the long-extinct Natchez Indians.

Camille had listened in fascinated horror, her heart crying out for the awful suffering, but full of the excitement and the perils of those events and times that had shaped the character of the land she now dwelt upon.

She wished she had lived then—perhaps she might have been able to do something to prevent the terrible tragedy—the annihilation of the magnificent Natchez.

These and many other memories continued to occupy her mind as she bid the servants good-night and retired to her room, never knowing she had been closely observed as she made her way home.

Immediately after Camille had left the Copelands', Charles had mounted his stallion and followed at a distance behind her. He had in mind only to assure himself that she got there safely and then he would take his dirty, exhausted body on home for a much needed bath and sleep.

But Camille had loitered along the way, her eyes sweeping the fields. As he watched, he could feel her pain as though it were his own. His mind flew back to the day of her father's funeral, when as a child, she had stood so alone, so sad beside the grave. His heart twisted. Then he saw again the straightening of slender shoulders, the stiffening of the spine. She was a tough little thing—a survivor. She would make it. And how he hoped he might be around to see it.

With a grin of self-mockery and a shrug of his wide shoulders, he wondered why he should feel such tenderness for the little spitfire, who could be selfish, and who cared nothing for him—other than some dutiful gratitude perhaps. But it was her strong independence as well as her remarkable courage that so enchanted him. He wondered again what he was to do about her—this intriguing child-woman who was his wife. The status quo of their relationship was unbearable. He could no longer be merely her guardian and friend.

Either he must be more, or perhaps he should be much less—for his own peace of mind.

He saw Camille give a quick shake of her head and turn toward home. He had seen her make the same gesture at the cemetery. She would handle whatever came her way, for she came from Beaufort stock, and she was made of pure steel.

Reluctantly he turned his horse back toward Natchez. It was becoming harder and harder to leave her, and he did not like the things she was doing to him.

He needed a diversion—something to get his mind off his wife. Justine was not the answer. Since the ball when Camille had danced that damned flamenco, he'd returned to Justine's arms twice, thinking to relieve his mind and body of the strain, but had been disappointed, realizing on both occasions all too clearly that the answer to his problem could not be found in making love to another woman.

He had cared for Justine, and would soon have to explain to her something he didn't understand himself. He suspected she already knew that something was amiss, but still he postponed the unpleasant scene, though he knew it was only fair to be honest with her, and the sooner the better.

In the meantime he could occupy himself with business, and perhaps a little hunting and an occasional horse race. It would just have to do. He smiled, recalling that a race was planned for the next day over near St. Catherine's creek. Just what he needed!

THE DAY FOLLOWING the fire was another gorgeous summer day, and Camille ordered the carriage prepared for "calling." She dressed with care, choosing one of her most attractive walking dresses of blue and white silk, belted around her small waist with a rose-colored sash. The underskirt exposed in the front was of blue silk with a deep, fringed border. A bonnet of straw with rose-colored ribbons was jauntily tied to one side under her chin, and a blue parasol completed the ensemble. She felt pretty and carefree.

Some traditions Camille flagrantly violated—those she considered ridiculous and of no value whatsoever. Others she tolerated, because there was something in them for her. Visiting or "calling" was one of those that she found a little silly, but she enjoyed any excuse for conversation and catching up on the latest gossip.

Josef helped her up the mounting block into the carriage, but he would not be driving. Those honors were reserved for a pair of brothers in full livery who sat proudly atop the carriage. He called out to them, "Jonah, Josiah! Yo' take care with Miss Camille now, y'hear? Keep a steady han' on them high-steppin' hosses!"

A team of four matched chestnuts were hitched in fine harnesses of leather with silver fittings. They pranced, full of high spirits, as Jonah, with a wide white-toothed grin, nodded his head in acknowledgment.

A flick of the reins was all the horses needed and they stepped out smartly. Camille called at several neighboring plantations, including the Copelands, who seemed to be coping in the aftermath of the fire. She either visited for a few minutes at each place, or left her card in the customary way.

Becoming bored with the chore after an hour or so, she instructed the drivers to turn the carriage toward home, and twirled her parasol, wondering what she might do next. Life had settled into a rather tedious routine and except for the business she conducted in town, Camille found she was frequently bored and at loose ends.

ROWDY LAUGHTER ricocheted across the tree-lined lane, about a mile away from Camille. Bits of hearty conversation echoed back and forth as a group of mounted men, resplendent in their finery, made their leisurely way in her direction.

"John, hope you've brought a heavy pocketbook today, old man," one of the riders shouted with good humor.

"Indeed not. What I have brought is the best Mississippi racer in the whole damned state! You'll have your chance to put your money where your mouth is shortly, dear Robert."

"Say, Charles, what about Reaper? Do we get to see him in action today? Heard he had a gimpy leg."

"Reaper?" Charles laughed heartily. "Tell me, boys, does this magnificent animal look gimpy to you? Of *course* he'll run today—and he'll take anything you can muster up to run against him!" Proudly, Charles patted his stallion's finely arched neck, thinking what a good idea this outing had been. He loved sporting events of all kinds, loved the game, the competition, and best of all, he loved to win. Reaper's time for the mile had never been beaten and Charles felt confident about the outcome of the day's races.

Many wealthy Natchez planters and some of the young blades as well spent vast sums securing the best breeds from Europe and won and lost fortunes on the monumental bets they made when they felt certain of a winner. Some of them made regular trips to Europe to add to their string of race horses.

Charles had only Reaper but so far the matchless bay had been all he'd required. He loved the animal as much as he'd ever loved anything or perhaps any *one*, he thought with a small smile.

Love was a word never spoken in the Scottish hovel where he'd grown up. Love was not shared by his parents, nor was it implanted in their children. *Poverty* was a word they all understood and the daily struggle against starvation required the total efforts of each of them. Charles had begun doing his part in small ways from the time he was able to walk, as had his older brother. Scratching out a meager garden and laboring for scraps from the tables of the upper class had been his life. Until he was fifteen, he had not known there was any other way of life.

Then one day an American family visited his village. They had everything they needed or wanted. To Charles, they seemed prosperous and satisfied. He wanted it all for himself—for his children—if, God forbid, he ever had any! He knew he would never, *never* bring a child into the kind of life he'd known.

Soon other young men of the village began to leave one by one, in search of a better life. Why shouldn't he? It would only be one less mouth for his parents to feed and he knew they wouldn't regret that.

Charles left for America as soon as he was able to save up passage money. His parents' calm acceptance that he'd be leaving them, perhaps forever, hurt more than he would ever admit.

He had promised to send them money, though, when he could, and had done so faithfully all the years he'd been away. But never once had he received a single communication from them or even one word of thanks. He might have thought some disaster had befallen them or that they had moved away, but the one person in the village who did write to him kept him informed of their circumstances.

His parents had moved into a small, neat cottage on the edge of the village and seemed content, though they still worked hard, as if afraid their good fortune that had come so suddenly might just as easily be stopped. Charles's brother had disappeared, and no one had heard from him in years.

"Charles!" came a challenging voice. "How about a little side bet? Just your Reaper against this new beauty of mine?" John Markham smiled as he patted the muscular black stallion that moved restlessly beneath him. "Demon here needs a little warm-up. How about it?"

"You're on! Fifty dollars!" shouted Charles, anxious to leave his troubling thoughts behind. "To that big oak at the bend in the road yonder."

"Right! Robert, you call it!"

The two men lined up in the center of the lane, controlling their restive beasts with firm hands until Robert called out, "On your marks, gentleman. Get set . . . now . . . Go!"

The dust flew as the horses dug in and barreled down the straight lane. In the first quarter of a mile it looked as though the challenger might take them, but Charles was holding his mount in check. When Reaper was given his head, he surged past the other horse, easily outdistancing him. Reining in and slowly cantering to a stop, Charles looked back. John was waving the money in the air as he and the others rode to catch up with Charles.

"Looks like you two are in fine form today," he grumbled, handing Charles his winnings. "But Demon here takes a while to get warmed up. You remember, I told you that? But just you wait, Charles Longmont.''

Charles laughed heartily. The day was going very well indeed. Just the diversion he needed. They continued merrily on their way, exchanging anecdotes and puffing on the Havana ''segars'' they all enjoyed.

''Hey! What's this?'' John was pointing at a carriage that had just come into view as they rounded a bend in the road.

''Oh, no,'' Charles muttered.

There was no mistaking the elegant coach nor its liveried pair of drivers. Charles remembered the interior from his brief ride in it on the night of Beaufort's death, and he remembered settling Camille and her sister in its comfortable interior on the day of their departure for school. Yes, he was all too familiar with this particular coach, and knew before he looked inside precisely whom he would see.

Adopting a nonchalant air, he rode alongside, sweeping his hat off in a salute to the young lady who sat smiling inside. ''Why, Mrs. Longmont, to what do I owe this unexpected pleasure? I hadn't thought to see you today.''

I'll bet you hadn't, she thought, the smile glued to her lips while her mind whirled. Where could he be off to—with this group of rowdies? Her eyes took in the young gentlemen with Charles, some whose reputations had been somewhat tarnished by their gaming and womanizing.

John Markham had broken more hearts and been threatened by more irate fathers in Natchez than anyone she knew. But in spite of his less-than-savory reputation, he was still highly sought after as an escort and was probably one of the most eligible bachelors in town. His family were third generation Natchez planters and a mantle of wealth and respectability covered his unseemly exploits. John's father and his grandfather had used their combined influence to bail him out of more than one potentially disastrous row. His twinkling brown eyes and rich crop of auburn hair lent him a deceptively charming appearance.

Robert DeVry had grown up on a neighboring plantation to the Markhams' and his family were equally revered in the nabob society of Natchez aristocrats. Robert, as the middle child, would inherit little, the family's house and lands passing to the firstborn, his older brother Kent. Since childhood, Robert had been scrappy and intent on nonconformity. He always did things his own way, including the choice of his friends. Charles Louis Longmont was several years his senior, and so little was known of the man that Robert's parents had frowned on the relationship, but Robert had been unaffected by their opinion and had merrily gone on his way. A streak of rebelliousness ran deep in him, as well as a burning need to prove himself. Robert was the handsomest of Charles's friends with his head of jet-black hair and mustache, and eyes that sparkled with vigor and mischief.

David Renault was the quietest of the four men and little was know of him or his background, other than that he had arrived in Natchez some years earlier with only a pocketful of change and a bony mule. With his sheer persistence, intense desire and a little luck, he had scratched out a fortune from the rich Mississippi earth, and was now free to do anything he might wish. His one sorrow in life was the death of his young wife, whom he'd loved devotedly. Her memory was sacred to him, and he neither courted nor flirted with any of the Natchez lovelies. Those who had come to know him and call him friend could count on him for life.

Actually, Camille thought the sandy-haired slender young Renault did not even belong in Charles's circle of friends, but he was ever-present with them, and had the same high respect for Charles as did the others.

The last of the entourage was "Ace" McGuire, who'd gotten his nickname for his abilities at the card table. For years he had plied his trade as a riverboat gambler, and was widely known up and down the Mississippi. The death of relatives in Natchez and his unexpected inheritance of Six Pines plantation had catapulted him into a new life-style, one that was entirely agreeable to him. Still, his greatest pleasure was a swift and cutthroat game of chance. And he loved horse racing with a burning passion, particularly if his horse was winning. Ace dressed with a conscious flamboyance, diamonds flashing prominently on both hands and at his wrists and throat. He could be seen regularly Under the Hill with an assortment of handsome women, equally stylish and game for an evening's lively entertainment.

Camille liked Charles's friends and was accorded the utmost respect and courtesy by them. But today she knew they were up to something; they looked like nothing so much as little boys with their hands caught in the cookie jar!

"Why, Mr. Longmont, I'm out payin' my calls, doin' my duty as a good citizen, you might say." Her drawl was more pronounced than usual and Charles's eyebrow shot up. But she continued politely, "And may I ask the same question of you, sir?"

"Of course, madam. My friends..." His arm swung back to include the four who rode with him. "My friends and I are out for a pleasant afternoon ride, for some sunshine and fresh air, you might say." He chuckled.

And you might also say on your way to a horse race, she muttered under her breath before turning her gracious attention to the other men.

"Well, you fellows have a pleasant *outing*." The emphasis on the last word was not unnoticed, and the young men who were so impatient to be under way bid her a good day.

Now why didn't he come right out and say they were going to the races? she wondered as her carriage rolled homeward. There must be something he was hiding, some reason he didn't want to admit where he was going, at least to her.

There was nothing like a good mystery to get Camille moving. Jumping out of the carriage almost before it had stopped, she called for her own horse to be saddled. Holding her skirts high, she flew up the stairs to her room.

"Get my riding clothes, Indigo!"

"Now, ma'am?"

"Now, Indigo! And hurry!"

"But...but...ma'am...it's time for tea."

"No more buts. No tea. Just move! But first help me unlace this frazzlin' dress. Why can't *somebody* make a dress one can get out of *alone* for a change?"

"Now, now, yo' jest calm down, Miss Camille. I have yo' out of dis dress in no time—ef yo' jest stan' still!"

"Oh, all right, but hurry!" Camille did stand still, except for her foot, which tapped impatiently. She did not want to miss a minute of the activities. Father had always refused to let her go—saying it was no place for a lady—most especially not for a child! But she knew he dearly loved the races himself, and she knew that her mother had accompanied him on one or two occasions at least, though she had more than likely remained discreetly in her carriage.

In less than a half hour Camille had mounted her horse and was ready to be off.

"Jest a minute, Missy Cam." Josef had ambled over and placed an aged hand on the reins. "Yo' can't go ridin' off all alone."

"Oh, yes, I can, Josef. Now, you turn me loose. I won't go far and I won't be gone long." Thinking she'd spoken too harshly, she placed her hand over his and patted it before removing it gently from the reins. "I'll be fine, Josef." Her brilliant smile won him over as usual and with a rueful smile, he stepped back.

"Yo' be careful, now y'hear?" The young woman who galloped away from him was no longer a child, he thought with pride, and she had done a fine job of running the plantation. No, he had to stop thinking of her that way.

Camille enjoyed a brisk gallop through the back roads toward Pharsalia plantation. When she neared the clearing on St. Catherine's Creek where she knew the circular track to be laid out, she slowed her horse, planning her arrival. It would be best if Charles didn't see her right away, so it was important she see him first.

The creek was narrow and deeply bedded where it wound a serpentine path through the verdant countryside to an outlet into the Mississippi twenty miles below Natchez. The track followed the natural lay of

the land along the creek's bank. Ash trees grew thick
and tall around the clearing, and that was where
Camille remained, hidden from sight.

She saw him. Her mare slid to a stop in response to
her harsh, unconscious yank on the reins. Her breath
caught in a ragged gasp. Charles was magnificent; yes,
that was the right word, magnificent. One of Magnolia's young black servants held Reaper and Charles
stood alongside the track not more than fifty feet away
from her.

He did not see her, but she could not take her eyes
off him. Something in the masculine grace of his stance
and his tanned, rugged face caused her stomach to
plummet to the vicinity of her toes and her pulse to
quicken until the blood was racing wildly through her
veins. She could only recall having felt this way one
other time in her whole life—when the Gentleman
Bandit had made his nocturnal appearance on the
Trace.

Her eyes widened, clearly registering her emotional
response and inner turmoil. Luckily there was no one
to see, and she kept her eyes trained on the tall, strik-
ingly handsome figure of her husband.

She blinked. Her husband! Oh, God, there went her
stomach again!

Charles Louis Longmont stood out in a crowd. He
towered above the others and his commanding presence revealed his position of leadership. Camille noticed his easy friendliness and felt the camaraderie of
the men who strode about with spurs jingling, placing
their bets and urging their chosen horses on to victory.

She was not surprised that Charles was a leader of
men; she'd just never given it much thought before.
His tall black hat failed to protect him entirely from the

sun, which dappled over his bronzed face and bare forearms. His vest hung open and his shirt revealed that enticing dark patch of hair that had so intrigued her at the ball. She wanted to reach out her hand and wind her fingers in the curls that she knew would be wiry and soft at the same time.

His lashes were entirely too long for a man and opened to reveal the warmest brown eyes she'd ever seen. The sturdy, gentle hands that had held her in comfort in the past negligently held a pocketbook and an impressive amount of loose bills that fluttered in the warm breeze. She held her breath as she watched him place a sizable bet on his stallion, next to run.

It was important to him that his horse be a winner. Somehow she knew that, as indelibly as she knew her name, and suddenly she wanted the same thing—for him—so badly she ached with the wishing. She held her breath as Reaper and two other well-bred racers lined up.

The signal was given and the horses, all ridden by small black jockeys, were off to a good, even start. A roar went up from the men standing around the edges of the track as first one then the other took the lead. Halfway around, Reaper was back by a full length.

Camille could not believe Charles's horse might lose. Her heart hammered with the excitement of the race. Finally the small jockey gave Reaper his head and the big, gallant horse gave everything he had. He began to pull away, at first only by a nose, then by a head; at last leaving the others well behind, he crossed the finish line a clear winner.

Charles gave a whoop of joy and threw his hat high into the air. His cry was echoed by Camille, who impulsively shouted her joy, unaware that in doing so she was giving herself away.

With a brilliant smile, Charles turned in the direction of her exclamation and recognized her in the shadows. For a minute he grinned at her and they shared the exultation of the race. She felt closer to him than she ever had and a new, wonderful feeling swept over her.

Nudging her horse with her knees, she moved toward Charles, anxious to congratulate him. He took a couple of steps in her direction before a tap on his shoulder stopped him and he turned back, away from her.

The smile disappeared from Camille's face and her hand tightened on the reins, bringing her horse to a stop.

Holding Charles's arm in a familiar way, Justine Blanchette stood there, looking very beautiful and sophisticated. Where had she come from—and what was she doing there? No other woman was near the track, though a few awaited their husbands at a distance in their carriages. But here was this...this woman, walking boldly up to Charles as though she had every right to be there!

Confusion, bewilderment and anger flitted across Camille's face and she seemed frozen where she was, unable to move, until Charles looked at her once more.

He held out one hand and took a step toward Camille, but before she could read the concern in his eyes, she whirled her mare in a tight half circle and urged her into a headlong gallop back down the lane.

She was oblivious of the breakneck pace she set and the thin branches that slapped against her skirts and brushed her arms and face. She only knew she had to get as far away from him as possible.

Why had she gone there? It had been a foolish thing to do and she regretted it heartily. But she couldn't change that now. And what she had seen was more hurtful than she could ever have imagined. Of course, she'd heard the rumors about Charles and Justine. Natalie, the town gossip had made sure of that, and soon after she'd returned from Maryland, too. But that had all been so long ago—before they were married. And, she admitted, she had expected him to be as faithful to their marriage as she had been, even though it had been arranged and was a marriage in name only.

It hurt desperately to think he had still been seeing Justine while she was away, that he was apparently *still* seeing her!

Two can play this game, Charles Longmont, she muttered, slowing her horse to a canter and coming to some definite conclusions about her future behavior. There had never been much of a chance for the marriage, she supposed, though she had harbored a fragile hope it might work out. *There are plenty of eligible young men out there who'd be happy to be mine, just mine,* she continued, her one-sided conversation aimed at her absentee husband.

For the next hour Camille rode without paying much attention to the direction she took. It was nearing sunset when she realized with a start that she had wandered into the ancient Natchez Indian burial mounds. The fading glow of the sun bathed the overgrown mounds of earth with an ethereal light, and shadows in the trees surrounding the clearing were spooky and ominous. Camille shivered, frightened to find herself alone where the Natchez had carried on their religious rites and ceremonies. She could almost see them dance, hear them chant in the utter stillness.

"Let's go home, Sadie," she said, giving her little mare a swift, encouraging kick.

The rustling of branches alerted her to another presence. She threw a worried glance back over her shoulder. Just breaking free of the line of trees, she spied a dark horse and rider, who seemed intent on catching up with her.

At her insistence, Sadie increased her speed, but the other horse covered the distance separating them quickly with his longer stride. Camille heard him gaining on her, and would not turn to look back again, but applied her whip, squeezing a little more speed out of her game but thoroughly outclassed mount.

Soon the unidentified rider was right behind her and then right beside her. Before she realized what was happening, he had reached over with a strong, jacketed arm, and snatched her easily from her saddle, settling her smoothly in front of him.

"Do not look around, my lady." She heard the throaty voice with a shock of recognition. The strong arm wrapped around her waist so firmly belonged to none other than the gentleman bandit!

"What are *you* doing here?" she managed to choke out, her voice barely above a whisper.

"I've come to see you. I've thought of little else but you, dear lady. A vision of you is before me, both waking and sleeping."

"What fancy words for a bandit, sir!" Her fright was quickly dissolving into anger now that she knew who held her.

"You are a fancy lady, my heart. And I have traveled a long way to be near you."

"Yes! And robbed a few unfortunate souls along the way, I warrant."

His deep chuckle sent unwelcome chills through her and she wondered if his amusement was for the victims of his crimes or for her, a victim of his charms.

Warning her not to turn around, he whispered into her ear, and his suggestive words blended with the sensual unreality of the ancient place almost hypnotized her.

Later she would wonder how he had managed to return her to her own horse without her ever having seen his face, and how she had then arrived safely at home. She could not remember the details, just the husky voice in her ear and the snug fit of his arm around her waist as he'd held her much too tightly.

Why had she allowed him to make love to her with his seductive voice? He was a rogue, and she *was* married! Camille wrestled with her guilt before finally deciding that she had done nothing wrong, really. There was nothing she could have done to combat the strong arms fastened about her. But the question was, had she wanted to? Her thoughts were a contradictory jumble as she prepared for bed that night.

Chapter Nine
END OF OCTOBER, 1859

"I'VE THOUGHT IT OVER very carefully, Charles. I want the annulment you promised me before I went away to school." Camille had dressed in what she considered her most sophisticated outfit for this meeting with her husband. It was a promenade suit of smoke-gray poplin trimmed with garnet cording and matching fitted jacket. A single garnet stone hung from a long, gold chain around her neck, and her soft kid boots were trimmed with garnet ribbon and flat bows.

It was vital to her that she appear mature in this discussion. And she vowed she would *not* lose her temper, nor in any way would she act like a child. She had, indeed, thought the situation over from every angle before she had arrived at this painful and difficult decision.

A message had been dispatched to Charles, asking that he call on her at seven, and she received him in the library, hoping to appropriate some of her father's calm authority in the room she still considered solely his.

They sat in duplicate overstuffed leather chairs, a tray with two glasses and decanters on the rosewood table between them. Though she rarely drank, Camille felt the need for extra courage and poured herself a glass of sherry when she refilled Charles's with brandy. He was frowning, but made no other sign he had heard her.

A grandfather clock's loud ticking filled the empty silence that grew as their eyes refused to meet.

The encounter with Justine had convinced Camille that marriage was patently unfair to women, and she'd decided she wanted no further part of it. Husbands could indulge in affairs without repercussions, but if a wife were to do the same thing, the outcry would be horrendous. Well, she still had a choice in the matter, and she chose to put an end to this pseudomarriage. She tried in vain to ignore the knot of helpless yearning that moved through her for what might have been.

She had also realized with a stab of pain that Charles, too, deserved his freedom. He'd been tied to a child for six years and had probably remained in the relationship only because of his loyalty and friendship for her father. He would not be the one to put an end to the relationship; it was not the gentlemanly thing to do. So she would do it for him, freeing him to live his own life.

"No!" His vehement response was a considerable shock to her, and she found herself stuttering incoherently.

"But... but... Charles. Why? *Why?*"

He looked long at her without speaking. In the depths of his brown eyes, an emotion flickered. Was it pain, or something else? She couldn't be sure. But whatever it was had been quickly replaced with a hard, brilliant glare of impatience.

"No!" he repeated firmly, his steady gaze fixed on her face.

Still he gave no reason, no explanation for his refusal to even consider the annulment she requested.

This was the last thing she had expected from him. Would she never understand this man?

All the hurts and misunderstandings that had been between them through the years bubbled up in her, and she fought down her pain with blinding anger.

How could he sit there so calmly and deny her very reasonable request? What recourse did she have if he refused to grant her the annulment? She would be forever bound to a man who didn't love her, who would never love her, who would blatantly continue his affairs if he chose to do so.

"I will live exactly as I choose, Charles Longmont. I'm no longer a child to be sent away whenever I get in your way. This is my home, and I intend to manage my own affairs, beginning right now! And...and... besides, I don't love you as a wife should. I—I...love someone else!"

Where had the lie come from? She hadn't planned to say anything so ridiculous or untrue. But seeing that he would be unmoving, she had to do something drastic. The words had spilled out before she could stop them, and now there was no calling them back. But it seemed to be working. A dark scowl made Charles appear more fierce than ever, and she was almost afraid of him. His eyes raked over her so unkindly, she thought surely he would agree to her request now.

At her words Charles had risen from his chair. "No." He took a step toward her as he spoke softly, but there was an angry iron will behind the quiet word. Camille shank back in her chair at his approach.

"Well, then, just tell me *why*!" she practically shouted at him, not caring any longer whether he thought her a child or a woman, or a thorn in his flesh! She had to know *why*!

"Who is it?" he growled, his hands clasping her shoulders and pulling her up from her chair. Camille felt his fingers digging into the soft flesh under the silken fabric of her jacket.

"No! I don't have to tell you anything. You *can't* make me!"

"Can't I?" His head lowered, and his lips met hers with a bruising, driving force. Her hands flattened against his chest to push him away, but he was much stronger. He pulled her to him so tightly her hands were pinned ineffectually between them. She tried to turn her head to one side to escape the punishing kiss, but he would not allow it.

"No," he murmured, his kiss gentling as her struggles lessened. "No, Camille." His hand crept up to embed itself in her thick curls. "No annulment. You're mine. You have always been mine!"

What was he saying? That she belonged to him—like a horse, like a slave? That she was his exclusive possession?

"No! Charles Longmont!" She gasped, having pulled away enough that she was able to speak, though his face was still much too near, his lips almost brushing hers, and the rest of their bodies, well, it was practically indecent, but also damnably pleasant, she admitted with great reluctance.

"I don't belong to you," she managed to continue, "or to anyone. You *promised* me an annulment. Don't you remember?"

His dark eyes were hooded by hawklike brows that bunched together in another frown. Again she thought she saw a glimmer of some well-disguised feeling below the surface. She wanted to pursue this expression, but it was gone, so completely and quickly she wondered if she'd imagined it.

"What kind of game are you playing, Camille?" His voice was gruff, and its peculiar timbre played up and down her spine, sending shivers racing through her. "At first you seemed content to be Mrs. Charles Longmont. Why the sudden change?"

She could not tell him how she had felt seeing Justine on his arm, nor could she reveal her contradictory feelings about the gentleman bandit. And anyway, was either of those the real reason behind her request? Or was it truly that she wanted her independence, wanted to prove what she could do alone? And then, of course, there was Charles's side of the question. Could she explain to him that she *really* cared for his position and was willing to let him go, even if it meant allowing him to return to another? No, he probably wouldn't believe it.

"It's . . . it's for the best, Charles."

Her cryptic answer seemed to shatter what remained of his control and he swept her up into his arms, muttering, "Bloody hell, Camille." Her breath expelled in a tiny grunt, her murmured denials silenced by his voracious mouth. He tasted of brandy, sweet and intoxicating and her head reeled from the kiss that deepened, stirring a dormant but powerful feeling inside her. She made a token murmur of resistance before giving in to the overwhelming demands of her heart.

He carried her up the stairs so easily she felt weightless, and all her strength seeped away when she realized his intention. Only her arms felt capable of any response and they were clasped tightly around his neck. Her head rested on his shoulder. As though from a great distance, she heard the peal of the dinner gong summoning the slaves to their quarters.

The upstairs hallway greeted their arrival with a soft creaking of the sturdy oak floor beneath his feet, but no other sound. The house was deserted. Camille, very aware of the hand that firmly held her midriff and the arm supporting her knees, knew that unless she summoned a servant, they would be completely alone for the long night ahead.

Charles would not leave. He meant to make love to his wife. Camille was almost giddy from the sherry and from emotions that were coming too fast. Strange how she hadn't known until this very moment how very much she wanted him.

"My love," he murmured into her ear as he lifted her onto her bed and cast aside the jacket he'd been wearing. "My dear, dear love." The warm amber glow of his eyes caressed her as he stood without moving.

"Charles." Her uplifted arms and the tenderness in her voice unleashed a dam of desire within him, galvanizing him to action. He advanced toward her, nimbly removing his vest, his shirt and belt and stepping out of his trousers, hopping on first one foot and then the other to strip off his boots.

His eyes never left hers as he came nearer. Camille sat very still, watching his every movement. Anticipation was followed quickly by delight as she found his proud nakedness magnificent. Her hands itched to follow the smooth contours of his shoulders, his arms, his trim, taut waist . . . She dared to look further; her eyes opened wide with shock and flew back to his face.

He chuckled. "It's all right, love. Really, truly all right. I will bring you only pleasure, never pain." As he spoke, his hands began deftly releasing the tiny buttons of her jacket and soft blouse. Both were eased off her shoulders and slid to the floor with a whisper. Only the brilliant garnet necklace winked at him from between her bare breasts as his eyes feasted on her lush softness. His hands slipped up over her rib cage, his thumbs tenderly stroking the sensitive fullness.

Her body arched toward his touch, and with a smothered gasp, he allowed his hands to fill themselves with her, his thumbs now teasing the rosy peaks unmercifully as his lips followed to continue the torment.

Camille felt an irresistible tug at the center of her being and was swept away on a tide of passion. She wanted his hands, his mouth, his body—everywhere, all over her, loving her, filling her, satisfying her, and relieving her of the painfully intense feeling building inside her.

"Darling, love." Her skirt and petticoats joined the heap of clothing beside the bed. Her body was now revealed to his searching gaze and the pain that filled him was a surprise as her innocent beauty wrenched at his heart. He had waited so long, and he had tried, he really had, to love her from a distance. Had he but known what beauty and pleasure awaited him, he would not have been able to withstand his urgent desires for a fraction of the time. She was a prize beyond measure, a treasure above price. His eyes worshiped her, while his body ached with driving need for her.

"Love me, Charles," Camille pleaded, asking for so much more than the physical fulfillment her body vehemently demanded. It was a request for a commitment, a love that would grow stronger with the passage of time.

They both understood and shared this overwhelming desire and when he moved over her, his love filled her in a way she'd never dreamed, carrying them both soaring to incredible heights of wonder. The earth fell away and there was nothing left save the two of them, their spirits and bodies united in a mystical union.

Replete, Camille lay against him, her hand resting on his chest. "I love you, Charles," she murmured, drifting into a contented sleep.

Charles remembered the other time when a child had placed all her trust in him and fallen asleep in his arms, wrapped in his cloak. His heart beat painfully and emotions welled up inside him he'd fought down for so long.

Camille Braxton Beaufort Longmont, the bewitching creature who lay curled in the circle of his arms, was his destiny. He had tried to escape it, to deny it, but everything in his life had been leading him toward this woman and this moment in time when she would be completely his. He was exposed and vulnerable where she was concerned, and could easily be hurt beyond healing. But hadn't she said she loved him?

He stroked her cheek with his knuckles, unable to resist touching her. It made him feel good just to look at her as she lay sleeping. His fingers traced the delicately arched brows, the pert upturned nose, and he buried his face in her silken hair that glimmered like onyx and smelled of sweet honeysuckle.

Her eyes flew open. Charles had touched her, caressed her as she slept! Even now his hand lay against her cheek. His golden brown eyes with flecks of amber were soft with tenderness and his lips split into a happy grin when she smiled up at him. He swept her into his arms and crushed her against him, as though afraid she might flee.

"Cam, my love." He dropped kisses on her hair, her forehead, her nose, and finally claimed her mouth with a sweet seduction she could not have resisted had she the smallest remaining desire to do so. This time, when they made love, it was an inevitable slow exploration, a claiming, an appropriation.

WHEN HAD HE FALLEN in love with this beautiful and sensuous child-woman? he wondered afterward. With a start, he realized he had always loved her! Always there had been the promise of her womanhood. It could be seen in the inky depths of those indigo eyes, in the haughty set of thin shoulders squared against the world. He would carry to his grave the sight of the small, courageous girl standing beside her father's grave. His heart had been ensnared since that day in some inexplicable way. But when he had seen her again as an astonishing beauty and a desirable woman after six years, his love, his longing and his passion had become centered upon her.

Oh, God! What have I done? he thought. He hadn't meant to take her like this—hadn't meant to take her this far—not this soon. But she had been so bewitchingly beautiful, and had antagonized him so terribly with her taunting about another man! His fury and his frustration at never being able to hold her, to love her, had blurred his common sense. He had suddenly needed to prove to her that she was his alone, and when he had kissed her, his overwhelming physical need for her had taken over rational thought. With a shudder, he remembered her sweet capitulation, her ardent response when first her lips, then her hands, then finally her body had moved against him.

None of this was any excuse for his behavior; he knew he had been a cad to take advantage of her youth and inexperience. But their lovemaking had been so earth-shattering in its intensity, her responses to him so loving and uninhibited, he admitted with a roguish smile that he would probably do it all again if presented with the same opportunity. After the initial pulling away, she had ceased resisting, and had responded with her whole body and soul.

Why hadn't he agreed to the annulment she requested? She'd had every right to ask, and it was quite true that he *had* promised. But that had been so very long ago—long before his wayward heart had been so firmly trapped, long before his every desire had focused on her lovely slender body, long before those haunting eyes and the crystal laughter stayed with him through the night, long before . . . everything!

What if he had said yes? Would she have turned away from him? Would that have been the end? He might never have experienced the rich feel of her satiny skin, the soft, dewy fullness of her lips, now swollen from his kisses. His loins ached with the need to have her again, and only with utmost exertion of will was he able to resist slipping his hands around the tiny waist and covering her softness with his demanding body. His eyes moved over the smooth planes of her face, but his hands kept still, rejecting their driving desire to claim her body once more.

He had overreacted to her request, of that he was sure. He should have gallantly agreed, giving her the freedom she obviously wanted so badly. And then, perhaps, he could have earned her love, not stolen it from her as he'd done so completely this night.

When she realized fully what had happened between them, she would hate him. She would resent what he had taken from her. But perhaps it was still not too late. If he agreed to give her the annulment, it might make up in some small way for his unforgivable actions. And then, if she no longer wished it, she could make her own choice, and he would court her then as he should have done, instead of his brutish behavior of this night.

He slipped from the bed they'd shared for those few moments of unequaled bliss and quietly pulled on his trousers and stockings. His chest still bare and his dark hair rumpled, he walked out onto the gallery, his tread soft so as not to wake her. Shielding his pipe from the soft morning breeze, he lit the aromatic tobacco in its bowl and puffed, smoke drifting around his head like a lacy cloud.

The sweet scent of freshly mown grass from below blended with the tobacco made a pungent combination that coaxed Camille from her dreamy sleep. Yawning, she stretched luxuriously, without taking her eyes from the form of the man who stood half-dressed, lounging against the balcony railing. Her bedroom seemed different now that Charles had been there. She would never feel the same way about it. She would never feel the same way about anything, she realized.

She was a married woman now, with a strong and loving husband. She smiled, feeling an absurd happiness. What a fool she had been to ask for an annulment—when all she'd ever really wanted was to love and be loved as he had loved her this night, to be held so tenderly, to be taken to such heights of rapture! She had never imagined it could be like this! Why hadn't her mother told her? Of course, she had been much too young to understand such things when her mother died—and her father too. And then there had been no one.

But now there was Charles. She could share these new emotions with him. He would understand, surely. Hadn't he flown to those same heights with her, urging her ever upward and still farther? Now they could share everything; they might even start a family, she thought with a quiver of excitement.

Camille had moved so silently across the plush carpeting that Charles was not aware of her presence until her soft hands lay against the corded muscles of his shoulders and stroked down the smooth line of his back.

He jumped as though her touch burned and whirled on her. "What are you doing?" Hawkish brows lowered over blazing eyes that not so long ago had been soft and warm with longing and passion. "God!" he cried. "Get some clothes on, Camille!" Harsh anger barely disguised a numbing pain as he forbid his eyes to travel over the lush curves, the alluring softness. Neither would he look in her eyes; he couldn't bear the confirmation of his fears. He swung away from her.

Her small, bare feet seemed riveted to the floor as she stood for a moment, trying to make sense of his unexpected reaction. What in God's name did he mean to reject her so completely after making love to her?

"Charles...?" Surely, there was a reason. He would explain, in just a minute, and everything would be all right. He loved her—he must! "Charles..." she repeated brokenly.

"You may have the annulment, Camille. I was wrong to deny you."

The words were a gauntlet flung in her face! He would give her the annulment—now! What a mockery! What an insult! She would never forgive him for this, never!

The hard peal of her laughter raked across his distraught nerves, and his hold on the railing tightened.

"Get . . . out . . . of . . . here." The words came from between clenched teeth as she stood close behind him. Though her hands had dropped from his bare back at his first words, she had not moved from where she stood, so close she still felt the heat from his sun-warmed skin.

"Get out of here, Charles Longmont. And don't ever set foot in this room again. I hate you!"

He winced. The angry blue light in her eyes as he turned back toward her convinced him he had made probably the biggest mistake of his life, a mistake whose consequences would haunt him forever.

"Cam, I'm sorry. I didn't mean it to hurt you. . . ."

"No, you really didn't mean anything, did you?" she said softly, vivid blue eyes brimming with the tears she'd vowed never to let him see. In the way an oyster would a tiny pearl, Camille wrapped her heart with layers of protective coating, shielding it from future hurt and rendering it incapable of feeling.

She shrugged off the tentative touch of his hand on her bare shoulder, as something offensive or aggravating. His eyes implored some softening toward him as he thought how lovely she was, her hair a blue-black cloud sweeping the satiny skin of her neck and shoulders.

There was nothing but blue ice in the depths of her eyes that never wavered from his. He had lost her—or perhaps he'd never really had her—but God, how he wanted her! How he loved her!

He could not leave without touching her even if she rejected him again, and his hands went of their own accord to either side of her face, his thumbs gently stroking her cheeks. She allowed him to hold her and even to kiss her, though it was a poignant sharing of pain and loss; it was goodbye.

It was the child Camille giving up her dreams of a handsome knight who would love and protect her from every wrong. The child-woman was gone; in her place stood a new person intent on making a way for herself, with or without a man by her side.

Charles gathered his boots and snatched his shirt from the back of a chair. He was out the door before she released the breath she'd been holding since their parting kiss.

He was gone! And she was alone. The stillness of her room after the echoing slam of the door reverberated around her.

A feeling of irrevocable loss swept over her as she splashed water from the bowl on the washstand onto her face and arms. But how could she lose something she'd never had? She toweled herself dry and pulled on a satin wrapper, belting it with an angry jerk around her waist. She slipped her feet into matching slippers and walked back out onto the gallery.

Down the lane, she could still see the outline of a dark horse and rider. He was galloping out of her life.

The annulment was hers. Wasn't that what she'd wanted? Yes, but that was before—before she'd realized how much she loved him. Before she'd been loved by him. No, not love . . . it had meant nothing to him. He had used her as a plaything, nothing more.

THREE WEEKS PASSED before thoughts of Charles Louis Longmont she had shoved to the back of her mind came forth one by one to torment Camille. She had not seen him in all that time, and though it came as a surprise to her, she longed for his warm smile.

How she hated to admit that! She had ordered him to leave, but had hoped against her better judgment that he'd come back, that the business affairs of Magnolia would draw him, even if her presence did not. He had not been seen in town in some time now. Probably, he'd disappeared on one of his unexplained "business" trips. But she missed him! And she knew she mustn't.

Since that night she had not allowed her thoughts to stray in his direction for more than a few moments, trying to avoid the hurt, the pain, the unanswered questions. She could no longer avoid dealing with it. Her mind must somehow be put to rest, the nagging doubts and guilt quieted.

Why had he made love to her so passionately, so tenderly, and then shut her out so completely, agreeing to the requested annulment? There had to be a reason, didn't there, other than the obvious one that it was what he wished? Only her overwrought emotions at the time had made her believe that. But then, why did he agree so soon after making love to her?

Of course! Because it was what she had said she wanted!

Why hadn't she realized before? He had done it for her! Or in his elaborate set of moral ethics, he had decided it was for the best that he get out of her life, and allow her to make her own decisions. Charles Longmont would always do what he thought best, regardless of what he wanted!

Of course! He had wanted her! She couldn't have been wrong about that. And he cared for her, too. Though he'd tried not to show it, she'd seen it in his eyes more than once. He only held back for what he considered her best interests.

She had been a fool. It was time to do something—to take back those hateful words she'd flung at him. What could she do, if he wouldn't come to her? Yes, she would go to him—wherever he was, she would find him, and she would show him the annulment was not what either of them wanted.

But where? And how? It would not be easy to find him, if he did not wish to be found. And once she found him, she knew how difficult it could be to convince him of anything. *Ah, but I have a little more negotiating power now,* she thought with a wide smile.

Two days later Camille discovered that Charles had boarded the *Natchez* for a trip to New Orleans. She also learned, to her delight, that the steamboat would not leave its port until sunrise. Plenty of time for what she had in mind. A satisfied smile curving her lips, Camille made final preparations to carry out her plan. She bathed and dressed with an unusual amount of care, applying liberal amounts of lotion to her already creamy skin, and dabbing expensive French perfume in secret places that brought a flush to her cheeks. She selected her finest cambric underthings and a dress that matched the inky blue shade of her eyes perfectly.

At last, with a final glance at her image in the mirror, she was ready. Her heart pounded madly; her pulse was soaring.

Dusk had settled in eerie darkness over the Mississippi when Camille made her way on board the steamship. Even in the dim light, Captain John recognized her and, enveloping her hands in his gigantic ones, guffawed and roared, "If it isn't little Camille Beaufort Longmont! All growed up, and a powerful lovely lady! Damned if I don't remember that first trip—you was just a little freckle-face tyke, but a spunky one! I knew we'd meet again. Yessirree! To what circumstance do we owe the honor of this visit?"

"Evening, Captain." Her smile was captivating as she continued, "My husband is aboard, and it seems I must see him about some business we never completed. Could you show me to his cabin?"

His eyes alive with good humor, the captain escorted her to Longmont's cabin.

Camille hesitated before Charles's door, frightened just as thoroughly as she had been the first time she'd sought him out as a child of thirteen, but the painful pounding of her heart and her dizziness had little to do with fear. Desire and longing coursed through her and she clasped her hands together to still their trembling before she raised one fist to knock.

Seconds passed. Footsteps sounded. The doorknob spun and the door swung open. Deep brown eyes swept over her silently, and he reached for her hands and gently drew her into the room, shutting the door behind her. He did not notice the captain's wide, knowing smile or his discreet departure.

Charles did not question her presence. Indeed he still had said nothing, but indicated with a sweep of his hand for her to move nearer. Slipping the cloak from her shoulders, he folded it carefully and laid it across a table. He turned toward her, but neither of them moved nor spoke. The powerful, unspeakable emotion between them radiated throughout the room, a third presence as vital and alive as the man and woman who stood there, communicating only with their eyes.

Camille's strong resolve quailed. Could she really do this? She had known only Charles, and her inexperience would surely be obvious. How would he react? She knew she would die if he rejected her. That would be the end of everything.

Charles was casually attired in a gold quilted smoking jacket, belted with a heavy silk cord, and soft, buff-colored trousers. His eyes in the candlelight appeared the same golden color as his jacket, but his expression was inscrutable.

Her deep blue eyes wide with trust and shining with love, she raised one arm, her fingers pulling at the blue satin ribbon holding her curls up off her neck. It loosened, and she let it slide through her fingers to the floor, her dark hair falling in shimmering waves to past her shoulders.

Charles stood motionless, but his eyes smoldered now with a wild, amber light. Camille took one hesitant step toward him, then another, moving slowly, seductively. When she stood in front of him, her hand reached toward the silken cord at his waist and gently tugged until it came loose in her hand, the lapels of his jacket falling open. Another tiny step, and her hands were inside, sliding through the springy curls covering his chest in a silken mat.

"Oh, God! Camille!" Arms he had held tightly to his sides flew around her and he gathered her to him, kissing the top of her head and then her tear-filled eyes, his voice soft and warm with love, "I love you, Cam. Oh, God help me, how I do love you!"

With a soft sound of pleasure, she clung to him, so grateful for his response, her heart leaped against her chest and then melted within her. Everything she was, everything she had or ever hoped to have, she gave into his keeping. She would be, for now and all time, completely his. "And I love you, Charles."

He reached to snuff out the candelabra and a glow of unreality enveloped them. They were lost in the wonders of their love and filled with a sweeping, encompassing rapture that knew no bounds.

Neither heard the lonesome whistle of the boat in the wee hours of the next morning, nor felt the small lurch when it slid into the river to begin its journey southward. They slept, nestled in each other's arms, all their cares far behind, and the promise of a bright future upon their faces.

NEW ORLEANS HUMMED with life, and with Charles by her side, Camille experienced its pleasures in a way she could not have imagined on her short visit there as a child. Proudly, he escorted her through streets crowded with shops and affluent shoppers, insisting she splurge on a new wardrobe since her unexpected honeymoon trip had caught her with only the clothes she'd worn aboard the *Natchez*.

When his eyes caught and held hers at odd moments, they shared the intimate exciting memories of that night. Charles said it had worked out perfectly; he'd always planned to take her to New Orleans for their honeymoon, and this was the perfect opportunity. With his help and opinions so freely given, her new wardrobe of exclusive garments was entirely to his liking, the fabrics and colors they selected perfect foils for her complexion and coloring. More than once, a carriage had to be hired to haul back to their elegant hotel the many boxes of shoes, dresses, hats, under-garments, ribbons and laces.

"Charles, we must stop!" She was smiling and ra-diant, out of breath from their latest expedition. "Or we shall need to book the entire *Natchez*, and possibly the *Mississippi Queen*, as well, just to get all our bag-gage home!" She had slipped off her shoes, and was looking up at him while she gingerly rubbed her com-plaining feet.

"Perhaps we shall never go home, Camille." His eyes locked on hers, and burned with passionate in-tensity. "I love having you all to myself here. And there's still much to see."

But as he swept her up in his arms, she knew with a secret stab of pleasure they would see no more of the enchanting city that day.

The next morning they strolled through the French market, revelling in the potent smell of steaming chic-ory coffee and feasting on the delicacy of *beignets*, a square donutlike confection lightly powdered with sugar.

The pace quickened as the sun rose higher, and soon the *banquettes*, or wooden sidewalks, were filled with patrons. Stalls echoed with cries of vendors hawking sweet potato cakes, fresh fish and live crabs, spices of all kinds, brown and purple figs, and even live alliga-tors. Black women bustled about with large bowls or heavy baskets on their heads, calling out, *"Belle calla. Belle calla. Tout chaude."* The rich aromas of their deep-fried rice balls flavored with nutmeg and cinnamon filled the air.

Horse-drawn buggies and wagons soon clogged the narrow streets, the clip-clop of horses' hooves and the jingle of harness bells adding to the growing cacophony. A milk wagon stopped in the middle of a block of houses painted in pastel shades of pink, blue, and lavender to fill the pitchers of waiting customers.

Camille and Charles paused before Jackson Square, the former Place d'Armes, and admired the twin spires of the stately cathedral, the symmetrical walks and gardens recently added to the square. They marvelled at the perfectly balanced statue of Andrew Jackson on his rearing steed, and admired the Pontalba Buildings.

Later they lunched at renowned Antoine's and afterward prowled through small shops along side streets in search of more bargains. Black iron lace adorned most of the buildings, some three stories high, and heavy grilled doors swung open into shaded, secluded courtyards.

Camille glanced inside one such area and shivered, suddenly cold in the midday sun. Shadowy, even though the sun tipped the tops of tall palms growing inside, it was narrow and long, with steep sides, one of red bricks, and two of mortar. Huge, flat paving stones formed the floor and grotesque masks sat on high pedestals, leering at passersby. A ceramic cat clung to one wall, as though it had tried to escape and failed.

Camille grasped Charles's arm, thankful at once for his strength and calm support. He asked, leaning toward her, concern clear in his face, "What is it, Cam?"

"It . . . it . . . looks so like a prison."

"Darling, it's only a courtyard." His arm had gone around her as he hastened to reassure her. Camille couldn't have said why, but the feeling of foreboding lingered throughout the rest of their stay in New Orleans and haunted her dreams for weeks.

Chapter Ten
MARCH, 1860

IT WAS THE BEGINNING of the very best of times. Since the tragedies of her youth, Camille had never dared to hope life could be so wonderful again—that love could be so wonderful. Happiness she had never thought to find filled her, and she constantly felt like laughing, dancing and singing roundelays at the top of her voice. All of her dreams were reality, and life seemed too good to be true.

In the months since she and Charles had returned from New Orleans to live at last as husband and wife, life on Magnolia had settled into a pleasant, comfortable routine. They entertained, throwing a spectacular ball and frequent parties; they attended the theater, performances of touring opera companies, and shows on the riverboats with a devoted circle of friends; they shared the responsibilities of the plantation; best of all, they shared night after night of rapturous lovemaking and they shared their love, denied for so long and now freely acknowledged and enjoyed.

Tonight they would attend the biggest ball of the year in Natchez. Everyone would be there. A chef was being brought in from New Orleans to prepare an elaborate feast for five hundred. It would be a celebration to end all celebrations.

Whispering Oaks, a palatial estate on the bluffs overlooking the Mississippi, was festooned with expensive hothouse flowers as well as the currently blooming local favorites, camellias and cape jasmine. Flowers were everywhere: trailing garlands wound their way up the spiral staircase and adorned the mantles of the fireplaces; a profusion of the fragrant blossoms filled porcelain vases and silver bowls.

Light from thousands of candles poured through the open windows and could be seen from the river for many miles in both directions.

For Camille, the best part would be that she and Charles would attend together, for the first time, as a married couple. Her happiness over the past weeks had been a burgeoning delight inside her, driving out thought of any obstacles or problems. Something had sprung to life between the two of them on their impromptu honeymoon trip to New Orleans. Whatever it was, and she still wasn't sure, it was heady, like a fine wine, and gave her a trembly, good feeling that had been with her ever since.

He cared for her! Surely he must, or he wouldn't have . . . She blushed brightly, recalling the abandonment of their lovemaking.

Now her arm was linked securely in his, and she was proud, so proud to walk beside him. She cast a sideways glance, taking in his tanned and handsome face, his luxuriant chestnut hair, the intriguing mustache of the same color, and the wide expanse of his shoulders. He was elegantly attired in a silver-gray frock coat and black satin vest. The points of his white, high-collared shirt turned down over a matching black satin cravat.

"You look lovely tonight, Mrs. Longmont." She had been about to say how handsome he was, and had indeed been so lost in contemplation of him she'd quite forgotten what she had worn.

She looked down self-consciously, her hand smoothing the cool red satin of her off-the-shoulder formal gown. She smiled up at him, "Thank you, Mr. Longmont. I was about to say that you look quite dashing yourself."

He smiled his unalloyed pleasure at her compliment, his hand covering hers in the crook of his arm protectively. His eyes played tricks with her as he looked her over, not missing a detail of her appearance.

It had taken Magnolia's well-trained seamstress a solid three weeks to get the dress exactly right. Camille had wanted everything to be perfect, and had spared no expense, ordering the best satin fabric available from New Orleans. Imported lace covered the inverted V-shaped panel in the front of the skirt; two bright red camellia blossoms were pinned to the lace, one at her waist and one near the floor. The brilliant crimson of the dress set off to a striking advantage her midnight-colored hair and creamy skin. The fitted waist narrowed to a tiny span before billowing out into petticoats stiffened to just the right degree to hold the voluminous skirt out in a perfect bell shape that rustled delightfully with each dainty step.

Charles was smitten. He remembered the other dance, when she had done the tantalizing flamenco. Now she looked every whit as voluptuous and desirable, but tonight she was every inch the perfect lady, the perfect wife. There was no hint of wild abandon in her behavior, though he knew her outward demeanor concealed a fiery and passionate nature. He was captivated, and heart-stoppingly proud of her.

Every eye in the ballroom was trained on them, either with pleasure and approval or in undisguised jealousy. They were, without question, the most handsome couple there. The spark that jumped between them when their eyes met or they touched could almost be seen and heard.

The elite of Natchez were a close-knit group of about forty wealthy planters with properties in and out of Natchez, but others from the surrounding countryside were included in festivities of this kind, making for large and festive gatherings.

A ball such as this was an "event," eagerly anticipated and carefully prepared for. It was a chance for socializing and for demonstrations of wealth—a good way to show off new coaches, glittering jewels, and the finest attire money could buy. It was also an occasion that might be used to complete a discreet business deal or make a special announcement.

Such an announcement seemed forthcoming, as Glory's father silenced the musicians and signaled for the large group's attention. Couples in and out of the ballroom quieted and looked expectantly toward Rourke Smythe.

"Good friends, one and all." His loud, almost theatrical voice rang throughout the large rooms. "Welcome once more, to our home. May your evening here be unforgettable and filled with many pleasures. This year, we have a happy reason for this ball, and an important announcement to make. It is with great satisfaction and pride that I announce the forthcoming wedding of my only daughter Glory Elizabeth to Dandy Martin Ashton, the son of my good friends and neighbors Mildred and Whitney Ashton of Pleasant Oaks."

Raising his glass, he saluted the couple who stood on his left, and was joined by other lifted glasses and shouts of "Here! Here!" which were soon drowned out by the hearty applause.

Camille stood near her friend and was among the first to congratulate her with a hug. "I'm so happy for you, Glory. Do be happy."

"Oh, I *will*, Cam, I just know I will! And I want you to be my matron of honor."

"Of course. When is the wedding?"

"In late May. And it will be *here*, of course. If the weather permits, we will have it in the garden."

"That sounds lovely. We'll talk later."

Camille turned to Dandy, whose eyes twinkled with mischief. When he embraced her, he whispered in her ear, "You missed your chance, lovey, by getting married as a child! I would have waited for you, you know."

"Of course you would, you rogue!" she said, laughing.

Camille had expected Dandy and Glory to be married soon after her return from school, and still wondered about the cause of their extremely long engagement. Glory would be the last of their circle of close friends to marry, and Camille had always assumed she would be the first.

A sumptuous midnight feast was laid out in the double parlors, its irresistible delicacies including fresh oysters in their shells, stewed fruits, and tangy mince pies in the flakiest of crusts.

The fine champagne and imported whiskeys flowed freely and the revelry continued until dawn, although it was mostly the younger couples who remained for the bountiful breakfast served on the gallery.

The party of the year was over, and the remaining guests began to depart. Coaches rumbled down the narrow road along the crest of the eroding bluff, one after the other, raising clouds of dust in their wake.

Camille leaned against Charles inside their coach, and closed her eyes with a satisfied sigh.

"Sleepy?" he asked, pulling her close.

"Mm-hmm," she murmured.

"How sleepy?"

"Well," she replied, looking up into brown eyes darkened with passion, "I suppose I'm not *terribly* sleepy. No, not that sleepy," she repeated softly as his lips touched hers.

Their love had become solid and complete over the months, and was developing into something beyond their wildest fantasies. Cooperation in business affairs and running the plantation had taught each of them a healthy respect for the intelligence and good sense of the other.

Charles had promised her Magnolia would always be hers, as her father wished. But he longed to build a house for her, one that would belong only to the two of them, every board and nail planned by them. She would design the interior, and have free rein in selection and ordering of carpeting, wall coverings, curtains, and the furnishings for every room.

Their house would be built on the property adjoining Magnolia, and it would be as though she had never left home. Surely she would be pleased, he hoped, as he secretly consulted with a Philadelphia architect, Lucas Brumley.

He would not tell her until everything was perfect. His warm eyes sparkled with affection when he looked at her and thought of their new home. He was so proud to be able to offer *her* something at last and, he admitted, this was important to him.

It was something his family never had, nor hoped to have: a home filled with love and happy children. Ever since he'd fled Scotland, putting an ocean between himself and his childhood home, he'd dreamed of one day having a real home of his own.

Weeks flew by, while he consulted with Brumley, and work commenced on the new house. Carefully, Charles worked out every detail. Satisfied with the way the building was progressing, he invited the bearded architect to his home for tea. Brumley would meet Camille and the two of them would spring the surprise.

Stunned at the announcement, Camille's eyes flew from the dowdy architect to her handsome husband, whose nervousness had him practically pacing the veranda, hands clasped behind his back.

In an instant and without further explanations, it was clear to Camille how much Charles had put into this project and how important it was to him. But how *could* she act overjoyed at something designed to take her home from her! In her heart, she knew she would never be happy living anywhere except on Magnolia.

Could she tell him that? His heart showed so clearly in his eyes, she decided that she could not.

Haltingly she answered, "The plans are so carefully thought out and the idea is intriguing. It's very sweet of you, Charles. But . . . I mean, it's such a big decision . . ." Perhaps if she could forestall the plans, a compromise might somehow be reached. Her heart jumped to her throat while she waited for his reaction. Had she been too blunt, said too much, even while she was trying to spare his feelings and avoid a disagreement?

"Of course, Camille." His clipped words revealed much, and sent her hopes plummeting. He was furious with her, or was it pain she saw flicker in his eyes before the implacable mask dropped in place? "Mr. Brumley, my wife advises caution, so I'm sure you'll understand if we table the matter until some future date."

"Well, that's fine, just fine, Charles. And of course you understand I can return at any time you would like to continue."

"Yes, thank you, Lucas. The plans you've developed are excellent and as close to my wishes as is humanly possible. You have put forth an extra effort and we both appreciate it, don't we, Camille?" He took her hand, drawing her into the discussion.

"Yes, Lucas," she agreed softly, "if the reality can compare to the design, it will be a masterpiece."

"That it will, Mrs. Longmont, that it will, I assure you. Perhaps the reality may even exceed it. Your husband has exacting, but exquisite tastes and a far-reaching vision few can match." He had, indeed, been impressed with Charles's suggestions and ideas. It was an interesting project and should prove to be lucrative, as well. He certainly hoped her hesitation would not be a major setback, and that the construction would continue.

"But now, I really must be on my way. Circumstances at home require my immediate attention, or I would be strongly in favor of accepting your kind invitation to remain, Charles."

"You mentioned you are a delegate to the Republican convention in Chicago next month. What are your predictions about the outcome?" Charles had been watching the political scene carefully, and was more concerned than he'd yet been willing to admit about the presidential election of 1860.

"Old Abe Lincoln's a shoo-in to win the nomination and with the Democratic party split, is almost certain to win the election."

"Yes, I agree." Charles's brow furrowed as a sudden, clear vision of the chaos ahead for his country wiped thoughts of home-building from his mind. "And when he's elected, there's sure to be serious trouble on the slavery issue. Those hotheads in South Carolina will be screaming for secession and others will follow suit, I fear."

"But, Charles," Camille protested, "surely you don't agree that the government has the right to dictate to the states whether or not they have slaves. And surely, a state that disagrees has the right to withdraw from the Union?"

Her dear face was so intent, something plucked at his heart in spite of himself. He wanted to reassure her, but he had little hope the country could avoid a violent confrontation over these divisive issues.

"Clear heads can often avert a disaster, Cam, and it is vital that Southerners think clearly and consider the situation carefully before jumping to follow their very healthy consciences."

Camille heard Charles's words with a stab of foreboding. Could there really be a war? No, surely their statesmen would be able to keep the South on a steady course.

When the architect took his leave, neither of them seemed willing to broach the subject that had already driven a schism of misunderstanding between them. They would discuss the plans for their house later.

"BRETHREN! Examine your hearts and you will find them black with the vileness of sin! You must cleanse your conscience and make your peace with an angry God!" The strident, high-pitched voice disturbed the peace of late evening on the Natchez Trace fifty miles north of Natchez.

A few listened willingly, the rest continued their activities, but though they wished to, were unable to escape the range of the preacher's voice.

Clement Masters stood on a large rock in order to be able to see over the heads of the small crowd he'd managed to gather. He was soon moving among them, hat in hand, to collect their offerings, saying in a singsong voice, "Thank ye, ma'am. God bless ye, sir. Amen!"

Jacqueline Longmont stood nearby, watching, but not taking part. She was relieved Clement had not yet demanded her assistance; she was much too shy to take part in his "services."

He did, however, always expect her attendance and her rapt attention to his words. She dared not fail to do so, for she heartily feared his temper. As long as she did as he wished, he was amiable enough and seemed pleased to be with her.

For her part, Jacqueline still held him in some awe and trusted his healing arts. Her attraction to him had been growing until she was listening more seriously to his future plans for them. He had convinced her he'd never meant to marry and only his strong feelings for her might change his mind.

He was in a hurry to get to Natchez for some reason he did not share with her, and had insisted they travel along the Trace. One of his reasons for that mode of travel was soon apparent: he fed off crowds, both literally, as their meager offerings supported him, and figuratively, as he seemed to draw vitality from their impassioned responses.

Jacqueline was fascinated by the wild light in his eyes following one of his particularly successful oratories.

"Would you care for nourishment, Clement?" she'd asked timidly, almost afraid to interrupt, to disturb his almost trancelike state.

"Nay! I require nothing!" He sat, hunched against a tree, his black cloak wrapped snugly about him, the flicker from the camp fire illuminating his dark face briefly, and then sending it into oblivion once more.

She feared to stay near him, yet she had nowhere else to go, so she hovered, hopeful he might turn to her, accept something from her. But he seemed unaware of her presence and retreated entirely into himself.

He still sat thus, hours later, when Jacqueline tried once more to reach him. "Clement, you must rest."

Fiery, bloodshot eyes impaled her, ripping the breath from her with their consuming heat. "Yes, Jacqueline." His voice was soft, but no less deadly than when sharp and wicked with anger. "A good idea, my dear. Come, help me up. I fear my strength has drained from me."

But the hand that gripped hers hurt, eliciting a sharp cry of pain. He came to his feet nimbly, with a light-footed grace that seemed out of place.

A sharp flare of desire coursed through Jacqueline, and her knees trembled. He had claimed her body before, and each time she had come to a shuddering climax. She did not understand her response to this wild, ruthless man, nor did she question it or try to deny it. It was as natural to her as breathing. She would take any abuse, suffer any indignity to avoid arousing his ire. She dared not risk his rejection: she could not bear it if he withheld himself from her. He had become her life.

She sighed with relief when he turned her toward the wagon they shared, his hand pressing relentlessly against her straight back. They would be together this night.

He grabbed her from behind, his arms reaching around and his hands fastening to her breasts tightly and kneading them pitilessly. She was pinned helplessly against him and felt his heated arousal through the thin fabric of her dress.

Her pulse beat so rapidly she felt sure she would faint, and her heart thudded painfully against her chest. She rubbed herself against him, hating her wanton response, but unable to do otherwise. She felt like a harlot in his arms, but knew she would do whatever he asked of her, regardless of how base the act. Her hands, her lips, her body sought to do his will, to pleasure him—in the end always bringing the utmost pleasure to herself as well.

They entered the wagon, hastily discarding their clothing, and fell with hungry passion upon their hard pallet, pale bare legs and arms entwined, grappling, seeking a quick relief to the heated flame that possessed them.

Spent by the brief, but violent encounter, Jacqueline lay staring up into the darkness alone. He had rolled away from her as he always did. In a few days, she thought, they would reach Natchez, if the hungry animals that howled in the distance didn't make a meal of them first, and she would be reunited with her sister.

Camille—she dreaded to face her, to try to explain the presence of Clement Masters. Camille could be so . . . so . . . unmoving, so unbending, and so opinionated. Jacqueline knew Camille had made up her mind about Clement on their first meeting, and nothing would persuade her to change it.

Well, she would just have to accept him, and if and when they decided to get married, she would have to accept that, too. Camille was so accustomed to having everything her own way, had probably never known a moment's doubt in her entire life.

Was that why Jacqueline hadn't written to let her sister know of their impending arrival? Was she hopeful she might surprise Camille, catch her off balance and take advantage of some temporary weakness?

She smiled at the prospect, but doubled over when a spasm of pain swept through her midsection. She whimpered, but dared not cry out and risk wakening Clement. He was in his foulest mood when roused too suddenly from a deep sleep. The recurring pains she suffered and her frail paleness were the only remaining symptoms of her lifelong illness. Surely, Camille would see that Clement had helped her, as he had promised, and she would be grateful.

A bony arm was thrown across her chest, knocking the breath from her lungs and pinning her to the thin mat so that she was incapable of motion. The strength disguised beneath the thin frame of Clement's angular body never failed to amaze her. She had caught the brunt of it many times in the past, and had steeled herself to withstand future outbursts. She had never attempted to resist, knowing inherently it would be futile and would only anger him further. He had been driven to a blinding rage only once since she'd known him, and she would do anything to prevent that ever happening again. Anything, she thought, shivering from the cool night air but afraid to reach for the covers.

A sharp stone gouged her, but, terrified of waking him, she lay still. The long night was nearly spent before she closed her eyes for a brief time of restless sleep.

At the first sign of daylight, he shook her shoulder roughly, his fingers biting into her skin. "Get up. We shall be leaving soon. And I must have my breakfast."

Groggily, she pulled herself to her feet and set about to comply as quickly as possible. How she longed for Magnolia and for servants who would do her bidding, and for a soft, warm bed. Soon, she thought, very soon.

SPRING CLEANING was an annual event in most of the Natchez plantations. For the first time Camille was directing Magnolia's staff in the very thorough procedure that involved practically stripping the walls and floors and to make way for the cooler decor of summer.

Since early morning, Indigo, Essie and the other housemaids had been joined by a small crew of manservants directed by Josef, who was too aged and held too high a position in the household to do the menial, physical tasks involved in the process, but who was a most capable supervisor.

The bedding had been stripped from all the beds, and the moss-stuffed mattresses carried out for freshening in the sun, a regular procedure. It was thought that the heat of the sun would drive bedbugs to the bottom, making for a more comfortable night's sleep. The heavy curtains were dismantled from the tester bed in the master bedroom and the half-testers in the girls' rooms, and were replaced with mosquito netting, which could be pulled back and tied when not in use.

The dirty job of cleaning chimneys and smoke from the walls and ceilings was handled by the twins Josiah and Jonah, who whistled and sang as they worked through the long afternoon. Camille had given them specific instructions for cleaning the wallpaper, and supervised closely to see that they brushed downward with the hairbrush. Then she handed them three-day-old bread, and watched as they held it by the crust and rubbed down with long light strokes, then crosswise.

"Well done," she commended them, before going on to show Indigo how to clean the keys on the square grand piano.

"Yes'm, I 'members now. First, yo' use dis fine cologne water on de softest of cloths, den you sets dat piano in da sun ta bleach dem keys some more!"

"That's right, Indigo. But I think we can skip the sun today." Camille smiled, but before she moved on, cautioned, "And do be sure and rub the cracked keys with some olive oil."

"Yes'm." Indigo was shaking her head in agreement and set herself to the task.

Turning back to the parlor, Camille noticed dust rising from the carpets being swept by the diligent twins.

"No! Jonah!" she cried, hurrying over. "You have forgotten the dry salt." The salt was important to brighten colors and check the ravages of moths when

the heavy rugs were rolled and dragged to the attic for
storage. Dust, thoroughly taken up by the mixture, did
not rise.

"Yes'm, I truly did fergit. I'se sorry, ma'am."

In place of the heavy rugs, light straw mats soon appeared. Sheer lace curtains replaced the heavy damask at the windows, their primary usefulness keeping
out mosquitos, the cause of some of the worst problems in Natchez in late spring and summer.

Jib windows were raised and the bottoms thrown
open to catch the fresh spring breeze, and make a
doorway to the surrounding galleries. The twelve-foot
ceilings, designed to be twice the height of the tallest
man, would be cool and airy now. Even the big Belter
rosewood furnishings took on a daintier appearance
with their light airy carvings, sometimes referred to as
wood-lace.

Camille inspected each room thoroughly and ordered a few additional chores, then pronounced herself satisfied with the results, releasing the servants
from their duties for the rest of the evening.

A tall glass of cold lemonade in her hand, she collapsed into a chair on the veranda. Her hair had been
pulled back and tied with a colorful bandanna, and she
tucked in a few black curls that had crept out around
her face and ears. She still wore an apron, and a
smudge on her cheek gave mute testimony to her day's
work.

Since she rested on the southern veranda, Camille
failed to see a wagon roll from the lane into Magnolia's long, oak-shaded drive. Nor did she hear the rat-
tle of its wheels or the hungry whinny of the thin nag
who pulled it.

"Miss Camille, ma'am." Jonah's eyes were wide where he stood at the bottom of the steps, twisting his hat in his hands. He hesitated, as though not quite sure how to begin. "Sorry to disturb yo', ma'am, but I knowed you'd want ta know. It's Miss Jacq'line, ma'am . . . and a man. She say not to bother 'nouncin' her. I'se afraid she done gone up to her room."

Camille had leaped to her feet with a happy smile at the first mention of her sister's name, but stopped short at Jonah's mention of a man. It would be Clement Masters. So, Jacqueline had actually brought him back with her, then. And with not a word of their impending arrival.

"It's all right, Jonah. I'll tend to it. You did the right thing. That will be all for now."

"Josiah done seen to da wagon. Shall I take dey bags up ta Miss Jacq'line's room, ma'am?"

"Not just yet, Jonah."

How would she deal with her sister and this unwelcome guest she'd dragged home with her? Surely Masters couldn't be planning to stay at Magnolia! She would be firm and suggest in no uncertain terms that he would prefer staying at a local inn.

Why had Jacqueline gone straight to her room without a word for her sister? The action stung Camille with sharp pain until it occurred to her that Jacqueline might be embarrassed to face her, knowing her feelings for Clement Masters.

Camille drained the last of the lukewarm lemonade from her glass and set it back on the table as she considered how to handle the situation. Stripping off her soiled apron, she let it drop to the floor. Thoughtfully she pulled the bandanna from her head, and shook out her thick curls.

It had been such a long time since she'd seen Jacqueline, and they had not parted under the best of circumstances. The desire to see her sister overwhelmed her, and Camille turned and hurried through the parlor and up the stairs.

She paused outside the door to her sister's room that was slightly ajar. The voices she overheard were angry, though she was quick to notice the note of subservience in Jacqueline's softer tones.

"You shouldn't have come up here," Jacqueline whispered.

"And just where else was I s'posed to go? I don't see the fatted calf or anything! But I'm just sure there's a nice comfortable room fixed up for me down the hall, right?" His voice was heavy with sarcasm as he continued, "Or did you fail to notify your dear sister of our arrival like I told you?"

"I'm sure she'll prepare a room for you, Clement. She must not have received my letter, that's all." Jacqueline spoke in a placating manner that Camille found quite unpleasant.

"Yeah . . ."

Camille had heard enough. She moved into the doorway and her presence was quickly acknowledged.

Clement had stopped in midsentence and stood with his mouth open, his hand still possessively on Jacqueline's arm.

Camille was dismayed by her sister's unkempt appearance. Her dark curls were dirty and in disarray, and the dress she wore could easily have belonged to one of Magnolia's servants.

Self-consciously, Jacqueline pulled out of the clutches of the preacher, and looking down, smoothed her skirt.

"Jacquie." Love and welcome filled Camille's voice and broke the reserve that separated them. Jacqueline rushed into her arms. Camille hugged her tightly, stroking her hair. "I've missed you. And I'm so glad you're home." Neither saw the look of loathing on the man's face as he observed the reunion.

"Oh! So am I, Cam! So am I!" For that short span of time, she rejoiced in her homecoming—until a muffled "Harumph!" reminded her of another presence in the room. Slowly, Jacqueline stepped back and extended her hand to Clement Masters, who stepped forward to stand beside her.

"You remember Clement Masters, don't you, Cam?"

"Yes. You should have had Jonah fetch me—and I could have given him a proper welcome on the front veranda." Camille's soft statement was a rebuke and Masters realized she was telling him he had no business in Jacqueline's bedroom.

Camille thought quickly. Obviously he planned to stay. And perhaps it might be best to have him remain at Magnolia. That way, she could observe him closely and discover what he was up to. Charles would not put up with anything untoward from this creature, of that she was certain. She just wished he were home now.

"If you'll give me a few moments, Mr. Masters, I'll have your room ready. I was not sure of the exact time of your arrival, so I've only made preliminary preparations," she lied, protecting her sister. "Please follow me to the parlor. You may wait there. Jacquie, why don't you ring Indigo for a hot bath?" She gave her sister a kiss and, making sure Masters was behind her, turned for the door.

Reluctantly the little man trailed behind her down the stairs. In spite of his outward bravado, he was not ready to face the formidable Camille alone, not just yet.

In the parlor, she motioned for him to be seated, but stood with her back to him for several seconds. When she turned on him, her eyes snapped with barely restrained anger, her words were biting. "What in God's name have you done to my sister, *Reverend*?" Her voice accentuated the title he bore so proudly. "And what is it exactly that you seek here?"

"I have merely escorted your sister home for you, my dear young lady—"

"My name is Mrs. Longmont," she interrupted.

"Mrs. Longmont, of course," he continued smoothly. "As I was saying, Jacqueline was anxious to come home, and lacked a proper escort—"

"Which service you provided," she broke in once more, her voice shaking with anger. "And you consider yourself a *proper* escort, I presume?"

"Why, certainly, due to my esteemed position, and to our long acquaintance—"

"Explain to me how she has arrived at her own front door practically in *tatters*, that is, if you can, *sir*!"

"I'm afraid I really can't, uh, that is, she seemed comfortable enough in that clothing. It was rough terrain, and all that."

"How *did* you travel here, may I ask?"

"On the Natchez Trace, the same pathway you chose for your own trip, if I recall." His smirk told her he thought he had an unanswerable argument.

"I, sir, was forced to travel a portion of that despicable roadway in order to reach home. But you have dragged my sister across six hundred miles of the roughest country ever dignified by the name 'road,' and without the slightest apology, I see. To what purpose? I repeat, Mr. Masters, what is your reason for being here?''

He bowed. ''Merely as I have said, Mrs. Longmont. My motives are of the purest, I assure you.''

Chapter Eleven

APRIL 21, 1860, was a glorious day for a wedding. A spring breeze blew the ruffled heads of brilliantly blooming flowers filling the Smythes' garden, which had been elaborately decorated for the occasion. An arbor of fresh greenery marked the spot where the bride and groom would repeat their vows. It was flanked by candelabra interwoven with more greenery and vivid red and white camellias. Red velvet covered the long aisle wending its way through neatly spaced rows of hundreds of chairs brought up from New Orleans for the event.

Guests were beginning to gather and their happy chatter could be heard inside the house where Glory made her last-minute preparations, much the same way Camille had done several years ago.

"Wedding jitters?" Camille asked, looking over Glory's shoulder at her reflection in the mirror.

"No, not really. But it's just all so...so...*final*, isn't it?"

Camille smiled at her friend's worried expression and agreed, "Yes, it is."

Glory turned, her powder-blue eyes looking deep into Camille's darker blue ones. "You *are* happy at last, aren't you, Cam?"

"These last few months with Charles have been the happiest of my life," she answered honestly. "And

you'll be happy with Dandy, too, Glory. He loves you
very much.''

''Do you think so, Cam? Do you *really* think so? Of
course, I know he *says* so, and he acts like he does, most
of the time, anyway.'' Glory nervously applied a little
more color to cheeks already pink with excitement, and
patted her golden hair into place. It had been softly
pulled up and tied with a satin bow, luxuriant curls
cascading over her shoulders and well down her back.

Camille thought she'd never seen her friend look so
beautiful. The gown Glory wore surely was the most
elegant ever seen in Natchez. A cream-colored satin,
it had a scooped, ruffled neckline with the tiniest hint
of a sleeve over the very edge of her shoulders. Fitted
snugly around her small waist, it was tied in an oversized satin bow in the back; lacy rows fell from the bow,
making her train. Elbow-length gloves of the same
color and a matching single strand of pearls completed the ensemble.

The couple repeated their vows with Camille at
Glory's side, half-turned toward the crowd behind
them. Touched by the look of devotion in Dandy's
face, Camille searched for Charles. Her face must have
revealed more of her emotions than she realized, for
when her eyes met and held those familiar brown eyes
of her husband, a look of sadness washed over his
handsome face. He knew she thought back to their
wedding, and in her heart regretted never having a
proper one. She smiled and winked to let him know all
was well. Things had worked out for the best. *You chose
well, Father,* she thought as her eyes continued to sweep
the large gathering of Dandy's and Glory's family and
friends.

Marguerite and her husband William sat with their four children, almost filling a whole row by themselves. Camille suspected Marguerite was expecting again, and she was happy for her. They seemed content with their life, and their house was always full of love and laughter.

Glory's parents sat proudly on the front row, eyes fastened on their only daughter and soon-to-be son-in-law. Rourke was almost surely dreaming of grandchildren, future heirs for Whispering Oaks.

Camille's glance skittered over several more rows of their childhood friends, before they collided with a mocking pair of beady black eyes, set close together over a hooked nose. Clement Masters! He had been staring at her! She was sure of it, though she couldn't have said how she knew. He had laid one thin arm possessively along the chair behind Jacqueline, who seemed completely at ease at his side and lost in the ceremony.

A sense of imminent disaster, a terrible foreboding sent Camille's heart plummeting, and made it difficult for her to breathe. This shifty little Easterner who called himself a preacher was a threat, a very real and dangerous threat to all of them.

Glory nudged her, jerking her attention back to the wedding, and she reached to take the bridal bouquet. Minutes later the happy couple were pronounced man and wife, and shared a lengthy nuptial kiss before starting back down the aisle.

Camille kept seeing that dark countenance superimposed over the fair face of her sister. She could not shake the feeling of impending doom all through the reception and the traditional wedding dance that followed.

Charles's hand slipped around her waist and he pulled her into the comfort of his strong shoulder. "What's wrong, Camille? You're not sorry Glory's getting married?" There was a trace of regret in his voice.

"Oh, no! It's not that at all, Charles. It's just . . ." Her voice trailed off when she saw her sister and Clement Masters leave through the garden gate, hand in hand.

"I'm afraid of him, Charles."

He laughed softly. "I've never known you to be afraid of anything, Cam." Placing a soft kiss on her lips, which had opened in protest, he continued, "I won't let him hurt her. I promise." Charles spoke with reassuring confidence, and Camille looked up at him in gratitude. He was strong and good and dependable, so much the opposite of the man her sister had chosen.

"But what can I do?" she asked.

"Nothing, Cam. I said I'd take care of it." Those undeniable shutters dropped over his eyes. There were still a few areas in his life she had not been able to penetrate, some part of his mind and heart she was never allowed to enter. And that troubled her, whenever she thought of it.

"Well, enough bad thoughts for this happy occasion." She shook off the feeling, demanding playfully, "When were you planning to ask your wife to dance, Mr. Longmont?"

"Right at this very moment, Mrs. Longmont."

He pulled her to him, and led her smoothly into a romantic waltz. She gave herself over to the sensual delights of the music, the occasion, and the embrace of a loved one, allowing her mind to be swept clear of troubling thoughts for the moment.

Unnoticed, a dark form lurked in the shadows of the garden, watching them with malicious envy, nervously pulling at the edge of a dingy black frock coat several sizes too big for him. With a muttered curse, he turned and melted away into the dark night.

SUMMER CAME TO NATCHEZ on the heels of a pleasant spring filled with a whirl of social activities. Parties had been a frequent and welcome diversion. In addition to Glory's wedding, Camille had attended two others, and discovered to her delight that Marguerite was indeed expecting; the baby was to be born in November.

The soaring heat and humidity now sent everyone in search of cool balconies and shade trees. The temperature had climbed to 104 degrees in the shade, though reflection from the streets and *banquettes* doubtless drove it even higher in town. Even the interiors of the high-ceilinged homes might reach 98 degrees. It was not a time to be outdoors.

On a muggy afternoon in July, Camille, Charles, Clement and Jacqueline sought the relative comfort of the south veranda, hopeful of a breeze that had as yet refused to blow. They sipped mint juleps and lemonade. Charles quoted the *Natchez Daily Free Trader*, which said, "'Really the weather is excruciatingly hot.'" He went on to share with them the report that several persons in Vicksburg had died of sunstroke.

The newspaper, consisting mostly of ads for local businesses, miracle cures and rewards for runaway slaves, was full of news and support of Breckenridge and Lane, the Southern Democrats' solution for the

November election. Charles read these reports without comment, knowing his political views clashed with those held by Clement Masters, and wanting to avoid argument. It was just too hot.

An uneasy peace had settled among the four of them. Masters had been at times overbearing, but had done nothing overt to provoke their outright hostility. Although they still suspected his motives and the sincerity of his affection for Jacqueline, he had not engaged in any questionable activity. It was apparent, however, that his head was being turned by the easy wealth, the social life and gaming that was a way of life on the plantations. He had developed a passion for horse-racing exceeded only by his apparent laziness. He often slept till midday, sat around with a glass in his hand until evening, and then disappeared until the wee hours of the next morning.

Jacqueline, being frequently ignored by him, was petulant at times; but the more distant he became, the more enamored of him she seemed, following him around whenever he would allow it and seeking to please him in every way. Camille was at a loss to understand her sister's irrational behavior where he was concerned. Had she never really known her, or had Jacqueline changed so drastically during those years in Baltimore?

A crust of politeness toward his hosts almost hid from view Masters's greedy jealousy and lack of any redeeming human quality. Camille was hopeful he would soon tire of Jacqueline on his own, and leave. He had such a powerful hold on her sister, she didn't think she could ever convince Jacqueline to give him up willingly.

"No races today, Charles?" he asked abruptly.

"Not on the Sabbath."

"Oh, it *is* the Sabbath, isn't it? I'd forgotten." Clement's pursuit of religious duties had decreased in proportion to the increase of worldly pleasures he enjoyed more with each passing day.

"Clement, don't you think . . ." Jacqueline had begun, reaching for his arm.

He shook her off, and silenced her with a sharp retort. "No! And neither should you . . . think, that is!" His hand grasped her arm, and she winced in pain!

Charles leaped to his feet and grabbed the smaller man's lapels, lifting him off the ground. "You hurt the lady," he ground out.

"Surely I did not, did I, Jacqueline?" Masters spoke calmly, waiting for her denial.

"No, not really, Clement. I'm sure he didn't mean to, Charles. P-please let him go."

At her timid request, Charles released him and the preacher hit the floor with a thud, shaking himself and reaching for his battered black hat.

"Well! I've never been treated so rudely! I'm going for a walk—alone!" He sent Jacqueline a quelling look that clearly revealed she was not welcome to join him. Still her eyes followed him as he marched off toward the river.

Before Camille could protest, Jacqueline was out of her chair, and had disappeared into the house. Seconds later, they heard her bedroom door slam.

"She is so dependent on him, Charles, and a worse blackguard I've never seen. Whatever shall we do? You don't think he'd actually hurt her, do you?"

He hesitated before stating firmly, "Not if I have anything to say about it. His life is worth nothing if he ever lays a hand on her again."

"Charles! I just remembered, the other day I did notice some bruises on her ribs and her arm. She explained them away, but you don't suppose...?" Camille could not fathom the kind of man who would treat a woman so harshly. Why, the slaves on Magnolia were never browbeaten or bruised. Her sister deserved better.

"We will demand that he leave here once and for all, at dinner tonight."

"You're absolutely right, Charles. We shouldn't have allowed him to stay this long. Only because Jacqueline, well... she seemed to feel so strongly about him. She will be angry with us, but she'll get over it in time, if we can only get her out from under his influence."

But that night at dinner Jacqueline and Clement presented a happy, united front, holding hands and discussing their plans for buying a racehorse. Some of Beaufort's estate had been left in trust for the girls' discretionary use until they reached maturity, and Jacqueline, at the preacher's urgings, had rapidly been depleting hers.

"Let's go to Europe and choose one for ourselves. That's what all the planters do!" she suggested, her eyes bright with excitement.

"An intriguing idea, for sure." He seemed to have no qualms about her spending her inheritance on him.

"I've always wanted to go," she continued. "Let's do it! And when we return, we can build our very own racetrack, just like you've been wanting."

"Jacqueline, you can hardly go off to Europe with Mr. Masters and no chaperone. You can't be thinking clearly." Camille's stomach churned, and she had given up trying to eat. She merely sipped her glass of wine.

Jacqueline giggled. "Always the worrier, Camille. Of *course* not—I wouldn't thing of such a thing. But," she paused for effect, "*if* I were to go as Mrs. Clement Masters, surely no one would object to that."

"I would!" roared Charles, on his feet in an instant, the table settings of Sevres china clattering from his abrupt movement. "Jacqueline, I'll never allow you to marry this . . . this person! Don't you forget for one minute, I am still your legal guardian!"

Tears welled in her eyes and trickled down her cheeks, and Camille hurried over and put her arms around her. Clement Masters did not spare a glance for Jacqueline; his eyes locked with Charles's, as each felt the other out, seeking strengths and weaknesses. Apparently satisfied, Masters left the table without a backward glance or a word to anyone.

He left the house and did not return for three days, when he came back to retrieve his meager belongings. On his way out, he found Camille alone in the library. Stepping inside, he pulled the door shut behind him.

Camille instinctively moved toward an open window, where she felt a little safer; she never wanted to be backed against a wall by this man. He was evil and capable of anything; she saw that clearly in his eyes now that he was making no effort to conceal it.

"I'm leaving. I suppose you will be satisfied to know your illustrious 'Southern hospitality' has driven me away at last," he sneered. "Oh, but I won't be far; I have managed to make a friend or two in these parts. I can promise you, *Mrs. Longmont*, that you haven't seen the last of me!"

He spun around on his rundown heels, and yanked the door open viciously, stomping out of the room. He called back to her over his shoulder, "But the one you should really be afraid of lives right here in this house with you. Do you know where your husband is, Mrs. Longmont?"

"Wait! What do you mean?" she cried, rushing after him.

"I daresay you will find out soon enough. But if I were you, I'd sure keep an eye on that one." His cackling laughter floated back to her as he shuffled around to the stables. Minutes later she watched him trotting down the drive on the horse Jacqueline had bought for him.

"Good riddance." She couldn't resist the barbed farewell, though he couldn't have heard as he cantered away, the tails of his ever-present black coat flapping behind him in the breeze.

CAMILLE'S THOUGHTS returned more than once to the preacher's innuendo in the weeks that followed. At first she had angrily discounted his parting words, but as time went by and Charles became more uncommunicative, and he was absent for longer and longer periods of time, she couldn't prevent a feeling of uneasiness—not suspicion, she hastened to reassure herself, just unanswered questions.

One evening she chanced on a meeting that was apparently being held in the stranger's room, one of Magnolia's rooms with an outside entrance that was always prepared for wayfarers. Charles had pushed her gently, but firmly, out the door and insisted she return to their rooms before she was able to identify any of the faces in the dim candlelight. When she attempted to question him later, his answers were cryptic, even impatient.

What had they been doing at Magnolia? What was Charles's part in it? Why had he been so adamant about excluding her? He must have something to hide, she admitted reluctantly.

It hurt to realize there were things he didn't trust her enough to share with her. Were his activities illegal—as the preacher had hinted? Surely she knew Charles better than that. . . .

But did she really know him at all—or had she only thought she did? Perhaps she had been fooling herself all this time, just as surely as he had been fooling her. And just as surely as her sister was being fooled by Clement Masters.

There was no one else she could turn to—for either advice or help. She would have to work this out for herself, as she had done time and again in the past. She would begin by learning exactly what Charles was doing—and why.

That was a lot easier said than done, she discovered, as several weeks went by and nothing else happened. During that time Charles was as loving and attentive as he'd ever been; he was the perfect gentleman she'd married, and his activities could have withstood the closest surveillance without any doubt of his honesty and fidelity.

They heard nothing more from Clement Masters, and Jacqueline's tears seemed to have abated somewhat, though she still wore a long face and had little to say to them.

One afternoon, after trying in vain to convince Jacqueline to join her, Camille decided to go calling alone, as had been her custom in the past.

Only Josiah would drive, as Jonah was ill. Josef had wanted to go along, but Camille refused, saying it wasn't necessary and that he had duties to perform at home. She tried to spare him as much as possible these days, as his health had been poor during the long winter months.

Josef frowned as they drove away, and wished it had been Jonah who drove the mistress rather than Josiah, who was not as capable of controlling the headstrong horses. But ever since he'd stepped out of his place on the night of her father's death and argued with his mistress, he'd vowed never to do that again. A good servant did as he was told, without interfering.

Still, he worried about young Camille, and knew he would die should anything happen to her. His watery eyes followed the carriage until it was long out of sight. Shoulders bent with age, he turned toward the house.

Camille had opened the windows to catch the fresh afternoon breezes and settled back to enjoy the ride. Of course, she much preferred riding horseback, but a brisk carriage drive could be a pleasant diversion, too.

A soft wind teased her curls, pulling a few free of the flat, derby-shaped hat she wore. Josiah had instructions to deliver her first to the new home of Dandy and Glory. Their wedding present from Glory's parents had been a plantation-style home very near Whispering Oaks on the bluffs they had playfully called Gloriana.

Recent rains and erosion had made the narrow road in front of the new home quite treacherous. Had Jonah been driving, he would have known to take the old cemetery road and come up to it from behind, but Josiah started up the front way, urging the horses to more speed for the steep climb. Camille held her breath as the trees whipped by, tearing at the carriage.

The rim of one back wheel dipped over the edge and Camille felt the carriage lurch sickeningly to the left. Hastily she scrambled over to the other side and screamed at Josiah to stop, but the wind snatched her words and hurled them away. Her heart pounded with the wild swaying and bouncing as she fell back on the seat.

With a sigh of relief, she felt the wheels once more gain a solid purchase on the narrow road. If he would only slow down and keep a tight rein, they might live to see another day.

The frightened whinnies of the horses filled the air: they were about to bolt. A sinking fear washed over Camille as she remembered a hole up ahead where a portion of the road had fallen away. It would take a steady hand and good control of the horses to guide them around it. Apparently, Josiah had neither.

Camille closed her eyes, helpless to do anything to stop their headlong rush to disaster, bracing herself for the inevitable hard bump that would more than likely flip horses, carriage and all over the bluffs to fall through the air to the swampy ground two hundred feet below. If they were lucky, perhaps they might land in the Mississippi instead.

The rapid beat of the horses' hooves echoed directly outside her window. "Hold on, Camille!" came the warm, strong voice she so loved. "I'll stop them." Charles streaked by her on Reaper and leaped from his horse onto the back of one of the runaways hitched to the carriage.

In response to his firm strength, the horses soon slowed to a canter, then a trot, and finally a walk.

When Charles had brought them to a complete stop, he jumped to the ground, and ran back to lift Camille down. Her legs trembled so badly she would have collapsed had he not gathered her in his arms.

She felt the deep shudder of fear go through him, and wrapped her arms tightly around him.

"Cam! I saw Josiah turn the corner and start up the hill and I *knew* he was sure to lose control. I could see you flying over the edge, and I wasn't at all sure I could reach you in time." He pulled back and looked deep into her midnight-blue eyes. His own were shining with tears. "I don't know what I'd do if I lost you, Cam."

"I love you, Charles," she'd said before his lips slanted across her, tasting her, reassuring himself she was really safe and in his arms once more. He crushed her to him so tightly she could hardly breathe. His lips ceased their gentle assault, and he smiled his relief. "And I love you, my little Cam. You'll ride with me." He helped her to mount in front of him, and carefully led Josiah and the carriage to safety.

"Take me home, Charles," she had whispered to him, unwilling to give up the comfort of his arms. He dipped his head and claimed her lips in another long kiss before he acquiesced and turned toward Magnolia.

They spent the next few hours locked in their rooms, lost in the fervor of their love for each other. Servants moved about quietly, their brows raised, but not presumptuous enough to say anything about the unconventional behavior of their master and mistress.

The rays of the evening sun bathed the couple in a golden glow as they lay wrapped in a passionate embrace, each unwilling to leave the other's arms. The dinner delivered and left outside their front door went unnoticed.

The next morning, however, they were ravenous and in high spirits when they came down for the breakfast buffet. Jacqueline was the only one who exhibited any disapproval, and she dared not do it overtly, only in small, reproving glances at her sister as they ate.

Camille's joy was so complete, she almost laughed out loud. "You know," she said, turning to Charles, "Glory once described you as my 'knight in shining armor,' and that's just what you were yesterday!" He had also been very handsome and so very loving, she thought with a painful pulling at her heart. How could she ever have doubted him for a moment? Her dear Charles would never do anything to hurt her, never anything dishonorable or illegal! He was her dear, gallant love. She smiled at him across the table, thinking how lucky they were.

Chapter Twelve

NOVEMBER, 1860

THAT FALL, news of the election of Abraham Lincoln swept through the South like a thunderclap. It had been expected, but the reality of it brought renewed consternation and the fear of a confrontation over the issues that split the two sections of the country.

Natchez was divided in sentiment, some favoring the Confederate cause and some the Union, as serious trouble appeared imminent.

Talk in South Carolina and other states that leaned heavily toward secession had become more and more heated and with the election of Lincoln, it swung toward violence and action. The president was a threat to them and their way of life. Men crossed the line from pacifism and "Let's wait and see" to militancy. Had they but realized what lay ahead, surely cooler heads would have prevailed, and a compromise been reached.

But in their youthful exuberance and sectional pride, they heartily believed they could quickly win a war with no danger to themselves or their way of life. Little did they know that their country, particularly the South, hovered on the brink of almost total disaster.

Demonstrations of support for the resistance, in favor of secession, spread through Southern cities, and young men began to enlist, afraid that if they tarried too long, the battle would be over before they had a chance to fight.

Some, like Charles, cautioned reason and careful thought, but they were most often ignored and even ridiculed by the hotheads who were so anxious to enter the fray.

In her mind, Camille agreed with him, but her Southern heart yielded to the zeal and patriotism intensifying around her, and she could not completely dismiss her old doubts about Charles's loyalties. If war broke out, would he choose to fight for the South? Somehow, she doubted it. How would she feel about his refusal to openly espouse the Southern cause?

By the time the inauguration rolled around, seven Southern states no longer called Lincoln their president. Beginning with South Carolina, they had met at their state houses and voted to secede. At first no one knew how Lincoln and his new government would react. But there was little doubt he would permit such a withdrawal from the Union without a struggle.

His inaugural speech was a strong and pointed statement of just how far he and his government were willing to go. He spoke of the dangers of dissolving the Union. He had no authority, he said, "to fix terms for the separation of the states." His most pointed remarks were directed at secessionists:

"In *your* hands, my dissatisfied fellow countrymen, not in *mine*, is the momentous issue of civil war. The Government will not assail *you*. You can have no conflict without yourselves being the aggressors. *You* have no oath registered in Heaven to destroy the Government, while *I* shall have the most solemn one 'to preserve, protect and defend it.' "

The battle lines were clearly drawn. Men began to align themselves on one side or the other. When it became apparent the North would invade the South as a result of the shots fired at Fort Sumter, four more Southern states cast their lot with the Confederacy: Virginia, North Carolina, Arkansas and Tennessee. Now that Virginia had joined their ranks, the Confederate government moved to Richmond.

The war, for the most part, was welcomed. Slavery was not an issue in these early days; the North fought to preserve the Union, the South for the rights of states to determine for themselves how they would be governed.

Turmoil and unrest prowled the streets of Natchez, as was the case in the majority of Southern cities. Opinion was often divided, but always strong. Conversation inevitably turned to the topic of war. The secure, happy future that had almost been theirs was about to be shattered by the tyrannical finality of war.

Families were sure to be torn asunder by divided loyalties and business would suffer, but the burning patriotic spirit grew stronger day by day in the sons and daughters of the South.

Men's fortunes and their very lives hung in the balance. On a twist of circumstances, so much might change. A fine thread suspended the fate of a nation, a people.

INEVITABLY, THE WAR CAME, as inescapable as the passage of time. As the guns rumbled nearer, what else could the Southerners do but live as they always had, with the sharp edges of their desperation camouflaged beneath a surface gaiety? At President Jefferson Davis's first call for volunteers on March 6, most of the able-bodied young men of Natchez had willingly signed up. They had marched out covered with epaulettes shining in the sun, their heads held high and their bows to the ladies low. Each was sure he was equal to at least three Yankees, and anxious to prove it.

Everyone assembled to see the troops leave from city hall. Women and children, old men and negroes all hurried along, some with their arms full of flowers, others waving flags. Somewhere a band played.

Soon the procession started down Silver Street where the men would meet the steamboat that would take them far away from their families and into the conflict. Soldiers in uniform marched; mothers, sisters, sweethearts and wives rode along in elegant carriages to see them off. All of them tried to crowd aboard the boat until it listed badly and nearly capsized. Lovers clung together for one last kiss. Though some of the women cried, most of the men were smiling, certain it would soon be over and they would be home.

As they pulled away from the dock, the "bonnie blue flag" waved proudly, and strains of the popular tune, "The Girl I Left Behind Me," floated back to the relatives wildly waving handkerchiefs and trying to be as brave as the men who were leaving them to serve the South. But too soon they were all gone, and with them, their high excitement and youthful exuberance.

Camille had been puzzled and concerned about Charles's refusal to become involved in the furor and his reserve in any discussions of the war. There were those in Natchez who questioned his sentiment and doubted his loyalty. Though she did not share their feelings, still she wished Charles would explain his attitude and his activities, which seemed to become more covert with each passing day.

She had watched Marguerite bid farewell to her husband, and felt a distinct guilt in her own happiness that Charles would not be going to serve on the front lines of battle. Whatever his motives, she felt sure they were honorable.

But Charles's unexplained absences had increased and he was gone for longer periods of time, returning home bone-weary and dirty, sometimes covered with mud. Once he'd had an arm wound she had treated, but he refused to talk about where or how he'd gotten it. Regardless of what he told her, she feared his activities were dangerous.

He had been gone for several months, and she had no idea when he might return, or even if he still lived. She missed him desperately.

Thankfully, Clement Masters had also disappeared, a fact Camille found not too surprising. She had always thought him to be a coward.

Camille's few friends who remained in Natchez included Glory and her husband Dandy, who was commander of the small force stationed in Natchez, Marguerite, David Renault, and a few others. Some older men with medical exemptions and a few widows and unmarried girls completed the dwindling circle.

They tried to maintain some semblance of ordinary life, "as if there were no damn Yankees!" Glory often said. It was an embattled and brittle merriment, but if it helped in some small measure to ease the pain of their losses, so be it.

One such occasion had been a small party at Magnolia, given in honor of David Renault's birthday and in hopes it would swing his mood to the brighter side. The severe depression that engulfed him made them all fear for his ability to cope. Camille would never forget the picture of Charles's friend as he'd hobbled back into Natchez, a bitter invalid, beaten by the war. He had lost a leg in a river battle on the ironclad *Louisiana* near New Orleans, and his days of carefree fun and horse races were now a thing of the past.

Renault usually attended their gatherings, having no family and, as he said, nothing much to do, though he always drank heavily and never seemed to have a good time. At least they could count on his being there for this party in his honor. If only he could see how much they cared for him, maybe he would start to see his life as more meaningful.

Preparations for the party had kept their minds off war and its hardships for the past three days as Glory, Camille and Marguerite had their heads together, trying to make it special, and to be sure everything was just right.

Happy Birthday banners printed by hand were plastered over the parlor, amid the other handmade decorations. A few precious candles cast a pleasant glow over a buffet table spread out in the dining room. Though the table was beautifully set, the usual delicacies were absent and the fare sparse: a bowl of berries and cream, some of the last slices of ham from the smokehouse, and the ever-present biscuits.

A bottle of Madeira found hidden away in the empty wine cellar and saved for a special occasion, cooled in a bucket of ice that Glory had contrived to get from a passing riverboat.

Dandy played the few tunes he knew over and over on a small fiddle. Glory's eyes were fixed on him in pride, and Camille thought what a good match they'd turned out to be. With a smile, she remembered his flattering remarks about waiting for her on his wedding day. As though he followed her train of thought, Dandy smiled at her and winked, causing a becoming blush to spread over her cheeks. Those carefree days seemed a lifetime away.

A flurry of hurried activity followed by complete silence greeted David's arrival. Camille opened the door to him.

"Where is everybody?" He looked solemn and puzzled at the empty house. Late as always, he had expected the festivities to be in full swing. "Do I have the wrong night?" He looked so woebegone Camille pulled him in, and taking his arm, led him quickly into the parlor.

"No, David, you have the right night and the right place, and everything's all right!" she assured him.

"Happy Birthday! Surprise!" They all spilled from their hiding places with wide smiles, congratulations and applause.

Camille still held his arm in hers and she looked at him closely to judge his reaction. She had not been sure if he'd be pleased or hurt by all this attention he'd been seeking to avoid.

She was chagrined to see tears jump to his eyes and she felt a trembling in his arm. Catching her breath, she waited. There was a brief, tense silence as others in the room shared her doubts and earnest wishes.

After a long pause, he spoke in a choked, emotional voice. "Thank you, my friends." A slow smile spread across his face, his first genuine smile since his return.

A sigh of relief swept through the room, followed by strains of "For He's a Jolly Good Fellow," accompanied hesitantly by Dandy on his out-of-tune instrument. They gathered around for some back-slapping and handshaking, and David was treated to enthusiastic kisses from the ladies, which brought another reluctant smile to his lips.

A toast to his health preceded the meager but very merry dinner, served by Essie and Josef with as much pomp and ceremony as though it were one of the elaborate occasions of the past.

Their spirits lifted by David's heartwarming response and mellow from the wine, the guests talked of any subject except the war and laughed uproariously at their own bad jokes.

At the height of the gaiety, the front door swung open. An unseasonably cold spring wind swirled through the hall, causing the candles to flicker. Charles stood there, obviously fatigued, his hair limp and matted and his dark clothing caked with grime. Even in his unkempt state, Camille still thought him the most wonderfully handsome man she'd ever seen, and the most welcome surprise. With a glad cry of welcome, she jumped up and was about to rush over to greet him, but something in his demeanor stopped her.

A startled silence greeted him as every eye turned in his direction. For long seconds, his weary eyes took in their party apparel, the decorations and the empty wine bottle resting in melting ice.

His arm moved outward in a half circle, indicating all the trappings of the celebration. Pain etched its way across his face, drawing his lips into a thin line. His brows arched together in an angry frown and, looking straight at Camille, he growled, "Woman! Don't you know there's a war on?" She had never seen Charles so cold, so fiercely angry. His totally unexpected arrival and reaction had caught her unprepared and she stood frozen, with no idea of what to do next.

His harsh expression eased somewhat when he noticed David with his cane and saw the quick tears welling in Marguerite's soft gray eyes. "I'm sorry," he apologized to the unwelcome guests in a softer voice, "but go home, all of you, please." Without another word, he turned his back and made his way up the stairs. The slump in his wide shoulders was sad and uncharacteristic.

Stung by his open rebuke, Camille looked helplessly from one friend to another. There was another long silence before, one by one, they bid her goodnight, with words of sympathy and understanding. The wonderful party had been spoiled, but David gave her a lingering hug, and his smile made it all worthwhile.

Charles refused to discuss the matter further, and left the next day with no reconciliation between them. Camille was at a loss to understand his attitude. She knew their entertainments were harmless and vital to their survival. Even in the face of Charles's displeasure, they would continue. It was not fair to the others to stop. Probably, Charles had been weary and discouraged and had taken it out on her. Surely he hadn't meant the harsh things he'd said. The next time he came home, she would somehow make him understand and would make it up to him. She knew she could. Charles had always been a reasonable man. What had caused the strain that had lately made his face grow harder, and was responsible for the gray that streaked his honey-brown hair?

April 7, 1862

Night crept upon the encampment gently, like the touch of a lover's hand, its peace and softness decrying the horrors and obscenities of war the weary soldiers had witnessed that day upon the battlefield of Shiloh.

Nothing, no matter how wondrous or how beautiful, could ever erase from their memories the screams of agony, the sudden, violent spurting of blood from a severed artery or a severed limb, the horrendous roar of cannon and musket fire, the acrid smell of gunpowder mixed with the foul odors of death. Time might bring some lessening of the pain, some dimming of the gut-wrenching fear, but not one soldier who had drawn his weapon against another that day would ever be the same. Youth and innocence were but a small portion of war's high cost.

As battle followed weary battle, they had learned the only way to cope, the only way to survive, lay in their memories of the past and the occasional letter from home that managed to catch up with them on the long marches. They no longer dreamed of a future. There was only today—and one more night to be gotten through before another battle must be fought, and then another....

This was a war of no moderation, with no quarter given on either side, both of which had surprisingly proven to be in deadly earnest. Because they were soldiers, the men kept on fighting. War became normal for them; their homes, wives or sweethearts were a world, a lifetime away. For many, the army was all that was left to them after their plantations and farms had been looted and burned. They had nothing to call their own but their pride, their courage, and their unwavering dedication to a lost cause. These they had in abundant quantities, and it was enough.

An owl hooted in a tree overhead, and somewhere in the distance, an animal screamed, the eerie sound sending a tremor through the tall man who stood in the shadows, separate from the others. He was not an officer, nor even a soldier, though that day he had stood shoulder to shoulder with them, firing with a borrowed gun the meager ammunition he had scavenged. The men in the battalion knew little of him. Nevertheless, he had earned their admiration with his courage and daring, as he had fought tirelessly beside them.

Charles Longmont knew he would be gone by the morning, with not one of them, save their commander, having learned his name. It was always the same, and a sad loneliness clawed at his soul. He made no friends and knew no camaraderie, as he went his secretive way back and forth across enemy lines. But the worst part was his desperate longing for Camille. She had so quickly become a habit, as necessary to him as food or sleep, and the loss of her was a consistent physical pain. Not only her physical presence had been denied him by the demands of war, but their closeness had been undermined by her doubts and growing suspicions. The harmless birthday party for David he'd spoiled with his angry remark had been only one manifestation of the impotent frustration building in him as he watched the senseless suffering and death brought on by war, day after day. When he'd returned home from a particularly bloody encounter, expecting to be loved and comforted by his wife, and found instead a gala party, something in him had snapped. He had not been able to explain or apologize later, for fear he might reveal too much of his very secret role in the war. He hoped, no, he prayed, Camille would somehow understand regardless and find a way to forgive him. But for now there was nothing he could do, except watch helplessly as her love for him diminished along with her trust.

Midnight stars twinkled overhead, calling to mind the blue-black sparkle of her hair, the fathomless mystery of her indigo eyes. In the silence of the darkest night, her image came easily before him, their forced separation fueling the fires of his fantasies into an all-consuming blaze. He was tortured and nearly undone by the possibility he might never see her again, might never touch her again, might never be loved by her again.

He pulled out a pocket watch and by holding it just so in the light of the moon, was able to see the Roman numerals indicating it was well past midnight.

Time to be on his way.

CAMILLE GAZED OUT her bedroom window at the same midnight sky. Where was Charles tonight? Her arms ached, no, her whole body ached with her need for him. Parting with her husband had been like losing something of herself; she was incomplete, and would never be whole without him.

Problems on the plantation had multiplied in his absence and at times seemed more than she could bear. Some of the slaves had run away at the first promise of freedom and a better life, leaving her short-handed, and making it difficult to tend to the crop. Josef had had a setback and had taken to his bed for the past two weeks. The doctor could not seem to help, no matter how many times Camille insisted he visit her elderly servant. She had always thought she could run the plantation by herself, but now she had cause to wonder.

Many of the things they had all come to depend on and take for granted were no longer available due to the blockade. There had been shortages of so many things, and the few goods available were sold at vastly inflated prices. They'd had to learn to make their own candles, pillows and linens. Camille supervised an enlarged garden and the smokehouse that was so vital to their survival.

She had done her best to keep things running smoothly. She had begun practicing new economies and teaching the servants to do the same, training the household staff gardening and caring for the animals, tasks previously assigned to field hands. Cutting back on expenses whenever she could, she had still managed to get some sugar for canning and they would have the luxury of jams and preserves for a while longer. Supplies for the house as well as those for the servants' quarters were closely rationed. Though none would go hungry, there were few extras.

Clement Masters had been lurking about, and Camille was sure Jacqueline had been sneaking off to meet him, but there was little she could do about it.

Camille had learned to hate this war. It was so horrible, with cousins fighting against cousins, and even brothers who found themselves enlisted on opposite sides of the conflict. A confrontation between unmoving foes, it would be a death struggle to the very end, till all of those laughing young men, the bright promise of the future, lay buried in unmarked, unmourned graves across the vast land, hundreds of miles from home.

Camille grieved for them all, for those she knew, for those she would never know, for those who had no one else to sorrow over them. War was a despicable thing, and this war was the worst of all, the ultimate in honorable futility.

High moral ideals and expectations that it would be a brief skirmish soon ended now seemed but childish dreams. It dragged on and on, strewing in its path the maimed broken bodies of its young men and the countless dead, cut off in the prime of life, men who would never plant fields and watch cotton spring to life and flourish, who would never give life to future generations.

The war had never really been an issue of slavery versus freedom, nor even the protection of one's homeland, though this had drawn many courageous and loyal sons of the South into the fight. The issues were much less defined, and were determined by elected officials who, for the most part, stayed safely hidden behind their roles of leadership, claiming moral rights and wrongs, and inflaming the populace to fight.

Men with deep pockets to line with gold had been responsible for this holocaust, and those gallant men who fought for freedom only pawns in a larger game, a game in which there were no clear-cut rules and to which there seemed to be no end.

Camille feared for Natchez and Magnolia, knowing nothing would be the same after the war was over. Even if they escaped destruction as they had so far, and remained standing, and there was someone left to live and love there, it would be all gone: the gentle, easy way of life; the carefree balls and entertainments; their unfettered plans for the future.

The South was crumbling around them and much of it lay in ashes. Memphis...Fredricksburg...the roll call of doomed Southern cities continued to lengthen. Would Natchez be next?

Life that had once been as grand and glorious as it might ever be was now barren and hopeless in a way few had foreseen. A people who had been the luckiest and happiest in the world now suffered the awful penalties of war, their age of innocence ended with the firing of that first shot on Fort Sumter. Would they be forever haunted by "what might have been"?

Camille saw her way of life disintegrating before her eyes and she remembered Charles's prophetic words that this war would cost them all dearly. His had been the calm, reasonable voice amidst the cries of the young men of Natchez for justice, for honor, for war. They had raised their brows at him, wondering at his lack of patriotic fervor. Now his words rang clear and true.

"The stakes of this war are the life and death of a people and a country," he'd said. "It will bring grievous wounds, and it is a conflict the South can never win." His statements had brought howls of angry disagreement from those who optimistically saw their beloved South as invincible, from those who had refused to look realistically at the numerical and industrial strengths of the North that would at the last crush them.

Life had turned out so differently than they'd all planned.

One of the daily realities of war was a trip to town to examine the lists of the dead, to discover if hope remained that a loved one might still live. Camille had watched in sorrow as anguish spread over familiar faces and she had shared in their losses. She'd also seen disbelief and hard stares as one or another of her neighbors or friends struggled to deal with their grief.

She had suffered with Marguerite when she read her husband's name on the list. William had been killed at Manassas, leaving her friend a widow with five small children, one still an infant.

To make matters worse, for the past ten days a dismal rain had fallen, dampening their already dreary spirits. Several of the black children were down with lung congestion, and although Camille cared for them tenderly, her heart moved by their misery and discomfort, they did not seem to improve.

Had Charles been out in this incessant rain? Had he been wounded, or even killed? She had no way of knowing if he had remained near Natchez or if his business had taken him far from her. She could only pray he would come home safely.

The weather cleared after a couple of days and, to give her spirits a lift, Camille donned her white muslin gown with pink ribbon knots. Indigo fastened her hair up in curls and added some perky bows. She felt almost human again, but how she longed for Charles's appreciative looks!

She paced the length of the parlor, fighting the urge to climb on her mare and ride off somewhere—anywhere, so long as it was away from here. Magnolia seemed so big and so empty without Charles. But it was foolhardy to ride out alone and it was courting disaster to leave the comparative safety of Natchez.

The afternoon stretched endlessly in front of her. All the daily chores were done and for once there was no pressing project to demand her attention. Had she forgotten, then, how to enjoy leisure time?

She smiled. Surely not. She had always been quite good at it, in fact. Perhaps she'd call for a carriage and visit Glory. But no, she hardly enjoyed Glory's company for fighting her jealousy because Glory's husband was close at hand and could be home every evening, while Charles was off, God only knew where.

She had long since ceased trying to ferret out his mysterious comings and goings. Whatever he did, he had to do and there was nothing she could do about it, except love him when she had the chance. Which, since the outbreak of this cursed war, was rare indeed!

Camille wandered into the library and sat in her father's overstuffed leather chair. She could always feel his presence there, and it comforted her as nothing else could. She ran her hand down the heavy, gilt-edged volumes on his bookshelf. Maybe she would read; some new books had recently arrived by steamboat. Since she had read everything in their large collection, a new book was always a thing to be prized and she savored the joy of reading them. Picking up several that rested on the desk, she thumbed through them, looking for one she might lose herself in.

"Need something to fill your idle hours, my love?"

Camille ducked her head, almost afraid to look up, afraid the possessor of that wonderfully familiar voice might vanish or prove to be a figment of her imagination.

"Cam?" He spoke softly, his warm voice full of so many things: longing, desire, entreaty.

Her eyes flew to the dearly beloved face and immediately filled with tears. "Charles!" Her joy knew no bounds; he was safe—and he was home! The books tumbled from her hands and she ran heedlessly into his open arms. "Charles, it's been so long!"

"Yes, my love," he murmured into her hair. He kissed her soundly and deeply until the blood rushed crazily through his veins. He needed her like the ocean needed the rain; she was life and sustenance to him.

Holding her at arm's length, he cried out, "God, Cam! How can you look so damned lovely? Don't you know there's a war on!" This time there was no rebuke in the words, except for himself; they were a plea for forgiveness. He crushed her to him again, reveling in the way her soft curves molded into him.

"Oh, Charles! I was so afraid you might never come home!"

He swept her off her feet and into his arms, covering her face and finely arched neck with kisses and whispered endearments. He strode with firm steps out of the room, across the wide hall, and took the steps two at a time, daring anyone to try and stop him.

He kicked the door to their room shut behind him and stood, his eyes devouring her, unwilling to release her. His lips plied hers with a sweet torment, as though he could make up for all the kisses they'd missed.

He set her on her feet slowly, allowing her body to slide down his. Gentle hands stroked her shoulders, found their way to her waist and swiftly unfastened the tiny buttons and loosened her stays. She stepped out of the dress and petticoats and they fell in a silken heap at their feet. Only her chemise concealed that which he longed to see so badly he ached from the desire.

He savored the delight, squeezing pleasure out of each moment, allowing the already unbearable tension to mount a while longer, as he deliberately removed his own clothing, his eyes the brown amber of desire.

"Now," he whispered, reaching for her and making swift work of removing the last impediment of her underclothing. They stood then, facing each other, as God had made them, rich in their love, their bodies hungry for fulfillment that only such a love can bring.

"Cam." He cradled her head in the hollow of his shoulder and loosened her curls so the blue-black silkiness fell freely. He gathered a handful and gently tilted her face upward. "You are so lovely. I wanted to wait, to go slowly. I wanted to sit and talk with you. But I find that I cannot. Oh, God! I cannot! Love me, my Camille."

Her hands threaded through his thick hair, and his lips lowered once more to claim hers. With a strangled gasp of pleasure, she guided him toward the bed. They fell across it, unable to wait any longer, their bodies voracious in their starved need.

His knowing hands moved over her, as though to memorize every beguiling inch. Her body hummed with the erotic tunes he played on her and her response stoked the steadily building fires inside him.

Their lovemaking was familiar and yet new; a whole world waited to be explored; gourmet delights to be held on the tongue and savored, a cascading waterfall, followed by the gentle flowing of a summer steam.

For the long night, they never left each other's arms, but they did talk at last, of many things. He shared with her what he was able, telling her some of the places he'd been and some of the things he'd seen. She took a part of his grieving heart into herself, lightening the heavy load he carried. Faraway places she'd heard of during the conflict became more real as he spoke of them: Charleston, Richmond, Shiloh, Manassas. He told her of young men who'd marched gallantly into the very teeth of death, never to return. She laughed with him at some of the sillier episodes: a cow almost shot for an enemy, a girl dressed as a boy who'd enlisted to be near her lover, a respected general who'd told them hilariously funny tales all through one long night of tension.

So, he had to have been with the Confederate troops, didn't he? His heart supported the cause much more than he had ever admitted and he was doing his part, though perhaps in an unorthodox way. She was angry with herself for the doubts she'd struggled with for so long.

Charles prodded her for the truth about how things had been at Magnolia, asking penetrating questions that required honest answers, though she would have spared him knowledge of her difficulties.

"I'm sorry, Cam. You know I never wanted to leave you. It's not fair for you to have to handle everything alone. I'll be here for a few days; perhaps I can help put some things to rights, and see that you're provided for before I must leave again."

"Ah, Charles, must you go?" But she'd known from the first moment she'd seen him standing in the doorway of the library, that he would soon be leaving. It was the way of things. She would not make him feel guilty for following the dictates of his conscience.

The few days Charles spent at Magnolia were an unending joy and Camille reveled in every second of his presence there. She arranged his favorite meals, as best she could with the shortages, and catered to his every wish. They spent long, pleasant evenings on the veranda, storing up memories to be pulled out and savored on the long, lonesome nights of separation that would soon face them.

Only one unpleasantness spoiled their time together. Clement Masters made a most unwelcome appearance, in the company of a group of ruffians. If possible, he was even more gaunt than ever, and it was obvious things had not been going well for him.

"Well, well, well . . . home from the war, I see," he taunted Charles, knowing that he had not enlisted, anxious to cast doubt on the man who had insulted him and driven him from Magnolia.

"That's more than you can say for yourself," Camille snapped. "Just what *have* you been doing, Clement Masters?"

"Oh, I dabble. This and that, you know. But it's all very interesting. Yes, indeed. I learn a lot of *secret* things that way." His gaze settled on Charles with obvious meaning.

Charles's eyebrow shot up, and he nailed the little man with a sharp look. "Just what do you mean?" he asked slowly, the threat in his voice so real it sent shivers up Camille's spine. Her husband would not be a good man to cross, she realized in that instant, discovering a facet of him she'd never seen before.

"Oh, nothing partic'lar, Mr. Longmont. I was just speaking in general terms, if you get my meaning."

Charles looked as though he did indeed get his meaning, and was not pleased by it.

When Clement rode off, Charles soon made some excuse and rode off after him, leaving Camille to wonder what would transpire between the two of them in private. She shrugged her shoulders helplessly and went inside.

Too soon, Charles prepared to leave and Camille steeled her heart for the parting. He made no promises about when he would return and she knew there were no guarantees he would return at all. Wherever he went, it was near the front lines of battle, that much she'd ascertained during his short visit. And it was important, at least to him, and more likely than not to the Confederacy. Clement Masters's thinly veiled innuendo had some connection with Charles's covert activities, but Charles had not mentioned either the man or what he'd said again. He had seemed intent on forgetting the entire incident, and was concerned that Camille do so, as well.

Dressed to leave, he looked so tall and ruggedly handsome Camille's heart lurched inside her chest. Where would she find the strength to let him go? His muscular shoulders seemed to invite her to lean against him, leave everything to him. His arms, powerful but so gentle, beckoned her into his embrace. Only the deep pain in his brown eyes and a muscle that worked in his jaw revealed his own struggles with their leave-taking.

Charles's expression was serious and thoughtful as he left directions with the household staff and Josef, who had made some progress toward recovery. He had done all he could, for now at any rate, and he hoped things would go well on the plantation for a while.

Reaper was brought around and stood pawing the gravel. Well fed and rested, the big stallion was ready to go. Charles put a comforting, protective arm around Camille's shoulders as he talked and she stood so near his heart she felt its irregular rhythm, and knew his control over his own emotions was only outward.

Her arm was wrapped securely around his waist and she was loathe to release her hold even as he turned her toward him, putting both his hands on her shoulders.

Looking long into her eyes so full of love for him, he said at last, ''I'll be back, Cam.''

''Yes,'' she acknowledged his promise, a catch in her voice the only sign of her distress, as she said softly, ''Go with God, Charles.''

He bent to kiss her one last time, pulled himself away and snatching up the reins, threw himself on his horse and galloped off down the drive. Where the lane intersected the tree-lined drive he reined in and lifted his hand in a last farewell salute. Camille put her fingers to her lips and returned his gesture. Her eyes strained to see him long after he was out of sight, leaving only dust and her empty heart behind.

Back straight and head high, she turned toward the house. Picking up her skirts, she walked steadily up the stairs. No one saw the tears that sparkled in her deep blue eyes or heard the sobs that wracked her slender body when she reached her bedroom and fell across the bed.

As THE WAR DRAGGED on and the North tightened its net around them, necessities as well as luxuries became harder and harder to obtain, even if one could afford the exorbitant prices. Damask curtains hastily sewn into imitations of the latest styles began to appear at the theater and there were ''starvation soirees,'' parties where there were no refreshments but dancing and revelry that might go on until dawn.

Two wealthy Natchez families fled to Europe, never to return, and others of the previously well-to-do were reduced to letting out rooms in order to pay their taxes. Proudly they did what was necessary, gripped by a singular fatalism, and a burning will to survive.

A small group of young women gathered regularly to roll the bandages Charles had sadly predicted "would be useful in surrendering."

"There's not a decent shoe in the whole town!" wailed Glory at once such session, wiggling her toe through a hole in the side of her well-worn shoe, now long out of style.

Camille smiled at her friend, but her heart ached with a raw pain. Sometimes it was the little thing, the mundane, everyday thing that hurt more than all the major catastrophes they faced. And Glory's remark had that effect on her.

Seeing the expression on her friend's face, Glory asked, "Cam, do you really think the South might *lose*?"

"Oh, I do so hope not, Glory!" But Charles's prophetic words echoed in her mind. "Then it would all have been in vain, wouldn't it?"

"Dandy says we may still have a chance if we can hold the river."

But they both knew that less than three hundred miles south, New Orleans stood on the brink of disaster, and the tenacious General Grant threatened Vicksburg, their neighboring city on the north. They were, in effect, surrounded by the enemy. Camille suspected the few successes of their own army only prolonged the agony. But she was proud, like her fellow Southerners, of their brilliant generals: Robert E. Lee, Stonewall Jackson, Joe Johnston. In her heart she grieved already for the outcome she feared. So many had sacrificed so much. And to what end?

Should they lose to the North, the future looked bleak indeed. And for her, there would be no future without Charles. God, bring him home safely, she prayed, knowing similar prayers were being sent heavenward all over the land, both in the North and the South. Many were being denied, for some inexplicable reason. Why did it seem God had turned His back on them just when they needed Him most? She felt a jolting return of the doubts she'd expressed to Charles when her father died so soon after her mother and her brother. Was there really a God? Did He really care for them, as she'd been taught to believe, or was He as indifferent as He seemed?

Chapter Thirteen

CAMILLE STOOD in the fading sunlight on the bluffs overlooking the Mississippi. She'd gone farther than she had planned on her walk by the river and as she turned to make her way home, darkness was fast approaching.

Twilight shadows distorted everything and there was something eerie about the sudden blanketing of darkness across the wide lawn and drive. Knowing the path as well as she did, she had no trouble negotiating it, but foreboding caused her steps to lag, and become more tentative.

As she drew nearer she was relieved to see the usual lantern hanging on the back porch, its golden glow bathing the cypress steps. But even the familiar scene failed to overlay the tension of the night.

Every step toward the haven of her own back door was made with supreme effort. She felt weighted down by some evil portent. Something was afoot in the moonless darkness of the late evening, and without understanding why, she knew it involved her. Could she escape by dashing madly for the back door and latching it behind her? Perhaps not. Her shoes seemed filled with lead; she could not run. She could barely move. It was as though her muffled steps were taken through thick, wadded cotton. She seemed to make no progress at all toward the door.

To her right, along the veranda, a cloaked figure suddenly appeared and faded away, swallowed up in the night shadows. Could her eyes be deceiving her? She blinked once, twice. No, it had been no illusion. For another dark shape exited the stranger's room, followed quickly by a third and a fourth.

What was the meaning of this late-night intrusion in her home? These shadowy people were abusing the gracious hospitality of Magnolia. Anger replaced her pervading sense of fear and released her feet. She strode toward the door of the stranger's room to discover the cause of the furtive meeting.

Her hand fell to the silver-plated knob, but it twisted from within. Someone was coming out! The impetus of the door opening threw her off balance and she would have fallen but for the strong arm that clamped firmly about her waist.

Her body neatly meshed with the lithe, masculine form that prevented her fall with an easy grace, but whether the contact had been a natural result of his reflexive action or some sinister design on his part she couldn't have said.

For the length of a heartbeat, they stood thus, she struggling to regain her balance, he in no apparent hurry to release his steadying hold on her, intimate though it might be.

A deep rumble of laughter revealed his delight in their circumstances before a hauntingly familiar voice mocked, "Didn't I tell you we would meet again, dear lady?"

His hands spanning the narrow circle of her waist, he held her so close she could not look up at his face. But she knew she was in the arms of the gentleman bandit. He placed a kiss on the top of her head.

"Lovely wraith of midnight," he murmured, his seductive voice low. "One day our destinies will bring us together in more fortuitous circumstances." He hesitated before continuing, "But for now, I'm afraid I must leave you once more." With a casual twist of his strong arms, he turned her from him and set her inside the room he'd just vacated, closing the door firmly.

By the time she was able to snatch it open with shaking fingers, he was gone. She heard only the rapid beat of his horse's hooves on the gravel. Standing on the portal, alone and frustrated, she peered into the darkness after him, fighting an incredibly strong urge to follow him.

Just once, just one blessed time, I'd like to do exactly as I please, she thought. She had moved from the carefully protective custody of her father into the equally protective care of Charles Longmont, having had no chance to experience life on her own. She had been coddled and pampered, and restricted by the expectations of the men who loved her and the times in which she lived. But tonight she was intrigued by the idea that she was free to follow the gentleman bandit if she wished. There was no one to stop her!

Without another moment's hesitation, she flew toward the stable, grabbing a stable boy's pants and rough shirt from a hook inside the door. Hastily discarding her gown, she stepped into the pants and yanked the shirt down over her head, shoving a weather-beaten hat down over her head and tucking as much of her hair as she could beneath it. She stepped into boots, well-worn and much too big, and reached for Sadie's bridle.

Quickly she bridled her little mare and led her out of the stall. She chose to ride astride and bareback.

Climbing up on a rail, she swung her leg over. Grasping the reins tightly in one hand and clamping her knees around Sadie's sides, she urged her to top speed as they bolted through the stable doors and down the wide drive toward the lane. Thinking she knew which direction he had to have taken, she whipped Sadie to her right and plunged off into the darkness.

Galloping through the cool night was exhilarating. Camille loved the feel of the responsive horse under her and the wind whipping her hair wildly where it escaped the floppy hat. With a soft cry of gladness, she spied the bandit up ahead on the open road. Did he know he was being followed? It did not matter. She had to get to the bottom of this and find out what was going on between this handsome, but maddening stranger and her husband. She would not admit to her equally strong longing to discover what was going on between the handsome bandit and herself.

Suddenly the gentleman bandit left the road and completely disappeared. Where could he be? And what in God's name had he been doing in her home? Did he have some connection with Charles? From the time she'd first seen him leaving the stranger's room, she'd been sure he was bent on some dark deed. What unwavering purpose had propelled him in and out of the shadows on this lonesome road beside the city cemetery where she had doggedly pursued him?

Camille slowed as she neared the forest opening where she had lost sight of her prey. Slipping down from her horse, she cautiously made her way into the undergrowth. The tangled, trailing vines clutched at her, snagging her hastily donned riding clothes, scratching her arms and face, tearing at her oversized boots. She stumbled over a rotted log and almost fell.

Crouching behind a thick growth of bushes, she shivered recalling the local legend of the Devil's Punchbowl. It was said to lie somewhere past the cemetery. Those who claimed to have seen it, described it as a mysterious gully, shaped like a giant cup, as much as five hundred feet across and two hundred feet deep.

The thick, almost impenetrable growth around its rim made it a perfect place of concealment, favored by pirates and runaway slaves. Boatmen claimed when they passed the opening to the Punchbowl their compasses behaved crazily. They told stories of buried treasure, hidden there by early French and Spanish pirates and of the men who had gone in search of that gold, never to be seen or heard from again.

Camille blinked, fearful of seeing a barefoot pirate, earrings jangling, pass by in front of her when next the moon reappeared. Stubbornly the moon remained hidden behind, refusing to show itself anew.

Trailing tendrils of smoke drifted up from a camp fire, and giant puffs of fog clung to the tops of trees, probably somewhere near the river's opening. Was that where the bandit had gone?

For the moment she had time to wonder why she had come here. It had been a whim, utter foolishness on her part. Like the night she'd gone Under the Hill, she fervently wished herself back home. That night, at least, she'd had a mission, some purpose behind her foolhardy act. But tonight? Tonight it was only curiosity—or had it been more than that? She convinced herself she needed to know what the gentleman bandit had been doing at Magnolia. And if he were somehow connected with Charles and his frequent meetings in the stranger's room, well, she must find out about that, too.

But then he had completely disappeared, and now she crouched in the brush, afraid to go on, but too stubborn to go back.

A waiting, breathless silence hung around her and she scarcely dared to breathe for fear she'd give herself away. She was light-headed from the chase that had brought her here, her stomach queasy with a potent mixture of fear and excitement.

A cricket chirped from a thicket nearby and Camille started, her heart hammering wildly. She listened for any other sound foreign to the deep stillness of the night. Branches rustled softly. Someone was there— just inches behind her! Before she could whirl to see who it was, a muscled forearm fastened around her throat, cutting off her breath, and a foul-smelling rag was clamped firmly over her nose and mouth, finishing the deed. She felt and heard no more.

CAMILLE'S HEAD POUNDED unmercifully, her arms ached from their unnatural position, and the rope bit into the tender flesh of her wrists and ankles.

Willing her eyes to move around the room as she could not, she discovered little. She lay on the floor in a dark room. There was no furniture, nothing to break the sheer monotony of roughened planked floors and walls. Barely enough light filtered through the dingy windows for her to see that her prison was quite small, and she its only occupant. The narrow door, she suspected, would be solidly bolted from the other side— there seemed an absence of any kind of latch on the inside.

Why was she a trussed-up prisoner in this claustrophobic cell? What had she done, except follow an almost irresistible curious urge? And even then, she had seen nothing, nothing at all! She could hardly be a threat to anyone because of information she'd learned or faces she'd seen, could she? Certainly not—all she'd really seen had been the diffusion of camp fire smoke through a thick canopy of trees!

What was the meaning of all this? Someone must have followed her when she rode out after the bandit. Then she recalled watching through the brush, and she felt once more the firm strength in the arm that circled her neck like a steel band, inhaled again the noxious odors of the rag clamped over her nose.

After that, nothing but a cloudy haze of scattered bits of memory. A harsh guttural voice and the reply, soft but in a voice teasingly familiar. A rough, bouncing trip thrown uncomfortably across a horse's back, her legs and arms dangling. The jolt of being dumped in this damp, barren room. The skittering feet of—what could it have been?—mice, even rats! She shivered at the thought.

Whose feet pounded forcefully overhead? Where was she anyway? The floor seemed to fall away below her and then slam back into her! The continuous rocking motion, the damp, musty odor, the saltiness of her lips . . . led to one conclusion—she must be on a boat! Probably heading downstream, and in the middle of the night, a treacherous undertaking on the constantly changing Mississippi. There were sandbars; downed trees lay hidden below the surface; and other dangers lurked in the depths of the mighty river. Also, there was the additional menace of Yankee gunboats that prowled the waters. Only a wise and experienced captain could make such a voyage safely, and she doubted such a man was in charge of this vessel.

Camille looked up toward the small porthole, cloudy with grease and dirt. She made a movement toward it, but was stopped abruptly by crude bands of heavy rope looped tightly around her arms and feet. Testing, she rubbed her wrists back and forth against the rope. They were tied securely and she could not loosen them. She was immobilized and helpless.

Would her captors reveal themselves? Or would they leave her hidden in this hole, alone, for the whole trip? Where were they going? New Orleans? It seemed the most logical destination. Almost at the mouth of the Mississippi, it was a busy harbor town where a person could easily drop out of sight. But what reason had anyone for wanting her gone? She had harmed no one. Frantically, her mind sought for someone who might have a grievance against her.

Clement Masters! But he was gone, wasn't he? Besides, what would he gain by having her kidnapped? It would never open the way for him to the Beaufort inheritance—not with Charles around! But what if something happened to Charles? What if something already *had* happened to him? He could be lying in a ditch somewhere, and she would never know!

Camille struggled anew against the ropes that bound her, but succeeded only in pulling them tighter. Her breath whistling painfully through her throat, and her head throbbing unmercifully, she ceased. She would have to use her wits or she might never leave this tiny prison.

Her stomach heaved and, helplessly, she retched. No sympathetic servant stood by to offer her a drink of water or wipe her brow with a cool cloth. Dear God, how she longed for a drink! The rancid taste in her mouth made her stomach roll once more, but this time only dry heaves shook her.

Exhausted and still feeling the effects of the drugged cloth, she slept fitfully.

Sometime later, when she awoke, a faint increase of light suggested daytime. If anything, she felt worse than ever. Something drew her attention to her feet. There, firmly planted on the swaying floor were two big, booted feet, two thickly muscled legs. Hesitantly her eyes moved upward. If she'd longed to see the familiar white whiskers of Captain John, she was sadly disappointed.

Though equal in stature, this man bore none of the humor or softness of the captain she'd known for so many years. Her heart sank. Before her stood her captor, her jailer. She could hope for nothing from him.

"Mornin', my lovely." His booming voice echoed through the small room and caused a furious banging in her already throbbing head. She stared at him, but refused to answer. He did not deserve a polite response.

He saw her frowning reaction to his loud voice, and noted her resolute decision not to speak. With a quirk of his black brow, he studied her inquisitively. "So that's the way 'tis to be, hey? Here I'm thinkin' p'rhaps ye'd be glad for a little company! In that case . . ." He threw her a mocking glance and stomped out the door, dropping the bolt into place. Heavy, booted footsteps shook the floor as he strode purposefully away.

"W-wait." Her weak protest had been too late to stop him. She was alone again. Why had she been so foolish? She'd lost in the first round with this man, but she hoped there would be others. And the next time she'd call on her intelligence instead of her obstinate stubbornness. She would find a way out—she had to!

How different this voyage was from the one undertaken when she was but a child—how painfully different from the one made in the arms of her husband after her seduction of him. With an agony of helpless longing, she recalled the pleasurable delights of long nights in his arms, breakfast in bed, strolls aboard the deck of the magnificently outfitted *Natchez*. And now she was a captive on this rickety tub that would most likely not make it past Baton Rouge!

She slept, to dream of Charles, but dreams of her husband were overshadowed by another powerful presence—the bold strength and dark good looks of the gentleman bandit. Were they always destined to meet, then part so quickly? Despite the strong feelings he stirred in her, she knew she should put him from her mind. There was nothing for the two of them. She was married and she truly loved Charles.

Why, then, these vague restive doubts about her emotions for a highwayman? What could she be thinking? It had probably been he and his rowdy band of outlaws who'd had her kidnapped so she couldn't learn the truth of their secretive business!

But what an urgent longing she'd felt when he'd pulled her to him in that brief moment before he'd disappeared into the night. And the strange, tender kiss he'd placed in her hair. Her head reeled when she recalled the wanton response of her body to the demands of his, as she'd lost herself completely in his embrace. Was it for that reason she had followed him, and not to settle her suspicions as she'd told herself so righteously? Would she even now give herself to him? Had he but to ask? No! She shook her head vehemently back and forth, anxious to be rid of the thought of him, the temptation of him.

Her response to him had been caused by Charles's most recent desertion, and her abject loneliness, combined with a desperate fear of the future. He'd been only someone handy to cling to in the storm of her emotions, nothing more. With these thoughts, she tried to console herself as she drifted once more into troubled sleep.

When she awoke, she was startled to find herself in different quarters. The lumpy pad beneath her was no soft down mattress, to be sure, but much better than the rough hardness of the floor. Her wrists and ankles had been freed of their bindings and she rubbed the feeling back into them with relief. A washstand was the only other piece of furniture besides the crude, narrow bed on which she lay, but, with a thankful gasp, she saw that it held a bowl with clean water and a cloth.

Testing her feet, confined for so long by the ropes, she found she was able to put some weight on them. Shakily, she stood up. Her eyes still on the precious water, she took one hesitant step and then another, placing her feet gingerly on the swaying floor, falling against the wall when the boat rolled more violently.

A few more steps and she had made it! She grabbed for the edge of the table to steady herself, and hung on until her head stopped its wild spinning. Greedily she plunged her hands into the water and scooped welcome handfuls to her parched lips. Almost as pleasant was the feeling of the damp cloth, rough though it was, against the skin of her face, neck and arms as she sponged off the dust and grime. After as thorough a cleansing as she could manage, she felt almost human.

Her spirits revived a little. Whoever had moved her and untied her must possess at least a shred of kindness that might be manipulated into her eventual release.

She paced the room, about twice the size of the previous one, trying out her new mobility, glad she was able to walk and move about. She rushed over to a small porthole, but found it out of reach over her head. Jumping, she couldn't reach high enough to even touch it with her fingertips. She must have something to stand on, and thought of the cot where she lay when she awoke. But even as she hurried toward it, she realized with disappointment that it was securely bolted to the wall.

She turned to the washstand, carefully setting the bowl with the remaining water on the floor, and dragged the table under the porthole. It was small and not at all sturdy, would most likely not bear even her slight weight. But it was her only chance since no other furniture decorated the bare room.

Placing her hands against the wall, she lifted one foot and set it cautiously in the center of the little table that shook and creaked beneath the weight. Her hands slid up the wall as she set her other foot on the wooden surface. She swayed, her fingers grasping for the rim of the porthole. If she could only regain her balance and pull herself up the slightest bit more, she could see out!

But the overloaded table gave way with a loud crack, its legs splaying out beneath and sending her tumbling to the floor, her fingers sliding down the rough wall. Oh, if only she could have managed to see out, she knew she would have felt much better. She huddled miserably on the floor amid the broken bits of the table scattered around her. What she wouldn't give to know where they were going, and what lay in store for her!

Camille sank down on the edge of her metal cot and, for the first time, realized she was ravenous. Her empty stomach lurched threateningly, and she feared she would be sick again. *Oh, no!* she thought, *not here, not now!* Willing her stomach to cease its churning, she sat very still. *It will pass, it will,* she repeated to herself as she felt the sickness abate.

Creaking against its heavy iron hinges, the big door swung inward, and a huge form stood silhouetted in the dim light from a narrow hallway.

"Well, well, well." His laughter roared. "Aren't we looking pert this mornin', my lovely?"

She bit back an angry retort and congratulated herself when she saw a makeshift wooden tray in his big hands. At that moment, the welcome aroma of coffee reached her.

"Thought ya might be needin' a bite, now." His knowing eyes were watchful, careful, as he set the tray down beside her. "Some hardtack and a bit of stewed meat. I'm afraid it's the best we can do, my lovely."

His black eyes moved over her in obvious appreciation. Despite her ordeal and the disheveled condition of her clothing, he clearly thought she was a beauty.

Hungrily, Camille made quick work of the simple breakfast, and savored the coffee, even though it was the strong chicory she'd never developed a taste for. Her stomach settled down uneasily, and she felt almost in control of her body once more.

She returned the captain's curious stare, but this time she would not antagonize him, not if she could avoid it. There was much she wanted to learn from him. He could be, she thought, a dangerous foe, if provoked, or perhaps a reluctant ally if handled properly.

Her new attitude of cooperation won him over little by little, as well as the members of his small crew. He soon decided the pleasures of her company were worth the slight risk of her being able to escape the ship in the middle of the river. She was delightful in conversation and fetching to look at, a welcome addition to his poor boat. He would deliver her to New Orleans and his job would be done. That was all he'd agreed to do. They hadn't actually said he had to keep her under lock and key, had they? No, just that he bring her safely to the contact in New Orleans—then he could collect his money and be on his way.

On deck for the first time, Camille discovered the boat was a little nicer than she'd expected. It was a small stern-wheeler, swabbed clean and kept on course by a four-man crew that included the captain, a first mate, a boatswain and a cook, of sorts.

Both deckhands were young and pleasant enough, going out of their way when the captain wasn't looking to make her as comfortable as possible. A crude wooden bench appeared and then a piece of tattered canvas, tacked up for a shade. Here, she spent hours in the fresh air, watching the shoreline, ever hopeful of finding someone she might signal for help, or some other way out of her unhappy situation.

Though she no longer felt threatened or in any real danger, her heart pined for home. Also, the uncertainty of where she was being taken and what ultimately lay in store for her gave her cause for concern. When they docked, as eventually they must, she would find a way to get ashore, to get away, and would make her way home, somehow.

Until then there was nothing at all she could do, unless she could catch the attention of a passing boat. But the captain had evidently considered that possibility, and she was hurried below whenever any vessel came in sight, or when they passed too near the shore.

Looking into the swirling currents of the Mississippi, she knew there was no hope should she throw herself overboard, as she'd been strongly tempted to do. She had never been a good swimmer, and her sodden clothing would very likely pull her down to a watery grave. No, she would have to wait patiently and hope for a way out.

Bored, she offered to help the boat's cook, and the nearly inedible fare improved markedly, for which all aboard were silently grateful. Even Cook himself did not disapprove, though he mumbled something under his breath about her "high-handed ways." He blustered around, rattling pans and complaining, but keeping a close eye on her, all the while learning how to prepare dishes that were more palatable and how to make a little go a lot further.

His fat cheeks puffed out and the big wart on his nose wiggled when he was able to use what Camille had shown him for the first time. The appreciation of the crew brought a rare smile that revealed his crooked, yellow teeth.

"I don't think I ever seen Cook smile," said Johnathan, the first mate.

"Naw, but he sure never had nothin' to smile 'bout before!" guffawed the other mate, Billy Whipple. "An' neither did the rest of us, eh?"

"This is good grub, mate," agreed the captain, with a knowing wink at Camille, who smiled her pleasure. They sat in the long, narrow dining room off the galley, gathered around a rectangular wooden table, carved with the initials and exploits of sailors who'd drawn up chairs there in the past. A lantern swung from a hook in the wall over the captain's left shoulder, casting eerie shadows over the incongruous group.

What strange set of circumstances had brought her to this table? she wondered, more in curiosity than fear. Camille suspected the next sunrise would bring them to New Orleans, and the thought of what might happen then brought a knotting to her stomach. They would not release her. From Billy she'd learned that the captain had been paid by someone to steal her away and deliver her to New Orleans.

He'd said he wasn't sure who, and when she'd questioned him closer, had clammed up and refused to say anything more. His first loyalty was to his captain, and he was aware he'd probably said too much already. Though she'd tried repeatedly, Camille had been able to learn nothing more from either Cook or Johnathan.

Her last resort was the captain himself, and her last chance was that very night as he had stood with her on deck watching a colorful sunset paint the sky.

"Beautiful, ain't it?" he'd asked.

Surprised at his appreciation of nature's glory, Camille nodded her head and looked up at him. She found his eyes on her, the expression in them unreadable but not unkind. It was almost a fatherly look, she thought. Perhaps she could reason with him after all.

"Captain . . ." she began.

"Now, Miss. Ain't no sense in ya askin'. I gotta do what I gotta do. Tomorrer I'll be turnin' ya over to somebody else, just like I was told."

"But why?"

Why, indeed, he thought. It had been a paltry sum he'd agreed to, but he'd desperately needed it to feed his crew and to keep his boat in the water. And the man had assured him no harm would come to her—it was only a temporary necessity that she be sent away from Natchez. Then she would be released and free to return home.

Did he really believe that? Recalling the dark eyes of the man who had offered to pay him for the kidnapping, he doubted it. But if he let her go now, the man had promised he'd never see the rest of the money, and that his reputation on the river would be forever ruined when word leaked out of what he'd done.

No, he couldn't turn back on the deal. But when he saw her young loveliness, listened to the soft rhythms of her kind voice, and thought of her helpfulness to him and his crew, he knew he could not abandon her to her fate.

He would have to find a way to help her.

He would have Billy follow her and find out where she was being held. Then, without letting his part in it be known, he could send someone back to her husband with the information. That way, his conscience would be clear. Yes, it would be a simple matter and easily arranged.

The captain had a moment's doubt, however, when he was met by the contact to whom he was to deliver his prisoner. The man sat hidden from sight in a coach pulled by four fine horses. He did not meet them face to face as the captain had expected, but ordered his footman to escort Camille from the boat into his custody in the curtained coach. The footman returned with a bag of coins, but before the captain could summon Billy and tell him of his plan, the coach careered away from the dock and was quickly lost in the crowded streets.

"Damn!" he muttered. All he'd be able to report to her husband now was that she was in New Orleans—and a big place it was. Damn near impossible to find someone there—especially someone who did not want to be found. That man was crafty all right, staying hidden like that and whisking her away so quickly, almost as though he expected some pursuit.

"Damn!" he cursed again, kicking his foot against the gangplank. He had come to like the young woman and he didn't like to think she might be hurt or kept a prisoner indefinitely. Her new captor might not choose to be as kind as they had been to her on his boat, and he doubted her gentle nature and slight body could stand much abuse.

He sent Billy running down the street, though in his heart he knew it was too late. There was nothing more he could do but notify her husband of what little he knew. Surely, if the man loved her, he would leave no stone unturned until he found her, no matter who held her prisoner. But the captain would be delayed in reaching Natchez for several weeks and unable to communicate his vital information to Camille's husband.

CAMILLE RECOVERED QUICKLY, after being hastened inside the carriage, and straightened in her seat, curious to see who rode with her. The interior was dim due to the heavy curtains and she could not make out any distinct features. Two impressions jolted her: her captor was a man who was both large and fiercely dangerous. Unlike the gruff but malleable riverboat captain, this stranger was a true adversary, someone to be respected and feared. A deadly, lethal power revealed itself in every line of his formidable body.

As the horses raced unchecked through the streets of New Orleans toward their mysterious destination, Camille could see nothing outside, no landmarks to show the way. The man across from her sat unbending and silent, an almost regal air about him. Not a word was spoken between them until they lurched to a stop after a ride of some distance.

Camille did not move, but awaited the instructions she felt sure would now come. Still, he said nothing.

When the door was pulled open, a shaft of late-afternoon light fell across the plush interior of the coach. The first thing she saw was a vicious, jagged scar etched across the length of his face from one corner of his mouth to his hairline, in a half-moon shape. A shock of dark hair fell over his forehead, brushed his ears, and fell to the top of the cloak he whipped around himself as he prepared to step down.

The deference paid him by the coach attendants and by the servants who waited at the door of a large, imposing house indicated his exalted power and position. Camille saw only the one structure, but assumed it to be a large estate in the Garden District, where she'd stayed with friends of Aunt Emily on her stopover in the city as a child.

The man reached back to her with a black-gloved hand. She hesitated before placing her hand in his, and then recoiled at the strength and vitality that coursed through his hand and into her like an electrical shock at his touch.

His head was turned toward the house and she still could not see his face. Such seemed to be his intent. She had no difficulty stepping down with the firm support of his hand. He did not release her then, but maintained contact as his hand slid to grasp her elbow securely.

Aside from the potent threat of that touch, there was nothing to reveal her status as prisoner. She might have been an honored guest, and the servants bowed to her as they swept inside, halting momentarily in a wide, marbled hallway beneath a glittering chandelier.

The expressions on the faces of this man's household staff soon quenched any hopes she might have had for help from that quarter. They were in his employ and firmly under his domination. They seemed to idolize him.

Before she could realize what was happening and before she'd clearly seen his face, he had led her up the ornate, free-standing stairway, past the first landing. They continued to spiral upward until they reached what must have been the third floor.

He whipped a heavy ring of keys from his pocket and efficiently dealt with three sets of locks. The massive door opened inwardly. Camille was firmly shoved inside and the door slid softly closed behind her. She whirled, but before she could reach it, distinctly heard each of the locks engaged. She was now truly a prisoner, as she had not been up to that time, even though she had been bound hand and foot on the boat. A debilitating depression such as she had never felt before descended on her as she realized how foolish her plans of escape had been. There was no way out!

That man, whatever his wicked intentions might be, would never let go, not willingly. How she knew that so surely she could not have explained. But know it she did and a hard, convulsive shudder of real fear claimed her. Unable to support her own weight any longer, she slid down the door into a crumpled heap, her head on her knees as painful, deep sobs of hopelessness broke from her and filled the room.

The man who stood motionless outside the door heard. With a casual lift of his wide shoulders in a shrug, he turned toward the stairs. A thin smile distorted his almost-handsome face.

When Camille at last raised her head to look around, she was astounded. Apparently a turret, the room's shape was a semicircle, its sides steep and high. Only one window broke the symmetry of the smooth walls and it was at least ten feet above her head and very small. She thought, but could not be sure, that small bars crisscrossed the crystal panes of glass on the outside.

The furnishings were elegant and expensive, designed for comfort. Two high-backed chairs were drawn up before a stone fireplace. A huge tester bed and a mirrored wardrobe occupied the other side of the room. Candles burned brightly on scattered tables and illuminated an assortment of current books and magazines, including the latest in fashion from Paris. For whatever strange intent, there were even writing materials available on a teakwood desk. She laughed harshly. Perhaps he would post a letter for her! Let's see...she could say, "Dear Charles, having a fine time in New Orleans! Hope to see you soon." Tears of frustration welled in her eyes. How she longed to see the familiar twinkling brown eyes and be held in those strong arms.

Camille looked around in awe and disbelief. Where was she? A finer prison she could not have wished, but as it was in fact a prison, none of its beauties or comforts brought her any pleasure. And who was that horrible, forbidding man? More to the point, what were his plans? Surely not to keep her here indefinitely. No, he had some other dark motive and it would be in her best interests to find out what it was as soon as she could.

Almost without her knowledge, her hardy spirits began to revive and from somewhere deep inside she drew on a reserve of hope and courage too strong to die. Perhaps she could somehow get word to Charles. He would fly to her aid and rescue her from this elegant prison—but would he be a match for the strength and cunning of the one who held her captive? Or would he be putting his own life in jeopardy in a foolhardy rescue attempt? Charles had probably never dealt with anyone as cruel or as powerful as the dark, scarred man who held the keys of her imprisonment.

She stood up, and only then did she realize she still wore the servant's riding clothes she had grabbed so hastily in her pursuit of the bandit. Though she'd been able to clumsily launder them on the boat, they were a shabby and bedraggled mess, and their rough texture abraded her skin painfully. With a smile, she thought of the servants' refined response to her entrance here. What a sight she must have been, indeed! She chuckled, relieved at the return of her almost-normal feelings. There was nothing to be done about it, though. This was the way she looked, and there was nothing she could, or would, do about it.

An impulse drew her toward the wardrobe and she pulled it open cautiously. Inside, to her surprise, was a collection of gowns and dresses almost to equal her own wardrobe back at Magnolia. Whose? she wondered, fingering the fine fabrics: silks, laces, satins, velvets. Below them, in neat rows, stood pair after pair of handmade shoes of the finest leathers and cloth, and a pair of soft kid riding boots with the high tops she personally favored. She pulled the drawers open one at a time, and finding an assortment of fine lawn underclothing, she hastily pushed them shut again.

This room belonged to someone then? A daughter, a sister, a wife, perhaps? Someone coddled and treated to life's finery, that much was for certain. And she was an intruder here, albeit a helpless and reluctant one.

Thoughts spun through her head, darting first in one direction and then another. Before she could collect them to any reasonable conclusion, a knock came on the door, followed by the grating of a key in the first lock, the second, the third.

The door opened slowly and two manservants entered, carrying on their shoulders an ornate ivory tub. They departed quickly and almost immediately two uniformed ladies' maids entered and began filling the tub with steaming hot water. Another older servant, probably the housekeeper, brought a fat cake of sandalwood soap and two oversized towels, leaving them on a high stool beside the tub.

They were gone before Camille could utter a word of thanks. A puzzled frown on her face, she was drawn unwillingly to the fragrant steaming water. Even though she didn't want to seem overly anxious to partake of this man's "hospitality," she could not possibly resist such a bath!

Wrinkling her nose, she quickly unfastened her dark clothing and tossed it aside. With a sigh of satisfaction, she stepped over the rolled edge of the tub and lowered herself into the deep water, enjoying the satiny feeling of its warmth as it rose up to her chin. Reaching for the cake of soap, she scrubbed her body hard, trying to rid herself of the awful dirt and lingering odors from her enforced trip downriver. Loosening her hair, she gladly felt it fall around her shoulders and with a cry of delight, soaped it and rinsed it until it squeaked.

She stood and rinsed herself, letting the water dribble deliciously all over her, before grabbing one towel and wrapping herself in its soft folds. She stepped out and lifted the other one to her head, rubbing at the long, tangled curls and finally tying it around her head, turban style. How much better she felt!

Her eyes fell to the tawdry heap of clothing she'd discarded on the floor. Fingering it, she knew she couldn't bear to put it back on now that she felt so clean and wonderful. She'd rather sit here clad only in the clean, soft towel.

Another knock sent her scampering behind a Chinese screen placed across one rounded side of the room. Conveniently hanging over its edge lay a monogrammed silk robe in luscious shades of peach, rose and pink. Hastily she wrapped it around her, dropping her towel, just as a servant she had never seen before entered with a tray filled with a tempting assortment of delicacies. Depositing it without a word on a small, round table, the girl quickly withdrew.

How many servants did this man command? She had yet to see one she felt she might talk to, possibly appeal to for help, nor had she seen any one of them

more than one time. They were all so dour and busi-
nesslike, extremely serious and unapproachable.

Thinking how foolish it would be to refuse such
nourishing food when she was famished, she approached the table with relish. Pulling up a chair, she
sat and enjoyed her solitary dinner, as she couldn't remember having done in some time. Sipping the glass
of fine wine that accompanied her meal, she sat fingering the initials on the pocket of the borrowed robe
she wore.

Intrigued, she looked down to read the monogram,
curious about the owner of all the fine clothing in the
room. Her heart stopped for a full heartbeat, then
hammered wildly, causing her to feel faint in spite of
her recent nourishment.

C.B.B.L.—they were her own initials! A coinci-
dence? No! That was hardly possible. With deliberate
steps, she strode to the wardrobe and yanked it open.
Angrily she slipped first one foot then the other into
pink satin slippers that matched the robe she wore,
knowing before she did so they would be a perfect fit.

She snatched a gemlike turquoise dress from the rod
and shrugging out of the robe, slipped it over her head.
Silken fabric whispered down over her curves like a
second skin. She did not have to fasten the gown to
know it had been custom-made for her!

The whole wardrobe would fit her perfectly! She
knew it! And it was done in the colors she adored and
always preferred in her own clothing.

As though it were a hot poker burning her fair skin,
she snatched the blue-green dress back over her head
and hurled it across the room. She wouldn't wear it—
any of it! She felt violated by the cruel stranger who
knew too much about her.

Choking back tears of frustration and helplessness, she grabbed up the robe once more and flung it around herself, her one concession. But on second thought, she tossed even that aside, and ran for her own discarded clothing. She would show him her opinion of his elegant clothing! Let *him* wear them! She never would!

But her clothing was gone!

The servant who had brought her dinner must have gathered it up before she left. Camille's attention had been centered on the food and she hadn't noticed. She stared at the floor, as though she could will her miserable stack of clothing back, as though she could will none of this to be happening. Naked, but unaware of it, she stood without moving, hardly breathing, for long minutes.

Footsteps sounded in the hall. Camille shivered. A key turned in the lock. Then another. In dismay, she looked down at her nakedness. She sped back across the room to the robe and slipped into it, belting it around her. The last of the locks was released and the door flew back on its hinges.

It was him!

Chapter Fourteen

NEW ORLEANS—LATE SPRING, 1862

QUIVERING WITH ANGER and helpless frustration, Camille stood straight and tall. If he expected her to grovel, or be sweetly grateful for the clothing, he could think again. She had not been afraid of the riverboat captain, and she refused to be afraid of this man. Nor would she be manipulated. He might hold her body captive, but never her spirit.

A blue fire sparked from her eyes to his, dark and enigmatic, but revealing nothing of what he was thinking. Their bold black depths were strangely calming, almost hypnotic. They seemed to see right through her. Slowly, against her will, Camille felt her anger seep away, leaving her eyes deep blue-purple pools.

The man stood a full twenty feet away and had not touched her, still his look had the soothing effect of a gentling hand stroking her hair. What magical powers lay in his control? How could he calm and still her overwrought nerves so easily, without a single word or touch?

She had never experienced anything like what was happening to her under the brooding gaze of this man she'd never seen before today. She could not speak, nor did he as the exercise of his will over hers continued.

If she didn't do something soon to stop it, she would be completely lost, in his control and rushing to do his bidding as readily as one of his many servants!

With a determined shake of her head, she pulled her eyes from his and turned her back on him. Thankfully, she felt a relaxation of the high-strung tension, an easing of the elemental force of his personality. She could not look long into his dangerous eyes.

Why, then, did she feel a powerful, almost irresistible urge to turn back toward him? Holding her crossed arms tightly against her waist, she fought down the disturbing desire and heard his knowing chuckle.

"Ah, so I shall have my work cut out for me, *chérie?* You will fight me, yes?" His deep voice had a smooth resonance and a hypnotic power not unlike that of his eyes. "But, perhaps," he continued, "nothing is worth having if it is not worth fighting for, *non?* And you, *ma chérie*, are definitely worth having. Most definitely."

The words, heavily accented and flavored with French expressions, sent a chill of fear through her and she hugged her arms even tighter.

"Turn around, *s'il vous plaît.* I will not harm you, but I would look on your lovely face. Ah, yes," he greeted her compliance with a sigh of satisfaction. "You have found your robe, I see? It is the perfect complement to your complexion of ivory and peaches."

This time when she faced him, it was as though his magnetism had dimmed. He now appeared to be only a swarthy Frenchman of above average stature. Though his features were regular, his nose finely shaped and his lips full, he was cheated of being handsome by the slash the scar carved across his visage.

Where had he gotten such a grievous wound? Why did she long to trace its outline with her fingers? Was his hypnotic power at work on her once more, or was this merely the play of her own wild imagination?

They stood apart still, each measuring the strength of a formidable and worthy opponent.

"It will be a good fight, *non*?" He laughed then, a hearty, unaffected laughter that filled the room. "We will share our evening meal, you and I. And you will dress for dinner, *non*?" A nonchalant flick of his wrist toward the wardrobe indicated his awareness of her discovery of the clothing, and her decision to wear none of the finery. The intelligence in his black eyes was fine-honed, missing nothing. There was also in the jet-black depths a very potent threat. If she did not do as he commanded, the consequences would be dire. She had no doubt about that.

"And this—" He had crossed the room to stand next to her, though she was hardly aware of his movement. "This—" his hand reached to finger the dusty-rose collar of her robe "—will not do for dinner." A relentless pressure from his hand, like a hot brand against her skin, and the robe fell open, revealing her luscious softness. Mesmerized by his touch, by the hypnotic cadence of his voice, she stood still, unable to move.

He dropped his hand and stepped back, though his eyes continued their assault. She felt as though his hand still lay against her bare skin. How long they stood thus, she didn't know.

Then he left the room without a final word for her, releasing her from the spell he'd so insidiously woven around her.

She dropped her eyes to see if his heated touch had indeed branded her skin as she feared. Only then did she become aware of the parted robe that had revealed her nakedness to his look of calculated sensuality and possession.

Horrified at her response to him, and the totality of his control over her, she pulled the robe together with cold trembling fingers and flung herself across the bed. A feeling of self-loathing and disgust filled her and she gave in to harsh, rending sobs that tore through her small body, leaving her shaken and wrung out, and at last unable to cry any more.

She had no strength left, and surrendered finally to the surcease of sleep. Unmindful of the sun as it crawled high into the sky and then sank once more into its rest, she slept the clock around. Only a persistent shaking roused her at length. A servant stood over her, saying, "Madame, you must dress for dinner now. The master will soon be here, and he insists . . ."

Amazingly refreshed, Camille sat up. "No." The word was softly spoken, but her intent purpose and resolve could not have been clearer had she shouted.

"But, madame . . . I think you do not understand." A look of fear flitted across the lined face of the housekeeper before her expressionless mask fell back into place. "As you wish." Quietly, she had backed out of the room.

Why hadn't the servant continued her arguments—perhaps even tried to help by pulling out clothes? Did she have orders to desist? Did the hypnotic stranger perhaps hope Camille would defy his orders?

What would his reaction be if she remained as she was? Would he undress her himself? She shivered at the thought, feeling once more the firebrand touch.

Could it be his true desire that she disobey, thus opening the way for him to force her? Though what would stop him in any case, she hadn't any idea; she was his prisoner, and all the advantage lay in his hands.

But perhaps she could gain the upper hand in this instance by doing exactly as he'd ordered. With that thought in mind, she hurriedly dragged forth the beaded turquoise, shot with fine gold thread, that she'd hastily tried on earlier.

He wanted her to dress for dinner. Well, that was precisely what she would do! She snatched up gold slippers and slid her feet into them. Rushing to the oval mirror attached to a dainty dressing table, she pulled and twisted up her hair, fastening it high on her head with combs provided there. A jewelry box opened to reveal delicate gold filigree earrings and a matching necklace. In angry haste, she put them on, applied a little rouge to her high cheekbones, and appraised her work. She was ready.

Camille sat at the table laid out with a lace cloth and fine china and crystal, awaiting his arrival, her posture regal, her head held high. A scented candle in a golden candelabra cast a shimmer over her skin and light danced through her ebony curls and was reflected in her blue eyes, eyes that for this night at least, duplicated the deep blue-green of the dress she wore.

An entourage trailing behind him, the man burst into her room unannounced, and was seated across from her with a flourish by his manservant. White napkins were unfurled and placed in their laps, and their every need and wish was met promptly throughout the meal by the cadre of servants who hovered nearby in anticipation. Wineglasses were automatically refilled before they could be drained. One course was whisked away to be immediately replaced by the next and the next.

In spite of herself, Camille found she enjoyed the rich and abundant Creole foods flavored liberally with tomato and tabasco, and she was intrigued by the studied politeness of the man who shared her dinner. He made no attempt to control her thoughts or actions and he might have been merely any pleasant host, rather than a threat to her liberty. She could not judge his reaction to her decision to dress as he'd commanded. He had not mentioned it.

Camille could not tell if she'd caught him off guard, but she strongly suspected he could never be caught unaware. She had, at least, postponed the inevitable confrontation between them. Would it come after dinner, after the servants had cleared the dishes and taken their leave?

To her surprise, it did not come at all that evening or the next, which followed in much the same pattern. They shared a pleasant meal and he departed immediately afterward. Could she, then, lull him into a sort of false confidence in her agreeable nature and find a way of escape?

She was encouraged when he held out a promise of fresh air and exercise, due to her decorous behavior. But when she discovered that her outing was to consist merely of a stroll in an enclosed courtyard, her high hopes were dashed to the ground.

The courtyard, with its solid, outer iron gate and high walls, was a prison in itself, though a brighter one, as rays of sunlight penetrated the tall palms to dapple the brick paving stones beneath her feet. Besides the outer gate, the only other door was the one that led directly into his quarters and was closely guarded by the largest and most severe of his servants.

Camille paced back and forth the length of the pathway several times, her agitation growing with each step. Glancing up, she saw to her dismay a ceramic cat clinging to the wall, as much a prisoner as she. It brought to her mind her frightening premonition on glimpsing such a courtyard when she and Charles had so happily trod the narrow streets of the Vieux Carré.

So! Perhaps she was not in the American sector, as she'd thought, but in the French Quarter? She should have known immediately from the stucco masonry and the ornate iron fencing.

But it made no difference, did it? There was still no way out, and it would be perhaps even harder for someone to find her here because of the nature of the people of mixed blood who lived in this part of town. Was her captor, then, Creole rather than French? She had never heard anyone speak his name, and he had not mentioned it.

Surely by now, Charles had learned of her disappearance and was looking for her. He loved her and would never give up trying to find her. He would certainly come—was probably on his way to New Orleans right now. And, though she was very much a prisoner, she had not been harmed, nor threatened with violence.

BUT CHARLES HAD NOT returned to Natchez since Camille's disappearance, leaving the way clear for Clement Masters, who grabbed at the opportunity to install himself at Magnolia. He capitalized on Jacqueline's grief over the loss of her sister and her helplessness. He relished the role he usurped as master of

Magnolia, but it did not take him long to see that it would not be enough. He quickly arranged his marriage to Jacqueline, thus gaining the privileges Charles enjoyed, or so he told himself.

Though gossip among the townspeople was as disapproving as the loyal servants' of Magnolia, none could stop the very determined little preacher. Jacqueline seemed in a total daze and, as usual, went along with his every desire. Soon after their hasty wedding, he pulled field hands from their regular duties to work on his pet project, clearing land for the racetrack he coveted. He couldn't wait for it to be done, so that he might have races whenever he wanted—even on the Sabbath, if he chose.

A search party had been mounted after Camille's disappearance became known, and the men of Natchez had looked long and tirelessly for her. But after some time had passed, Clement Masters had insidiously planted false bits of information about town indicating that Camille had gone willingly—enough to arouse some doubt among even the most loyal of her friends.

If she did not wish to be found, she would not thank them for pursuing their search. This, added to an extensive search that had turned up not a single lead was enough to put an end to their efforts to find her.

"Your dear sister will *never* be found, Mrs. Masters," Clement sneered at his bride. "She is gone for good and Magnolia is *mine*!" He was oblivious to Jacqueline's pain, and thought only of his own gratifications. When she started to protest, he silenced her with a raised hand.

"No, I will hear no more of her! Do you understand? Your sniveling is getting on my nerves. It shall be as though she lay dead and buried. We are free to live as we please and enjoy those comforts denied to us for so long.'' His voice softened, and he put an arm around her, rubbing her shoulder and stroking down her arm, consciously gentling her with his touch, bringing her around to his way of thinking.

Jacqueline trembled and he pulled her closer, settling her on the sofa beside him. ''Dear Jacqueline,'' he intoned over and over, as his finger traced across the fine skin of her cheekbones, her arched brows, the outline of her quivering lips. Soon his fingers touched her earlobe and designed a circle on the sensitive skin around her ear. Her eyes were closed and her breathing labored as he continued his calculated assault on her senses. Oh, yes, he could be convincing when he chose to be. But that was not what his ''dear Jacqueline'' preferred, as he well knew.

With a sadistic smile of pleasure, he watched her as fingers curled into her hair and pulled hard. Her eyes flew open wide, dark with passion mingled with fear, and his mouth clamped down on hers, hurting her, his teeth biting into her lip, drawing blood. With a murmur of satisfaction, he licked away the blood and plunged his tongue into the soft cavern of her mouth. His grip on her hair had not loosened, as he held her head still. His mouth slipped from her lips to her ear, where his tongue slid in and out in an evocative rhythm that brought an answering moan from her. His hand slid inside her dress and squeezed her breast mercilessly, but she did not cry out.

Instead she writhed beneath him, begging, demanding for more of his harsh treatment that so excited her. Unmindful of the doors open to the center hallway and of their exposed condition in the parlor, they quickly discarded their clothing and came together on the floor. His thin, white body covered hers and he rode her fiercely to their shuddering, mutual climax.

Then, shaking her off as something troublesome, he rose to his feet and began methodically putting his clothes back on, as though nothing had happened between them. Without a parting word for her, he strode from the room and she heard him imperiously demanding for his horse to be brought around.

Jacqueline huddled there until he had gone, then scurried about, gathering up her own scattered clothing. Clutching them to her, but without bothering to put them on, she fled up the stairs to her room.

Clement Masters galloped off for his appointment. He was late already.

THE SHEER OVERWHELMING NUMBERS of the Northern army necessitated the formation of small, colorful bands of raiders, men sanctioned by the Confederacy though not actually recruits, who roamed freely doing their best to create as much havoc as possible among Federal troops. These men risked their lives repeatedly in bold strikes against supply and communication lines, dynamiting strategic railroad bridges and interrupting movement of matériel toward the front lines with whatever means available to them. They also acted as carriers of vital information and intercepted communiqués from the enemy whenever possible.

The leader of one such group conducting raids in the far western theater of the war was Charles Louis Longmont, who had been awarded the commission of colonel for his "unique service" to the Confederacy. Charles had personally instigated plans for such a group to operate along the Natchez Trace and had petitioned General Robert E. Lee for approval in the very early days of the war. His endeavor was sanctioned privately by the Confederacy, but was to remain highly secretive.

The brave men chosen by him were incomparable horsemen and, for the most part, plantation owners who were excellent marksmen from their days spent hunting game. They lived as civilians, but at regular intervals met to carry out strategic raids invaluable to the Southern army. It was a way of life that could be exciting and even immensely profitable, but to Charles and his men, it was an inescapable duty, their way of serving their country.

They followed the conflict across the land, watching for opportunities to harry the adversary, making life so unsafe the Northern army was forced to move for the most part only in large companies.

One final raid remained on their latest lengthy excursion before they would allow themselves a brief visit home. Dressed in their usual dark clothing, Charles and four others stealthily poled a small raft across the Tennessee river. On the far bank, Yankee sentinels trod back and forth on their lonely watches. An occasional voiced salute drifted across the murky, silent waters, joining the night noises of singing frogs and locusts.

The men on the raft used hand signals, fearing even the slightest whisper might be heard and alert the sentries. Their mission was twofold: first, to circumvent the patrols and come upon the sleeping Yanks unobserved, causing the utmost confusion and panic; then they would skirmish with them, taking out as many as they could, but more importantly, confiscating a corral full of prime horseflesh needed so badly by their own cavalry.

They slid noiselessly up on the sandy bank and abandoned the raft, swiftly making their way in the prearranged direction, two to the left, three to the right. Without a sound, they surrounded the enemy, who remained undisturbed, most of them sleeping soundly.

Through the dim light of a sliver of moon, Charles spied the rough planks of the hastily constructed corral and the outline of the restless horses. Soundlessly, he crept toward the gate. He placed one hand carefully on the length of rope that held it closed. His fingers worked to loosen it. Suddenly, he stopped what he was doing and froze, the hair on his neck standing up in alarm.

A voice spoke from the darkness, a cultured voice and with a definite Yankee accent! Had he been discovered? If so, he would probably die as a traitor or rot away in a Yankee prison. His throat dry at the thought and his pulse beating more quickly than normal, he waited. He would do nothing to give either himself or his position away. If someone had spotted him, it would be up to them to make the first move.

His mind flew to his companions and what each would be doing at that moment. He was certain their careful plan was being efficiently carried out. It allowed no room for mistakes in judgment or execution.

Had he made a mistake? Had he done something to signal his presence in the Yankee camp? God, how could he bear it if an ill-timed action of his should bring defeat to their mission and perhaps death to his dedicated band of men?

His hand still poised on the rope, Charles reassured himself he had done everything exactly as planned and without the slightest noise. No, the fault did not rest with him.

An answering casual remark from nearby eased his escalating tension. It had been only a late-night game of cards ending, its participants heading for their tents and bed.

He stayed his hand until all sounds of their departure had died away and then made quick work of untying the knot and freeing the gate. It could now be opened with the slightest pressure.

Turning his attention to the quiet camp, he drew his gun from its leather sheath, feeling the cold steel against his palm. He would never become accustomed to taking another human life, but he did what his conscience required of him skillfully and efficiently. He was a crack shot and rarely missed a target, even a moving one, or perhaps especially a moving one. Soldiers in combat were in that regard like the wild animals he'd hunted—generally moving rapidly in evasion, self-defense or attack.

Their signal echoed through the night and Charles's voice joined the others in the wild and eerie rebel yell as they swooped into the camp. Curses and screams filled the air as men struggled from their beds, grabbed feverishly for their weapons and scattered, firing as they ran. Stampeding horses added to the building confusion and noise as they plunged toward the river.

The element of surprise combined with the noise and repeated firing from all sections of the camp gave the impression of an invading force much larger than it actually was. The Yanks fought at a disadvantage, but nevertheless fiercely for some time before they began slipping away into the cover of the surrounding trees, leaving behind supplies that would be heartily welcomed by Confederate troops.

Charles stood in the middle of the camp, waiting for his men to gather and hoping against hope they had all survived. One by one, they came forward, their arms full of medicines, ammunition, foodstuffs; wide smiles on their faces, happy with themselves and their successful mission.

"Well done, men," Charles commented, his quiet words of praise of obvious importance to them all. "Now, let's go home!" This was greeted with a loud "Hurrah!" for it had been long months since they had seen their loved ones, and they were anxious to do so.

Making fast work of it, they rounded up the horses, commandeered a wagon, and loaded it with everything they could scavenge. As two of the men drove the wagon away in the direction of their front lines, the rest sent along with it a prayer for the sick, hungry, poorly armed soldiers the supplies were meant to assist.

Once more they poled across the river, this time with no attempt to be quiet, but singing "Dixie" at the top of their voices. They retrieved their own mounts, hobbled at various spots in the woods and regrouped, galloping into the night toward Mississippi and home!

Chapter Fifteen
MAY-JUNE, 1862

THE LONG DAYS Camille spent as a prisoner in her deceptively comfortable cell had settled into an uneasy routine. On a calendar provided in her writing desk, she marked the time, hoping, longing, for Charles to come for her. But day followed weary day, and still he did not come.

Each morning, the New Orleans *True Delta* was delivered to her with breakfast and she was able to follow the progress of the war. Encouraging was news that General Robert E. Lee had assumed command of the Army of Northern Virginia. He was highly respected and the majority of Southerners pinned their hopes for the outcome of the war on his good sense and leadership and the brilliance of his tactical knowledge. Some few days after that, Jeb Stuart had completed his daring and flamboyant ride around McClellan's entire army, thumbing his nose at the Yankees, and the South had loved it—and him.

New Orleans had fallen to Northern occupation in April, after David Farragut and his Union fleet had successfully run the guns of Fort Jackson and St. Philip. The forts had surrendered following the fall of the city, and soon afterward, General Benjamin Butler moved in to set up a hated and corrupt administration.

Citizens chafed under the grip of this fanatical Northerner who delighted in their sufferings and sought to punish them for their audacity in standing up for their rights. He was roundly denounced by his countrymen for his insufferable General Order Number 28, the infamous "Woman Order." Outraged by the behavior of Southern women toward the occupying force, he declared that "when any female shall, by word, gesture, or movement, insult or show contempt for any officer or soldier of the United States, she shall be regarded and held liable to be treated as a woman of the town plying her vocation." Any local woman could be arrested and held overnight, treated as a common prostitute, on the complaint of any Yankee soldier!

Prostitutes resented the law as much as the more respectable ladies, and posted Butler's picture on the bottom of their chamber pots. When he discovered this defiance, the general had some of the offensive pots confiscated and personally smashed them.

With women no longer safe in the streets, Camille wondered how she would make her way through the city, even if she were able to escape the clutches of the man who held her locked away in his home.

Raphael Montaigne, her Creole captor, had revealed to her that his obsession with her had begun when she and Charles had honeymooned in the city, saying, "When I saw you, I knew I must have you, *chérie*."

"But surely you must have realized that I belonged to another?"

"Of little matter." He waved his hand as though her marital ties were a pesky fly, easily brushed away.

"Not to me, certainly," she'd said softly.

"So I see. But that will change. I am a patient man."

"How do you propose to accomplish such a feat?" she'd asked with some trepidation, aware of the power he could wield with his eyes and his voice.

"Ah, you shall see, *ma petite*. You shall soon see."

Her heart fluttered wildly when his finger stroked down her cheek, his black eyes holding hers an unwilling captive.

With a shudder, she stood and deliberately turned her back to him. "No, you are the one who shall soon see, sir. My husband will come for me! I know it!" But her voice trembled, revealing her hidden doubts. Would Charles really ever find her and come for her, or was she destined to live out her days as this man's plaything, to be toyed with by his magnetic eyes?

She paced the room in agitation, her head up, but still not daring to look at him, as he sat with impervious calm, his eyes following her appreciatively, admiring her spunk as well as her incomparable beauty.

"Come, *chérie*. You have spoiled our lovely dinner. You are mine now." His voice hardened with purpose. "I will never let you go. Your dear *mari* perhaps may come...." His tone of voice indicated he found that doubtful. "But even should he attempt to rescue you, it would be to no avail. And he would most certainly risk his own *dear* life in the process. Do you not see? There is no way out of here for you. You must resign yourself to your fate, which shall, perhaps, not be *très terrible, n'est-ce pas?*"

He had come up behind her silently, and his hands gripped her shoulders, abruptly putting an end to her restless pacing. Though his touch was light, there was domination in the caress, and she felt shock waves again darting through her, weakening her knees.

Camille did not resist when he pulled her back, supporting her trembling body against the sinewy power of his own. Her head reeled and, though she fought the waves of dizziness that rushed over her, she seemed to have no control. Blackness clutched at her and, fainting, she slumped in his firm embrace.

With a muttered curse, he swept her up in his arms and stood holding her for a moment, his eyes trailing from her beautiful, innocent face to the soft voluptuous curves of her body he carried so lightly in his arms. Unconscious and helpless, she was in his power as she might never be otherwise. She was a vixen and a fighter, and would not easily surrender. He knew that, and exulted in the knowledge.

With a satisfied smile, he walked over to the bed and snatched back the delicate lace coverlet. Gently he laid her down. She would be his soon, and willingly, he assured himself while he stared down at her. And it would be forever.

Seating himself on the edge of the bed beside her, he tenderly bathed her face with a soft, damp cloth and as she began to stir, lifted a cup of cool water to her lips.

She sipped, her eyes wide, deep in thought. Finally she said quietly, "I've never fainted before."

"I expected so," he replied, setting aside the cup and the cloth. "Perhaps there is reason for your 'indisposition'?" His black brow arched inquisitively. "Could it be there is some 'secret' you have not shared with me? I would know all, *chérie*." His voice tightened as he spoke, and she saw the hard intent in his all-knowing eyes. It would not be wise to try to hide anything from him, but what he was talking about she hadn't the slightest idea.

She had no "indisposition," at least none she was aware of. Of course, she had been violently sick on the boat, but surely with just cause. As she thought back over the days of her confinement, however, she remembered fighting a losing battle with a queasy stomach on more than one occasion. And she had truly never fainted before today. Had she contracted some dread disease aboard the boat that had brought her to New Orleans?

Her deep blue eyes widened with concern and flew to his face. He still regarded her closely, alert for any hint of subterfuge. Was it possible, then, she didn't know? True, she was still young and recently wed. He decided there was no duplicity in her eyes, only fear aroused by his questioning and her puzzling symptoms.

"Then I shall, I suppose, be the bearer of tidings— be they good or bad, that is for you to decide. My *chère petite*, it would seem that you are in what is commonly known as the 'family way'."

Camille's mouth opened to protest the shocking announcement and snapped shut. It *was* possible! she realized with a bubbling of joy deep within her. And she had not even suspected. What marvelous news! Charles would be so delighted, and he would make such a good father. Oh, Charles! she thought, as despair brought quick tears to her eyes at the thought that he didn't know, might never know—about their child!

Her eyes sought those of her captor and held them. What did he plan for her? Was he angry she was expecting Charles's child? What would he do about it? Protectively, she placed her hand on her stomach.

"I shall have my baby, and I shall take it home to its father and Magnolia." Her voice was resolute, determined.

He smiled, flashing brilliant white teeth, their perfection marred by a small gap in front. "Of course, you shall have the baby and who is to stop you, *ma chérie*? But as to the second part, that I very much doubt. No, it shall never be allowed. You *and* the child will be mine."

"And you will keep us both under lock and key in this room forever, I presume?" she challenged.

"No," he said thoughtfully, "I have other plans, long-range plans that will involve an eventual change of scenery for you—for all of us. But for now, I must apologize, this is the best I can offer."

"You can't keep me here!" she shouted, her anger rising with each passing minute. "I will find a way out! Just you wait and—"

Her words were cut off by the uncanny power of his gaze. Again, as on her first day there, he soothed and gentled her with a look as powerful as a loved one's touch. This inescapable magnetism seemed at his disposal to call upon whenever he wished. She had no defenses against it, and felt all the emotion drain from her.

"Now, you must lie back, *chérie*, and rest. I will send Monique with something to make you more comfortable, and we will discuss this another time."

Her eyes fluttered shut at his soft command, and the rapid beating of her heart steadied. She was sleeping before he silently left the room.

He had left the house immediately, more disturbed than he'd allowed her to see by her condition, and its associated problems. It might, indeed, it would cause a complete change of his plans.

"To Old Absinthe Room!" he shouted to his coachman, climbing into the carriage. Built in 1806 by two Spaniards, it was a place where he frequently went for an evening of drinking, occasionally mixed with business. Tonight he planned to concentrate on serious drinking, to try to forget the bewitching innocence of those blue eyes and the unconscious sensuality of her slender body.

Camille Braxton Beaufort Longmont had haunted his days and nights since he'd first seen her on the arm of her husband, strolling the streets of the French Quarter where he owned three city blocks of shops and rooming houses, as well as a large warehouse on the waterfront. Camille had purchased items in several of his shops, and it had been a simple matter to reconstruct a wardrobe for her with information gleaned from salesclerks in his employ.

He had followed the happy couple back to Natchez where he had a fortuitous meeting with Clement Masters. The two men found they had a mutual interest in the young woman, and had worked out a deal to benefit them both. Satisfied, Raphael had returned to New Orleans to wait.

Every waking moment since that day had been spent in preparation for making Camille his. Now he had her within his grasp, only to find she was to have another man's child!

He could, he knew, secure a voodoo potion and do away with the unborn child, but for some reason as yet unclear to him, he found he was unable or unwilling to do so.

He would allow her to have the baby. Since he would never father a child of his own, he saw no problem in simply claiming the child and raising it as his own. Not in New Orleans, of course, but somewhere far from there. He knew just the place!

Seated at his usual table alone, he sat swirling the absinthe in his glass. The strong liqueur made from wormwood was one of his favorites, but he knew it would take several to loosen the coils of his nerves this night.

On his third, he glanced toward the door to see a man enter the establishment, his serious brown eyes sweeping over the regulars scattered throughout the room. For a second, they exchanged a look and then a nod of restrained greeting. It was Charles Longmont!

Revealing nothing of his recognition, and secure in the knowledge Charles did not know him, Montaigne turned his attention back to the brilliant emerald liquid in his glass. Charles was never out of his sight, though, as he made his way around the room, stopping at each table, questioning any who would speak to him.

The men in the room were all acquaintances of Raphael; some were his business partners, and he felt sure they would reveal nothing. But should the man continue to question and search in this part of the Vieux Carré, he might stumble across something that would lead him to his wife.

How had Longmont managed to have gotten this close, this soon? He must have elicited information from someone—the riverboat captain? Somehow, he thought not. The greedy little preacher, so anxious to take over the Beaufort fortune? Perhaps. And if you have let slip a word, even the slightest clue, *Reverend*

Masters, you are doomed! he thought, slamming down a coin and making his way out the door without returning a single greeting.

The night air did not cool the heat of his growing anger. He strode along, rattling the *banquettes*, the fierce brooding look on his face enough to clear the way for him. No one who was abroad this night wished to tangle with him. He headed for the waterfront.

CAMILLE PICKED UP the silver-backed brush from the dressing table and absently brushed her fine hair, tangled after a good night's sleep. She had slept soundly thanks to the *tisane* potion brought to her by Monique.

This morning, she felt rejuvenated, with no trace of yesterday's illness or dizzy spells. The awesome knowledge that she carried a new life born of the love she and Charles had shared was an exquisite pleasure, marred only by the fact that he was not here to share in it. How proud he would be! And his eyes would sparkle with happiness, crinkling at the corners in that endearing way she loved. Just the thought of that smile warmed her, bringing bright color to her pale face. If only she could see him, be held by him, be loved by him!

Raphael had not returned last night, or so she'd been told, and would be out of the city for several days. Her pulse quickened as she realized this might be her chance to escape. There had to be a way out of here, and she would find it! She had to do it—for herself, and for the child she carried. She would use the long hours of the day stretching before her to form a plan and then, under cover of darkness, she would carry it out.

Camille sat on the *meridiènne* with her feet tucked under her, sipping *café au lait*, the rich coffee liberally laced with cream she enjoyed each morning. The apple-green satin of her dress was a bright contrast to the rich crimson color of the linen-covered daybed, part of a parlor set that occupied one large area of her spacious prison. Her arm lay along the curved back of smooth mahogany as she considered her predicament.

She saw the futility of trying to escape from this elegantly furnished room, where every precaution had been taken to assure the failure of such an attempt. The window was much too high and small to be of use, at any rate, and there was no other way out except for the heavy, triple-locked door.

Her only hope lay in her ability to persuade one of the servants that their master intended she continue her walks in the courtyard even in his absence. Then, a distraction of some kind would be necessary to divert the ever-present guard, and she could climb over the lowest portion of the wall and be off! It seemed ridiculously simple as she thought of it. By this time tomorrow, she would be on her way home!

After she was out of the courtyard, she would make her way to the waterfront, and somehow convince one of the riverboat captains he would be well paid if he could wait for his money until they reached their destination at Natchez.

Prowling through the magnificent wardrobe provided for her, she first decided on a dark riding habit, gloves and boots. Though she couldn't imagine why they'd been included, they would be perfect for the night's adventure.

As the afternoon waned, however, she began to doubt the wisdom of her choice of clothing. The servants would be suspicious of such a costume, and that foolish idea would surely bring a swift end to her escape attempt. No, one of the plainer walking dresses, such as the dark burgundy, would be more sensible for a stroll in the gardens. It would have to do for climbing over walls and running through the streets as well!

Carefully, Camille dressed for dinner, pulling her hair back into a bun. The absence of her host and her escalating tension made the dinner hour seem maddeningly long.

"Monique," she addressed the servant who came to clear the dishes, "I'll be ready for my evening walk soon. Please ask one of the menservants to escort me." She kept her eyes averted while she tried to make her request seem a casual, expected one. Did she imagine the girl's hesitation before she made an affirmative reply and departed?

Minutes crept by while she waited to see if her request would be honored or ignored. She paced. She talked to herself. She worried.

At the sound of a key in the first of the set of locks, she held her breath, waiting anxiously, almost afraid to hope. What if it was *him*? If he had returned, she knew she had not a prayer. All would be lost.

But as the door swung open, she barely disguised a sigh of relief. It was only one of the servants, and she was glad to see it was not the big brute of a man who usually escorted her to the courtyard and kept watch at the door to his master's suite of rooms. That one must have gone with Raphael. A point in her favor, surely. The load that had been weighing her down all afternoon lightened considerably. It might just work!

With buoyant steps, and already light-headed with the taste of freedom, she followed him down the twisting stairway. It would soon be over and, like a bad dream, could be pushed to the back of her mind and forgotten with the passing of time.

Strolling the paths of the courtyard alone, she decided she would fake a sudden attack of illness, hoping her guard would go for help, leaving her a few precious minutes of solitude. But she knew the plan was risky. Either he might refuse to go altogether, or he might return before she could scramble over the fence, catching her in the act.

Just then, she heard the muffled tramping of many feet, accompanied by a musical sound of horns, noisemakers, and whistles. She stood on tiptoe and in a few short moments, she glimpsed the glowing flambeaux, tall torches that accompanied carnival floats, lighting their way! A parade!

It was not the Mardi Gras season and parades had practically ceased because of the war, but New Orleanians, particularly Creoles, loved festivals and used any excuse for a parade. They would have their parade and dare General Butler to do anything about it.

Surreptitiously she glanced toward the man who watched her from the perimeter of the courtyard. He had heard the sounds also, and his expression indicated his obvious interest.

"I think I'll just watch from here," she called to reassure him as she climbed onto a nearby bench, though all she could see were the tops of the torches and the very tallest of the floats.

He seemed pacified, however, and turned his head to answer a call from inside. She scarcely dared to breathe and barely inclined her head so she could see where he stood from the corner of her eye. He was gone!

Perhaps only for seconds, but it was her chance, and if she didn't take it, there might not be another! Gathering her skirts in her hands, she jumped down from the bench on which she stood and bolted for the corner of the garden where the fence was the lowest. Her feet flew across the brick-paved walk. Hoping it might conceal her briefly should he return, she dodged behind a tree as she made a grab for the cracked concrete at the top of the wall.

She reached for the hem of her skirt and hiked it up, tucking it under the belt at her waist. Finding a toehold in a wide crack, she kicked herself up until she precariously straddled the fence. The increasing shadows of the night shielded her from the sight of the revelers drawing near on the street.

With one final thrust, she pulled her other leg over and dropped to the ground, hastily releasing her skirts to a more modest length. A glance around the corner revealed her guard and the other servants gathered on the front porch to watch the parade. She was suddenly very glad for the Creole love of festivities, but she could not move for fear they would spot her immediately.

As the spectators and participants moved steadily toward her, they overflowed the streets and the *banquettes*, spilling into the yard, and giving her a perfect shield. Stepping into the shouting, happy crowd, she was quickly swallowed up, her escape neatly covered.

For several blocks, she remained a part of the boisterous crowd, being propelled along by their momentum. Torches danced merrily over their heads, illuminating awesome masks in vivid hues of reds, blacks, yellows and whites. There was a mad scramble along the way for the beads and doubloons tossed out in response to cries of "Throw me something, Mis-

ter!'' from the crowd. Camille clasped some of the
beads in her hand for luck as she walked quickly along,
trying to think what to do next.

Finally she decided her best course was to stay with
the parade until she was as far away from that house as
possible. By the time they discovered her missing, and
realized what she must have done, it would be too late
for them to find her.

As soon as the parade reached the busiest part of the
Vieux Carré, she turned away, and hastened down one
of the side streets toward the river. She picked her way
along crude *banquettes*, trying to ignore the sickening
stench of garbage and refuse in the ditches that ran
alongside. Doors stood open to a variety of rowdy bars
and gambling establishments, noises and aromas
flowing out unhampered, swirling about her. She had
only been in the French Quarter one time, and that
during the day. At night it was very different, both
amazing and alarming! In her dark clothing, she did
her best to melt into the shadows.

Nothing looked familiar as she walked the narrow
streets. She made several wrong turns, before at last
she was rewarded by the sight of tall masts, and the
mixed notes of foghorns. The river was up ahead!

Having not paid much attention before, she was
truly astonished by the multitude of boats docked on
the far side of the levee. In places, they were five or six
deep. There were flatboats and steamboats from
upriver, and from faraway places, sloops, schooners,
and streamlined clipper ships.

But what was she to do? The only thing she *could* do
was try to find a convenient gangplank on a boat that
looked promising, go boldly aboard and request passage. But first she would see if there were any boats she

recognized, for she was familiar with the *Natchez*, the *Princess*, and one or two others that made regular runs up and down the river past Natchez.

Though there were any number of imposing paddle wheelers, she was not acquainted with any of them or their captains. Should she wait until morning, when her appearance and request might seem a little less startling? It would probably be best, but that would leave the urgent problem of where she could safely pass the night.

Looking around in the darkness, she could not think of a single solution to that dilemma. There were no respectable boarding houses or hotels where she might seek a night's lodging; besides, she had no money. No, she would have to board one of the boats, and soon. Though she tried to be inconspicuous and keep to the shadows, an occasional roustabout acknowledged her presence with a lusty whistle or a crude comment that made her flesh crawl. She could almost hear Josef say, "Ain' no place for a lady, Missy Cam." But Josef wasn't here, and she had only herself to depend on.

She hurried along the wharf, eyeing each boat at length. There were all shapes and sizes, with a wide range of cargo: some were stacked high with cotton; some she suspected still transported slaves; some brought into New Orleans the fine wines and whiskeys from across the ocean. One seemed better outfitted and brighter than the rest, and its gangplank was extended in welcome. The *North Star*, she read in fancy script on its side. Yes, it looked perfect, or at least the best she could expect on such short notice!

"Cap'n! Lady comin' aboard!" sang out the friendly tones of a crew member as she hesitantly placed a booted foot on the plank. Giving her head a haughty shake, she strode up the gentle incline with all the assurance she possessed.

Waiting to greet her at the other end was a tall, slender man wearing the uniform and insignia of a captain. Bowing formally, he extended his hand to her, "Welcome aboard the *North Star*, ma'am. Cap'n Wilkins at your service."

Nothing in his demeanor indicated surprise at her late and unannounced arrival. A real gentleman, she thought, allowing him to take her hand and assist her up the last few steps.

"To what do we owe the honor of a visit from so charming a lady as yourself?" In the dim light she could not make out the features of his face, nor see his eyes clearly beneath the brim of his hat, but his voice reassured her that all was well, and her choice a good one.

"I am Camille Beaufort Longmont of Natchez, Captain Wilkins. I have been in this city not by my own choice, but as a result of the most unpleasant circumstances." She would not elaborate unless necessary. "And now I intend to make my way home to Natchez and in the speediest way possible."

"At your service, ma'am."

"Do not answer yet, sir, for you've not heard the whole story. It seems I'm embarrassed by a temporary insufficiency of funds. But I do assure you that you will be amply rewarded for your trouble by my husband when we dock at Natchez."

"This is rather unusual, Mrs. Longmont. But I think we may be able to be of service. I do have a nice berth available that will satisfy your needs, I feel certain. If you'll follow me, please?"

Tears of gratitude in her eyes, Camille followed him down a stairway and then a long, narrow hall. On the far end, he indicated a room on their left, and threw open the door for her. He pointed out several things for her comfort, and left her alone, closing the door firmly when he went out. She had not seen the look of malicious intent on his face, nor did she know he had hastily gone ashore and vanished into the night soon after leaving her.

CHARLES CROUCHED in the bushes and stared at the massive, fenced house. She was in there! He knew it as well as he knew her name—Camille Braxton Beaufort Longmont—his wife! But was she a captive, or had she come to New Orleans of her own free will, as he'd been led to believe? He had to find out before he could put to rest the demons of doubt that had plagued him since he'd learned of her disappearance and begun his search for her.

He remembered every small detail of his return from the horse-stealing raid, when he had first discovered that Camille had been kidnapped. Striding through the front door of Magnolia, his mind happily planning a reunion with his wife, he'd known immediately that something was dreadfully wrong. Flowers he'd brought her were strewn across the marbled entryway where he dropped them in his anxiety, striding from room to room, calling her name, demanding to know what was wrong. "Damn it!" he called out. "Where is everybody?"

She was not in the house. Something terrible had happened. His premonition of disaster on the long ride home had been real. Camille was gone!

He charged up the stairway and snatched open the door to the bedroom they'd shared, intent on finding some clue to her whereabouts, or the reason for her unexplained absence. A blind fury engulfed him at the sight of Clement Masters ensconced in the huge, high bed he'd shared with his wife. Each heavy, booted footstep reverberated as he deliberately marched to the bed and bodily lifted the near-naked preacher, dumping him unceremoniously on the floor.

He cast a pitying glance at Jacqueline, who shivered alone in the bed, a sheet clutched to her chin. Then his black gaze fastened on the miserable creature pulling himself to his feet.

Charles demanded, "Where is she?" his voice a hard, cutting blade of honed steel. Violence vibrated through him and only his need for information kept his hands at his sides when they twitched with the burning need to fasten themselves to the bony neck and squeeze the life from the man.

Cadaverous, his bones thrusting from beneath thin, blue-veined skin, Clement Masters withered under Charles's murderous gaze. His small eyes darted about the room as though seeking a way out or a weapon with which to defend himself.

Then it occurred to him that his cunning, as always, was the most powerful weapon he had. He would con his way out of this death trap and in the process point fingers of doubt at the ever-perfect lady, his dear sister-in-law. For the long months of Charles's absence, he had carefully worked out the details of his fabricated story. Others in the tightly knit community had at last come to accept it, and he was convinced her husband, masculine pride wounded irrevocably, would buy it, as well.

"She's gone," he spit out, glad to see the look of pain on the handsome face of Camille's husband as hearing the words spoken aloud confirmed his worst fears.

A look of implacable purpose replaced the fleeting vulnerability and Charles demanded, "Where!"

"Well, if the young woman had wanted you to know that, I presume she would have told you, or at least left you a message, some word of her whereabouts. Course her not knowing when—or if—you'd ever return, mayhap she just thought it was no use."

The preacher took a step backward; his gut tightening to see the corded muscles flexing in Charles's strong arms, his fists clenching and unclenching in an unspoken but very real threat.

"Liar!" Charles bit out the word and there was no apology, no backing down in his expression. He waited for Masters to call him out, the gentlemanly response to such a direct challenge to a man's honor.

But Masters continued slowly backing toward the door, shaking fingers pulling his black coat about his emaciated frame, unable to fasten the buttons.

"No! It's all true. Ask anybody—she just took off. Packed a few bags and left. But she didn't go alone, nosirree! With my own eyes, I seen her go, like it was all a lark, a picnic to her. Did she say a word of good-bye, to me, to anyone? Hah! She never even looked in my direction. Hah! Hah! But she never looked in yours, either, did she, Mr. High and Mighty?"

Charles swung toward Jacqueline, who had crept from the bed and slipped into her robe. "Jacqueline." He spoke softly, but it was clear he would brook no half-truths or diversions. "Where is your sister?"

"Charles... I—I honestly don't know. She never said goodbye, just like Clement said. She was just gone. The men from town looked for her, but there was no sign of her, nothing at all. That was when the rumors started.... Finally, they—we—all gave up." Nervously she chewed at her bottom lip, her eyes darting to Masters, who threw her a scathing glance.

"What rumors?" Charles's blood had turned to ice. Camille had been gone for so long her trail would be cold now and almost impossible to follow. Of course, he would never believe the gross lie that she'd left willingly. Still, he repeated, "What rumors?" He had to know everything.

The sniveling voice of Clement Masters drew his attention back to where the man stood silhouetted in the doorway. "After we discovered her things missing, I started to ask around. Surprising what you can find out with a word here, a word there. But soon, I was able to put the whole story together, yessirree, I was quick to get it all figured out." He looked ridiculously pleased with himself, and Charles had to bite back a bitter retort and let him continue his bizarre tale.

Clement eyed him closely before going on, "Seems there was this good-looking stranger come to town, and she took up with him right away. Later, I heard the two was real friendly back in Baltimore and he come all the way out here to find her. Now ain't that romantic? And, though I couldn't say for certain, I think word might have reached her delicate ears that Justine Blanchette's sudden disappearance was connected to your own!"

Charles lunged for him, but before he could reach him to give him the beating he deserved, the little man had made his escape. Deciding it would be a waste of precious time to pursue him down the stairs, he turned back to Camille's sister. The confirmation of everything the preacher had claimed was evident in her eyes, filled with pity for him!

Was it possible Camille had left willingly? She had certainly been given good reason to doubt his Southern loyalties, but worse than that, to doubt his faithfulness to her, or so the preacher had sworn. Though Clement Masters's cleverly concocted story seemed plausible, Charles was beckoned by the haunting memory of her silken touch and the loving glimmer in her midnight-blue eyes, which drew him helplessly after her, regardless of the circumstances of her disappearance.

Like a man possessed, he searched for her endlessly, up and down the Mississippi, in every town, every shanty, every cave. In his worst nightmares, he heard her cry out for him, pleading for his help. All anyone seemed to know was that she had been taken aboard a river vessel. Charles had spent a small fortune in bribes to the rough men who plied their trade on the water before he discovered one small lead. A young man, who claimed he'd tried to locate Charles for some time, told him in apologetic tones that Camille was being held in New Orleans, but swore that was all he knew.

Charles's anger had flared to think the man possessed such knowledge and yet had done nothing to rescue her, and he shook him roughly, swearing to thrash him soundly if he ever showed himself around Natchez again.

With the help of his band of raiders, Charles swept through the city of New Orleans, leaving a trail of broken chairs, black eyes, and a few contented smiles of those they were able to bribe, before they found the information that had led him to this place—the right place!

As he watched from across the street, Charles knew he must make careful plans before he made a move. On his visit to Old Absinthe Room the previous night, he had unearthed some provocative information. Several more bars, and a score of bold lies led him eventually to one name. Raphael Montaigne! It took him a little longer to investigate the strange tale of a mysterious young woman who lived with the influential Creole. Several hundred dollars had revealed the address of this house, a virtual fortress, with its air of seclusion, high fences and formidable menservants.

His mind was in a turmoil as he struggled to come to a decision. He had no fear for himself, but he would die if any harm should come to Camille because of his own rash actions.

While he watched, a tall man in a black cloak alighted from a carriage and made his way inside the house. It was the Creole!

Chapter Sixteen

CAMILLE HAD NO IDEA of the hour of the night when there came a loud knocking on her cabin door. Though she was still fully clothed in the rumpled burgundy dress, she had dozed off and was not mentally alert as she opened to the summons. Mistakenly she had assumed it would be the captain.

A gracious smile froze on her lips as she recognized the dark face of the last person she expected to see. Raphael!

Had he been the devil himself, he could not have inspired more fear in her. Belatedly, she tried to slam the door she'd so carelessly opened to him, but his flat palm slapped against it, his strength easily overpowering her. The door flew back, slamming against the wall. She fled to the far side of the small room, terrified, trembling in the worst fear she'd ever known. She could not bring herself to look in his direction.

The door closed with a thud, and the latch dropped into place. He did not move toward her. He did not speak. He stood aloof, silent, as he had been in the carriage the first night she'd seen him. The awful tension multiplied in his grim silence until it became unbearable, but still he did nothing to relieve it. He had anticipated her fear, and he toyed with it, apparently willing to use it to his own purposes. She sensed that he was actually pleased she'd run away and brought about this confrontation, though underneath that pleasure lay the bedrock of his implacable fury.

All of this she knew before a word was spoken between them, and before she managed to raise her eyes to his by sheer force of will. His black eyes were the dull cast iron of a Creole skillet and revealed nothing. Gone was the magic spell he could so easily weave around her.

His soft voice when he finally spoke had the effect of a whip lashing through the stillness. "We shall go home, *non*?" His enchantments were not necessary to convince her of the wisdom of obedience. Camille did not answer, but, squaring her shoulders and looking past him, she walked toward the door.

The carriage ride back was infinitely longer than the first one she'd made over the same route with him. As before, it was a completely silent journey. This time, however, her active mind played out several possible scenarios that might follow, each more horrible than the last.

As they entered his home she was not surprised when his hand fastened on her arm inescapably. He steered her not to her third-floor prison, but to his own quarters on the main floor. Her heart skidded almost to a stop, though her reluctant feet continued to move, her steps ringing on the tiled floors.

They were met by no one in the long central hallway. The whole house seemed empty, devoid of life. Inside his spacious apartment, the only light was provided by candles flickering in wall sconces. Camille noticed nothing else, not even the chair where he deposited her, none too gently, before turning his back to her. She heard the clink of glass on glass as he poured himself some wine. He turned and held a glass out to her. Wisely, she drank it without protest, but slowly.

Camille watched fearfully as Raphael tossed down glass after glass. As he drank, he paced and loosened his collar, shrugged out of his coat and tossed it onto the bed. Finally he began unbuttoning his shirt, stopped pacing and stood in front of her.

Now the reflected light of the candles burned in his eyes, and his fiery gaze moved over her as she tried to disguise the full extent of her terror. Sensing her futile efforts, he smiled. Then the hypnotic power of his ebony eyes held her captive while they soothed away her trembling anxiety, bit by bit.

"You should not have attempted such a foolish, foolish thing, *ma petite*. A *faux pas*, was it not? I had presumed you were much too intelligent for such games."

"It was no game!" She had found her voice and though his charismatic spell still spun its way around her will like the iridescent web of a giant spider, she found the strength to challenge him. "I intended to leave here and never come back. And my intentions have not changed." This time she fought his mental domination though her insides quivered from the conflict.

"But surely they will." He spoke as if there were no question of it and he seemed so unshakably certain that her resolve faltered. Would it be so much easier, then, if she gave in, surrendered to his overwhelming power? He had promised her a life of wealth and ease in the distant West Indies. She knew he would pamper her and provide for her every wish if she gave in to him. It was appealing and, suddenly, almost irresistible.

Her hand fell to her lap and brushed her stomach. A quiver darted through her as she thought of her child and that small reminder wrenched her from the trance into which she'd been falling.

"Never. I will never cease. Either I shall leave here, somehow, by myself—or Charles will come for me. Either way, you lose, Raphael."

"No, *ma chérie*, it is you who is lost."

Her smoky blue eyes widened. She jumped to her feet. "What do you mean?"

Standing very close, so close she could feel his breath when he spoke, he looked down at her, a sadistic smile curving his lips. "You chose such a bad time to run, *chérie*. Suppose you could guess who paid me an unexpected visit in your absence?"

Camille's mind spun. What was he talking about? Who could have come that she cared about? Charles! Her eyes lit up with the knowledge he still cared for her. He had followed her all the way to New Orleans and had actually found Raphael's house?

"*Oui, chérie*, your powers of deduction are astute, I see. Yes, it was your own dear Charles Longmont. Here, on my front steps only last night, not long after your departure. Tsk tsk. For him to travel all that way and find you out for the evening. How sad! *Pauvre diable!*"

He would be back! Charles had not given up; he had come for her. And he would be back! Perhaps tonight.

Hope illuminated her face, and her eyes sparkled with new life. Raphael grew more stormily angry by the moment as he studied her reaction. It would not be easy to break her free of this man's spell. Perchance, he might have to kill Longmont to accomplish it.

"It pains me so to see your happiness which must unfortunately, be snuffed out, when I tell you the rest."

Slow realization crept over her, and she sank back into the chair while he continued, "Mr. Longmont was quite persistent and insisted he be allowed to search the premises."

He paused, letting that fact sink in, and smiled to see the dawning awareness on her pretty face. Cruelty was no stranger to him, and she had made him furious by her near-successful attempt to escape.

"I showed him every room in the house, of course, and even insisted he examine my seldom-used turret." His teeth flashed in a feral grin.

Surely, she thought, Charles had been suspicious then....

As though reading her thoughts, he continued, "Oh, yes, he was suspicious at first, but I hastened to assure him, in my own convincing way, that the room was kept for my niece who visits regularly from her plantation up around Baton Rouge. When he saw all the clothing, the jewels and other personal things, it was evident he believed me. For what kidnapper prepares for a captive in such a fashion, or keeps her in so grand a style?"

"If you expect my gratitude . . ." she began.

"Oh, no, never that, *ma petite*, merely your adoration, perhaps eventually your love."

"Never!"

"Oh, then perhaps you would be interested in the rest of the story? Yes, I can see you would. I extended an offer of help to your dear husband, in whatever way I could be of service. He was convincingly apologetic and left soon after finding nothing in the servants' quarters or the stables. I'm sure we will not be troubled by him any further. But just to be certain, I had some of my men follow him until he was outside the city.''

''Raphael! You wouldn't hurt him? Please, please, leave Charles alone.''

''Perhaps we could strike a small bargain, *ma chère*?''

A bargain with Raphael would be a bargain for her soul, of that she was certain. But she had no choice. With the snap of his fingers, he could have Charles killed. He could disappear and never be heard from again. Charles! her heart cried out, what am I to do? For she knew only too well what the bargain would entail.

The sound of his laughter raised gooseflesh on her skin. She brushed past him, and walked to the window that opened onto the courtyard. ''Wh-what would you have me do?'' she asked hesitantly, sure she knew what his answer would be.

The ticking of the grandfather clock matched the heavy pounding of her heart in tone, but lagged behind in speed. The scent of roses in a vase beside her mingled with the sweet aroma of honeysuckle from outside, the combined fragrance cloying and unpleasant.

She stared into the night, lit only by a gas lamp in the street and the reflected candlelight pouring from the windows of the house that was her prison. Charles! It's not too late! You could still come back for me!

''He will never be back. My men would not allow it, would never permit him inside. They have been ordered to stop him, in whatever way is most expedient, should he be so foolish as to try.''

She whirled, picked up the cut-glass vase full of roses, the nearest thing to her hand, and hurled it at his head. Agile and forewarned by the fierce look in her eyes, Raphael sidestepped and easily avoided the blow. The glass splintered against the marble fireplace behind him, flowers scattering and water running down to puddle on the bricked hearth.

Raphael's back was to the light, casting his face in brooding shadows. Angrily he stalked toward her. His arm shot out and yanked her to him. Only when she was a prisoner in his tight embrace did she remember his half-nude body.

Her hands had fallen on his bare shoulders. In vain, she pushed, trying to break free of his grasp. The muscles in his upper arms tensed and his hold tightened about her waist, fitting her snugly to him. There was no room between them for her chest to fill with air, even if she were capable of drawing breath.

Her head tipped slightly back, she could see his wicked smile as his mouth lowered toward hers. She could not pull back, or break free, she could not even turn her head aside. Helplessly, she waited for his plunder of her lips and her body.

Surprisingly gentle, his lips brushed hers, lingered briefly, moved away. The clock pealed out three plaintive strikes.

''Our pact has been sealed, *chérie*, with the earnest of your lips.''

Had she kissed him back? Surely not, yet she knew she had not resisted. She hadn't the strength.

Once more his head dipped, and his lips claimed hers. The energy and passion of the kiss, combined with the power of his embrace sent her head reeling. Had he not swept her off her feet, she would have collapsed in a nerveless heap on the floor.

He covered the distance toward his mammoth bed with long strides. Camille's heart hammered from fear. To her surprise he sat on the edge of the thick feather mattress, cradling her in his lap.

Even in this man she had found to be without conscience and single-minded in his desires, there lay buried a small redeeming quality that made him human, at times almost likeable.

Raphael loved the way she felt in his arms and had been unexpectedly thrilled by her response. He would not tell her of Charles's vow to begin all over, to continue looking everywhere until he found his wife. His own plans for Camille would have her far removed from New Orleans before Charles's search led him back to them!

The look of utter desolation on her lovely face had almost softened him to pity, but she would get over it and one day she would care for him in that same way. The very thought made his pulses race. He would not take her by force as he'd almost done tonight, but would be patient and wait for her to come to him. Her capitulation, when it came, would be worth the wait, however long. His confidence in his power over her, and his patience, were unlimited.

Much to Camille's shock and everlasting relief, Raphael strode to the door and shouted for one of his servants. When the man arrived in his nightclothes, Raphael commanded, "Take her to her room. And be sure she's locked in."

Alone upstairs, her feeling of relief at her narrow escape from his wrath and his far more threatening ardor was soon replaced by a miserable unhappiness. Charles had come and she had not been there! Would he ever come for her again, or was it true as Raphael had said, that he'd given up and gone home? She knew how persuasive the Creole could be when he set his mind to it. Her heart sank. Charles would not be back. What more could he do? He had come and searched. He had seen the empty rooms and been convinced by Raphael's silvery words of his innocence. And even if he did come back, they might very well be gone.

SEVERAL MONTHS PASSED and Raphael made no move toward a relocation, except for a temporary trip to his plantation north of New Orleans where he took Camille for relief from the oppressively hot summer. He did not mention the fulfillment of their "contract".

Camille's first sight of La Montaigne filled her with homesickness, but she soon learned there were many differences between a sugar plantation and a cotton-producing plantation such as Magnolia, just as there were differences in his attitude toward slaves and the one she'd grown up with.

The main house lacked the majesty of Natchez plantations, but boasted a certain charm in its simple design. Long and low-slung, it was a shade of palest yellow and had balconies all the way around. A tree-lined road led to the sugar mill out back, and a thick planting of cypress trees separated the main house from the slave quarters.

The slaves lived in wooden cabins grouped around a central square that bustled with activity. The overseer, Daniel Trotter, had a cottage off to one side. On La Montaigne, he was in complete charge in the absence of the master, and used the stocks and the whip indiscriminately.

Due to the isolation of the place, and the thick alligator-infested swamps that surrounded it, Camille was given more liberty than she had been previously. Raphael placed more trust in her, and had become almost complacent, certain she wouldn't try to run away, or perhaps assured she was intelligent enough to realize there was no escape from La Montaigne.

Consequently she was free to roam the grounds, and with much leisure time, felt herself consistently drawn to the slaves, whose treatment aroused her pity and her anger at the needless cruelty of Trotter, and their less-than-adequate living conditions. She had never seen slaves so poorly treated. Their food rations were pitifully meager and the hovels in which they lived were tiny and poorly ventilated. It was a wonder they were even able to work! Trotter constantly prodded, pushed, and punished any of them unable to meet his harsh demands. When she could bear it no longer, Camille complained to Raphael.

"Do not concern yourself, *ma petite*. It is the way of life here. Trotter is responsible for getting the sugar harvest in and the burden rests heavy on him, as does the blame if he is not successful. He uses whatever means necessary to accomplish that. You must not think to interfere."

He looked at her closely to be sure she understood and would comply, noticing for the first time her hollow cheeks and the faint dark circles under her eyes. His finger traced the delicate bones of her face, and he murmured, "Such unhappiness, such beauty."

"I want to go home, Raphael, please."

His eyes were shadowed pools as he seemed to consider her request. She thought for a moment she saw signs of relenting there, but his firm words dispelled the notion. "*Non, ma chérie.* I have told you before.

That which you want most is the one thing I will never grant. Never! You are destined to be mine.''

She whirled away from him and fled down the path in the direction of the stables, her desperate need to get away from him making her act imprudently. With a few long strides, he caught her and swung her up in his arms. Pivoting, he strode toward the main house.

The brief freedom she had enjoyed was over, and she remained a prisoner in her room for the remainder of the summer. It was an added cruelty that from her bedroom window she could see the slave quarters, and the beating post frequently used by the hateful Trotter. On Magnolia, there had been no need for an overseer, and she was glad. But her visit to La Montaigne opened her eyes, as they never had been before, to the evil that slavery could be. Camille began to question her sublime acceptance of the practice and longed to help the poor souls under Trotter's control.

Magnolia! Who was tending to things in her absence? Had Charles returned? Was he gone again? Jacqueline had neither the stamina nor the sense for it, and poor Josef was too old and infirm to be of much use. Had they somehow managed to get in a cotton crop or had rampant weeds been allowed to encroach upon the cleared fields? Was someone tending to the gardens, the sick slaves, the smokehouse, the animals? A kaleidoscope of questions with no answers. If only she were home, she would see to it all.

Camille passed her time during the months of summer with memories of the past, worries about the welfare of Charles and Jacqueline, and the anticipation, in spite of everything, of the birth of her baby.

On their return to New Orleans, Raphael had surprisingly seemed content to carry on business as usual.

He continued to share the evening meal with his captive, who grew larger with child each passing month. Nothing more was said about the West Indies. Resigned that she could do nothing more until her baby was born, Camille retained a distant, but civil attitude toward her captor. It would not do to anger him, now that she had the child to consider.

The daily newspaper still gave her a tenuous link with the outside, but she feared more and more for her beloved South and her home as she read of the direction the war was taking. One bright spot had been the removal of the detested General Butler from the leadership of New Orleans. The city had celebrated and though they remained under the heel of the conquering North, the load on its citizens lightened with the end of his hateful reign.

The time of Camille's confinement and the birth of her child, for so long her only reason for living, was fast approaching. A local midwife had already visited and was standing by ready to assist. Though Camille was small, no problems were anticipated.

On the night Caroline Beaufort Longmont made her appearance into the war-torn world, a raging winter storm blew in off the Gulf and almost prevented the arrival of the midwife. Raphael locked himself in his chambers with a good supply of Havana cigars and rye whiskey, leaving orders he was not to be disturbed.

As Camille writhed and tossed in her pain, she thought for certain, perhaps even hoped, that she would die. When Monique approached her bed with a kitchen knife, she screamed out in terror. What in God's name was the girl going to do?

Monique hastened to reassure her as she slid the knife beneath the mattress of Camille's bed, "'Tis only for luck. It is said to *couper les douleurs*, cut the pain, of childbirth.''

And to Camille's surprise, the pain seemed to diminish from that moment. The *sage femme*, as a midwife was called by the Creoles, came at last, and the remainder of the delivery went smoothly. Before the sun rose on January 24, 1863, Camille held in her arms a healthy baby girl, her dainty porcelain beauty and shock of bright hair causing her mother's heart to jump painfully.

''Caroline. My darling little Caroline,'' she whispered, clutching the precious bundle to her breast.

Camille had wondered more than once during the long, endless days of her pregnancy why anyone would want to bring a child into the world, a world torn apart at the seams and apparently crumbling around them.

But now, as she touched the infinitely precious chubby fingers and toes, and looked into the baby blue of her daughter's trusting eyes, portents of a future that just might be worth living for and fighting for, a tiny hope sprang to life.

Caroline's chubby arms thrashed the air. She was a fighter already! Yes, they could rebuild their lives and the South would live again! Would it be any better for the struggle? Who could say? But if they had not been willing to stand and fight for what they believed to be right, there might have been no real future for them at all. For what one thought of oneself was the most important thing of all, wasn't it?

And what will your father think of you, my Caroline? she asked softly, her finger tracing the outline of a single, fetching dimple. And what will he think of your poor mother after all she's been through?

Would Charles still love her after so much time? The thought that he might not brought her greater pain that she could remember. The tearing pains of labor did not even compare to that bitter, aching hurt. Raphael had seemed so convinced Charles would abandon the search. Could he have been more right than she'd ever been willing to admit, even to herself? No, she had to believe he would come—or that she would somehow get free and make her way home to him. And she had to believe that everything would be as it once was.

The next few weeks passed in a blur, full of many impressions as Camille watched her baby thrive and grow, and as she busily began to plan a way to gain their freedom. This time her plan would work, for she had help. The midwife, who had visited her several times since Caroline's birth, listened sympathetically to her plight, and reluctantly agreed to help. Between them, they concocted an elaborate scheme that should have mother and daughter safely out of New Orleans and on their way home, a couple of weeks hence.

But one night when Raphael entered her room for dinner, Camille was distressed by his air of barely restrained excitement. Something was about to happen! He strode over to the lace-draped crib and looked long at Caroline before joining Camille at the table where she waited for him. He did not eat, but lounged back in his chair, sipping his *vin rosé*, his eyes following her as she tried to eat as though nothing were amiss.

At last, unable to choke down another bite and unwilling to wait any longer, she demanded, ''What is happening?''

''Yes, I suppose it is time you knew, *chérie*, as you must prepare yourself and the little one for travel.''

"Travel?" she repeated incredulously, as though by saying it she could erase the dreaded meaning of the word.

"We shall leave at sunrise tomorrow for the Indies." His black eyes challenged her to argue. Knowing there was nothing to be gained by such a reaction, Camille sat quietly, her eyes never leaving his. Any shouting or crying would be done after he left; he would not have the satisfaction of witnessing it. She had long since learned that such responses were ineffective on him, in any case.

"What makes you think I am recovered enough to travel?" If she could stall for only a short while, she could summon the midwife and accelerate their own plans. She must escape *before* he could take her away!

"My dear, the blush of supreme health is on your features. Nothing I have seen gives me the slightest doubt of your ability to travel. And as for the little one, she will be well provided for on the journey, and should have no difficulty at all. Was there some reason why you do not consider yourself fit enough to leave?" His eyes drilled into her, ready to pounce on the smallest sign of weakness or deceit. When she said nothing, he continued, "Urgent business demands my immediate departure, so I'm afraid there really is no choice in the matter."

It was a nightmare! What Camille had dreaded, what she had seen as a permanent end to her hopes for freedom—was about to happen!

Raphael was taking her to the West Indies, and she would never get home again. Two-month-old Caroline, so robust and healthy, and so infinitely precious, would never know her father, would never see Magnolia and come to love it as her mother did.

The question that had haunted her for months once more came to mind. Why hadn't Charles come back for her? How could he have been so easily duped, given up so quickly? It must be true that he'd never really loved her, or she would be home now, home where she belonged.

And Raphael? What kind of warped mind drove him? What would he do to her once they were safely out of New Orleans and she sufficiently recovered from childbirth? After the night of their "contract," he had never repeated his intentions, but they had been clear in his obsidian eyes from the very beginning. He meant to have her. She shuddered at the thought.

If only she could reach the midwife—but he would be watching her closely tonight, so that seemed an impossibility. Her only chance might be to break away at some point on their way to the ship the next morning. She could throw herself out of the carriage. But then what of Caroline? Or she could scream for help as they made their way aboard and cause such a row he'd have to let her go or do a lot of explaining. That idea was also full of holes, and had little chance of success. Who, on the docks, would hear her screams, or care to interfere if they did?

With a heavy heart, she bundled up Caroline's few belongings and chose from her wardrobe a minimum number of outfits for the journey. She managed to get it all in one carpetbag he had sent along with the trunk. She didn't want anything else. If he did, let him pack them!

The night was interminable! Thinking it might never end, she welcomed the passage of the endless hours. But she did not welcome the summons from

Raphael that inevitably came—it was time for them to go!

With a last look at the prison she'd come to know so well, she gathered up her young daughter and her bag and followed a servant out the door and down the stairs.

Raphael waited for her at the foot of the stairway. "Hurry up, *chérie*, the boat is scheduled to leave at sunrise. We have a long journey ahead and must be under way as soon as possible."

Though he tried to maintain his usual calm demeanor, a thread of nervousness showed in his short speech, and he rushed her out of the house and into the carriage. She suspected a reason for this haste, but could not imagine what it might be. Still, she would be alert and perhaps find a way she could use it to her advantage.

He seemed to relax once they had set out in the carriage. As usual, though, he did not speak during the drive.

The scene when she stepped out of the carriage was much the same as on the night she'd run away. Goods from all over the world were being unloaded and boats were taking on additional cargo for their return trips. Many of the vessels appeared to be making ready to cast off, and some were already sidling out into the current in the middle of the river. She watched with longing as a steamboat pulled out and headed north. It would pass very near her home, would more than likely pull in Under the Hill. What she wouldn't give to be on it!

As they walked toward the waiting boat, gaslights in the early morning darkness flickered around them. A dense mist rising from the river dampened her exposed skin, the rivulets indistinguishable from her tears, and brought a chill to her bones. Camille wrapped her cloak more securely around her. She could see little, her vision partially blocked by the hood that framed her face, and by the big man who walked beside her, keeping a firm grip on her arm. Along the street were a few wagons, and a carriage or two beside the one they'd arrived in. In the water, ghostly ships rested at anchor; the few visible deck hands busy about their assigned duties and paying no attention to the small boarding party.

Was there to be no help then? Was she doomed to a life of servitude with this man? God, no! she cried silently. She stumbled over a curb and was righted by the virile strength of the arm that supported her and held her firmly.

Inside her cloak and clutched fiercely against her heart lay her sleeping baby daughter. Caroline had not wiggled since being tucked inside her warm cocoon, where she lay content, lulled by the rapid beating of her mother's heart.

Chapter Seventeen

THE SWAMP was a collection of sordid dives, one-night hotels, gambling dens and bars. It was a New Orleans hangout for drunks, gamblers, pimps, prostitutes and cutthroats in general; violent crime was routine; shootings, stabbings, and bloody brawls were a nightly occurrence; and police enforcement was nonexistent.

The masked gentleman bandit was a figure at once feared and respected here. He had come to New Orleans to find and free Camille Beaufort Longmont, and into the Swamp for information. He had learned that her captor was the powerful Raphael Montaigne. He also knew that by now Montaigne, afraid her husband was getting too near, was preparing to leave the city with her and her baby. But how, when, and where, were the things he must find out.

He ducked his head and entered a shanty constructed of rough cypress planks salvaged from flatboats, where watered-down drinks were served to criminals of every sort. The floor creaked under his weight as he strode to a rough table laden with bottles of spirits.

"Whiskey, Nell," he ordered, slapping a coin onto the table and propping his foot on a stool while he waited for the portly, snaggle-toothed harridan to pour him a drink.

"Well, if it ain' *hisself*," she cackled. But as always, she was glad to see this man. He might be a thief, but he had a courtly manner, and had charmed her out of her socks more than once with his deep husky chuckle and his kindness to her.

"Yes. And how've you been, Nell? Keeping all these ruffians in line, as usual?" With a smile, he indicated the motley crowd in various stages of drunkenness lounging about small, rickety tables or at the bar, which consisted of wooden planks resting on two kegs. A dog wandered in through the open doorway; when no one seemed to notice or care, he wandered out again.

"I try, I surely do try." She rubbed dirty hands on an equally dirty apron, and smiled her uneven grin. "And where've ye been keepin' yerself, sport?"

"Oh, here and there. Up and down the river, across the Trace and back again. I stay busy, Nell. Anywhere there's pockets to be picked, mules or slaves to be stolen. You know how it is. A man has to make a living."

"A fine rogue ye are, sir. But sure nuff a perty one, fer all that!" He always made her feel like a girl again, with his smile and gentle banter. "Drink's on the house, my handsome bandit!"

"You're too kind, Nell. But I will pay for my own drink, if you don't mind. There is something you might do for me, though."

"And what might that be, luv?"

"I need information."

"Yer *allus* needin' infermation! And don' I allus give it to yer, when I can, that is?"

"Yes." He smiled, then continued, "But this time it's different. I'm looking for someone. A very nice, lovely young lady, Nell. She's being held in New Orleans against her will."

"How awful!"

"Indeed. I knew you'd feel that way about it. Now, here's how you can help. The man who kidnapped her is Raphael Montaigne."

"Montaigne!" Her eyes widened and gapped, blackened teeth snapped together, her lips sliding over them. "Don' know nothin' bout Montaigne!" she said sullenly, the name *Montaigne* spoken in a whisper.

"Now, Nell." His voice softened to a whisper in response. "I know you know him, and I know and understand that you are afraid of him—as is most of New Orleans. But I promise no harm will come to you if you help me. I only need to know where he might be planning to take the lady, and when. It is very important, Nell. The lady's life and that of her small baby may well depend upon it."

"A babe, huh? Well…" She had weakened, but was still reluctant to be involved. Montaigne's reputation for cruelty and merciless retribution was widespread. "If yer'd promise, I s'pose I cud trust yer."

"Of course you can, Nell."

She turned away to carry a tray of drinks she'd been fixing to a corner table, but soon shuffled back to where she'd left him. Wiping the table, as though unaware of his presence, she said under her breath, "He's got a clipper called *New Moon* that makes reg'lar runs to th' Indies. Contraband, yer know. If I wuz him, thet's what I'd do to a perty little thing I wanted ter keep hid. Boat leaves th' last Friday of th' month, us'lly fore daybreak!"

Friday! Only two days hence! Montaigne would be sure to make a move quickly, knowing Charles had been around again asking questions. Now he only need find a way to stop him!

"Thanks, Nell. You've been a big help, and you'll not regret it, I promise." He tossed her an extra gold coin, and she smiled.

"Thank yerself, good-lookin'!"

He stood outside in the deep bayou darkness lost in thought, oblivious to the night calls of swamp creatures, and the rustling of a damp wind through the treetops.

"Camille, my love, you will soon be free," he whispered into the wind.

He felt, rather than saw, someone come up behind him, whirled and drew out his knife in one motion. "What the . . . ! Why, you're only a boy!" The reed lantern hanging in the doorway of the bar he'd just left outlined the slight figure of the lad.

"I'm seventeen, sir! And a riverman, too—for the past three years!"

"Oh, I see." The bandit smiled. "And why do you not value your life more than to come sneaking up on me like that?"

"I don' want nobody to see me talking to you, sir. So I followed you outside. And besides, I-I'm not afraid of you, sir."

"No?" He chuckled. "A lot of people feel differently, I'm told." Putting his arm around the boy's shoulders, he led him away from the bar. "Now what is so damned important you'd risk your life to tell me?"

"Well, I—I . . . heard what you and Nell was talking about. The *New Moon*. See, I hang around down on the docks and I hear a lot. Usually, nobody pays me no mind, see? So's I knows a lot of things. The *New Moon* sails tomorrow morning, before dawn, not Friday!"

He continued carefully, "I think I know the young lady you're looking for—and if she *is* the same one, she don' deserve to be kidnapped and she sure don' deserve to be taken away from her home! I'll help you save her, sir!'' His chest puffed out in importance.

"How do you think you know the lady?" The dark man's voice was deceptively quiet. Something in the question caused the boy's hands to tremble before he answered hesitantly.

"She . . . she . . . was on a boat once, sir. The same boat as me. And she was kind to us all, sir. I wanted to help her then, but I couldn't."

"Why?" The question lashed at him. "Why didn't you help her?"

Billy Whipple haltingly explained the long story and hoped he made clear his innocence and his inability to help the lovely woman who seemed to mean so much to this gentleman bandit.

The man in the mask studied the boy for a long time before speaking. Billy knew he could be dispatched with the lethal blade at the man's waist in the blink of an eye should he be judged guilty of wrongdoing in regard to the lady in question. He held his breath as the bandit assimilated the information and made his decision.

"All right, Billy," he said slowly. "Tell me everything you know about this boat and her crew. If your information helps me rescue the young woman, you might just be off the hook, and earn a reward, as well."

"I want no reward, sir. Jest to see the lady safe."

"All right. Tell me everything."

The bandit listened, not missing a single detail. When Billy finished, he sent him on an errand with instructions to meet again two hours before dawn on the wharf. Feeling proud to be of service, Billy had scurried off into the darkness, determined to be successful, though he didn't understand why the bandit wanted a length of heavy rope, an anchor, and a horse.

The night was still and deep and dark when the two met as planned near the *New Moon*. An unusual amount of activity was taking place as some of the crew loaded cargo and others readied the ship for sailing.

"They are leaving early," the bandit said softly.

Relieved that he had been right, Billy answered happily, "Yes, sir!"

"Only one reason for that."

"Yes, sir!"

"We have to work quickly. We may only have one chance."

Billy stared at the sleek boat with his heart in his mouth. It boasted a crew of at least seven, possibly eight, brawny men. The light of a single lantern revealed their forbidding shapes, but not their faces, as they moved around on deck.

The man who knelt beside him could easily carry his weight in a fight, that much was certain, but Billy was painfully aware of his own limitations, and any fool could see they were greatly outnumbered.

A hand fell lightly on his shoulder and the bandit pointed down the street, along the levee. "See that, my young friend?"

Billy's eyes widened until the white rims showed clearly even in the darkness. "Yes, sir! I sure do!" A band of four heavily armed men rode slowly in their direction. When they reached the corner of the next block, they dismounted and slipped away into the night. "Who *are* they, sir? Friends of yours, I hope?"

A soft chuckle. "Yes, indeed. My friends, Billy. And just the help we need, huh?"

"Yes, *sir!*" Billy said, with a noticeable increase in enthusiasm. "Yes, sir!"

A few seconds passed before they were joined by the four men, creeping along in the shadows of the warehouses and other deserted buildings along the street behind them.

"Welcome, men," the masked man spoke softly. "Our young accomplice here is called Billy. Now, here's what we do...." They huddled around and nodded occasionally as he outlined the plan. It was simple. Billy would create a diversion on the wharf. One of the band would secure the boat with the anchor he'd found so it couldn't cast off, and the rest, on signal, would board the craft, deal with any opposition, locate Camille and get her safely off the boat.

But was she aboard? It seemed likely, since the ship would sail within the next couple of hours. But there was no way to be sure. They would have to proceed as though she were, or lose precious time. One of his men slipped out of the shadows and crept away to secure the anchor.

On his return, their leader raised his hand, about to give the signal to swing into action, when something caught his eye. Poised in midair, his arm did not drop. A small group of four people made their way swiftly toward the ship riding at anchor. The large one was no doubt Raphael's bodyguard. The tall man in the middle had one armed hooked around the waist of the petite cloaked figure on his left. He appeared to be urging her to walk faster. Another petite figure straggled along behind, hurrying to keep up. As they neared the ship, they were hailed by an unseen crew member, and the gangplank lowered.

"Camille!" breathed the man with his hand still uplifted. He cursed his luck that there had been no time to make a move before they boarded, but stared intently after them to see where they would take her.

To the left and below deck!

His hand slashed downward through the air.

Billy staggered out into the open, singing a bawdy tune at the top of his lungs. The three men on the forward deck acknowledged his presence with loud guffaws and jabs at each other's ribs.

As one, the bandit's men sprang into action, running for the boat. No alarm was given as two of them swung over the side and ran toward the three men ogling Billy's capering. An immediate battle was joined, knives were unsheathed, and fists flew. Grunts and oaths sullied the peaceful night.

The bandit and the other two men ran boldly up the plank, each with a knife in one hand, a loaded revolver in the other. They split up, the bandit heading for the stairs where Camille had disappeared.

A light was extinguished. A whispered command given. A door slammed shut, close at hand. The bandit took two careful steps down into the darkness, before he heard the ominous click of a hammer being drawn back.

He held his breath, trying to determine the direction of the sound. He could not. Whether he saw the flash of the gun firing, or ducked first, he wasn't sure, but the bullet lodged in the wall behind him with a soft thud.

He leaped in the direction of the shot and rammed against a brick wall, a wall that moved and aimed a chopping blow at his neck! The blow glanced off harmlessly and the bandit bowed his head and dove at what he thought was the man's stomach.

"Ooof!'

"A-ha!'' He kicked up savagely and connected with soft flesh. He heard the man scream and with some satisfaction, delivered a last numbing blow with the butt of his revolver to the man's head.

Above him, he heard scuffling feet, blows being landed and cries of pain. A splash. Someone overboard! The crack of a pistol. Someone dead? Not one of his good, loyal men!

A muffled cry came from his left. He lifted a booted foot and smashed it against the door, which crashed back into the wall. Pistol levelled, he jumped through the opening.

A disembodied voice spoke from the darkness. "My revolver is pointed directly at her head, and if you do not drop your weapon immediately, I shall not hesitate a moment to shoot, first the lady and then yourself, *mon ami*.''

A mirthless chuckle sounded hollowly through the room after the bandit's gun dropped loudly to the floor at his feet.

"Now, shall we see who it is we have here, *chérie*? Do be a dear and light the lamp beside you." Shaking hands reached to do his bidding and a golden glow filled the room. As he'd said, Raphael's gun was aimed at Camille, who sat close beside him on one of the room's two narrow cots.

"You may untie the scarf from your lovely mouth now, *ma chérie*. Perhaps you would speak with the man who has failed so miserably to rescue you?''

Camille reached to the back of her head and struggled with the tight knot, her eyes fixed on the man of her midnight dreams, the object of her secret desires, and the man who cared enough for her to risk death at the hands of Raphael Montaigne.

"I'm sorry," she said softly.

"No need, dear lady. The fault is all mine." From the mocking smile on the bandit's lips, one would have thought Raphael the one being held at gunpoint rather than the other way around. "Are you all right?" he asked, the concern eloquent in his rich, deep voice.

"Y-yes . . . and you . . . you're not hurt?"

"My, my, my, how sweet. Almost like reunited lovers, but you're not, are you? I understood the lady to be wed, with a husband she loved so dearly she could not bear to be parted with him." His voice angry but tightly controlled, Montaigne motioned the bandit to the far side of the room.

Grudgingly he gave up ground, moving farther from the door and farther from Camille, his gaze directed at the dark Creole holding the gun at her head.

The ruckus continued unabated overhead. It was unclear who was winning, but the fighting was ferocious.

"Aren't you going to invite me to sit down?"

A flush of rage spread over Raphael's countenance, outlining in relief the jagged scar across his cheek and jaw.

"No, I suppose not." Continuing to taunt the man with the gun, the bandit lounged against the wall. Though he appeared relaxed, every muscle in his lithe, athletic body was tense, poised for action. All he required was the tiniest opening, the smallest distraction.

He glanced at the doorway. "C'mon on in, Billy, the party's just getting started." He smiled and spoke in a jovial tone.

For a fraction of a second Raphael allowed his gaze to stray from the bandit to the door. It was an almost-fatal mistake. In that instant the soft-spoken bandit lunged and Camille knocked the lamp off the table, plunging the room into darkness once more.

Camille made her way toward the dim light filtering into the room through the doorway, painfully aware of the sounds of the heated battle between two well-matched opponents behind her. She felt around on the floor for the bandit's weapon, though she hadn't a notion what she'd do with it if she found it!

Success! Her hand touched the cold steel, and she hefted it with both hands and turned, aiming it toward the two bodies thrashing about on the floor. She could not shoot! She'd be as likely to hit one as the other! She could only wait to see who would be the victor. If it proved to be Raphael she would shoot him without a qualm, and answer to the consequences. She would be no one's prisoner—ever again! She would die first!

Caroline! Where was she? Her heart pounded with a new fear. Raphael had taken her and the nurse to another cabin after bringing Camille here, evidently planning to have her to himself this night.

She ran out the door and down the hall, pounding on each door as she went, crying, "Monique! Monique! Caroline! Where are you? Answer me!"

The only noise in the narrow hallway came from the unending strife above. Which door? Which one could be hiding her daughter? Every door she tried was securely locked. At last, she was rewarded by a loud squawl. Finding the right door after following the crying, she pointed the gun shakily at the knob. "Open the door, now, Monique—or I'll shoot! I swear I will!"

Inside the small room, the servant stood pressed against a wall, her hand over her mouth in fear. The wild passion in Camille's voice impressed the girl into action. She hurried to the door and released the bolt.

Camille pushed by her, demanding, "Where is she?" Too frightened to speak, Monique pointed to a small room off the main chamber.

"She'd better be all right!" Why wouldn't she be? Camille asked herself as she hurried past the shivering Monique and into the other room. Her daughter's fair skin was pale and she lay motionless in her crib. Camille's heart thundered in her chest. Had that monster already done something to her helpless child? Her hand tightened on the weapon she carried. Slowly, Camille lowered her left hand, holding it in front of the tiny bowed lips.

A sigh of sweet breath escaped the lips, brushing Camille's trembling fingers. She almost dropped the heavy gun with relief. Her baby still lived! She breathed, "Thank God!" Scooping Caroline up in her arms, Camille somehow managed baby, blanket, and gun until she reached the doorway. She stopped, still inside the room.

Footsteps echoed loudly through the hall. The battle between Raphael and the gentleman bandit was over and one of them was coming for her. Nestling Caroline in the crook of her arm, she pointed the gun at the doorway, willing her arm to remain steady enough to hold it. *All I want, dear God, is just one good, clean shot,* she prayed.

Monique sniffled in a corner. Waves splashed outside. The stench of gunpowder still burned Camille's nose. And beyond that, the sweet, powdery smell of her baby.

The steps grew louder and did not slow. Whoever it was would not stop or hesitate until he found her. Resolutely she forced herself to hold the gun firmly.

When the familiar masked form appeared in the doorway and turned toward her, the relief she felt was so sweet, her gratitude so great, she dropped the gun and rushed at him, catching him off balance and almost knocking him off his feet.

"Whoa," he whispered as she clung to him, the baby squirming in between. "Whoa, now, dear lady. It's all right. Montaigne is in no shape to bother you now." His hand stroked her hair, and she remembered the particular delight his touch always brought her. "Lady with the midnight hair," he soothed. "You're safe now. But I'll feel better when we're out of here." He laughed, picked up his gun, and turned with her toward the steps.

Signs of a struggle littered the quiet deck above. A bloody hat. A spilled cask of wine. A body draped over the rail. Another doubled over, hand still on the anchor lines. Twisted lengths of rope scattered about.

"Quite a row, eh, boss?" All four of his men, some looking a little worse for the wear, drifted out of dark nooks and crannies.

Camille held out her hand in friendship to one of the men. "Thank you, all of you!" Her eyes moved over each of them, returning to those mysterious eyes behind the mask.

His hand lay protectively, possessively, lightly, on her lower back, just above her waist, and his touch burned through her clothing. She was relieved and yet disappointed when he removed it to help her off the boat.

Someone stirred on the boat behind them. Quickly they mounted the waiting horses and split into two groups. The bandit and Camille headed north. The others waited for them to leave before setting off in the opposite direction, hoping to draw any pursuit after them.

A feeling of euphoria swept through Camille as their horses galloped through the sleeping streets of New Orleans. She was free and on her way home!

Through the fog-laden night, the two riders raced, hoping the dense, swirling mist that hampered their flight would also slow any pursuit. Camille rode astride, her skirts bunched up under her, and a length of leg showing shamefully. The responsive mare she'd been provided was fleet of foot and she kept an easy seat in the Spanish saddle as they sped up the river road out of New Orleans, following its serpentine path along the Mississippi.

She hazarded a glance at the man on the big chestnut who rode as though born in the saddle, cradling her tiny daughter so lightly, yet so securely in the circle of one arm. In his dark jacket and mask, he was as shadowy as the night, draped in its trailing remnants of fog.

The gentleman bandit was a name long feared by travelers, yet it was he who had come to her rescue like a knight on a white charger, snatching her and Caroline from under the very nose of Raphael.

After they had ridden some distance north of town, he cast a concerned glance back over his shoulder. "Someone is behind us. Damn! I didn't think it would be so soon. Can you ride faster, dear heart?" His deep voice teased her, even while urging her on to greater speed.

"I can keep up with you!" Digging her heels into her horse's sides, she put feet to her self-confident words and the mare jumped past his larger mount and spurted ahead. Camille lost a stirrup but clamped her legs firmly around the horse's middle and hung on tightly.

The pace of their pursuit picked up, as well.

"We'll split at the fork; I go the left and you to the right!" he shouted across the noise of accelerated hoofbeats.

"Not on your life, bandit!" she shouted back. "I'm staying with you two."

He looked down, having forgotten the child, who, incredible as it seemed, still slept in his arms. "Hold on, little one, here we go!" he whispered, yanking his horse hard to the left. Camille remained close behind him, the wind whipping her hair wildly. His burst of laughter at her stubbornness and courage was snatched away by the wind. She had never missed a step as they had fled the waterfront, cutting a zigzag path through the narrow streets of the Vieux Carré.

When they had broken free of the city, and onto the open river road, he'd thought they were out of danger. But now someone rode hard behind them. He motioned for Camille to turn off onto an overgrown road to her right, and he was close behind. They reigned in their mounts and moved off the path into a thicket of bushes and overhanging trees. Long minutes passed. The fog had lifted, and now the road on which they'd been riding could be clearly seen, under a blanket of moonlight. Without speaking, they both waited to see what rider would pass.

Camille recognized Raphael at once. He rode like a madman with no thought of his own safety or that of his horse, already lathered from the hard ride. In his left hand he held a pistol, cocked and ready to fire at the slightest shadow. Camille was sure he would not hesitate to kill either or both of them if given the opportunity. His obsession with her had been converted into a passionate hatred and he would stop at nothing to avenge his loss.

She held her breath until he was well down the road and then slowly expelled it, feeling the energy drain out of her. Her head swam with a light giddiness and she tried to think when she'd last slept, or eaten.

A pair of strong hands closed about her waist and she let herself slide, depending on him to catch her. Her feet barely touched the ground before he was lifting her, cushioning her against his chest, and walking with her in his arms to the grassy knoll where he'd already laid the sleeping baby.

"I think we've lost him." He sat with Camille cradled in his arms and into her hair he whispered, "Shhh . . ." to silence the protest he expected. With a soft murmur, she surprised him by snuggling against him, slipping an arm around his neck to steady herself on his knees.

Her fingers toyed with soft fabric of the mask that covered his face and kept his identity from her. She leaned back to look up at him, and to her surprise, found his dark mysterious eyes a mask behind a mask. What was he hiding from? Who was he? For she knew he was no mere bandit!

"I would see you, sir." Her fingers played across the mask, outlining the lines and contours of his face.

"Close your eyes." His voice was husky with desire.

She did as he asked and felt the silken fabric of the mask slide over her own face. When she opened her eyes, she found she could not see, and reached to adjust the eye holes.

"No. See me this way." His warm hand guided hers to his face where she felt skin tightly fashioned over bone, roughened by sun and wind; high, strong cheekbones; a classically shaped nose; a rough growth of beard that scratched her hand but was nonetheless a pleasant feeling; a pair of lips, full and smiling now and meant for kissing.

"I've wanted you from the first night I saw you, Camille. And you . . ." His lips found hers under the mask and moved over them with a barely restrained passion that tugged at her heart and pulled at some cord buried deep inside her. "You, my lovely, have wanted me, too. I've seen it in your eyes." He dropped kisses on her eyes, covered by the mask. "I've felt it in your touch." He kissed the sensitive palm of each hand, his tongue teasing playfully. "I've heard it in your voice." He kissed her neck where the pulse was jumping wildly.

She had been drifting in a sensuous void behind the safe darkness of the mask, enjoying the mystery, and deeply, erotically moved by his caresses. But now panic seized her for what was about to happen between herself and this highwayman, and she tried to pull away.

Since the first time she'd seen him in the deep woods of the Trace, slapping his whip against a muscled thigh, Camille had been helplessly drawn to him. There was something about him . . .

And later, when his small band of men had stopped the wagon in which she rode with Zeb and he had jumped up to sit beside her—she recalled too vividly the feel of his leg brushing hers—the fiery touch of his fingers on her skin when he'd snatched off her necklace.

"My locket," she asked, "where is it?"

The familiar throaty chuckle. "In a safe place, dear heart. One day soon you will have it back."

He had kept it—all this time! He cared for her, too. Of course! He had cared enough to risk his life and his men in his bold rescue of her. She saw him again as he had tenderly held her baby daughter in her arms—almost lovingly, she thought with a start. And now those same gentle arms held her next to him.

And Charles, she asked herself, what of him? He had not cared enough to come for her, had left her to languish in her prison for all those months, to have his baby alone and in a strange place, far from home. Where had he been? What had he been doing that was so important he had never come back for her? Once he had loved her, she was almost certain. But not anymore.

As though he shared in her dilemma, and knew when her decision was reached, the bandit held her firmly in his arms and settled her alongside him, laying her back in the soft grass, fragrant with early morning dew. "You are mine, my love, if only for this one night. Every lovely inch of you—mine. In a way, you have always been mine."

With a sigh of defeat, Camille released the dam of feelings she'd held back, letting them rush over her in never-ending waves as she molded her body to his. He was her lover, her savior. Tonight he was everyone, everything to her. There was nothing, no one else. She owed her life to him, and there was but one thing she had to give him in return—herself. And she would give—unreservedly, but she would not fool herself into thinking she acted only out of gratitude. She longed for him with every fiber of her being.

Leaving the mask in place, intrigued by the idea he could see her but she could not see him, and that she could only "see" him with her hands, she slid out of his arms and one by one, stripped off every article of her clothing. She lay beside him, naked and unashamed.

In his presence this night, she was wanton, free of the inhibitions placed on her by society. She was his. She felt only a primitive, exultant pride in their shared intimacy. She stood and held her hand out to him, and when she felt his hand in hers, she tugged, bringing him to his feet. Still holding his hand, her fingers entwined in his, she took a couple of steps until she was very nearly touching him. Then she slipped her hands under his coat and pushed it off his shoulders, pulling down on the bottom of the sleeves until it slid to the ground. Tentatively, but with unwavering purpose, her fingers worked on the buttons of his soft broadcloth shirt, releasing them one by one until his chest lay bare to her touch. She leaned against the corded muscles, running her fingers through the softly curling hair, and breathed deeply. His scent was wild, musky, redolent with the night and the excitement. A thin sheen of perspiration gave him a masculine aroma that nearly drove her wild with desire, and was vaguely reminiscent of another time, another place.

Shaking fingers moved to his waist and slipped inside his trousers, stroking his hard, flat stomach. His hand that had been restlessly idle, supporting her back, while allowing her tender torture to continue, whipped around to make quick work of the final impediment to their lovemaking. He had watched her, barely reining in the desire that hammered through him while she took off her clothing. She was so lovely, so delicate, his hands itched to touch her, but he had held back until she reached for him. No more!

Stepping out of his trousers, he kicked off his boots before once more laying her back on the ground, this time on a cushion of their discarded clothing. He dropped to his knees beside her, his eyes roaming over her freely, dark with longing and repressed desire given free rein at last.

Camille, who still reveled in her dark world inhabited only by shadows, images, impressions of her mysterious lover and herself, reached for him and drew him down over her. Their bodies were a play of light and shadow, her ivory beauty against his brooding darkness; a primeval dance between man and woman, as their bodies sought and found what they so desperately desired—in that time when night shadows are chased away by the early light of the sun.

She was a forest nymph and he her satyr, as they moved in an exotic rhythm of love and passion as old as the ancient river that flowed nearby. The world spun crazily, like a waterspout, out of control. Her fingers moved over the knotted muscle of his back in a ritualistic dance and he spiralled with her through the night sky, out of the moon's orbit and into another dimension, brilliant with light and saturated with joy.

In a peak of mindless ecstasy, they found mutual delight and a surfeit of satisfaction that settled over them like a warm blanket in the early morning chill.

"You're cold," he said softly, drawing his jacket over her and tucking it in around her hips. She hadn't realized she had shivered, but was thankful for the warmth he provided.

"Turn your back to me," he commanded.

She complied, rolling over, but snuggling back into him, enjoying the feel of his bare skin next to hers. He slipped the blindfold off her head and back onto his own. His hand gently stroked her tousled hair.

There had been no question of denying what was between them. Some part of her had belonged to him in a deep, mystical way since the night he'd first appeared to her on the Trace, a tall, arrogant, but totally sensuous stranger.

With Charles she'd had a warm, mutual love, but only a promise of the wild, abandoned lovemaking she'd shared with this bandit who, though a stranger, was in many ways her friend, probably the best she'd ever had, as well as a mysterious and exciting lover.

Reality crept back over them with the rising of the sun and the hungry cry of her babe, whom she nestled to her breast. The bandit watched with no apology, and she felt no embarrassment as they shared another intimacy in their peaceful hideaway.

"We must go," he said quietly, when she'd finished nursing her child. "Raphael passed by a little while ago, going back toward New Orleans. I have to go after him. If I'm not back by midday, you take the child and go north. There's a landing about five miles up the road. Wait there for a steamship that will take you home."

Silencing her protest, he'd put his fingers to her lips and placed in her hand a small bag of gold coins. "I'll be back soon," he promised.

He tenderly took Caroline from her and bounced her lightly in his arms while Camille reluctantly settled herself on her horse. With one last long look at the child and her mother, he held the baby up to her, making sure she was secure and comfortable before turning to his own horse.

Mounting, he wheeled his horse, and with a final salute, galloped away, back in the direction they had come.

Camille had shared with this remarkable bandit a rare blending of bodies and souls, and she thought she would never be sorry, for what had been between them had been inescapable.

Would he overtake the Creole? And could he beat Raphael in another contest? She prayed no harm would come to him. For in a very real way, she loved him, though how she could love two men, each so different from the other, she was at a loss to understand.

Chapter Eighteen

RAPHAEL MONTAIGNE woke with a huge lump on his head that pounded savagely. He had been bested by a masked bandit and a woman! He was furious. He would not sleep—or rest—until he found them. And when he did, they would pay. Oh, how they would pay.

Especially *her*! What had he done to Camille, except love her, provide for her, and wait patiently for her to learn to love him? But he'd been such a fool! The worst of fools! And if he ever got his hands on her lovely body again, he would not know the meaning of the words *patience* or *mercy*. "Beware, *ma chérie*," he whispered as he rode north on the river road, scanning the stretch of road ahead, pausing to examine each side road and pathway. He had ridden for a long time before he sensed they were no longer ahead of him.

Somewhere, he had lost them. They must have turned off the main road. But sooner or later they would have to come out and continue their northward journey if they were to reach Natchez. He could not sit idly by and wait, but neither was he one to rush off chasing shadows.

Just then, he saw a rider approaching on a sway-backed horse, and had an idea. A short, animated discussion was followed by a quick exchange of clothing and horses. Pocketing several gold coins, the happy stranger rode off in the opposite direction.

Raphael congratulated himself. When Camille and the masked man saw this man go by on his horse and wearing his clothing, they would foolishly think themselves safe. He could then double back and catch them off guard. They would be at his mercy!

CAMILLE STOOD BACK from the landing slightly, as she'd been instructed by the bandit, so she could see the river without being seen. Yankee gunboats made their way up and down almost without challenge now, and it was best to stay out of their way.

The steamboat should arrive by midafternoon, or so he'd thought, and she tried to wait patiently, watching the sun tiptoe higher into the sky. Mosquitoes made a feast of her exposed skin, though she'd fashioned a crude fan from a big leaf, which she used with vigor on herself and her child.

Mostly, she paced and, when too tired for that, sat on the hard ground. Camille shielded her eyes from the sun and peered downriver as she'd done many times already, unsure of how much time had passed. When the bandit had not returned, she'd left their hiding place as he'd told her, and made her way to this landing. He would have come back if he'd been able. What could have happened to him? She had tormenting visions of him battered and bleeding, perhaps even dying, along the road. She quelled the urge to go after him only by remembering what he'd said to her.

She became more and more tense as the long minutes crept by, her apprehension rising with the steady ascent of the sun. Something was wrong. Something was definitely not as it should be. Her heart began to beat faster, and her throat and mouth were so dry she couldn't swallow. Why? She hadn't heard anything unusual, or had she?

Standing perfectly still and trying not to make a sound, she listened. Her back was stiff from the effort before she finally relaxed. No sound in the woods around her. No sound from the road a few hundred feet away. No hoofbeats. Nothing!

Turning her back to the road and the woods, she walked toward the river. When she reached the edge, she knelt and scooped up a handful of the muddy water, which she splashed on her face, suddenly warm and feverish. Much refreshed, she wiped her wet hands on her skirts, and reached down for Caroline, who lay smiling up from her bed in a clearing between some bushes. Fed and changed, Caroline was ready once more to lie quietly, waving her tiny fists in the air.

"Where is that boat?" Camille demanded as she paced, continuing her nervous vigil. Her rebellious thoughts returned more than once to the events of the early morning. She wondered briefly why the bandit had said nothing about what had happened between them, and why he had felt it necessary to go after Raphael. Why couldn't he have just let him go? She would have time once she reached home to look for answers, but waiting for a boat that might not come in this unfamiliar place, with Raphael still out there somewhere, well, that was enough to think about right now.

Was that—could it be—a steam whistle? Oh, please God, let it be, she prayed. She ran to the edge of the water, leaned out as far as she dared and was rewarded to see a bulky shape in the distance. Too far to tell if it was the *Vicksburg*, the *Natchez*, or the *Princess*.

But it was a steamboat! She thought she had never seen a sight so welcome!

Camille raised her hands and waved wildly, but the boat was still a long way off, and it hardly seemed to be moving. She waited impatiently.

A terrible foreboding swept over her once more. Someone was out there! But where? Hiding in the thick growth behind her? She whirled, but could see nothing except shadows.

"Is anyone there?" she called out, and felt utterly foolish, hearing her voice echo in the emptiness, the unearthly quiet that was becoming more and more oppressive.

Still unsettled by the feeling, she snatched up her baby, who wailed loudly in protest. "Hush, baby," she tried to comfort and silence her, but found that her own voice trembled.

"A touching sight." The words, heavy with sarcasm, struck her a harsh blow, though she could not see the speaker.

Where *was* he? Her eyes searched everywhere, but she could not see him. Raphael was out there! And she was exposed and at his mercy in the clearing where she stood. How she wished for the bandit's gun! The boat was not nearly close enough to help. Her eyes flew to her horse. There would probably not be time enough to mount and get away from him that way. She could see no way out.

He was too close, his voice even louder, when he spoke again. "A foolish thing, *chérie*." She felt the repressed anger vibrating in his low voice. He would kill her this time. But not quickly, no, not quickly.

"Raphael!" she cried, "I did nothing to you. I *needed* to go home. You know how *badly* I wanted to. Let me go, please."

Silence. He would not. He had vowed he would never let her go.

She glanced down the river anxiously. The boat plowed its way through the water in a leisurely fashion. It was still such a distance away, no one would be able to see her.

"It's too late for that, *chérie*. I have you now."

She saw him, then, standing at the edge of the clearing. He was less than ten feet away from her.

"Come here, Camille." He extended a hand to her, and his eyes snared her. As though a whip had coiled around her and drew her inexorably toward him, her feet moved, closing the distance between them.

She was lost! Incapable of resisting him. And she'd almost been home. Home! The thought gave her new purpose, new strength.

"No!"

She backed up a couple of steps, her mind fighting him. "I . . . won't . . . go . . . back, Raphael."

"Oh, yes, you shall, *mon amour*, you shall indeed." He advanced a step toward her, and held out his hand as though expecting her to walk willingly back into his arms.

Every ounce of her strength was required to resist him as she backed steadily away. She did not take her eyes off him—this time she would not look down, she would not back down.

"Your bandit cannot save you now, *chérie*. He is on his way back to New Orleans, on a wild-goose chase that will take him farther and farther from you. A clever trick, *n'est-ce pas*? One designed to leave the two of us alone, for one last time.''

The finality suggested by his words and his tone of voice sent a hard shiver of fear through her. He meant to kill her! And Caroline? What would he do to her? She hugged her child tighter, turned, and ran toward her horse. She had to get herself and her daughter away from him! Reins clutched tightly in one hand and her child in the other, Camille struggled with the stirrup.

He grabbed her. ''Ah, no, *chérie*. It is no good, you see?'' He pulled her from the horse and turned her to face him.

''And now let's discuss the terms of the contract you have broken by your precipitous flight!'' She backed away, stepping into the line of trees around the clearing, but he steadily advanced on her, driving her further and further into the forest.

From the river she heard the lonely whistle of the boat as it slid past the landing.

''No, PLEASE, MISTER. I didn't mean no harm.''

''You had better tell me what you know and make quick work of it!'' the masked man said between gritted teeth. His hand fastened on the man's arm as he hauled him off Raphael's horse. ''Tell me where you got this horse and those clothes.''

''All right, all right. I ain't done nothin' wrong, I swear. I was just ridin' along when this here fellow stopped me.''

''Where?''

'''Bout five miles north of Peachtree Landing, I guess. I ain't exactly sure. Anyhow...'' The fierce look behind the mask encouraged speed in the telling of his tale, so he continued breathlessly. "Anyhow, he paid me—in gold—to trade horses and clothes with him. His was much better 'n mine anyhow, so's I did, willin' enough. And that was the last I seed of 'im, I swear!"

The deadly light in the masked man's eyes moderated and he released his grip, bringing a wash of relief over the man in the baggy, expensive clothing. Had his answers not been acceptable he knew he would have been barnacle bait at the bottom of the river!

"Tell no one about our little talk, understand?"

"Yes, sir! I won't say nothin' to nobody!" Released from the grasp of the bandit, he snatched up the reins, mounted his new horse and fled, not looking back, grateful to escape with his life and limbs still in tact.

"Damnation!" the bandit cursed softly, throwing himself back into the saddle and tearing out in the direction he had come. Raphael had tricked him!

And he, fool that he was, had left Camille alone, easy prey for the Creole. "No!" he shouted into the wind as he rode. "You shall not have her, Raphael!" But his heart was clamped in the harsh vise of fear, even as he raced up the road. He might already be too late to help her!

He had almost reached New Orleans in pursuit of this decoy before he realized his mistake. Now he only hoped he could reach her in time. He pushed his already winded horse almost beyond endurance on the long, return trip. He had to get to her before Raphael found her. There was no telling what that demented man would do now, after what had been done to him, his ship, and his crew in the rescue.

Some rescue! he berated himself—to turn the captive back over to the kidnapper so easily. He would never forgive himself if anything happened to her. He shuddered to think of her delicate body, her silken skin in the grasp of that madman again. He slowed when he passed the side road where they had taken refuge and made love, but only long enough to be sure she wasn't still there. He had not wanted to let her go, ever, but he'd had to go after Raphael, knowing the Creole would never leave Camille alone.

By now she should be at the landing. Perhaps she'd already gotten safely aboard the steamship. He heard the lonesome whistle in the air as he made the left turn onto the road leading to Peachtree Landing. With a sinking feeling in the pit of his stomach, he saw the boat in the middle of the river, moving steadily upstream. It had not pulled into the landing! Of course, since there was no one in sight to signal it to shore.

Where was she? God, where was Camille?

His exhausted horse slid to a stop at the water's edge and he looked anxiously around, everywhere at once. A soft nicker pulled his attention to his left. The horse she'd been riding was tethered there, just as he'd instructed her. But what was that bundle in the bushes? It was small and blanketed.

His heart in his throat, he ran toward it. There, in the dappled sunlight, lay tiny Caroline, sleeping peacefully. Charles pivoted, his eyes searching. Her baby was here, surely Camille was here somewhere, too. Maybe she had gone off for a minute and missed the boat? No! She would never leave the baby alone. He was only fooling himself.

A desperate fear was building in him as he strode about looking for some sign, some clue that would indicate what had happened, where she might be. Then he saw the other horse, well back from the landing.

Raphael had come back! He had probably been able to sneak up on her while her attention had been on the river, watching for the boat. And she would have had no way to defend herself. Why hadn't he at least left her a gun—a knife—something!

They had to be nearby. There couldn't have been time for them to have gone far. His ears tuned to the slightest noise, he stood motionless, listening intently.

A breeze rustled in the tops of tall trees, the water lapped in the rushes at the shore. A bird called. There...what was that? A muffled cry? This way...yes, there a broken branch that had been stepped on. And here, the leaves were flattened. Stealthily he made his way through the brush, careful not to make a sound.

If she were still alive, he was not too late. Oh, God! he prayed, please let her be alive!

A grunt reached his ears, attuned to any sound out of the ordinary. Another. A muffled curse. What in God's name was happening? He picked up his pace, petrified by the uncertainty.

CAMILLE'S MIND RACED as she backed farther and farther from this man with the gleam of madness in his eyes, black like bits of hard stone. Relentlessly he came after her, pushing her backward. She tripped over a log and fell to the ground. With nothing to block her fall, the force of it slammed through her, and the blackness that claimed her was brightened only by shooting stars of pain.

Minutes later she opened her eyes and found herself looking up into the horrible countenance of his hatred. The jagged scar and evil smile made his face a carica- ture of the devil. Raphael towered over her, his shape blocking out the sun, casting a giant suffocating shadow over her. She had never felt more helpless. His hypnotic eyes bored into her, and her heart gave a terrified leap, jumping against her ribs. She was trapped!

"Back away from her." The strong, masculine voice brought an immediate response from Raphael, who straightened his back but did not take a step. Camille's heady rush of relief on hearing the gentleman bandit's voice was replaced immediately by a new fear.

Deadly purpose shone from Raphael's eyes, and the gun he held was in front of him where the bandit couldn't see it. Camille cried out in warning, "Look out! He has a gun!"

Two explosions roared through the clearing almost simultaneously as Raphael whirled and fired in one motion and the gun of the gentleman bandit discharged. He had aimed high, afraid of hitting Camille, and when Raphael turned and sidestepped, the shell missed, lodging harmlessly in a tree. Raphael's shot had been more effective, knocking the weapon from his opponent's hand.

Camille scrambled to her feet, grabbed a stick and swung it at the Creole's head. She missed her target, but the blow landed hard on his shoulder, sending his second shot wide of the target.

"Get back, Camille!" the bandit shouted, running at the Creole who clutched his right shoulder, a grimace of hatred and pain distorting his features.

Camille edged backward a few steps, appalled at the blood lust controlling both men as they grappled in a macabre dance. Rigidly she held herself in check, forced to watch the deadly combat. First, one seemed to gain the advantage, then the other. She bit her lip to hold back a cry when Raphael slipped a knife from his boot and aimed for his opponent's heart.

The bandit grasped his wrist and twisted. They rolled over and over, and she could no longer see the silver-handled knife. She could not bear to watch, but she could not look away. They seemed to move in slow motion as it became a trial of strength, a battle of wills. Finally a scream rent the air. It was over.

One body lay very still, blood oozing from a chest wound, staining his shirt and soaking into the ground. Camille took deep breaths to calm her racing heart. A hawk sailed by overhead, its shadow swooping over her. She remembered the duel on the Vidalia sandbar she had once watched in horror. This one had claimed a life as well, but this time it was either her captor or her rescuer whose blood darkened the soil. Though she had desperately wished to be free of him, she would not wish Raphael dead. He was driven by demons she couldn't begin to understand, and often had aroused her sympathy. Yet she couldn't bear to think it might be the bandit. . . .

As she watched, one man disentangled himself from the other, and pulled himself slowly to his feet. He turned in her direction, but stood without moving. Across the distance that separated them, his eyes beckoned her and, with a glad cry, she ran to the bandit and wrapped her arms tightly around him.

He laid his cheek on the top of her head and clutched her fiercely to his heart, which beat out a stronger, steadier rhythm than her own. His arms around her were bands of steel, his broad shoulders a safe refuge she never wanted to leave.

It was he who ended the embrace, setting her aside at last. She looked up at him, her eyes pensive, questioning. There was much to be said, much to be answered between them.

"It's all over." The deep voice spoke words of comfort, but not the words she wanted to hear. She longed for words of love.

Her pride covered the turmoil inside her and she spoke with quiet firmness. "Thank you. It seems you've rescued me twice."

His voice carefully controlled, he replied, "You need have no more fear of him."

But what of you, gentle bandit? she thought. *Shall I have no fear of you?* "Are you all right?" she said aloud, a quiver in her voice.

"Yes. But we must hurry. You can still catch the steamship at the next landing, I think. Besides," he added, a smile easing the tension between them, "someone seems to be rather impatient for her mother's return."

Her mind confused and heart aching with new hurt, Camille smiled back and followed him to the clearing where she thankfully gathered her baby up in her arms. He helped her mount the horse he'd led out of the trees, his hand at her waist once more sending a chill and a spark of hungry longing through her.

She leaned toward him, the kiss she gave him replete with pent-up longing and awakening love. His eyes were soft, vulnerable, and she thought he would reach to pull her back into his arms, but he shook off the temporary weakness and turned to swing up on his own horse.

They rode rapidly up the road, speed making it impossible to speak, which was just as well, since neither of them knew what else to say. Too soon, they reached their destination. The boat was approaching. They would say goodbye and she knew with a pang of loss that she might never see the bandit again.

He left her then, leading her horse behind him, and her last impression was the straight line of his back as he rode off down the road.

CAMILLE SAT ALONE, except for the baby she held in her arms, in the bow of the *Princess* as it steamed upstream toward Natchez, toward home. Her mind reeled with a confusing array of images from the past months. Especially vivid were those from the past few days.

Most compelling was the recollection of dark eyes filled with tenderness, eyes hidden behind a mask. A husky voice that played over her emotions like the caress of fine velvet. The touch of warm, strong hands and a length of smoothly muscled body that turned her heart upside down.

He had been dangerously exciting and completely irresistible. And his concern for her and her daughter was very real and touched her deeply.

And where will you go, my bandit? she wondered sadly, watching a waterspout off the side of the boat. Her thoughts whirled in the same circular manner, never reaching a conclusion, yet never ceasing their tumultuous motion. So much had happened. And so many questions remained unanswered.

The one thing she knew for certain was that she would soon be home, and she was so glad! With every mile, every familiar aspect of the countryside, she grew more and more excited. She talked to Caroline as though she expected her to understand, to absorb her mother's love for the land, the river, for Magnolia.

"Caroline, my darling, see up ahead? Spanish moss and the live oaks—the lovely wildflowers! Look, there are the bluffs!"

Her eyes drank in the beloved sights. Even the familiar shanties Under the Hill and narrow Silver Street, bustling with life the same as ever, seemed beautiful to her. Glancing up, she could barely see the tops of tall trees, the lofty heights of several plantations.

"It's Natchez, Caroline," she whispered. "We're home!"

Chapter Nineteen

HOME! CAMILLE WAS HOME at last! Up ahead, sprawling in all its majesty, stood Magnolia. Her first glimpse of ivory columns in the buttery afternoon sun sent her tumbling back into her childhood, summoning golden memories of carefree times, overlaid by her passionate love for her family, for Magnolia. It was so good to be back!

Flowering yellow jasmine and late-blooming azaleas filled the air with a sweet nectar, their brilliant colors a feast for the eye. The glossy green of the magnolia tree, the ancient live oaks with their trailing whiskers of Spanish moss, all seemed to reach out and envelop her with welcome.

"Missy Cam come home! Missy Cam here!" The happy cry was raised by Josiah, echoed by his twin Jonah, and the chorus quickly joined by others until all the dearly loved faces of Magnolia's household servants were gathered on the front steps.

Camille felt that her heart would surely burst from the unrestrained love spilling forth in their wide smiles and words of welcome.

She spoke to each one warmly, proudly showing off her daughter to a chorus of appreciative comments.

"She's a beauty, Missy. Why, she look jest lak yo' did!" Josef's face lit up and he looked almost young again.

Essie clicked her tongue, this time in approval, and Camille didn't mind at all. Indigo danced about, hardly able to contain her excitement. "A baby! We gonna has us a young'un at Magnolia!"

Jonah and Josiah stood without speaking, white teeth sparkling in their open smiles.

"Welcome home, Missy Cam." Josef spoke for all of them, tears filling his eyes, his white head shaking with emotion. "We missed you, ma'am. We sorely did!"

"Thank you, Josef. I can't tell you how glad I am to be here." Her smile was brilliant, and included each one of them, but her eyes searched for Charles, for Jacqueline. "Is Mister Charles here, Josef?"

"No, ma'am. He come home jest last night. But he and dat Masters person done had a ter'ble argument. Den Miss Jacq'line lef' wi' Masters sometime during the night. And Mist' Charles, when he find out, he took off after 'em. Hain't seen one of 'em since." Josef said he thought they had taken the steamboat to Vicksburg, but he knew nothing else.

Camille's face fell in disappointment. "What was Masters doing at Magnolia?" she asked softly, afraid of the answer.

"Oh, I guess you din' know, ma'am. He an' Miss Jacq'line . . . dey was married a while back."

Camille fought to control her expression in front of the servants, but the news was a harsh shock. Jacqueline married to that preacher! And then to go off with him! Her mind could hardly cope with the distressing news. And Charles had gone after them! This morning? Then she had only missed him by hours. Charles! Her heart ached with the hurt. How could it be that she had waited for so long, wished so desperately to be in his arms, to see the sudden laughter in his eyes, to be held in his strong, yet gentle embrace, only to find him gone? It did not seem possible he was not here. Not when she had dreamed so many times of her homecoming, a return welcomed by more than servants, as dear as they were. Of course, he had no way of knowing; there had been no time to notify him. Perhaps she didn't deserve for him to be there, after what she'd done. Would she tell him? Could she jeopardize their marriage with the truth? She honestly didn't know. But when, oh, when, would he return?

Camille settled her baby down for a nap, and roamed through the house, feeling and remembering. Magnolia was much the same as it had been before she was abducted, though she herself had undergone drastic changes. The bedroom she shared so briefly with her husband brought on a sense of disquiet, though. She rested for but a short while and then called for her mare Sadie, who had wandered back home after the kidnapping. She was glad for the feel of her own mount beneath her.

It had been so long since she'd ridden wild and free across her land. She rode hard, enjoying the feel of her horse beneath her and the lengthening shadows of late afternoon as they crept across the winding pathways of Magnolia. She did not return until almost dusk. None of her questions had been answered, but she knew what she must do. In her absence and that of Charles, her home had become sadly run-down. She saw many evidences of it during her ride. Since she couldn't bear to see it that way, and could only wait to hear from Charles, she would channel her energies into setting things to rights.

Camille began her task the next morning. Soon she had servants trimming and weeding the lawns and flower beds and Indigo and Essie set to work on the inside, dusting and scrubbing.

"Jest din' seem no use with yo' all gone, Missy. And Miss Jacq'line and dat Masters person din' seem to care—jest stayed in dey—yo'—room mos' of da time," Indigo remarked.

"Well, I'm home now, and I expect Mr. Longmont back any day. Move their things out of my room today. I want everything perfect for my husband's return."

Camille learned of the siege of Vicksburg with a terrible sense of foreboding. Charles and Jacqueline were there! Would they be trapped and unable to get out? After the initial reports, news from their neighboring city to the north—dropped to a mere trickle of information.

Camille could only wait, and pray, and tend to Magnolia and the thriving Caroline, who grew more winsome with each passing day.

WHEN CLEMENT MASTERS FLED Natchez with Jacqueline, he had no idea where they would run—only that it was no longer safe for him there. Charles Longmont had returned unexpectedly and knew of his part in the kidnapping of his wife. The avenging husband would stop at nothing to make Masters pay.

He shivered, swallowing the bitter bile of fear. Longmont was mad! Clement had been lucky to escape with his life and nothing more than a badly sprained arm, which he had miraculously been able to wrench free from Charles's grasp as he leapt aboard the steamship pulling away from the dock and landed in a quivering heap beyond the railing.

Jacqueline was waiting there to help him up and they stood together, her arms wrapped tightly around him, watching Charles and Natchez Under the Hill fade into the distance. For one insane moment he'd been certain Charles was about to jump into the water and swim after them. He held his breath until they had safely rounded the first bend, heading upriver. He was safe! For now, at least, until Longmont discovered their destination and came after him.

Masters planned to go west, as far as possible, and start a new life. But since his funds were insufficient for the undertaking, he would stop at Vicksburg to search for another way of financing the expedition.

He thought with greedy longing of the fabulous paintings, the fine silver and crystal at Magnolia, treasures that would bring a king's ransom on the black market. If it hadn't been for Charles, he'd have had a boatload of them, and be set for life. The more he thought of that man, the more his passionate hatred multiplied until it became a blinding rage. His ears rang with it.

His fists clenched so hard his nails bit into his flesh, bringing blood, and his body was rigid, every sinew and ligament stretched to the limit. He was like a guitar too tightly strung, with the strings about to snap, one by one. Such a breakdown was a luxury he could not afford, not now. By conscious exercise of will, he opened his fists, loosening his fingers one at a time. Then his brain sent a message to various muscles of his body to release their hold and, grudgingly, they reacted. His arms and hands were first to relax their tension, then his neck, which allowed his head to move once more. Then his chest, alleviating the excruciating pressure that had been exerted on his heart. Then his midsection, and from his trunk down through his thighs, his calves, his ankles, his feet, he felt the response of his body to his brain waves carrying the message to relax.

He could easily have slid to the deck, but remained upright, conscious of Jacqueline's hands adding their encouragement by gently kneading his shoulders, his neck, his lower back, his buttocks. She knelt and her hands worked up and down his legs, moving to the inside of his thighs. His legs squeezed together tightly, clamping her hands between them in a vise.

The one sure way to work out what tension remained! He released her hands and taking them under his arm, compelled her along toward the cabin they would share. Thoughts of his narrow escape from Charles were pushed to the back of his mind for the present, as insatiable and cruel lust took the forefront.

"We'll see who's the servant and who's the master this night, my young heiress!" he said, his voice heavy with sarcasm. He had never been able to touch but the smallest portion of the Beaufort fortune. Though he hadn't given up, Jacqueline's presence was a constant reproach to him. And, though he had gotten rid of Camille, Charles continued to be an impediment to his schemes.

But a word in the right place would bring the Yankees down on Charles, for his part in the raiding bands. When they had executed him, or at least locked him away in a Northern prison camp, the way would be clear for him to get at the Beaufort fortune.

"Words of gold, words of gold..." he muttered, falling on his wife's naked body, already arching to-

ward him. He pounded into her mercilessly, until he
felt the overwhelming tension run out of him along
with his seed. Collapsing on top of her, he was snoring
in a deep sleep almost immediately.

The next morning brought them to Vicksburg on the
last civilian ship allowed to dock as General Grant
tightened the screws of doom on the once proud city.
No one would enter or leave freely for over forty days.
The siege of Vicksburg had begun.

GENERAL ULYSSES S. GRANT, the brilliant veteran
commander of the Union forces in the western theater, recognized the strategic importance of Vicksburg. He saw the city as the key to the end of the war,
an end he longed for as much, perhaps more, than
anyone. Regardless of the cost in human life and suffering, he knew he had to have Vicksburg.

He had made several attempts to gain access to the
city, but had been repulsed time after time by the brave
Confederate troops under General Pemberton, who
had dug in around the city to protect it.

Surrounded on three sides by swamps and bayous
and on the fourth by the river, Vicksburg seemed im-
pregnable to Northern assaults. It was a powerful fortress protected by its guns that dominated the river
from atop a 250-foot cliff. It would, indeed, take
General Grant an intensive campaign, months in
length, followed by a final all-out bombardment of civilians, to bring the noble city to her knees.

No one realized in those early days what a horrible
time of captivity lay ahead for the inhabitants of
Vicksburg. Masters and Jacqueline had joined their
number at precisely the worst possible time. When
they discovered their mistake and that there would be

no way out of the tight box Grant had constructed around them, it was too late. By that time Charles had himself entered the city in search of them, intent on rescuing Jacqueline from the clutches of the preacher as he'd promised Camille long ago.

Charles remembered Vicksburg as it had been when he'd first seen it, sitting high on the horseshoe bend of the river, staring regally down at passing ships. Much like Natchez, this city was a collage of lofty elegant heights and below-the-bluffs rowdiness. Now he saw beautiful Vicksburg being reduced to rubble, and viewed the devastation with a heavy heart.

Caves were dug into the sides of every available hill, where whole families—or what was left of them—cowered in abject misery, or bravely tried to make the best of impossible living conditions. Howling, hungry dogs. Galloping horses. Looting, fighting, and burning. Broken hearts, broken lives, broken dreams.... Vignettes of a world gone mad.

In the midst of this confusion and terrible suffering, Charles finally found Jacqueline and Masters. Their tiny cave, hacked out by hand in the hard earth of a hillside, was barely visible from where he now stood staring up at it. A ragged curtain hung over the gaping opening. There was no sign of life as he drew nearer, the sun beating down on his head. He stopped just outside the entrance.

"Jacqueline!" he called, and louder, "Masters! I know you're in there! I want to talk to you!" There was no response; the curtain hung limp in the stifling stillness. Charles wiped away a rivulet of sweat that ran down his temple, dampening his shirt collar.

Mixed odors of cooking grease and dried sweat swirled forth from the cave when the curtain was pulled

back, and a hooked nose and pair of black eyes could
be discerned in the opening. Charles caught the glimmer of sun on a blade of steel peeking out about a foot
below. He backed off just in time as the blade ripped
upward, missing his stomach by inches.

"That does it, Masters. I'm going to put an end to
your worthless life, once and for all. Jacqueline, come
on out. You're going home with me."

"Stay where you are," the little man snarled over his
shoulder at the young woman inside.

"You can't keep her here, Masters, if she doesn't
want to stay."

"Oh, she wants to stay, all right. You can ask her
yourself. You *do* want to stay, don't you, *Mrs. Masters*?"

A muffled whisper from inside.

"She's *my* wife, Longmont, and you can't take her
away. She doesn't want to leave." The smile on his lips
didn't reach his dark eyes and he waved his weapon.

"Now I'd suggest you get on out of here!"

"I'll be back, Masters. Jacqueline," he called, "be
ready to go with me. I'll be back at eight tonight."

"Don't waste your time," Masters called to him as
he turned and made his way down the hill.

Charles Longmont had never killed a man in his life,
except in the service of the Confederacy, but what if he
had to kill Masters to save Jacqueline from him? He
wasn't sure he could do it. Even after what he had done
to Camille—the evil pact he'd made with Montaigne
that led to her kidnapping and might have caused her
death. Masters hadn't cared what the Creole did with
her as long as he got his gold and his chance at the
Beaufort fortune.

Charles would try to talk Jacqueline away from him, and if that failed, he'd use the threat of going to the authorities, or of violence, only as a last resort. He had seen enough of suffering and death in this damned war.

A howling, screaming charge of rebels against overwhelming odds. A drummer playing on determinedly even as the dead from his company littered the ground in grotesque, bloody shapes. A young Union soldier eye to eye, as frightened and as disillusioned as he and knowing he had to pull the trigger—to kill first or be killed. A lonesome soldier talking wistfully of home, children, flowers and spring against a backdrop of the pop-pop of musket fire, and the roar of cannons.

The sun was setting, sliding down beyond the Mississippi, but the enervating heat had not lessened by a single degree. Charles returned to the hill where Jacqueline and Masters had taken refuge from the constant shelling and mortar attacks falling on the city. It was a pitiful hovel, but only one of many in the besieged city.

"Come out, Masters!" he shouted.

The curtain was yanked back, and the thin form of the preacher appeared. "You'll have to come and get me, Longmont."

"Jacqueline!" he yelled. "Come on out of there. I won't let him hurt you anymore!"

"Ah, the great and gallant Charles Longmont— protector of Southern causes and Southern womanhood! Couldn't even protect his own wife! What makes him so all-fired set on protecting mine? Better go on home and see to your own little love nest. By now, though, the Yanks will have taken it all! They know all about you and your *raiders*, Longmont!"

Charles's blood ran cold. Masters knew of his raiders and had gotten word to the Yankees? There were those who would hang raiders without a trial! The evasive bands were hated by the Yankees, who were always anxious to track them down and punish them. Could what Masters was saying be true? Were Camille and Magnolia in jeopardy because of him?

The preacher had disappeared inside, giving Charles a chance to digest what he'd heard. Suddenly he appeared again, with Jacqueline right behind him. Charles edged a little closer.

"You'll never take us, Longmont!" The mad satanic light in the man's eyes and the tone of desperation in his voice should have been enough warning, as he continued. "If you take one more step, I'll set off a charge that will blow us all sky high! I mean it!" he screamed as Charles took another step.

The man was truly mad. But still Charles didn't put any credence in the wild threat, and advanced a few more steps. He had to get Jacqueline out of there! He was close enough now to see the panic, the plea for help in her wide, dark eyes, so haunted by fear.

He held out his hand and said, "Jacquie, come here to me," talking slowly, as he would to a frightened child. She put her hand on Masters's arm as though she would get by him. At the same instant Charles made a lunge toward them, Masters turned to his left, and the world blew apart.

The force of the explosion ripped open the hill and sent Charles hurtling backward through the air. He slammed into a tree and slid to the ground unconscious.

When he awoke three days later he was in a Confederate hospital, his head bandaged and still splitting from the effects of the injury and the concussion of the explosives. His right leg bore a splint and seemed oddly bent.

Masters had not been bluffing and Charles realized he'd been an incredible fool to disregard the wild threat. His need to set Jacqueline free had led him up the side of the hill. Doggedly and stupidly, he had gone ahead, sure that Masters was a coward and would back down. How could he have been so completely, so horribly wrong?

Though he knew there was no way either of them could have survived the awful blast, he asked the nurse, "Do you know what happened to the man and woman in the cave?"

"No, sir. The soldiers who brought you here said anybody in there would be buried so far under the rubble... Oh! I'm sorry sir. Were they friends of yours, then?"

"In a way, nurse. One of them was my young ward, who was also my sister-in-law." His voice was replete with self-loathing. The nurse had seen much sickness and slow, painful dying, but the sorrow and haunted look of guilt in this wounded man's dark brown eyes moved her in a surprising way.

"If there's anything I can do, sir..." she offered helplessly, moving on to the next patient.

"Heard about that big blow," said the man in the next bed. "Though we're kinda used to loud noises around here. Sorry about your friend," he added, more kindly. "I'm Lieutenant John Mallory, at your service, sir."

"Charles Longmont, soldier. And thank you." He reached across to shake hands and noticed too late the man had lost his right arm. The other man only laughed at Charles's confusion and reached to shake hands with his left.

"Lost t'other one at Antietam, so I did! Coulda lost a lot more, though." He laughed again to cover the look of pain that shadowed his eyes.

"That why you're here?" Charles indicated the hospital room they shared with about forty other wounded men.

"Nah! Bad case of the dysentery, so's I couldn't stay on my feet anymore—that's what landed me here. Near good as new, now," he said, laughing harshly again, "or good as I can be, under the circumstances. Gonna rejoin my buddies tomorrow, I 'spect." His eyes showed new signs of life when he talked of his duty and his friends.

"Though why I'd wanna get back to them damn trenches, I can't imagine!"

The fighting in the sturdy redoubts constructed around Vicksburg had been intense, as musket fire from Yankee soldiers and cannon volleys from the gunboats in the river kept up an almost constant bombardment.

As he talked with the young soldier, Charles learned that conditions in the trenches were far worse than he had heard or could have imagined. Many of the soldiers had no shoes, and their uniforms hung in dirty tatters on painfully thin bodies.

"When yer starvin'," said the soldier, "a strip o' meat is a mighty handsome thing! You learn not to ask where it comes from. If it be an army mule too stringy-thin to live longer, or some kid's pet dog, it's all the same. It keeps you alive, and that's all that matters.''

But under fire the Confederate soldiers were steady and battle-hardened. Lieutenant John Mallory spoke of their courage with admiration. ''Yup! That rebel yell sure does things to a man's heart—and his head! It's the spirit of the army, see? It's revenge—'' his eyes grew hard as he continued almost in a whisper ''—for a buddy that just died in your arms. It's hatred—for the bloody enemy and what he's doing to your homeland!''

Many of the soldiers, he told Charles, had become insensitive to death and suffering in order to survive and were just holding out, hanging on for one more day, one more hour, one more precious minute of life. And they all hoped for one thing, for the wretched war to end!

Together, Charles and the one-armed lieutenant in the next bed, along with the other wounded in the crowded ward, heard of the surrender of the city.

It was over. Vicksburg had lost. The South had lost. As Charles had known it would. But they had fought with spirit and heart, and they'd fought hard, many to a brave and gallant death. With the surrender of Vicksburg, it would be only a matter of time until the war was over, and he hoped it would be a short time, so that what still remained of their Southern manhood could be saved. Rebuilding would be a tough and arduous process and the South would need all the resources left to it to pull through.

Charles learned then that it had not been merely for the end they all prayed, but for victory. The usual moans and groans from the hospital beds escalated to screams and cries of frustrated rage. He saw soldiers cry when word of the surrender had come, and he heard them curse and beg for one more chance to fight the Yankees. Even after all they had been through, they hadn't wanted to quit, hadn't wanted to give up. Surrender was unacceptable.

Turning their arms over to the enemy was a bitter, galling thing, but when 29,500 of them marched out to do it, Union soldiers cheered them in recognition of their bravery in the defense of the city. General Grant saw that they were fed, and allowed them to keep their personal belongings. The agreement between Grant and General Pemberton was a generous one, and the tired, beaten, Southern soldiers were paroled, free to return to their homes. The victors could afford to be magnanimous. They felt they'd won the war, and perhaps they were right.

Women, children, the old and infirm had crawled out of their hilly dens to join their husbands and fathers who'd survived. They would begin to build a new life for themselves.

But Clement Masters and Jacqueline would never come forth from the cave in which they'd taken refuge, and it was his fault.

Charles limped away from the hospital on a crutch fashioned from a tree limb. His leg ached miserably and had been poorly set. His head still pounded and he found it as hard to control his thinking as it was to control his uneven gait.

He plodded painfully down the road, leaving Vicksburg behind, as he wished he could leave behind the grim scenes of the war that danced through his mind, constantly tormenting him: Reaper shot out from under him, the beautiful animal screaming as he crumpled to the ground; a wounded soldier plaintively singing "The Yellow Rose of Texas"; the photograph of a pretty, smiling sweetheart in a dead soldier's knapsack; the look on Camille's face when he'd shouted at her in anger on the night of the birthday party; his friend David Renault, limping on his one remaining leg; Ace, whose body had been scattered in pieces across a Carolina battlefield. Oh, God! Would he never be free of it all?

Vignettes of a world gone mad!

A deep depression pierced Charles's soul. And he was almost glad for the pain, for at least he was able to *feel* something again. The cool, deliberate actions of war had, at times, made him callous, his heart unfeeling. He'd seen so many suffer and die and had learned the only way to cope with that was to allow the hardening to shield his heart from the terrible pain.

Under the shade of an ancient oak tree, he stopped, the scenes replaying in his mind again, as they had so many times before.

He was tired, bone-weary in fact, and wanted nothing so much as to go home. Home? If something had happened to Magnolia—to Camille—he knew he couldn't bear that.

Though Charles had foreseen the useless holocaust the war would be, he had not been able to stay out of it. He had fought for the only reason a man ever fights—to protect his home and family, to preserve their freedom and way of life. Was it all lost now?

Charles reached down to pick up a discarded journal lying at his feet. He scanned the dates.

April 27, 1863
We hear the Union soldiers are on the other side of the river below our city. Though they have

digged a canal and tried other means, they have yet to reach us! We have faith in our ability to withstand.

May 19, 1863
Our brave men have once more withstood the assault of General Grant with all his 33,000 men! He shall not have Vicksburg!

May 29, 1863
From my bedroom window, I can see crude trenches dug into the hillside by our soldiers. They have strong fortifications surrounding the city. May God help them—and us!

June 15, 1863
The last of our canning from last year's garden is long since gone. We are reduced to eating what can be salvaged, and most times that is poor indeed. The constant shelling wears one's nerves to the breaking point. We may soon seek refuge in the cave built by Cousin Matthew. The cannons seem to be coming nearer and nearer. Thursday, last, we lost a section of the porch, and spend much time in the basement.

June 30, 1863
Don't see how we can hold out much longer. Our men are scarecrows, so wretchedly thin. There is *nothing* left to eat! And water becomes an even larger problem. Please God, let it soon be over!

A sketch by some young woman of the siege from the beginning. But the writer either could not, or would not, write of the defeat—the end. No entry after July 3, 1863. Probably she hadn't had the heart.

Sadly, Charles dropped it, and a few pages fluttered out, plastering themselves to the mud and filth along the side of the road.

He was so hot that the perspiration rolled from his hairline down under his collar. His shirt stuck uncomfortably to his chest. He wiped his face, uncertain if he removed sweat or tears, for they had mingled on his suntanned skin. No breeze stirred, and the hot sun beat down unmercifully.

He had gone several miles before he realized his direction would eventually lead him into Natchez. Subconsciously he had given in to the desire to see her one more time, to be sure she was safe. Yet how could he stay there? A pain even greater than he'd been experiencing stabbed his heart. He had nothing left, not even his heart, which had been mutilated beyond repair. He was an emotional cripple, mortally wounded in his soul. Even his body was battered and beaten. Camille deserved better. She deserved someone with feelings, someone who could love and protect her, who would keep his promises—someone strong and whole. She deserved a man. How could he ever face her after he had failed her so badly?

Jacqueline—he saw once more the bewitching child with the raven hair and big, black eyes; heard once more his promise to protect her, made first to Braxton on his deathbed and then later to her sister. Camille had trusted him to keep his word. But he hadn't! Clement Masters had beaten him at last, even in his own death, for he had taken Jacqueline with him.

With a cry of rage and frustration, Charles drove his fist into the hard bark of the tree, bloodying and bruising it. Then he walked on, glad for the physical pain, the blood from his knuckles dripping unheeded to the ground.

Chapter Twenty

"GO BACK! Go back! The devils are in town!"

An old lady ran down the main street of Natchez, shouting, the ribbons of her bonnet streaming out behind.

Camille had driven her buggy in for supplies with Caroline nestled snugly beside her on the seat, sleeping quietly. At first she'd thought the old woman, whom she'd known for years, had gone completely mad. But then, looking beyond her to the bluff, she saw a big black puff of smoke.

A Yankee gunboat! Protectively she pulled her baby daughter into her lap. Had they come to take Natchez as they had Vicksburg? Camille had listened with growing horror to the stories trickling out of Vicksburg, even after communications had been severed, of the unspeakable terrors and deprivations of the siege.

Natchez had no strong line of defense, no earthworks, no trenches, no strong Confederate troops. The Silver Grays, a small force of citizen volunteers, were their only protection.

At the crest of Silver Street, a line of blue-coated figures materialized, marching in columns toward her. She sat where she was, too stubborn and curious to flee.

David Renault hobbled over on his crude, artificial limb and his one good leg, and led her horse to the side of the street, out of the way of the soldiers, just as the well-armed, well-groomed, well-fed Yanks marched past.

"It's happened, Cam. They've come at last," he said softly, standing beside her. "The foolish Silver Grays fired on them, I heard. And it seems they'd only stopped for water. But a volley was fired—the Yankee gunboat retaliated, and now we're lost. A little girl, an innocent child was killed."

"Oh, no! David!" she cried, pulling Caro closer to her. She let him help her to the ground and put her arms around him, wanting to ease the anguish she saw in his eyes, the helpless, impotent rage.

How long they stood there, she didn't know—but at last only dust remained to suggest the conquering force that had marched so determinedly by them.

Soon after, they learned that the mayor of Natchez had ridden out to confer with General Grant.

Within days, Charles Longmont rode into town.

"IS THIS THE HOME of Colonel Charles Longmont?" Brilliant mid-July sunshine reflected off the gold buttons of the soldier's spotless uniform as he stood with erect military bearing on the front portico of Magnolia.

Indigo had scurried to answer the door, giving Camille time to prepare herself for this unexpected visit from a Union officer.

"Yasuh, it sure is de home of Mr. Charles Longmont." Indigo stood in the doorway, blocking his entrance. She did not invite him in. Southern hospitality was not extended to include the hated Yankees who now occupied Natchez.

"Is *Colonel* Longmont in?" His emphasis on the military rank was this time obvious, even to the flustered servant.

"I don' know no *colonel*, suh. But Mist' Charles, he ain' hyah." She made the announcement triumphantly, hands on her narrow hips.

"I'm afraid I'll have to see for myself." The soft voice held the unmistakable tones of command.

Indigo stammered, "Da missus . . . she in da parlor, suh," as he impatiently pushed past her into the main hallway, and made his way to the room Indigo had indicated.

"Captain Peters, ma'am." He introduced himself, somewhat taken aback by the beauty and quiet dignity of the woman who stood in front of the largest gilt-framed mirror he'd ever seen.

"Camille Beaufort Longmont, Captain. What is it that you wish to see my husband about?"

"A matter of government business, ma'am. One which, unfortunately, I am not at liberty to discuss with you. When do you expect him, may I inquire?"

"Certainly you may, Captain, but I'm afraid I have no answer for you. You see, I haven't seen my husband in some time. I have no idea when he might return home."

"Perhaps you might know, then, where we could find him?" The tone in his voice indicated that he expected no cooperation from her, but only asked as a matter of procedure.

Camille was not fooled. This man was deadly serious about finding Charles. Her husband was in some kind of terrible trouble

"I'm sorry, Captain. I don't. And now if you will excuse me, I must see to my young daughter, who can be very demanding. Indigo will show you out." With a formal smile of apology, she moved toward the doorway, but the Yankee officer stood where he was.

"There's just one more thing for now, ma'am."

"And what is that, Captain?" Camille's patience was growing thin, her nerves were on edge, and Caroline was crying noisily from the nursery.

"If you *should* happen to see your husband, please relay to him that it is most urgent he appear at our command headquarters immediately."

He had clicked his heels, pivoted, and strode out the door, practically colliding with an anxious Indigo who hovered in the hall.

The stiffly proper young officer rejoined his small band of men waiting in the front yard, and they were gone as suddenly as they had arrived.

Camille was stunned. Why had they come looking for Charles? And why had he mistakenly called her husband *Colonel* Longmont? Charles, so far as she knew, had never enlisted in the Confederate army. And from the man's attitude, it was safe to assume he was not seeking a Union officer!

How could she find Charles and get word to him that he would be walking into a trap by returning to Natchez? She shuddered to think what would happen if he *did* come back, right into the teeth of a Yankee trap.

In the next few days, the Yankee captain made regular visits to Magnolia seeking Charles. And Camille suspected the plantation was being closely watched.

She knew she had to help her husband, regardless of what he'd done, or failed to do—and even if he no longer loved her. She loved him! She supposed she had always loved him, from the first time he had helped her climb onto her pony when she was but a child. Her love for him had intensified during the time of her father's tragic death, when Charles had stood by her and Jacqueline. She remembered the pain in his face at her father's bedside, his compassion for her and Jacqueline, how he had comforted her at her father's graveside. She could still see him as he'd looked the night she'd been sent by her father to find him, the warm smile on his face when he'd made his incredible offer of marriage, the look of pleasure and approval when he'd seen her again on the front steps of Magnolia after all those years.

Dear God! That's why it hurt so much when he sent them away! It wasn't just Magnolia or Natchez—it had been for Charles Longmont that her heart had pined during her absence, his face she longed to see most, his voice that could set her heart hammering, even now.

And those long, awful months in New Orleans, it had not been her freedom that she'd so sorely missed, but him! And that's why she hurt so badly now—with him gone. Why hadn't he come home, and worse, what would happen when he did come back?

She wandered through the vast, empty house once more, seeking some sign of him, touching the chair where he'd so often sat, lifting his pipe to breathe in the familiar aroma.

Charles might never again be hers, but at least she would see that he was safe, and she could tell him none of it meant anything, not even Magnolia had meaning for her, without him!

KNOWING HE WAS WANTED by the Yankees, Charles could not walk boldly into Natchez, but his need to see Camille and be sure she and the child were safe was a driving force inside him. He could not endanger them by letting Camille know he was home, not yet. Perhaps never, he thought, a shaft of hurt filling his chest.

He slipped into town, occupied his old rooms Under the Hill, and waited for nightfall before riding to Magnolia. Weaving his way through the back roads, he came up from the back of Magnolia so he could see without being seen. He cursed softly. Of course he could see nothing from the vine-covered thicket behind the house! Lace curtains covered all the windows and, though candles glowed brightly, he could not distinguish any of the shapes moving around inside.

He would not leave until he knew for sure. On foot, he crept closer and closer until he crouched outside the parlor window. An owl hooted, and he jumped nervously. Then he saw her. Camille, more beautiful, more womanly than he remembered. She sat on the sofa, smiling happily at the baby who gurgled back at her and reached for her mother's nose with chubby fingers.

His baby. His daughter. He could barely control the overwhelming longing to hold her in his arms. And Camille! He had never seen her more lovely, her face soft and tender with love for their child.

How would that face change when she learned of her sister's needless death, a death he could have prevented—a death, it might even be said, he had contributed to? He could see the deep lines of sorrow, even as he looked at her, and the condemnation that would follow. She would never forgive him!

He backed away and quickly covered the ground to his horse. Putting his heels to the animal, he recognized only the need to be away from here, away from her. Until the horse stopped, quivering from the hard run, he hadn't consciously known where he was going.

A shaft of moonlight speared a graceful curve of stairway. Charles took in the scene in a glance and his heart suffered a new agony. The beautiful symmetry of the stairs sweeping upward was all that remained of the house he had been building for Camille. Despite her lack of enthusiasm, he had wanted the place for their children. It would have been his legacy, and had nearly been completed before the war broke out.

Now there were only the damned stairs, leading to nothing. The rest of the house lay in blackened ruins. Masters had been right. The Yankees had beaten him home.

Doubtless they had seized his land and personal wealth, as well. He had nothing left that was his own, but he was thankful the reprisal of the Yankees had not reached as far as Magnolia. If he left now, the odds were good they would trouble Camille no more. But how could he go?

A harsh laugh echoed above the ruins. How could he not? He jumped on his horse and turned his back on his dreams and his hopes for the future. The damned war had stolen everything from him. The worst part was the empty cavity where his heart should have been. He would not be moved to fear nor to blinding sorrow ever again, as he would feel no exquisite joy nor contented happiness. It might be the only way he could survive. He would go away from here, as far away as he could.

UNAWARE OF THE DRAMA unfolding outside her window, Camille put her finger to her lips to silence Indigo, and rose from where she had been sitting, lost in thought. Quietly she made her way to the nursery and lay the sleeping baby down, tucking the covers in about her.

Blowing out the candle, she backed out the door, pulling it partly closed.

"I'm going to bed, Indigo. Good night."

"Oh! Missy Cam! I plumb forgot! A letter came for you today—from Vicksburg, ma'am!" She raced down the stairs to retrieve it, leaving Camille staring after her in shock.

Vicksburg! Where Charles had gone after Jacqueline and Masters! A letter from Charles? A letter—saying he'd soon be home? A letter—saying he still loved her?

"You should have told me sooner," came the gentle rebuke when Indigo returned.

"I'se sorry, ma'am, truly!" Indigo apologized again. Dismissed by her mistress, she hurried off to bed.

Camille stood in the hall with the letter in her hand, afraid to open it, afraid of what it might say, afraid of putting an end to her dreams. She knew that no one had been allowed to enter or leave Vicksburg for weeks. She also knew of the sad surrender, and hoped Charles was on his way home.

Trepidation slowing her steps, she entered her own room and settled herself near the candlelight spilling across her reading table. With trembling fingers, she tore open the envelope. Her eyes raced down to the signature—it was from Aunt Emily, not from Charles at all. Her disappointment was so keen she sat without reading for several minutes. Her eyes misted with tears—she missed him desperately and prayed daily for his safe return—and that of her sister. Jacqueline! The name jumped off the page to claim her attention.

Aunt Em wrote with a scratchy hand, obviously shaking as she penned the words. She told of Jacqueline's death in halting terms. ''A fire, an explosion of some sort...buried her in our family plot...a man with her, burned beyond recognition . . . and Charles...''

Charles! What about Charles? Had he been killed in the explosion? Dear God, no! She held the paper closer to the light and read on, though she could barely see for the tears. ''Head wound, in the hospital for several days...''

Charles had tried to save her, then, and almost killed himself in the attempt?

''He said his fault...'' the missive continued.

How could any of it be his fault? Charles might take the blame on himself, assume responsibility as he always did, but it could never, ever have been his fault. He would never do anything to hurt Jacqueline—or anyone!

''Left, I think...'' What? If he had left Vicksburg several days before, why wasn't he home? Where was he now?

Of course! He must have learned the Yankees were looking for him. That's why he hadn't shown himself. But couldn't he have gotten word to her somehow? At least to let her know he was all right? Didn't he long for her as she did for him? The doubts she'd had about his love while she'd been a captive in New Orleans came flooding back. Perhaps it was true he'd stopped loving her long ago.

She sat where she was long into the night, her heart grieving for her sister, the last of her family. Dear little Jacqueline, who had been so misguided and mistreated by Clement Masters. She shivered, thinking of the explosion. Another fire. Another death. Would it never end?

In her crushing sorrow, Camille fled the house and ran across the newly trimmed grounds of Magnolia to the family burial plot. Out of breath, she fell to her knees before the headstone that marked the final resting place of Braxton Beaufort. The undisturbed peacefulness of the place was external, a thing separate from her. It did not reach her heart. Unwilling to cope with the problems of the present, she closed her eyes and in her mind saw images. . . .

Images. . .of another time, another life—when there were no damned Yankees! When the whole word hadn't tipped wildly to one side. When life was graceful and beauty was everywhere. When laughter was more prevalent than tears and this all-pervasive sorrow. Images. . .of a tiny, raven-haired, younger sister, now forever lost to her. . . . Images. . .of her father, strong, decisive, loving. . . .

"Oh, Father, what am I to do now? What is there left for me?"

THE MORNING SUN designed a patchwork pattern across the lush, grass-covered mounds that marked the final resting places of her brother, her mother, and her father. A bird perched on a branch overhead trilled its merry song, unheeded by the young woman who knelt, seeking peace and solutions.

Magnolia, she seemed to hear him say, Magnolia. Looking around, she treasured the assurance that her home remained; thankfully, it had survived the rampages of the war thus far, and was much the same as always. But it was so empty. She was rid of the awful threat of Clement Masters, but in the process had lost the last of her family, her sister.

But not the last. The wailing voice of the tiny baby girl who lay in her own girlhood bedroom upstairs was a vivid reminder. Caroline! The hope of the future of Magnolia—the hope of her own future. Charles's daughter, who claimed his warm brown eyes.

Charles injured? Was he badly hurt? Her aching need to go to him, comfort him and reassure him of her love was so powerful, she jumped up and paced restlessly. She had to do something!

She would go to him. Even if he didn't want her, even if he didn't love her. She had to see him. She had to know he was all right. But where? And how?

Camille knew what she must do, and where she would start looking. She returned to the house, sent Indigo for Caroline, and called for her horse. If Charles wanted to stay out of sight, she knew where he would be—Under the Hill.

Camille made her way down Silver Street, clutching her daughter tightly to her chest, memories of the night she had come there as a child still vivid in her mind. Men's shouted curses sailed over her head, and she was oblivious to the gathering storm that began to pitch the waves on the Mississippi and blow her long curls into her face. She rode farther and farther down the hill, looking for a familiar face, trying desperately to decide where to go, whom to ask. Should she go to his old inn—perhaps she would find him there, or someone who could help her?

As she wrestled with her doubts and fears, she heard through the growing din a lonely foghorn. Her eyes drawn to the river, she spied in the dim light a ferryboat, apparently about to depart for Vidalia, overloaded with a cargo of men and livestock. Hardly daring to breathe, she looked, then looked again, her eyes arrested by a tall, hauntingly familiar form that stood out above the rest.

Charles! She wasn't even aware that she had shouted his name, until he turned slowly toward her. Their eyes met and held. Camille's tumultuous feelings almost toppled her from her horse and raindrops beat against her face as the storm began. It was really him! He had come back! But what was he doing on the ferry?

Charles made no move toward her. He was leaving without seeing her, or even once speaking to her! His head was bandaged and he leaned heavily on a cane. She wanted to run to him and take him in her arms, but she saw in his face no relief at the sight of her, no happiness. In his dark eyes, she saw nothing but pain and empty loneliness that cried out to her louder than the waves that now dashed against the boat with a deafening crescendo.

But what of their love? Her heart heaved from the pain. She saw no love in the familiar brown eyes. Once so warm and full of life, his eyes now had a haunted look, so emotionless, so hurt, so tired . . .

Had he ceased to love her? It would explain why he'd made only one aborted effort to find her, why it had been the gentleman bandit who had rescued her at last. Could love die so easily as that? She was certain her love for him would die a more lingering death. No, she could not give him up! She would not! If there was the tiniest spark of love still burning in him, she would do something to fan it into flames again. She would devote the rest of her life to that goal, if he'd only give her even one small sign that he had some feeling left for her.

What had happened to them? Had they lost everything? The war had come with its separations and sufferings and stolen away the happy, blissful days of their
innocence. Like dead leaves that flutter to the ground,
useless, fallen so far from their lofty perch . . .

"But the spring will come. . . ." Green leaves would
come to life to replace the old, it was true, and they
would make as thick a canopy, cast as pleasant a shade.

"The spring will come. . . ." Charles's words spoken to her grieving heart on their wedding day, so long
ago.

"Spring will come. . . ." An affirmation of life, of
love, of the future.

The certainty still existed.

The promise remained.

"Charles!" she cried. Her voice echoed across the
distance that separated them as she slid from her horse.

Camille watched his eyes as they moved from her
face to the cherubic face of their daughter and back
again. Yes! She saw there a glimmer of tenderness, if
nothing else. It was enough. In that moment she knew
that the spring *would* come again—to her heart, to
Natchez, to the South.

With a stifled cry, she moved toward him. She would
follow him across a continent if necessary, to the ends
of the earth.

He was her life, her destiny. Her tiny daughter's father. And, by God, he was her husband, even if he
tried to ignore or change that fact by running away!

Another step.

Still he did not move, but stood with one booted foot
on the dock and one on the boat, his hand on the railing.

His dark eyes fastened onto hers inescapably. Though he gave no indication of his desires or feelings, she felt a very real, very strong pull. She could not have stopped or turned back if her life depended on it.

Faster and faster she went, one foot in front of the other; step by step, the wind snatching her skirts and twisting them about her legs. A bolt of lightning illuminated her determined face and revealed the glow of love in her storm-colored eyes.

At last Charles broke free of the spell that bound him. With a cry of mingled pain and joy, he leaped from the dock and ran for the woman with the small baby cradled in her arms. Was it tears or merely the rain that dampened his cheeks?

He stopped when he reached her, his eyes questioning, searching hers.

Her husky voice caressed him as she placed one hand on his shoulder. "Where do you think you're going, Charles Longmont? Haven't you forgotten one small thing? I love you, above all else. I have made my choice. If you leave Natchez, we leave with you."

His voice breaking, he demanded, "You would do *that*? Leave Natchez, Magnolia, everything you love behind?"

"Not everything, my dear pigheaded Charles," she rebuked him, lowering her eyes to the wiggling form in her arms and raising them again to meet with his. "Not everything, my love."

Her fingers reached up to touch his face, and her deep blue eyes opened wide as she traced the sculpted lines of his cheekbones, his nose, his forehead, his clean-shaven face. Her breath quickening in her chest, she asked, "Charles?"

From his vest pocket, he slowly pulled out her locket and clasped it around her neck. "I meant to leave it behind, but I had to have something of you." The heated warmth from his fingers where they lingered against her skin seared into her soul. In that moment of awakening, she realized with a jolt something she should have known long before.

"Charles! He was—*is*—you! *You!* You . . . are the gentleman bandit! But how? Why?" Her mind flew back to their first meeting in the dark forest, then the next day when he'd stolen her locket, the daring rescue from Raphael, and finally their shared passion on the river road. A rosy flush of embarrassment crept up her face, but then she smiled.

"On second thought, I'm the pigheaded one. I should have known. Perhaps I *did* know. And that's why I loved you both!"

His lips curved upward and the smile reached his eyes. "We do need to discuss the rather wanton behavior of a very proper, married lady with a certain outlaw by the side of the road."

"And you, sir, have a bit of explaining to do yourself! But we will have years for that, won't we, Charles?"

Smothering a curse at himself for his foolishness, he wrapped them both in his arms, crushing them to him in an embrace that was at once tender, possessive and utterly wonderful.

The warm, crinkling smile she so ached to see began in his eyes and spread to full, sensuous lips. At that moment she saw in him both her dependable husband and the wild and exciting bandit who had so intrigued her.

"Let's go home, Cam," he said roughly, releasing her and snatching up the reins of her prancing mare.

Mindful only of her love and need and his answering passion and commitment, she turned with him toward Magnolia, where he would love her deliberately and thoroughly from that day forward. But for Camille, home was anywhere this man was, for as long as the spring would follow winter.

Epilogue

CAROLINE SLEPT IN the upstairs nursery. Magnolia slumbered peacefully, as well, the servants all abed, lamps extinguished, and a gentle calm settling over the household.

Camille stood in front of the window in the bedroom she shared once more with her husband, her body outlined by moonlight through her silken robe. Charles lit his pipe and, pulled by the love and attraction he had always felt for his lovely wife, walked over to stand behind her. One arm slipped around her waist and he heard her sigh of satisfaction as she settled back against him. He kissed the top of her head.

"The bandit once kissed me like that," she said softly, her hand covering his at her waist.

A deep chuckle sent chills racing over her as it always had. "He loved you, too, you know."

Charles had explained the necessity of the double identity. Even before the outbreak of the war, he had been actively at work trying to swing every advantage to the Confederate cause, knowing they would need it. Using the disguise of the bandit, he had been able to move more freely on his trips to New Orleans and up and down the Trace securing arms, ammunition and other supplies for the South.

Later he had formed his small band of raiders that had been so effective in harassing the Union troops.

Their last mission had been to cut the communication and supply lines of General Grant in his movement across Mississippi. They had been partially successful, but in the long run all the best attempts of the South had been fruitless and Vicksburg had fallen. After that, it had been only a matter of time until the war was over.

Magnolia, and Natchez as a whole, had escaped the worst effects of the war. Charles had been slow to recover from the wounds he had received in the explosion and had not actively entered the fighting again, though he continued to help in the war effort when called upon. He successfully avoided capture by the Yankees until the vindictive Captain Peters was transferred and Charles's activities with the raiding band forgotten.

Life was harsh. Reconstruction was, for the beaten South, a painful, often humiliating experience. For Charles, Camille and their daughter Caroline, things would never be quite the same. The boundless plenty of the prewar years was gone, but with hard work and courage they were able to live comfortably on Magnolia once again.

"Charles! What are you thinking?" Camille knew the horrors of the war and Jacqueline's death still tormented him, and that only their love had brought him healing and ease from the pain.

"I was thinking of the night you followed the gentleman bandit to the Devil's Punchbowl. I wish you'd caught him!"

"So do I," she said fervently, recalling the months of imprisonment in Raphael's house in New Orleans. "So do I."

"I felt so guilty when I finally learned what had happened—that you had gotten into trouble following me."

"It wasn't your fault." She smiled. "I *was* a little headstrong. And if it hadn't been that night, Clement would have found another way to get me out of his way and into the hands of Raphael." She shivered.

"Did he hurt you, Camille?" The words were spoken in a low growl, and his hand tightened its hold on her waist. He wondered why he'd never had the nerve to ask before.

"No," she hurried to reassure him. "He really treated me quite well, in fact. But if you hadn't come back when you did at the landing..." Her voice trailed off as she thought of the last, deadly battle between her gentleman bandit and the Creole.

"That time he would have hurt you," he finished for her, "perhaps killed you and little Caro, as well."

"Yes. He was a dangerous man, but I don't think he truly meant us harm, at least not until I escaped. It's strange, though, that I couldn't see that you and my bandit were the same, even then. I thought you didn't love me anymore, or you would have come for me."

She knew, now, that Charles had used his identity as the bandit to rescue her in order to get through Raphael's line of defense more easily, since they were expecting Charles Longmont. Also, it had been easier for him to move about and get information in areas of New Orleans like the Swamp, since the bandit was well known there.

After his first attempt to rescue Camille, Raphael's henchmen had turned Charles over to the authorities, and he had been locked up. It had taken his band of faithful men months to break him out, months he had been unable to help his wife or his countrymen.

"I never stopped loving.you, even for a minute, Cam. All those months you were in New Orleans and I was in a Yankee prison, you were never out of my mind. I was crazy at the thought of what might be happening to you."

"I know, Charles." She turned and looked up into his dear face, the chiseled lines of pain and suffering softened by the moonlight. "It's all over now, and we still have each other, and Caroline."

"Yes, Caroline, and each other," he echoed, his lips tasting hers. "And perhaps a brother or a sister for her, or two of each," he murmured between kisses, his hands caressing the smooth contours of her body.

"I would see you, sir." Her indigo eyes with their heavy black fringe of lashes were open wide, her lips curving into a smile. "And this time there will be no mask, my gentle bandit!"

His laughter was rich and deep as he swept her up in his arms and walked toward their bed, awash in moonglow and fragrant with the perfume of magnolias.

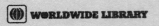